❦ NOBLE VISION ❦

❧ NOBLE VISION ❧

Gen LaGreca

Winged Victory Press, Chicago
www.wingedvictorypress.com

Winged Victory Press
P.O. Box 11307
Chicago, IL 60611
www.wingedvictorypress.com

This book is a work of fiction. Names, characters, places, and events
are either products of the author's imagination or are used fictitiously.
Any resemblance to actual events, locales, or persons, living or deceased,
is purely coincidental.

Cover illustration by Holly Smith of bookskins.net
Interior book design by Huron Valley Graphics
First printing 2005

ISBN 0-9744579-8-1
Library of Congress Control Number: 2003113981

Quality discounts are available for bulk purchases of this book.
For information, please contact the publisher, Winged Victory Press,
at (800)844-2114.

✄ DEDICATION ✄

To John

✌ ACKNOWLEDGMENTS ✌

I wish to thank Dr. Gail Rosseau, a Chicago neurosurgeon, for generously answering my questions and explaining neurosurgical techniques to me at the start of my research. I also deeply appreciate the medical editing that the book received from Chicago-based Dr. Robin Wellington, a neuroscientist, and Drs. Kirk Jobe and Juan Jimenez, neurosurgeons. These professionals gave me vital technical information and suggestions. We did not, however, discuss the theme or message of the story, which represents my view and not necessarily theirs.

The manuscript profited from two readings by Dr. Beth Haynes, a physician in northern California, and from the diligence of my excellent copyeditor, Katharine O'Moore-Klopf of KOK Edit. My opera partner, Dr. A. J. Mundt, a radiologist, patiently answered my numerous medical questions for several seasons during the intermissions. Other doctors, nurses, and hospital staff members kindly assisted me in my research.

Many books helped me in my writing, particularly those of three physicians: Dr. Kenyon Rainer (*First Do No Harm*), Dr. Edward Annis (*Code Blue*), and Dr. Jane Orient (*Your Doctor Is Not In*).

A very special thank-you goes to Dr. Michael Schlitt, a neurosurgeon in Seattle, Washington. His technical advice and creative ideas helped me enormously in molding the medical aspects of the plot. Any inaccuracies in the fictional adaptation of his ideas are my doing.

I am profoundly indebted to Dr. Edith Packer, a clinical psychologist in Southern California. She edited the manuscript, offering invaluable psychological insights into the characterization. And it was she—more than anyone else—who encouraged me to write fiction. When I did, it quickly became my life's passion.

❧ CONTENTS ❧

❧
PART ONE
Fire

❧
PART TWO
Thunder

PART THREE
Hope

PART ONE
Fire

❧ 1 ❧

The Dancer and the Phantom

The bus terminal was a study in gray, with its vertical steel beams, smudged windows, scuffed slate floor. Dusty cones of light descended from metal canisters along the charcoal ceiling. A concrete overhang outside the building kept the sunlight at bay. Lines of people waiting to be processed snaked around silver stanchions near the counters and boarding gates of the hollow station. One person in the crowd, a teenager with a child's long legs and woman's budding breasts, was tired of waiting, her restlessness apparent in the constant shifting of her weight and the tapping of her fingers in her folded arms.

As she approached the ticket counter, she saw gray-uniformed clerks boxed inside a row of booths resembling prison cells. The buses outside, pushing back from the gunmetal frame of the building like dead bolts sliding open, filled her with the daring hope of escape, for the destination of one of them was her future.

"Anyone traveling with you?" asked the ticket agent from behind his glass partition.

"No," said the girl.

"I need to see your ID."

She slid the driver's license of an eighteen-year-old under the partition, although she had just turned thirteen.

The agent's eyes darted suspiciously from the license to her face, making her knees tremble and her hands sweat. Fighting a quiet battle against a familiar enemy, panic, she forced her eyes to hold on the agent's unsmiling face. She had applied heavy makeup, worn glasses, pulled childlike blond curls into a frumpy bun, and practiced a deep voice so she could buy a one-way ticket across the country—and with it, a new life.

"What's your name?" The agent's words ground coarsely through the microphone.

"Nicole Hudson." The name and the license were one day old.

"Address?"

"Three-forty-three West 18th."

He waited.

"Here in Manhattan," she added.

"And what's your Social Security number?"

She recited the number she had memorized from the phony license.

"Which Motor Vehicles office did you go to for this license?"

Fear pulled her eyes down. Was there something on the license that identified the issuing office, or was the agent bluffing? The man selling her the phony document had not mentioned this matter. She had paid him eight hundred dollars with money stolen from her foster family, money she would repay, for she had never taken anything before.

Her fingers tightened around a small bag curled in her arm. The parcel contained the remnants of her first ballet shoes. She had preserved the tattered slippers like an heirloom in a fine leather purse, although the rest of her belongings hung from her shoulder in a cheap vinyl bag. During the split-second pause in the most important conversation of her life, she clung to the outgrown slippers the way a younger child might grasp a teddy bear.

"I asked you where you got this driver's license," the clerk squawked.

She knew of a Motor Vehicles office in the same building as the courtroom that heard cases brought by the New York State Department of Child Welfare.

"I got it at the municipal building on West 28th Street."

The tired entity that was the clerk returned the license. He didn't seem to notice the relief filling the blue eyes almost to tears and the tension draining from the slim shoulders. He didn't seem to notice that beneath layers of eye shadow were the wide eyes of a child.

"Where to?"

"San Francisco."

"Round trip?"

"One way."

When she'd felt driven to leave New York's stifling depot of foster care, San Francisco had become her destination. She knew of a great school for ballet there called the Benoir Academy.

Gracefully, she lowered her head to gather her cash, wondering if anyone had reported her missing or was looking for her. Apparently no one had or was. She paid the clerk and took her ticket.

Walking to her gate, she didn't hear the sterile music piped through the loudspeaker. Instead, she hummed a joyous melody from the first ballet she had ever seen, at age six, sitting with a group of vagabond children. Their unsupervised playground was Manhattan, except when they were gathered, washed, and fed by the nuns of St. Jude's, a parish in her neighborhood. Their ballet tickets were a gift from an anonymous church benefactor. Perhaps because many of the youngsters had entered the world trembling from one addiction or another or routinely visited relatives in jail or witnessed more violence in real time than on any movie screen, the supreme innocence of the ballet provoked in them only jeers.

But the little girl with the long blond hair never noticed their snickering as she sat hypnotized by the magic of the stage. She saw an enchanted forest of tall trees cut by a watercolor meadow of pastel pink and powder blue flowers. A lovely princess danced with a young prince in an unimaginable world of beauty and goodness.

After that day, the chaotic events of her life became simple. The ballet reduced all choices of true or false, right or wrong, life or death to one golden rule: To dance was good; not to dance was bad.

Her first ballet slippers were the child's bounty after weeks of rummaging through the trash outside Madame Maximova's School of Ballet, where the affluent children of a nearby neighborhood took classes. Worn and discarded by a young student, the slippers got a second chance at life—and gave one to the future Nicole Hudson. They became the one absolute in her otherwise uncertain world.

The slippers were with her the day her mother—never quite stable or sober—told her, "Get your things together," then left her on the steps of St. Jude's Parish. "Tell the sisters I'll be back for you soon," said the drawn figure whose unkempt hair and dark-ringed eyes added a troubled decade to her twenty-five years. The child of eight carrying a shopping bag of clothing stared at her mother blankly. "And don't be a pest and ask a lot of questions, Cathleen. Do what they say, you hear?"

Her mother never did come back, so the ballet slippers assumed the role of surrogate. They were the child's solid footing through a revolving door of foster families. When she was frightened, their soles whispered of a better life. When she cried, their cloth wiped her tears. The slippers were with her in the courtroom at age ten when she was pronounced abandoned and eligible for adoption. And the shoes were with her when she peeked at a paper in her file on a caseworker's desk that declared she was "maladjusted" and "unadoptable."

The slippers fit her feet in the early years when she danced on her first makeshift stage, the cramped living room of the tenement where she lived with her mother. To clear a space for her future, the child would push aside the clutter from her mother's disheveled life—the tattered armchair hauled there from a pawnshop, the chipped-veneer coffee table, the pages from a two-day-old tabloid strewn around the room, the soiled plates from the previous night's supper eaten before the television set, and an array of empty beer cans. Under a rust-colored water ring that stained the white ceiling like an old wound, the little princess would dance. Her mother, who had not yet decided what to do with her own life, could not understand how the child just knew what she herself would do with hers.

The girl became a persistent, uninvited presence at Madame Maximova's, searching for chores to do—sweeping floors, removing trash, cleaning locker rooms. The teachers objected at first to her unsolicited labors, chasing her home. But like a pesky squirrel hunting for food in its indomitable struggle for survival, the child kept returning. Eventually, the staff grew accustomed to her after-school assistance. Thus, she was allowed to take classes for free. Through the years, she continued to do chores—running the reception desk, enrolling students, issuing bills—without ever asking for money or receiving any. She just took the classes she wished for free, and no one stopped her.

When she learned her first steps, the slippers were on her feet. They arabesqued and pirouetted—and fell—with her. They and their successors covered frequently tired, sometimes blistered, but always nimble feet. They sat idle for periods in which she was sent to the dreaded suburbs, to foster families that comprehended nothing of the divine world of Madame Maximova's, which she missed desperately. Hence, she would run away to the shelter at St. Jude's and to her beloved classes. She returned to the sweet torture of exercises repeated hundreds of times until swollen, bleeding feet no longer could hold her. She took her lumps proudly, for pain was not a valid reason to stop. Then she would be retrieved by social workers who thought they knew best.

But that was in the past, when others were in charge. Now there would be *no* interruption of her training, she resolved, clutching her bus ticket, hoping it was not too late.

A toneless voice over the loudspeaker announced the most thrilling news of her life: "Gate sixteen to San Francisco now boarding."

Suppressing the wild cry of laughter swelling in her throat, she climbed the narrow steps into the musty vehicle, then found a seat. As the skyscrapers of Manhattan faded to a jagged gray backdrop in the rear window of the bus, she counted her money. Fifty dollars left. She smiled, unworried. She laid her head back and closed her eyes on the serene vision of fairies dancing in an enchanted forest where *she* was the princess. That day, an indifferent world barely noticed the last of Cathleen Hughes, homeless child of thirteen, and the first of Nicole Hudson, woman of eighteen.

On a July afternoon ten years later, the Taylor Theater of Broadway carried a hushed audience back to the dawn of mankind. A packed house formed a crescent of rows around the legendary stage. The chandeliers' starlike clusters of light slowly faded to black on the gilded ceiling of the historic building. With the luxurious rustle of soft velvet, the massive red curtain rose on a ballet that had become a Broadway sensation: *Triumph.*

The stage was divided into two opposite realms. On the left stood a white Doric temple rising from a grassy knoll into a slate blue night sky. Torchlights flanking the entrance cast a brilliant golden light over the scene. Ballerinas in sheer pastel gowns danced gaily to a pastorale. Male dancers joined them, clad in princely white tunics with full, flowing sleeves fastened tight at the wrist. The playbill described the realm as "an untroubled world of warmth, light, and beauty—Olympus, the home of the mythological Greek gods."

On the right, a dusty yellow stretch of barren field with shiny patches of frost faded into a charcoal sky. A straw hut stood swaying like an injured soldier. Icicles hung in slippery spikes from the roof. Missing from this world were the lively torches of Olympus, and with them the life-giving warmth, light, and gaiety of that world. Also absent were female figures to soften the stark landscape. Men in brown tunics shivered in the cold, dancing dispiritedly to a somber theme. They laid an animal carcass on a wooden altar, then, turning to the deities of Olympus, groveled on their knees, bowing their heads and offering their sacrifice. The playbill described this scene as "the first mortals on Earth in the Greek legend of man's creation."

On Olympus, an exciting male dancer with the sinewy body of youth and the tangled beard of old age portrayed the greatest of the gods, Zeus. He carried a giant torch whose flame streaked behind him with every leap. In a daring move, another male dancer, one with the beauty of a god and the anguish of a man, seized Zeus's torch. Before the indignant Zeus could stop him, the young rebel blazed to the Earth like a fiery comet. Flames raged across that bleak land, brightening the murky sky and melting the frost. Zeus's divine torch brought warmth, light, and a wondrous, new power to the men of Earth. Music of deliverance resounded as they rose from their knees and danced jubilantly around the fire. They removed the sacrificial animal from the altar, cooked the meat over their first hearth, and consumed it themselves. The Olympians looked on, aghast at their irreverence. The playbill announced: "Prometheus steals fire from the gods and brings it to man."

Enraged, Zeus hurled thunderbolts at Earth. The men in brown tunics, led by Prometheus in white, danced fearlessly against the piercing wind and rain of the ensuing storm. Imbued with a new courage, they withstood the tempest. Then, through theatrical magic, the men's brown tunics turned a shimmering white, resembling those of the deities in Olympus. Endowed with Prometheus's gift of fire, the men became godlike.

Zeus ordered his servants, Force and Violence, to seize Prometheus. The two nimble dancers tied him to a rock on a lonely Earth cliff. The curtain fell on the fiery figure of Zeus, dancing violently, vowing his revenge on mankind.

The next act opened on a rustic riverbed on Olympus. A lovely maiden appeared, dressed not in a gown but in a transparent hint of one that barely covered her shapely figure, evident underneath a skin-toned leotard. Flowing streams of lustrous blond hair bordered the delicate landscape of her face. She danced around Olympus with the weightless gaiety of a kitten. This was the being whom Zeus had created as his curse on man: the first mortal woman, Pandora.

Apollo, the god of the sun, placed a wreath on Pandora's head, bestowing the gift of curiosity. Zeus gave her a giant golden box, its lid fastened with a red ribbon, and told her to take it on a journey to Earth. The maiden attempted to lift the lid. Apollo urgently pulled her away, warning her never to open the box. Pandora did not seem to hear the sun god's admonishment but danced unmindfully around the chest like a child with a new toy.

On reaching Earth, she discovered the chained Prometheus on a cliff. They stared at each other with a dangerous excitement that overstepped the bounds of classical ballet. Pandora struggled to release the ropes that held the handsome young god but to no avail. As if emboldened by the ties that restrained his response, her own desire awakened. She danced before him with the grace of a ballerina and with a passion too physical for the fragile dance form, yet too spiritual for any other. She caressed his face daintily, then brushed her arms across his chest more ardently. With a flurry of staccato steps, she tiptoed away, frightened by her boldness. Then she again drew closer, pulled back by his arresting presence. The scene ended with Pandora's mouth raised to Prometheus for her first daring kiss. The audience did what it had done for eight months:

"Brava! Brava!"

The men of Earth gazed in amazement at Pandora, the first woman they had ever seen, and at her gift, the golden box. Endowed with a lively curiosity from Apollo, she pirouetted around the large chest, leaped over it, danced on it—and finally untied the ribbon. As the kettledrum roared, Pandora opened the box.

Monstrous creatures in grotesque masks and sleek bodysuits jumped out of the chest. The men of Earth recoiled in fear. Plagues of every sort escaped, casting colossal shadows against the blue backdrop. Pestilence, Misery, Worry, and Misfortune flew past the horrified Pandora to infest the Earth. Prometheus watched helplessly from the cliff. The men of Earth groveled once again, begging the gods' forgiveness for their arrogance. As act two ended, Zeus howled with laughter at the doomed human race.

In the final act, the inquisitive Pandora discovered a lone object at the bottom of the box, a female dancer in a pink gown—Hope. Like a flower bending over in the wind to pollinate another, Hope reached out to Pandora and placed a feather boa around her shoulders. The gift of Hope sparked Pandora with a new courage. She seized Zeus's torch and burned through the ropes binding Prometheus. In a fury of flying arms and nimble feet, the two of them chased the woes back into the box and shut the lid for good.

The playbill explained: "In the actual Greek myth, Prometheus remains chained to the rock and the miseries plague the Earth forever, demonstrating Zeus's mastery over mankind. However, in this audacious rewriting of the ancient legend, Prometheus and Pandora, armed with fire and hope, chase the woes back into the box and save the human race."

Warmth and light again bathed the Earth. A corps of ballerinas joined the men of Earth in a great celebration. Pandora and Prometheus took center stage for the final pas de deux.

The playbill concluded: "Man discovers woman and enters an age of innocence, goodness, and joy."

The creation of Pandora was also the making of the twenty-three-year-old playing the role, who, after a decade of poverty and struggle, exploded on a dance world that finally took notice: Nicole Hudson.

Sparkling reviews had poured in like champagne. "How did classical ballet become the stuff of Broadway, playing to record crowds for eight months?" one news program's theater critic had asked. "The answer is simple: Nicole Hudson."

"The sensational Nicole Hudson dazzled us with her virtuosity and exuberance," a reviewer in a leading newspaper had written. "*Triumph* is the unbridled spirit of Nicole, innocent and happy, untarnished by the world, the way we all start out in childhood."

A magazine devoted to the arts had agreed: "*Triumph's* vibrant new star, Nicole Hudson, is as radiant as a princess from a distant world where pain is banished and hope is the only passport."

With one willowy arm to her heart and the other sweeping out to the audience, Nicole Hudson bowed to wild cheers at the conclusion of the summer matinee. She wondered why, after eight months of a grueling performance schedule in *Triumph*, her desire to dance was never sated but only intensified the more she performed, like a sweet addiction nourishing itself. As she smiled at those she had stirred with her dancing, their cheering in turn moved her. She felt a burning rush of liquid fill her eyes and wondered why happiness could hurt. Bathing in the warmth of the spotlight, she knew that finally she, like Pandora, had entered a period of innocence, goodness, and joy, and nothing greater was possible.

Her dressing room smelled of men's cologne when she entered it. The scent emanated from a tall, dark-haired man in a fashionable suit—her agent, Howard Morton, who had gotten her the role of Pandora. The nervous lines on his face were in stark contrast to the calm radiance hers still held from the performance.

"Hi, Howie." She walked past him to remove her costume in the bathroom. "What are you doing here?" she called from the half-closed door.

"I want to be sure everything is prepared for your interview with Gloria Candrell."

Nicole reappeared in a silk robe that tied at her waist, emphasizing its slenderness. "There's nothing to prepare," she said, sitting at the vanity, facing the jittery figure perched on the arm of an easy chair. "Relax, Howie."

"Nickie, you're *too* relaxed. This interview's for *national TV*. And because you'll be in your dressing room, the viewers will form impressions about you from what they'll see here. I want to be sure those impressions will be good."

She glanced at the few furnishings in the room: a vanity, sofa, easy chair, coffee table, and taller table behind the couch. "It's a pretty average room, but it'll do."

"It'll do if we make one change—one small but very important change, dear."

She waited. He fidgeted, as if expecting resistance.

"There's one little matter, Nickie—some things we need to remove from this room just for the interview, then we can put them back—things that would not be understood and would make you seem . . . well . . . peculiar."

"What things?"

He looked pointedly at the table behind the couch. It was cluttered with a motley assortment of vases, bowls, and baskets, ranging from large to small, crystal to wicker, elegant to simple. Each container held the flaky remains of flower arrangements long dead. Her eyes followed his.

"I want them to stay, Howie."

"Why?"

"Because those flowers were gifts, the best gifts I ever received."

"But they are *dead* now, my dear."

"They are staying, my Howie."

"What if we remove just the rotted flowers and keep the containers? Though I haven't a clue on how to display such a hodgepodge."

"I want them to stay just as they are. Why do you worry so?"

"But you don't even know the guy."

"The flowers stay."

"Think of how preposterous it is, Nickie. He's sent you flowers and written you love letters for months now, and he never shows his face."

"They stay."

"There's something perverted about him. He could be a lunatic. I'm warning you."

"They stay."

"How do we even know it's a he?"

"The flowers *stay*. Read my lips, Howie."

"You know, you're acting like a schoolgirl with a silly crush. I thought you were smarter than that."

She seemed to be talking more to herself when she turned to the dead flowers and whispered: "I'd like him to know I kept them. I want the camera to pick them up. I wonder if he'll be watching."

"Nickie, really—you wouldn't want the public to think you're peculiar, would you?"

"I *am* peculiar."

"Be reasonable. You wouldn't want viewers to think you keep dead flowers. You wouldn't want America to think you're weird."

"I *am* weird," she said with finality. She grabbed a hairbrush and look at him through the mirror of her vanity. "If there's nothing else, Howie, why don't you excuse me, so I can get dressed?"

"Nickie, really! You need to let *me* guide your career. You can't run things for yourself."

Her arm made a wide arch to glide the brush through hair that almost reached her waist. She opened a drawer for a barrette. There she saw her first ballet shoes, the personal heirloom she had carried through the years. Whenever she had encountered something alien, the little slippers had brought her back to her purpose.

"I've run things for myself since I was thirteen."

"But Nickie—"

They were interrupted by a knock on the door.

"Come in," Nicole called.

A deliveryman entered with a gift-wrapped package.

"Oh, thank you!" Nicole sprang from her seat to grab the bundle, leaving Morton to grope for a tip to give the man.

She unwrapped a rectangular basket stuffed with dozens of wildflowers, spilling over the sides and tangling each other in a violent battle of fragrance and hue. Though they seemed to be wantonly thrown together, they were actually aligned in a procession of color: red, orange, yellow, blue, indigo, and violet—a rainbow. The perky blooms made Nicole feel like running through a sunlit meadow and rolling in grass so fresh that it pricked her skin.

"Now *this* will make a perfect centerpiece for the interview!" she said, placing the disorderly array on the coffee table.

"Oh, great! Couldn't the guy send roses? Wildflowers are so provincial!"

In the thicket of rowdy sprouts, Nicole found an envelope. Inside it was a letter in the precise script that was a trademark of the sender, the person she called the Flower Phantom.

"He has the most beautiful handwriting I've ever seen. Maybe he's an artist."

"Or a penmanship teacher," Morton added, peeking at the letter from over her shoulder.

Clutching the note to her breast, she brought it to the vanity, out of Morton's sight, then read to herself:

Dear Nicole,

Sunday I walked to the theater in the pouring rain. I watched stray cats crawl into empty doorways to shake the damp chill from their fur with violent shudders. I wished it were that easy to fling off the cold drops of despair seeping through my skin and condensing on my soul. If the season is summer, I wondered, where is the sun?

Then I reached the marquee and saw your billboard. The proud line of your head drawn back and your mouth opened wide in an exultant laughter shouted at me with another message, one that lured me in out of the rain.

For the next two hours, if the music played, I was deaf to it; if there were other dancers, I was blind to them. I could not stretch my awareness beyond the one presence that filled it, the vision of you whirling through the air with devilish eyes and flying hair, leaping and spinning with more power than was possible for such a slender creature. You seemed to relish pushing your body to daring limits that made the audience gasp. Watching you move with the boundless energy of a fawn at play, for the first time in weeks, I laughed. For the first time in weeks, I could feel a long-dampened torch rekindle inside me.

Can we really harness the fire of heaven and become godlike, as you so boldly affirm in your show?

When I left the theater, the dark clouds had thinned into slivers and the sun was edging its way through the slits. The cold rain, that misfit from another season, had given way to a more pleasing companion, a summer rainbow, to soak my path with color . . . and my dreams with hope.

As was his custom, the Flower Phantom left the letter unsigned. As was her custom, she lingered on the words.

"Nickie."

She did not hear Morton calling her. She saw only the extravagant rainbow of reckless blossoms.

"Gloria will be here in half an hour, dear. Don't you think you should dress?"

She was unaware of the entity called Howard Morton. Someone was pecking at the wall with which she kept the human race at bay.

The Flower Phantom stirred something inside her that she had never taken the time to notice: loneliness. For years she had been a fugitive, pursuing her dance training by day, holding odd jobs at night, and obsessively concealing her identity. She had never found time to date, nor did the disappointments of her early years leave her open to trusting anyone. But the Phantom somehow disarmed her. He wrote passionately of a great aspiration in his life and of obstacles thwarting him. Did she not have a passion and a struggle in her life? She wondered about the nature of his battle, but he never revealed it. How odd it was, she thought, to feel the presence of someone she had never met in the room. Would she ever meet a man who could arouse in her what Prometheus had awakened in Pandora?

"Nickie . . ." Morton tried again.

She replayed the argument with herself that had become routine after receiving a letter from the Phantom. She would find him, she resolved. No, she would wait until he came for her. No, she would find him and demand to know why he wrote to her. No, she would forget about him because he seemed to have no intention of appearing. And that was fine, because she did not need distractions!

"Nickie."

"Yes?"

"Will you be getting dressed now?"

"Yes."

She had tried to trace the Phantom before, but each time, he used a different flower shop, paid in cash, and left no record of his name. She had inquired, but none of the shops knew who he was. She glanced at his previous gifts on the table. All of them had come from the vicinity of the theater, where he evidently worked or lived. How many local florists could be left? She knew the ones he had already used; their cards appeared on the arrangements. She could find the remaining shops and offer their clerks money if they'd call were someone to order flowers for her. No, she would do nothing of the kind! He obviously did not want to be found. Then why did he keep writing? And why did his words stir the calm waters of her soul?

"Nickie . . ."

She reached into her closet and removed the clothes she intended to wear. "I'll get dressed now. Give me a minute, will you?"

"I'll wait outside."

As Morton left the room, she headed for the shower, and then stopped. She opened a drawer and removed a phone directory. Leafing through the pages, she found the listings for flower shops. She tore out the sheets and put them in her purse.

"To hell with waiting," she said, shrugging. "I'm going to find him!"

❧ 2 ❧

The Banquet . . .

The chandeliers in the grand ballroom, with their myriad of tiny lights, looked opulent, except for the scattered spaces where bulbs were missing. The great arched windows of the hall resembled a Florentine palace, but the velvet curtains around them were faded. Crystal glasses sparkled on eighty tables set for dinner, although many of the stems were chipped. The ballroom of the Rutledge Hotel of Manhattan seemed to be resting on grandeur from the past that was slowly slipping away.

Eight hundred of the state's business and government leaders were gathered there that July evening for a two-thousand-dollar-a-plate fund-raiser. Their tables curved around a flowered dais with a speaker's podium. Above the dais hung a banner that read "Reelect Governor Malcolm Burrow in November." The ends of the banner curled in a smile. The seals of New York State and its namesake city formed two bulging eyes above the grinning sign.

Dr. Marie Lang sat at one of the tables with the partners of Reliant Care, the large group practice that employed her. She looked poised in her black silk gown but for the persistent nervous tapping of slim tanned feet under it. Her sleek auburn hair brushed alluringly against her naked shoulders, while eyes of the same burnished brown darted anxiously around the room. Almost everyone found thirty-four-year-old Marie charming. The occasional more perceptive observer, however, found her puzzling, for when she smiled, her eyes did not follow suit.

She turned toward the entrance as if searching for someone, then frowned when she didn't find the person there. Her eyes fell irritably on the only empty seat at the table, the one next to her that was costing her group practice two thousand dollars.

"I know you don't support the governor, but I'm asking you to come to this dinner to support *me*," she had said earlier to the person supposed to occupy that seat. "I'm the only staff physician the partners invited. I'm probably going to get an award for being their best doctor."

"That's what concerns me" was the reply.

With a sweep of her hair, Marie shook off the troubling recollection. Turning to the officers of her group practice and their spouses at the table, she smiled broadly.

"Before the politicians give their speeches, let me make a statement of my own: I'm delighted—and honored—to be here tonight. Thank you for inviting me!"

"We're glad you could make it," said Dr. Paul Eastman, the stocky president of the fifty-doctor practice.

His youthful tan clashed with his sagging jowls to make him appear both robust and rotund. His perpetually racing eyes seemed to scan the world in search of the next task to tackle. He had entered medicine when it was easy to make a mid-six-figure income and left it for business administration when doctors' compensation became more regulated and took a sharp turn south.

"We didn't invite you just to toot a horn for Governor Burrow," Eastman continued. "We have our own drum-roll for the GP who's done so much to help Reliant Care reach its goals. Don't we?"

The partners nodded.

"Now whatever do you mean?" Marie asked gaily.

"You'll see."

Her innocent eyes belied the fact that she knew a bonus check had been cut for her that day. Her friendship with Eastman's secretary had paid off.

With one raised finger, Eastman signaled a waiter. With a circular motion of that finger he ordered a round of cocktails. "By the way, where's David?" he asked, as the waiter took the drink orders.

Marie's smile vanished. "Unfortunately, something came up. He was very disappointed he couldn't come. He said to thank you for your invitation and to send his regrets."

Everyone nodded sympathetically. Marie was married to a neurosurgeon.

"That downright ruins the aesthetics," said sixty-year-old Edna Eastman about the absence of Marie's very attractive thirty-seven-year-old husband, provoking a chuckle from the other women.

"Paul, I know you didn't invite me here so Edna could stare at my husband."

"Actually, we want *you* to be the center of attention."

"My goodness! Why?"

"Is this gal amazing?" said the head of the clinical staff. "She works her magic so naturally, she doesn't even know she's doing it!"

Marie knew that the second-quarter figures were in and that she had surpassed the goals set by the company for its physicians. Nevertheless, she was enjoying her little game with her employers.

"These are changing times for medicine," said Eastman. "Instead of pining for the old days, Marie is one doctor who adapts to change. Reliant needs MDs like you, my dear. CareFree needs them."

CareFree was the state's most celebrated public assistance program. Created by the governor two years earlier, the agency provided free health care to all New Yorkers. Subsidized by an approving federal government, CareFree took under its massive wing all patients formerly covered by national programs. This giant single payer of medical bills provided tax relief and other incentives to doctors for giving up solo practice to join groups, which the state thought were more economical and easier to monitor.

Recognizing the new trends, Paul Eastman had formed Reliant Care. The firm paid its doctors a salary as employees and collected a fee for their work from CareFree. Eastman spared his practitioners the necessity of dealing with the regulators, and the doctors in turn made a profit for the firm by working within the parameters set by CareFree. In the two years of its existence, his fledgling firm had grown to fifty doctors.

"My biggest migraine," Eastman complained, "comes from doctors who fight the system. The whiners want the old way back, but it's not to be. The whiners are stubborn. They don't want to take advice. They resist collaborating with the regulators and want to make all the treatment decisions themselves. But you, Marie, have a real knack for getting along with the administrators."

"I think other people have opinions, too. It's good to get their views," said Marie to the approving nods of the others. "I'm not always right, so I don't mind cooperating."

"Instead of getting lost in the weeds, we need to make our garden grow. And Marie has a remarkable green thumb." Eastman picked up her hand and held her thumb up.

"Oh, Paul, really—the new system isn't so bad. I don't like to complain. I'd rather get the job done."

"And so you do! We have our semiannual bonus for the doctor we select as Distinguished Caregiver," Eastman explained. "The numbers are in, and your record was unmatched, Marie. Of all the primary doctors in our group, you had the largest roster of patients, and you demonstrated the most prudent use of medical resources, with well-controlled hospital admissions, consults with specialists, and outside testing. Because of this record, you had no skirmishes with the folks at CareFree, which means no headaches for me."

Marie, who tallied her numbers the way a monk counts his prayers, tried to look surprised.

"If we could clone you, we would, kiddo," said the head of marketing. "I want to feature you in our advertising campaign to recruit new doctors."

"Oh, really, now!" exclaimed Marie.

"She's a natural healer!" added Eastman. "Some people are born with the gift." He threw an arm around Marie, his jowls shaking as he laughed.

The tension vanished from Marie's face. This time her smile did reach her eyes. The empty seat no longer seemed to matter; she rested her purse on it.

Eastman removed an envelope and jewelry box from his vest pocket, his midsection spilling over his cummerbund. He raised his voice, commanding the attention of everyone at the table. "Our selection for Distinguished Caregiver was unanimous—Dr. Marie Lang!" To the applause of the others, Eastman handed her the gifts.

Marie planted a kiss on his fleshy cheek and opened her presents. The envelope contained a check for ten thousand dollars, and the box held a gold pin engraved with the company logo and the words *Dr. Marie Lang, Distinguished Caregiver*.

"Thank you very much!" Marie placed a hand over her heart and bowed her head appreciatively.

"At a time when many of our colleagues are struggling, with independent practitioners becoming dinosaurs, Reliant Care is thriving," said Eastman. "Doctors like Marie prove we can expand our comfort zone and work under the new system."

"You did a great job, Marie," said the company's financial officer.

"And here's the booze. Perfect timing!" said another partner, as the waiter arrived. "A toast to Marie."

"And to the governor's reelection," someone added.

"To Reliant Care," said Marie, raising her wineglass.

Eastman grabbed his martini off the tray before the waiter could serve it. "To the future, which looks rosier every day."

Eight miles across the East River in Oak Hills, Queens, a man returned home from work, an unknotted tie across his chest and a suit jacket dangling from his shoulder. The soft silk coat crushed as he dropped it on a chair. He removed a note that his secretary had slipped into the pocket when he was leaving the office. He grabbed a beer, and as he entered the living room and lay across a couch, he drank eagerly without the benefit of a glass.

His legs, which he had never felt during twelve hours in surgery, now throbbed from the knees down. His neck cracked with the tension of craning over a microscope all day. His green eyes, which had spent hours locked on a section of protoplasm inside a human brain, now drooped. His exquisitely sensitive fingers, which had controlled countless minute tools, were stiffening. Even his forehead, under his boyish sweep of black hair, burned where the rim of the surgical cap had scraped. He felt as if his body were going on strike.

He lay with his head on a throw pillow, content in knowing he could finally relax. There was no longer a life at stake. Or was there? He glanced at the note from his secretary: "You have an appointment to present your project to the BOM research committee at 4 tomorrow afternoon."

He had waited months for an appointment with the state's Bureau of Medicine, or BOM, but wished he didn't have to go. The massive agency ran CareFree, the state's health care program, and also regulated hospitals, medical schools, and research. Nervously tapping the note against his fingers, he wondered how to get the committee's permission to complete his research. If his seven-year quest had led only to blind alleys, he could give up. But he couldn't cut the journey short just when he could see his dream, almost touch it, in the distance.

What if his proposal were rejected? Was there another way? He had exhausted every avenue. Should he move to another state? Conditions were becoming the same everywhere. Should he go abroad? The medical climate was no better there. What arguments could he prepare for the most important meeting of his life?

It seemed so much easier to fight the battle he had waged earlier that day against a benign brain tumor, a meningioma. He thought it misleading to call a meningioma benign when it could burgeon to the size of a grapefruit and kill as surely as its undisguised sibling, cancer. A meningioma forces the brain's blood vessels to service its cause. It feeds off human protein, growing larger and larger. To make room for its girth, it squeezes out the good brain tissue until its un-willing host can no longer function. Finally, the pressure of the intruder becomes so great that the brain one day quits. The "benign" meningioma murders its life source and therefore destroys itself. Such is its perverted aim.

There is only one cure: The unwelcome guest has to be thrown out. However, a meningioma is vindictive. It punishes its host for trying to expel it. If any mi-nuscule part of it remains, the vengeful alien can grow back faster and more deadly than before. The only way to stop it is to remove every last morsel.

His patient that day was a man of fifty-seven, twenty years his senior. The meningioma was easy to spot. There was the healthy yellow brain tissue with its pulsating web of blood vessels and nerves. Then there was the tumor, a dull gray mass resembling a tennis ball. He gently pecked at it, removing a piece at a time, careful not to disturb the delicate nerves and vessels adhering to it. Hours later, after he had removed most of the meningioma, he discovered something disturb-ing. He pulled his instruments out to rest his hands and decide what to do. The last bit of the tumor was attached to the command center that regulates respira-tion, blood pressure, and heartbeat, controlling life itself: the brainstem. The area where the meningioma had lodged seemed inoperable because the result of just one touch on the brainstem could . . . could not be very good at all. If he quit now, he thought, he would have given the patient ten years before the menin-gioma regrew to kill him. But if he could get the last recalcitrant bit of the tumor out, the patient could live thirty years, the full course of his life.

He sipped soda through a straw that the nurse slid inside his mask as he con-sidered the options. The last remains of the meningioma stuck to the brainstem like chewing gum on the trigger of a bomb. Could he remove it without touch-ing it? Coax it out? Wish it out? If he quit now, he had already bargained ten years from the invader. If he continued, the patient could live thirty years or die on the table. Ten years or thirty? Life or death? A nurse ran a dry cloth across his wet forehead. Finally, he stepped up to the brain, stared at the meningioma, and silently forewarned it: *One of us is going to get tired first, and it's not going to be me.*

Six hours later, he'd completed the operation. He had rid the brain of every vestige of the trespasser. The patient would fully recover and lead a normal life. That was easy. Meeting the BOM's research committee, however, was another matter. It was a foreign substance in the fabric of his life. It, too, pretended to be benign—but was it? How could he keep it from arresting *his* vital functions?

He glanced at his watch. It was eight o'clock, time for dinner. He wondered where his wife was, and then remembered she was attending a banquet. The prospect of spending the evening alone pleased him, but being pleased with her absence evoked guilt. He thought he should attend the banquet as she had so urgently requested, yet he couldn't bring himself to go.

He had not eaten since before entering the OR that morning. Was he too tired to eat or too hungry to sleep? His eyes decided for him. They closed.

Minutes later, his pager awakened him. A number he knew well flashed on the device. He reached for his pocket phone and dialed.

"Riverview Hospital Emergency Room."

"This is David Lang. I was just beeped."

"Yes, Doctor—hold on."

The next voice was that of a neurosurgery resident.

"Dr. Lang, this is Tom Bentley. I'm calling about my patient, a thirty-eight-year-old woman who was hit in the back of the head with a baseball five days ago."

"Yes?"

"After the injury, she developed headaches, sought medical attention, and was treated for migraines. As the week progressed, her headaches worsened. She recently gave birth and has been taking an anticoagulant for a blood clot in her leg. Her husband brought her in tonight because she was becoming harder and harder to arouse. Brain scans show a large subdural bleed in the posterior fossa. She's falling into a coma."

"Is her airway clear?" David Lang sat up.

"Yes."

"Is she intubated?"

"No. She's been breathing on her own, but her respiration is becoming shallow—"

David heard someone in the background yell, "Arrest!"

"My patient just stopped breathing," Bentley reported.

"Ventilate her, and give her K-35 in an IV drip to counteract the anticoagulant and restore normal clotting. Take her to the OR. I'm on my way."

The headpiece on the wall phone in the ER bobbed up and down after Bentley dropped it. David Lang's beer spilled across the carpet as he rushed to the door.

Bentley joined a wall of uniforms surrounding the almost lifeless woman. A gasping pump forced oxygen into her lungs. Monitors beeped, drawers slammed, voices sounded, wires trembled, and white jackets flew around her bed.

❧ 3 ❧
. . . And the OR

The clatter of conversation in the grand ballroom of the Rutledge Hotel faded when the man on the dais beside Governor Burrow took the podium. Sixty-five years had taken the color but not the thickness from the speaker's hair. He possessed the intelligent face of a scientist and the expensive clothes of a diplomat. His regal manner suggested a noble purpose, but his eyes seemed to be counting the number of television cameras following him. He was a former surgeon who had become the secretary of the Bureau of Medicine. Because the BOM's universal health care program, CareFree, was under constant attack by political opponents, the state's medicine czar was essential to the governor's bid for reelection. The secretary's job in the campaign was to defend CareFree. With his crest of white hair and tuxedo-clad trim form, he resembled a tall radio beacon emitting a message.

"Ladies and gentlemen, there are two things in the world that I cherish. One, which I made my former career, is medicine. I studied the glorious human body, discovered its mysteries, and defended it against attack. A doctor is a thinker, an explorer, and a crusader, a testament to the power of science in enriching our lives.

"But medicine is not an end in itself. We must use it to achieve a higher purpose. A proper health care system does just that. It frees medicine from the selfish concerns of business to serve the public. It guarantees care to every person as a right, the way our Founding Fathers guaranteed life and liberty. The other thing I cherish, which embodies this noble ideal, is our new system of medicine, CareFree."

Waiters watched from the sidelines, ready to serve the first course when the speaker finished.

"Contrary to our opponents' denials, private medicine has failed. Oh, it gave us dazzling technological advances and a standard of care unmatched in the world. But it failed on moral grounds. Patients had to pay for their care while doctors profited from the sick. The poor suffered the indignity of having to say 'please' and 'thank you' for someone's charity. Under CareFree, no one needs to rely on a doctor's alms, because care is guaranteed to all by law.

"At first the state did not want to manage doctors' business but merely to pay the bills for special groups like the older folks and the needy. But when the government picked up the tab, patients acted like sweepstakes winners on a shopping spree and providers behaved like retailers whose customers held the key to Fort Knox. The demand for care soared as people sought costly tests for every headache and fancy drugs for every stomachache. And the providers welcomed the increased business with expanded offices, new wings, elaborate equipment, and expensive tests. So there was a problem: People spent more when someone gave them a blank check. The solution was to keep giving the check—no caring person would dispute that—but to fill in the blanks.

"This is why the government had to step in to manage medicine. But did our providers accept the limits placed on them for the public interest? Regrettably, many fought us. To compensate for the lower fees they received for their public patients, the providers hiked the billings to their private patients. This squeezed the private insurance companies that were paying those bills. The insurers reacted by raising their premiums. This continued until the prices got so high that nobody could afford a policy. The problem was worsening. The solution was more management by the state."

The secretary's eyes caught the approving nod of Governor Burrow.

"So you see, private insurance also failed, and for the same reason," the secretary continued with conviction. "The government stepped in to regulate the insurers so that they would act with kindness, not actuarial tables; with sensitivity, not statistics; with the same rates for all; with no one denied a policy; with every condition covered. But did the insurers comply? More concerned with the ticks of their stock than the tears of the needy, they curtailed care and canceled policies faster than we could pass enough laws to stop them.

"The problem became a crisis. The solution was more management by the government. Finally, Governor Burrow, in his ardent compassion for the people, stepped in to save medicine with CareFree."

Like creatures stalking prey, television cameras covering the event fixed their lenses on the secretary.

"CareFree proudly is concerned not with finance, but with feeling; not with profit, but with pity; not with amount tendered, but with compassion rendered."

The secretary raised his head, his face imbued with a religious fervor. The governor looked confident that the secretary was the right man for his campaign.

"Our opponents claim that our ideal has been tried before and it failed. However, it was not the *ideal* that failed but the people entrusted with it. If a rocket could soar to Mars but unscrupulous people filled the fuel tank with sand, should we blame the rocket or the saboteurs? Unfortunately, some practitioners have failed in their responsibility to comply with our new program. They break the rules and overload the system with expenses!" He bristled, as if hitting a sore point. "I want to assure all New Yorkers that we will *strictly* enforce our guidelines for the medical profession! Let this be a warning: I will *not* allow malcontents to dump sand into our engine!"

A disturbing stillness fell on the room, most quickly on the doctors in the audience. They sat frozen, their eyes darting nervously. The governor's smile faded, and panic covered the secretary's face. Sensing that a change in course was needed to avoid crashing his rocket, the secretary quickly scanned his mind for a remedy. He noticed that the waiters had placed a glass of champagne before each person, so he picked up his and smiled.

"But let us return to our purpose," he said, his tone lighter. "Let us toast that which ended centuries of misery, transforming human existence from pain, suffering, and early death to health, happiness, and long life. A toast to modern medicine."

He raised his glass high and waited for the guests to follow suit.

"And a toast to the man who harnessed medicine to serve the public, the man who will be reelected in November. A toast to Governor Malcolm Burrow!"

Eight hundred gulps reverberated through the room.

David Lang's car hit the bridge to Manhattan with a loud thump, but his foot did not lighten on the gas pedal. The procedure would be a normal event of his life—he was called, he came, he worked, he left—except for one thing: This time he was angry.

A hot fuse of disturbing facts burned through his mind. Fact one: Bentley said the hemorrhage was subdural, below the dura, one of the layers of tissue between the skull and brain. David expected such a bleed to be from a vein, which flowed more slowly than an artery, providing time for diagnosis and treatment. Bentley said that the patient had sought medical attention prior to her emergency. Why did the problem remain undetected for days after the patient had seen her doctor? Fact two: The brain was sending warning signals with the worsening headaches. A blow to the head followed by progressively severe headaches, he thought, was a neon advertisement of trouble early on. Why had this symptom been preposterously misdiagnosed as migraines? And why had a scan apparently been delayed until so much blood and pressure mounted that the brain became a kettle about to blow its lid? Fact three: The patient was taking an anticoagulant, a blood thinner, for treatment of a clot in her leg. She had just given birth, and because pregnancy can worsen varicose veins and thrombosis, anticoagulants are sometimes prescribed. But any medical student knows that people taking blood thinners run a higher risk of hemorrhage after injury because their blood can fail to clot normally. Why was the anticoagulant apparently continued after the head injury and onset of headaches while the possibility of hemorrhage was ignored? He swore aloud; the prospect of senseless death was increasing the pressure on his own brain.

Was Bentley the doctor who had treated the woman earlier in the week? With general practitioners pressured by CareFree to reduce referrals to specialists, patients increasingly flooded the ER, where they could see such doctors more easily.

Bentley was the neurosurgery resident on call that week in the ER, and he had referred to the woman as "my patient." Had Bentley examined her earlier and sent her home to take blood thinners, with a subdural bleed? He swore again. *Stop it!* he ordered himself as he reached Manhattan. He ran a red light and headed west.

The air in the windowless waiting room of Riverview Hospital was hot and stale. Ten-year-old Billy Miller thought it was the stink of the hospital that made him sick to his stomach. A tall man in blue clothing, Dr. Bentley, was talking to his father. The doctor said that Eileen, his mother, was very sick, that her brain was bleeding, that a Dr. Lang was coming to operate. Billy could not take his eyes off the man's face, waiting, hoping . . . but Dr. Bentley did not smile. Billy wondered why he had played baseball outside their brownstone after his mother had told him not to, after she had warned him that someone could get hurt. He wondered why she was falling asleep so much and wasn't herself that week. Was it because his baseball had hit her that she was sick? Billy's father and older sister sat holding hands, but the boy remained by himself.

A door swung open in the operating room where Eileen Miller lay unconscious. The scrub nurse raised her eyebrows when Dr. Lang rushed in wearing street clothes. His eyes hit the shaved head on the operating table and the brain scans on the view box, and then he gasped.

"Get me gloves!"

"I'll have these instruments laid out in a few minutes while you change and scrub, Doctor," said the scrub nurse.

"We don't have a few minutes!"

"I need to insert this catheter," said the circulating nurse, trying to move around him.

"Forget that!" he said.

"I'll tape these tubes down," said the anesthesiologist, trying to get at the patient.

"Not now," said David, as the nurses threw a sterile gown over street clothes and sterile gloves over unwashed hands.

Someone managed to place a mask and cap on him. Soon the buzz of a high-speed drill and the smell of scorched tissue hit the air.

David had no time to question Tom Bentley, who was assisting him, because pieces of Eileen Miller's brain were about to explode. Clumped blood from the hemorrhage pushed structures in the brain, causing pressure to rise. David ordered drugs to reduce the swelling while trying desperately to contain the brain tissue in the skull, to remove the mottled clumps of blood, and to find the source of the bleed in a sea of red.

The brain David faced was raging. Spewing and clumping blood buried the normal pale color, gentle pulse, and delicate landscape of vessels and nerves.

Somewhere near the red deluge was the center that controlled Eileen's circulation and breathing. How much time would David have before the red menace reached the command post of the brain and began pushing and shoving critical areas? The threat haunted him. He evacuated the purple blotches at an alarming pace, with vital structures a hair's width from flying instruments. Could David find the source of the bleed and stop it in time? How much good brain would be lost on the battlefield? And what would remain of Eileen Miller, wife and mother?

Aromas of cognac and coffee laced the air of the grand ballroom after the meal. The crystal chandeliers cast a jaundiced glow on Governor Malcolm Burrow, rising from the dais to speak. His hair was neither black nor white but a tangle of the two, as if undecided between youth and old age. With thin legs and a paunch, he was both slim and chubby. His mouth smiled while his eyes drooped, his face seemingly unable to choose a mood. He wore cuff links handcrafted by an Iroquois descendant and a digital watch from a New York manufacturer. Malcolm Burrow was said to be all things to all people, an impression that he seemed to encourage, especially with an election looming. Television cameras followed him to the podium as the band played "Back Mack," a tune created for his campaign.

"Good evening, my fellow New Yorkers. I sincerely appreciate your generous support for my campaign. I see many among you who backed me four years ago in my first race for governor. I hope you all realize that your contributions helped us make history.

"My administration launched CareFree, the greatest public entitlement program ever attempted in New York. We're the first state to guarantee health care to all citizens. The president of the United States himself hailed CareFree as a model system. So now every other state in the nation is scrambling to copy what we've already accomplished here in New York!"

The audience cheered.

"Now, I'm going to ask you to make history with me again," continued the governor. "I have only one campaign promise this time, but accomplishing it will be another milestone. First, let me say that I was as shocked as everyone by the recent . . . questions . . . concerning one of our colleagues."

Burrow's tone softened. The lieutenant governor, conspicuously absent from the evening's event, was under investigation for accepting gifts and payments from construction companies awarded government contracts, and many voices were urging Burrow to choose a new running mate.

"We are thoroughly investigating the matter involving the lieutenant governor. Once the facts are known, I will act accordingly."

Burrow waved his hand as if to shoo away the scandal blackening the front pages of every newspaper in the state in recent weeks. Cameras panned to the secretary of medicine, the leading contender for the governor's running mate should the lieutenant governor be forced off the ticket. Prominent citizens lauded the secretary as a "man of honor," "pillar of morality," "impassioned servant of the people."

"This brings me to my promise to you and to all New Yorkers," Burrow continued. "I pledge that my administration will serve no cause other than the people's welfare. We will make history again, this time by having the most honorable government ever to serve the people. The public interest will be our only beacon!"

The governor's voice was a distant drone to alcohol-mellowed Marie Lang, sipping cognac and watching the waiter pour coffee.

"This coffee's stale," said the partner who managed Reliant Care's clinical staff, the tinge of petulance in his manner becoming more pronounced after the evening's drinks. He raised his hand to signal the waiter, and then lowered it. "Aw, what's the use complaining? Nobody listens."

The financial officer tasted his coffee, and then glanced around the room. "It's stale, but no one else is complaining. Who are we to go against the majority?"

"This is typical," said the head of marketing, tasting the contents of his cup disapprovingly. "The hotel makes a killing on the banquet, then serves us these dregs. There ought to be a law."

"I have just the thing," said Marie. She poured some of her cognac into the complaining partner's coffee. "How's that?"

"Actually, very good!" said the partner, sipping the brew.

Paul Eastman smiled. "That's a fifty-year-old cognac you just poured into stale coffee, my dear. One could say you ruined the cognac."

"Or one could say I improved the coffee."

"I'd say Marie's bent on making things work, even if it takes a little defiling," said the head of the clinical staff approvingly.

"The way Reliant's growing, we'll need to take on another partner." Eastman tapped Marie's hand. "Let's talk."

"Let's do, Paul," she replied.

Marie's silky hair bounced as she tossed her head back in enjoyment of the moment. Affixed to the thin strap of her gown was a gold pin. In the creamy light of the chandelier, one could read the engraving: *Dr. Marie Lang, Distinguished Caregiver.*

Disinfectants and sweat hung in the heavy air of the OR. Fluids that had been sucked out of Eileen Miller's brain filled a plastic container. Bloody gauze pads lay in neat rows on a blue cloth after a nurse triple-checked that every one put into the patient's brain had been retrieved. Bentley finished bandaging the patient's head. While David Lang shed a surgical gown resembling a butcher's apron after a day's work, the anesthesiologist removed the respiratory tube. David's eyes froze on Eileen Miller's still body. What would her lungs do? Within moments, her chest rose and fell in even breaths, an auspicious sign! Smile lines, the first of the evening, livened David's face.

He accompanied Eileen into the recovery room. Standing over her listless form, he waited for her to awaken. Would she? No device existed to spare him the anguished moments after surgery when only the limp body before him knew whether his best effort had been good enough. He waited for Eileen's body to confide in him its secret. Interminable minutes passed. Then Eileen Miller opened her eyes.

"Good evening, Eileen! Squeeze my hand."

Five frail fingers made the journey around the summoning hand. David felt a weak but discernible pressure.

"Good! Now squeeze my other hand. . . . Wiggle your toes. . . . Very good! . . . Now follow my finger with your eyes. . . . What year is it, Eileen?"

Although groggy and confused, Eileen responded normally to his various neurological tests. David laughed in exhaustion, relief, and triumph. But his laughter died when Bentley entered the room.

David stepped away from the bed and whispered to the resident: "Was a brain scan done on this patient before tonight?"

"No, Doctor."

"Do you know that a patient taking anticoagulants is predisposed to hemorrhage after trauma?"

"Yes, Doctor."

"Do you also know that persistent headaches after a head injury are a neurological sign to take seriously?"

"Of course," Bentley replied, confused.

"What has been done all week to treat this woman?"

"She was given a painkiller for migraines."

"Do you know the difference between a migraine and an intracranial hemorrhage?"

"Why, yes."

"Is this what I'm teaching you to do, Bentley?"

"Oh," Bentley said in sudden understanding. "But—"

"To observe symptoms and not to test?"

"But Dr. Lang—"

"To send a patient home to die! Is that what you're learning here?" David's fists tightened.

"But, Doctor, I—"

"Excuse me, Dr. Lang." A nurse had approached them, pointing to a man and two children standing at the doorway. "The Millers made their way back here. Shall I ask them to wait?"

David saw six desperate eyes staring at him.

"No, I'll talk to them right away." Glancing at Bentley, he added coolly, "I'll be back."

Despite the exhaustion apparent in his puffy eyes, David's handshake was firm. "Hello, Mr. Miller. I'm David Lang. I just operated on Eileen."

"You're smiling, Dr. Lang. Does that mean we . . . have reason . . . to . . . hope?"

"I think Eileen is going to be fine."

His words transformed three despondent figures into human beings. Mr. Miller jubilantly embraced his daughter. He paused to look for a small presence standing apart, watching them.

"Come here, son. Everything's going to be all right."

Billy tentatively walked toward them. The father and sister threw their arms around the little bundle, clutching him until the biting sadness lifted its grip on his small face.

David allowed them to talk to Eileen. He watched with a quiet thrill as they kissed the limp form with the bandaged head. He stood apart, allowing them intimacy, yet he could not avert his eyes, knowing he was part of that moment.

"Dr. Lang, forgive me—I haven't thanked you yet," Mr. Miller said when they left the patient. "You see, I'm still stunned. Eileen seemed fine. She complained of headaches earlier in the week, but they weren't bad at first."

"These conditions sometimes worsen, even though she might have seemed okay when you brought her to the hospital earlier this week."

"We never brought her to the hospital."

"You didn't come to the ER?"

"Why, no, we didn't think there was an emergency—until tonight when we couldn't arouse her from a nap."

"I guess I assumed you brought her here."

"We've never been to Riverview Hospital before tonight, except when Eileen gave birth."

"I was napping when Dr. Bentley called me this evening. I thought he treated her earlier this week."

"We never met Dr. Bentley until tonight."

"Oh, I see!" David said, relieved to owe Bentley an apology. He liked the resident. Then the fuse within him reignited, searching for the proper target to strike. "Who treated your wife?"

"She saw our general practitioner at the office as soon as the headaches started, the same physician who has been treating her varicose veins. We also telephoned our doctor when the headaches were worsening. We were told they were migraines and nothing to worry about."

"Who is this doctor?"

"Well, that's what we were wondering."

"What do you mean?"

"We were curious."

"About what?"

"Your name. We wondered if you were related. You see, our general doctor is Marie Lang. . . . Doctor, are you okay? . . . Is anything wrong?"

❧4❧
The New Frontier

To serve the public interest above all other concerns—this is the noble work of medicine. David Lang read the gold inscription over the entrance to the Manhattan offices of the Bureau of Medicine. His eyes dropped contemptuously to the
name under the quotation—that of the secretary of medicine.

In the serpentine lobby of the old brick building, he passed a mural of Antoni
van Leeuwenhoek peering through his magnifying lens in a moment of discovery. Leaning against the picture was the ladder of a maintenance man who was
changing a lightbulb. In the center of the lobby stood a statue of Joseph Lister
gazing into a test tube. Propped against its legs was a makeshift sign with directions to the information desk. A white marble tablet in the floor displayed the
etching *To the independent mind that is the wellspring of science.* The mural, the
statue, and the tablet were the remains of a bygone era when the building was
home to a distinguished medical school. David recalled hearing of students being
required to walk around the tablet, with the placement of one foot on the inlay
being grounds for punishment. Despite the building's history, countless shoe
prints now scuffed the inscription, the letters rounded from wear. As was his
practice, David walked around the tablet. Riding the elevator to the Department
of Medical Research, the man who spent more time in the OR than at home felt
that it was *he* who was now out of step in this building dedicated to medicine.

He arrived at a small, austere conference room whose gray walls and fluorescent lighting were as cold as the seven people sitting around its oval table. They
comprised the committee that would determine the future of his research—and
of his life, he thought uneasily.

Rising to greet him was the head of the committee, a petite, businesslike
woman in her forties, Dr. Alice Cook, the director of medical research for the
BOM. The shorthaired and long-waisted Dr. Cook, fashionably clad in a blue suit,
introduced David to the other members. With sweeping hand gestures and a
measured voice, she seemed to enjoy lingering in the moment of having control
over the fate of another. In an effort to establish what she liked to call a partnership with the community, she included in her group laypeople as well as health
care professionals. Thus, she presented David to a research scientist, a public-
health administrator, a retired gynecologist, a minister, a manufacturer, and a
homemaker.

When everyone was seated, Dr. Cook walked to the podium at the head of
the table and read from David's curriculum vitae: "Dr. David Lang is a practicing neurosurgeon and a professor at West Side University Medical School. He

has published dozens of papers and lectured internationally. He seeks permission to complete a research project he started years ago." She turned to him cordially. "Dr. Lang, please tell us about your project."

The man who approached the podium looked too young to possess the lengthy vita before Dr. Cook, except for an air of quiet confidence in his bearing. The aesthetic lines of his face made him seem too pure to deal with blood and death, but a ruthlessness in his eyes suggested that he could absorb such shocks. The silk suit he wore appeared too elegant for the grisly work of a surgeon, yet its tailored lines implied a laser-sharp focus on business.

"Thank you, Dr. Cook. Good afternoon, ladies and gentlemen." On a small table beside the podium, David rested a soft leather briefcase that he had brought. Eyeing the laypeople in the group, he decided to explain his work in simple terms. "My research centers around the thing that makes humans the supreme creatures of the world, characterized by remarkable feats and endless progress, from the cave to the skyscraper, from the wheel to the rocket, from the campfire to the power plant, from the stone tool to the computer. This thing makes humans superior to other animals because we alone can understand the world and harness the powers of nature to control our destiny. This thing is the most exquisitely complex object known, housing the massive power of two hundred billion cells engaged in countless electrochemical reactions, yet it is nothing more than a three-pound gelatinous mass that fits in the palm of your hand. It is, of course, the human brain.

"It might seem that the most powerful device in the world should be hard and indestructible, but the opposite is true. The human brain is soft and delicate. A blow could crush it; a germ could destroy it; a block in one of its arteries could choke it. Perhaps nothing needs and deserves protection more than the vulnerable human brain. A neurosurgeon is the man or woman who is the brain's defender."

Like the megalithic statues David had seen on an ancient island, the entities before him seemed to possess huge, lifeless heads atop short stumps for bodies. He tried to dismiss the vision that his future depended on reaching the unreachable.

"The billions of cells in the human brain comprise its intricate governing body, the central nervous system. This system holds the key to the brain's power—and also to its weakness. This nerve tissue ultimately makes possible every thought, movement, and process of the body. But however remarkable it may be, centuries of research and millennia of suffering demonstrate one thing this tissue can't do. It can't regenerate.

"When skin rubs off, the body makes more. When you lose blood, the body replenishes it. If you break an arm, the bone grows back. But what if a stab wound to the head severs your optic nerve? The nerve's function is lost forever.

What if you suffer a stroke? To the extent that the cortex is damaged, you will never again be yourself. What if you fall off a horse and injure your spinal cord? Because the spinal cord is an extension of the brain and has the same nerve tissue, the broken fibers will not reattach, and the movement they controlled will be lost forever.

"At birth, the brain and spinal cord essentially contain their full measure of nerves, each fiber like a strand of gold in a bank that permits only withdrawals. This is what makes nerve tissue precious and the brain vulnerable. Damaged nerves cannot be replaced; their assets are lost forever."

David could read nothing on the faces of his audience. The group neither took notes nor yawned but merely listened dutifully.

"The suffering caused by the refusal of the nerves to regenerate is gut-wrenching. Every neurosurgeon dreads finding an injured teenager in the ER, completely and permanently paralyzed from the neck down, unable even to breathe on his own. The only thing the kid can do is stare at you and cry, except when sleep brings a temporary reprieve to him—and to you.

"So much misery is endured because nerve cells won't grow. They once grew like crazy, at the rate of almost a million per minute during the entire prenatal period, when a few starter cells create the majestic human nervous system. After birth, however, this self-generating capacity of the nerves is lost.

"Some primitive species do regrow damaged parts. If you cut off the leg of a crab or the arm of a starfish, the animal makes another. These simple creatures seem more hardy than humans because *their* injured parts grow back."

David felt the chill of unquestioning eyes politely following him as he paced slowly before the group. Why did he suspect that the committee's conclusion was foregone and his performance merely a formality?

"If we could recapture the priceless capacity for nerve growth that we had before birth, we'd cross a new frontier. Victims of paralysis would discard their wheelchairs and skip across that frontier. But the problems are formidable. I've grappled with them for seven years. First, the nerves of the brain and spinal cord won't grow; if you put two severed ends together, the nerves won't extend to fill the gap the way broken bone tissue would. Then, scar tissue grows at the lesion site, causing a serious, further impediment.

"Considering how complex nerve tissue is, we can appreciate the difficulty of regeneration. Take the optic nerve, which carries impulses from the eye to the back of the brain, producing vision. This nerve consists of over a million fibers. It's like an unbelievably complicated cable containing a million wires, each color-coded with unique shadings and hues. When the cable is cut, each of the million wires on one side of the break must find its own severed end on the other side in order for the cable to work again. The nerves seem as baffled by this task as the researchers.

"But today I can tell you a secret . . ."

The secret crying in David's mind lured him like the music of the mythological Sirens, whose haunting songs ensnared all listeners. He forgot the audience, the BOM, the many obstacles plaguing him. His voice rose excitedly.

"The secret is that everything I told you is *false*."

He paused for water, the last word lingering in the air.

"These nerves *will* grow. They'll overcome the scar. They'll find their mates. And the horror of nerve injury will join the black plague as a forgotten nightmare of the past!"

The exalted vision of such a future radiated on the surgeon uttering the words.

"A lot remains to be done: more animal experiments, then human trials. However, my recent experiments show that we can regenerate the central nervous system and restore lost function."

David's pace quickened. He seemed unable to stand still.

"I discovered a protein in the nerve tissue of mammalian embryos that disappears after birth. It holds the secret of growth. When injured adult nerve is treated with this embryonic growth protein from lower animals, the tissue acquires a most extraordinary power to regenerate.

"Regarding the other hurdle, the barrier created by the scar, I isolated a substance that inhibits the scar from forming. Unfortunately, this substance also stops the new nerve from growing. However, the problem can be treated in two stages—that is, with two surgical procedures: one to regenerate the damaged nerve with the growth protein and the other, three months later, to remove the scar tissue produced and prevent any more from forming by treatment with the scar inhibitor. I have a presentation that demonstrates my study."

He removed from his briefcase a laptop computer, connected it to equipment in the front of the room, and projected an image onto a screen behind him. Someone dimmed the lights as he started the presentation. The first scene showed him in surgical garb standing over an anesthetized cat on an operating table.

"Here you see a complete transection of the spinal cord." His trim form was silhouetted in the darkened room as he narrated the scenes. The camera showed him cutting the cat's spinal cord.

"The first surgery is to reattach the severed nerve ends . . . " A camera on David's operating microscope showed him suturing the nerve ends together.

" . . . and to implant the growth protein at the lesion site." He positioned a capsule filled with a liquid at the point of the injury. "The growth protein is administered through a timed-release capsule that will introduce a continuous stream of the substance over a three-month period. The nerve tissue should then be fully regrown, and the empty capsule remaining will biodegrade and be evacuated by the body."

Next the screen showed the cat after the surgery. "As you see, the spinal cord transection left the cat's hind legs paralyzed." The poor creature struggled to move, powered only by its front quarters, dragging two hind legs like lead weights.

"During the three-month period after the first surgery, partial function will be restored as the nerve tissue grows back." The next scene showed the cat still using its front quarters to drag its body around, but now the hind legs moved, too, although the motion was limited and insufficient to enable the cat to stand.

"There will come a time when the partial restoration of function peaks. After that, it retrogresses because the growing scar tissue becomes an impediment." The cat on the screen showed less movement of its hind legs than before. "Without the second surgery, the interference from the scar tissue increases until the restored function is lost completely, leaving the victim no better off than before the first surgery."

The scene changed to the OR, where David prepared to operate on the cat's spine. "The timing of the second surgery is critical. It must be done after the nerve has grown and before all of the recovered function is lost to scar tissue. If the cat's hind legs retrogressed to full paralysis again, the loss of function this time would be irreversible."

Onscreen, David began the second surgery, with the camera showing a magnified image through the operating microscope. "You can see that the nerve ends have grown back together. There is no more break where the cord had been transected. However, you can also see why the repaired nerve tissue can't function. It's entangled by the scar. Now I'll remove it." Small, shiny tools delicately cut away the scar, bit by bit, avoiding the repaired nerve.

"This next shot, taken hours later, shows that the scar has been completely removed. The nerve tissue is now freed." The audience saw clean, glistening nerve tissue at the surgical site.

"I will inject some of the scar inhibitor over the nerve," he said, as a needle dispersed a liquid over the area, "and implant the rest in another biodegradable timed-release capsule. The scar loves to grow back and tangle with the nerve. However, the prolonged presence of the inhibitor from the capsule will keep scar from ever again appearing here, so this nerve tissue will remain unobstructed.

"After the second surgery, the cat can walk again. Here it is a month later."

The screen showed David playing with his furry patient. It ran and jumped with the energy of a kitten. A lively spirit had returned to the little creature. It seemed thrilled by its own bold leaps, performed effortlessly—thanks to the full use of its hind legs.

David stopped the presentation, and someone raised the lights. The expression that the committee saw bore the glorious contentment that results when a three-pound gelatinous mass harnesses the power of nature to control its own destiny.

"Ladies and gentlemen, this is the new frontier. This is the research that I *must* complete. . . . Thank you."

Dr. Cook raised an eyebrow, as if David's final words had overstepped the line from a request to a demand. The surgeon ignored her glance as he slid his computer back into its case.

Like an accused awaiting a jury verdict, David was escorted to an outer area while the committee deliberated. Minutes later, Dr. Cook retrieved him. Her unsmiling face foretold the verdict. She stepped behind the podium, as if to maintain a barrier between her and the green eyes staring insolently from a seat at the table.

"Dr. Lang, after careful consideration, the committee finds that although your work is valuable, it regrettably falls outside the scope of our more pressing social needs. Many people now question the wisdom of spending large sums for the benefit of a small minority when the majority funding universal health care has other concerns. We must weigh the relative value to society of offering one ground-breaking surgery to the few individuals needing it against providing, for example, one thousand pairs of contact lenses to those needing better vision."

She paused as if expecting a polite nod from David but received none.

"You know, of course, that your research has been attempted by countless others and always ended in failure, despite the initially promising outcome of a few isolated experiments. I'm afraid we have a responsibility to allocate public funds for projects benefiting more people and having greater chances of success."

David scanned the faces of committee members, who nodded in agreement. Like a jury in the presence of a judge, the others let Dr. Cook do the talking.

"Unfortunately, our budget is limited, and for every project we approve, there are twenty we must decline," Dr. Cook continued. "However, we want to thank you, Dr. Lang, for the opportunity to consider your research. Please feel free to submit other proposals to us. And we wish you success in your career."

Dr. Cook smiled, but David did not return the courtesy.

"Frankly, Dr. Cook," he said, his voice solemn, his eyes intense, "I don't want the public to fund my research. I don't want to have to fit in with what this committee thinks it needs or feels will succeed. I just want to be left alone to finish my work. I want to procure laboratory animals and conduct experiments at my own expense or with the aid of investors as a private venture. I'm prepared to do that. Now if my work doesn't cost the public a dime, then this committee should not have the power to object."

"But we do have that power, Dr. Lang. You know the law," replied Dr. Cook. Her voice remained coolly polite, despite the flush that formed on her cheeks. "Animals are protected. Their use in research is limited to projects approved by the state. We can't allow anyone who feels like it to butcher animals. That wouldn't be humane."

"Is it humane to squash seven years of research and stand in the way of progress?"

"It's not progress, Dr. Lang, when researchers go off half-cocked and are unaccountable to society," said Dr. Cook, her voice rising. "To conduct animal experiments without the proper authorization would be a serious infraction of the law."

One person folded his glasses into a case; another reached for her purse. Dr. Cook gathered her papers. The meeting was over for all but David.

"Where does that leave me and the thousands of patients who would want my new procedure, Dr. Cook? Would these patients think it humane of you to spare the animals and prevent me from properly testing the treatment on them first?"

"You know perfectly well that I don't mean you can experiment on humans instead. You first have to complete the animal trials."

"But thanks to this committee, I can't do the animal trials!"

"To perform your procedure and use your untested drugs on a human subject without first obtaining exhaustive animal studies and the proper regulatory approvals could expose you to serious consequences, Dr. Lang, including loss of your license"—Dr. Cook's voice dropped—"and even charges of manslaughter. Consider yourself warned."

David sprang from his chair and approached the podium to retrieve the briefcase he had left there. He walked unduly close to the petite woman, his tall form towering over her, his face hot with anger, his voice heavy with contempt. "Seven people sitting in a room don't have the right to tell me how to do my work. Seven people don't have the right to deny thousands of patients a treatment they'd want to have. Seven people can't run medicine for the rest of us, Dr. Cook!"

Cool air rushed into the stuffy room as David swung the door open and left.

Too agitated to be confined in a taxi, David walked briskly through the steaming city streets. But even his anger could not sustain his fast pace that hot day, and his steps soon slowed to a plod. The dank summer air had sapped his energy, just as the meeting at the BOM had sapped his spirit. He passed an outdoor café dotted with people sipping colorful summer drinks at tables covered with checkered cloths. Quitting time had arrived, and workers were spilling into the restaurants and bars to unwind from the day's tensions. Should he not do the same? But the bitter taste from the meeting combined with the rank smell of the city at rush hour left him feeling unable to eat or drink anything.

He phoned his wife to say that he would be working late. Despite his intention to go to his office, he seemed unable to steer his steps in that direction. Instead, they took him to the nearby theater district. His thoughts traveled back to a time when he had leaped out of bed each morning, eager for a fresh dose of the sweet addiction that nourished him, the surgeries that were his food, water, and air, with their struggles and victories. He felt that something was now vanishing. He still had struggles. But what was he losing and needing most urgently to reclaim? He stopped before a theater marquee that seemed to hold the answer. It said *Triumph*.

David Lang did not go to his office that evening. Instead, he bought a ticket to Nicole Hudson's show.

5

Hide and Seek

When he left Riverview Hospital at one o'clock the next afternoon, David Lang was unhappy. Despite his intention to remain busy until his mid-afternoon office appointments, he had swiftly completed his morning surgeries and hospital rounds without any complications, emergencies, or distraught relatives to detain him. Being ahead of schedule displeased David because it gave him time to do something that he had promised himself he would not do.

He stepped outside into the tropical forest of scantily clad people, hot asphalt, and smoking gridlock that was Manhattan in July. He walked for a few blocks until he reached the glass door of a flower shop where a puff of cool, fragrant air welcomed him. He strolled through the shop, surveying the store's colorful inventory with the intensity of a composer creating a theme. After careful deliberation, he beckoned the proprietor, a businesswoman in a tailored dress, standing nearby.

"I know what I want," he said, smiling.

Pointing to an array of exotic flowers in a display case, he described the arrangement that he envisioned.

"And will there be a note, sir?

"No!"

The proprietor looked curious at the sudden edge in his voice.

"All right," she said pleasantly, gathering the flowers.

The woman assembled the display while David directed the creation. With a boyish excitement, he watched the product of his imagination take physical shape.

"On second thought, I'll take a piece of your stationery."

When David received the paper, his smile vanished, his head dropped, and he stared intently at the blank sheet. Sitting on a stool at the end of the counter, he began to write. With a hand that controlled minutely accurate instruments in the exacting repair of the intricate human brain, he wrote in a script of such exquisite precision that the letter he composed seemed more like art than mere communication.

Five blocks away at the Taylor Theater, a leotard-clad Nicole Hudson had just completed a ballet class with her fellow dancers prior to the day's matinee. Returning to her dressing room, she sprawled across the couch to relax for a moment before showering. Her head rested on a pillow, her long legs extended past the armrest. Her eyes paused on a picture hanging on the wall. The photo captured her at age sixteen, in arabesque, playing the princess of her favorite childhood ballet. Nicole smiled at her likeness, remembering the thrill of her first leading role, a thrill she now felt every day as Pandora.

She was born Cathleen Hughes, the daughter of an alcoholic mother and a father she never knew. She had lived with her mother in a dilapidated building on Manhattan's West Side, in a neighborhood never visited by the tour buses. Whenever her mother spoke of her father's disappearance, the subject of Nicole's birth invariably followed. "Your father had a job. He gave me money. I thought he'd marry me once I had you. But, no, he wasn't ready for a little brat. He took off the day you were born," her mother would tell her resentfully. "That day's cursed, I tell you! It's the day I started drinking."

Because the mother tried to forget the cursed day, the child did not know when she was born. Sister Luke from St. Jude's Parish, where the neighborhood children gathered, had a practice of lighting a candle on a cupcake for a youngster having a birthday, leading the other children in singing to the honored one. "When's your birthday, Cathleen?" the nun once asked. "The Fourth of July," the child replied, because she liked the holiday's bands and fireworks.

What the mother failed to provide, the child tried to substitute. On the frequent days when her mother slept until noon, the child rose early, dressed herself, climbed onto a chair to search the kitchen cabinets for a stale cookie or bag of pretzels for breakfast, took her key, then went to school. Always draped over her shoulder was a torn serape picked from the trash behind a flea market. On occasions when she returned home to find the door locked from the inside, indicating that her mother was entertaining a male visitor, the child neither whined nor cried nor pounded on the door. In the silent, matter-of-fact manner that became her habit, she made do. She canvassed her favorite garbage cans for food. Wrapped in her colorful serape, she slept in the hallway of her building. When the dinner pickings were slim or the night was cold, the child went to St. Jude's to be sheltered by Sister Luke until such time as her mother noticed her absence and retrieved her.

When she was eight, her mother left her on the steps of St. Jude's with a promise: "I'll come back for you as soon as I can." She never returned. The child remembered the man waiting for her mother in a nearby car, the man who spoke of marrying her mother but who always referred to her as a "nuisance." Thus, Nicole was born in her mother's attempt to land a man and abandoned for the same reason.

Perhaps because the child had already acquired a stray cat's skill at caring for herself and a future star's dream of dancing on stage, she survived her gloomy predicament. The radiant sixteen-year-old princess pictured in the dressing room looked unscathed. Never one to take success for granted, Nicole instead always cherished every signpost of it. From her spot on the couch, she smiled at her likeness in quiet salute.

Just then the phone rang.

"Hello."

"Is this Nicole Hudson?" a voice whispered.

"Yes."

"This is Tony from Regal Flowers. You were in here a week ago—"

"Yes, Tony!" Her heart raced. She remembered the shop and the teenage clerk.

"You said to call if somebody came to buy you flowers."

"That's right! Is he there now?"

"You said you'd give me two hundred bucks—"

"The money's yours! Is he there? Can you speak up?"

"I don't want him to hear," the caller whispered. "The boss is making an arrangement for him that I'm supposed to bring you. He won't be here much longer."

"Did he give his name?" She flew into her closet and threw a pair of slacks and a blouse over her leotard.

"No, but he's tall, black hair, light gray suit, tie—"

"Is he . . . young?"

"He's pretty old," said the teenager. "But not wrinkled yet," he added encouragingly.

"Is he . . . handsome?"

"Looks like any other guy to me."

"Stall him till I get there! You hear, Tony? I'm on my way!"

Seconds later, as she rushed out the back door of the theater, the humidity outside flushed her face.

Hopes of hailing a cab vanished when she saw the gridlocked traffic. Walking would be faster. She tried running, but the lunch crowd was formidable. Her gazelle's legs were reduced to a turtle's pace as she skirted around people and wedged between cars. She remembered the flower shop; it was one she had contacted recently in her search for the Phantom. She wondered at the eagerness of her steps. What kind of force was pulling her? She could not answer. She only knew that she must meet it head-on. After walking one street west, she had four blocks left. She must hurry. But a red light and a caravan of vehicles barred her advance. Like a caged cheetah, she paced across the width of the walkway, ready to leap forward on the green.

The shop owner presented a lively, scented flower arrangement for David's approval. He examined it, touched it, turned it, smelled it, shook it. The proprietor thought he would taste it.

"It could use a little red here," he said, pointing.

The proprietor reached for flowers with the velvety richness of a prized Bordeaux. "Will these do?"

"Oh, yes!" he said, smiling.

The owner embellished the arrangement, and David proclaimed it perfect. He slipped a sealed letter into the wrapping and paid the bill.

Two blocks away, exhaust fumes thickened the air, horns blared, and pedestrians cluttered the sidewalks. With a football player's swinging arms and raised elbows, the graceful Nicole of classical ballet charged past the obstructions. She advanced only a few paces when a conveyor belt unloading boxes from a truck blocked her path. She joined the trickle of people winding into the street around the vehicle. Dainty feet accustomed to tiptoeing on pointe tripped over the heels of the protesting person ahead. Then Nicole collided with three tourists taking a picture. The world seemed to move in slow motion. She reached the corner, with only one more block north to walk. *You're not going to get away this time!* she thought. But then came another red light.

The husky youth named Tony looked more like a linebacker than a flower deliverer. With his hands on his hips and his legs spread apart, he formidably blocked David's advance to the door.

"Excuse me, Mr. . . . uh . . . Mr. . . . ."

"Yes?"

"I'm going to be delivering these flowers, sir, but I'm not sure where the Taylor Theater is."

David looked surprised, as the theater was well known. "It's three blocks south and two east. You can't miss it," he said, stepping around Tony to reach for the doorknob.

With one quick lunge, Tony blocked the door with his body.

"But, sir, I was . . . uh, wondering—is the Taylor Theater on the street with the construction? Is it that old building next to Harley's restaurant?"

"It's on that street, but a few doors east. Now, if you'll excuse me."

David's hand reached out to Tony's midsection, behind which lurked a doorknob.

"How much farther east?" Tony's body did not budge.

"You'll find it."

David and Tony faced off; David tried to reach the door while Tony stood stalwart against it. A line of scrimmage developed, attracting the attention of the proprietor. Her two raised eyebrows finally prodded Tony's body from the exit, and David was permitted to leave.

Nicole sprinted north, her voluminous hair waving behind her like a banner. She stretched her long neck to see the flower shop at the end of the block and across the street. What if she did not like the Phantom? she wondered. *Good,* she thought. *Then I'll be rid of this intrusion in my life!* Nicole had no experience dealing with intrusions.

As she reached the corner and stepped off the curb, she saw a tall man in a gray suit leave the flower shop and step off the curb on the opposite side of the narrow street, facing her across a distance of twelve feet. They both stopped and stared at each other in astonishment.

Somewhere on the edge of David's awareness, he now understood the reason for the employee's odd behavior. With reflexes primed for shocks, he remained expressionless, except for his eyes, which widened in amazement. He made no attempt to hide being caught. His glance fixed on her, and his astonishment softened to a look that was open, calm, almost tender.

Nicole eyed the starched collar of his shirt and the crisp lines of his suit. He seemed impervious to the stifling heat that wilted the figures around him. His hair formed a black backdrop for his face. His eyes seemed to hold center stage, two green magnets pulling her. His mouth was the mysterious part of the scene, its muscles drawn tight, its next move unknown. She found no trace of the despair punctuating his letters and wondered if she alone knew of an inner struggle he kept hidden from the world. His straight posture and penetrating face suggested a man possessing the capacity to write her letters. His countenance was so proud that it seemed as if a spotlight were shining on him, dimming everyone else by contrast. She thought that the stage, not the street, was the fitting place for such a presence. He looked like the prince of her favorite ballet, the one whose powerful kiss awakens her from a long sleep and delivers her to everlasting happiness.

But he was not a prince in a fairy tale, she reminded herself. He was a real man in the world—her world. She suddenly wanted to force him to blink, to make his eyes turn away first. She cocked her head and looked at him insolently. *I don't know anything about you,* she thought, *but maybe I know you better than anyone. I know your deepest longings and your worst despair. You tell me. I think you tell* only *me. You* need *me!*

He saw the meaning of his letters written on her face, a sight that did cause his eyes to break away from hers, but not in the manner she had intended. His eyes danced over her body in a momentary sweep, too subtle to be rude yet too pointed to be polite, a sweep so palpable it made her suddenly aware of her breasts beneath her thin blouse, her thighs against her slacks, the strange tingling down her throat. When his eyes again met hers, it was she who dropped her glance.

This was the first time he had seen her offstage. Without makeup, she looked younger—and more beautiful. He saw a slender young woman with a slim waist, a swanlike neck, and legs too long for a human form, legs suited to a graceful feline. He liked the contrast between the dainty body and the power of its movements on stage. She looked at once vulnerable and strong.

He was struck most by the arresting face that watched him. The firm set of her mouth showed no trace of the laughter that had enchanted him from the stage; the intensity of the giant blue eyes bore no hint of the gaiety he knew. He saw instead an earnestness that was more haunting than her joy, an earnestness he had not anticipated. He searched her face for a sign of levity, which he knew would set him free of her forever, but he could detect no amusement. He saw only a quiet solemnity that conveyed to him what his letters meant to her.

While they stared at each other, neither one seemed to notice that the traffic light was green and the street clear; either one could have crossed at any moment. They continued to face each other across twelve feet until the light changed and a city bus lumbered into the road between them. After the vehicle passed, Nicole was left with a question. Her eyes darted to the nearby subway entrance, to the stores along the street, to the crowded sidewalk, searching for an answer.

Where did the Phantom go?

❧　　❧　　❧

David returned to his office and arranged to take his wife out to dinner. He told himself that he had written his last letter to Nicole. He'd never intended to meet her. He'd certainly never intended to cross the street that afternoon, wrap his arms twice around the slender waist, and press his mouth against hers before any words could be spoken between them. That was just an impulse! Fortunately, the bus had passed, jolting him back to his senses.

"Dr. Lang, are you feeling okay?"

He realized that his secretary had been knocking for a few moments.

"What is it?" he asked the head peering through the door.

"It's about the chocolates you want sent to your wife. Do you prefer dark chocolate, milk chocolate, white choc—"

"Why don't you decide?"

"And would you like truffles or—"

"Whatever you think is good."

"And do you want a note or—"

"Have them scribble my name on a card."

"Okay."

She watched him through the shrinking slit in the door she was closing, puzzled by his uncharacteristic curtness.

Trying to tackle the mound of paperwork on his desk, he grabbed a document but instead saw across the page the immense innocence of Nicole's face. But that was the one thing he must not see, for the delicate figure had been dangerous to him from the start.

The previous summer, in a laboratory that he kept at the university, David had begun an experiment of great importance. By the fall, after hundreds of hours spent isolating his new embryonic protein and scar inhibitor, he hoped to overcome seven years of failed attempts in his research. On the brains of fifty rats, he performed the first of his two operations to regenerate nerve tissue. This experiment, he believed, could finally bring success.

In January, as he was ready to perform the second surgery on the rats to determine whether the new technique worked, he received visitors—inspectors from the Department of Animal Welfare.

"Dr. Lang," said the chief inspector, Daryl Denkins, a thin man with a colorful bow tie and lifeless eyes, "the approval period for your study is expiring, so we're here to reevaluate your research and discuss revisions."

Standing by the door, David stepped aside to let the officials enter, but the annoyance on his face conveyed another message. He remained silent while Denkins and two assistants analyzed his records, examined the animals, and surveyed the premises.

"These physical conditions are stressful, Dr. Lang," said Denkins after his investigation.

"The conditions aren't the best, but I manage."

"I didn't mean stressful for you, Doctor. I meant for the animals. There are violations here."

Denkins paused, as if expecting the customary explanations, excuses, apologies, and pleas, but he received none.

"The air vent is clogged. This air is unhealthy for the animals," continued Denkins.

"But I've been breathing the same air they have for months."

"There are insufficient vitamin supplements in the animals' feed, resulting in improper nutrition."

"More improper than the garbage they eat in the subways?"

"There's a leak in the ceiling, making it substandard."

"More substandard than the ceiling they have in the sewers?"

"And you haven't waited for a veterinarian's approval of your protocol before starting your experiments. That's a major violation."

"But I operate on *humans* all the time. Don't you think I can handle a few rats?"

"A veterinarian is needed to act in the animals' behalf."

"Who acts in my behalf?"

"Dr. Lang, you don't seem to understand."

"I don't."

"These animals have rights."

"I understand only that I have none."

"Of course you have rights, Doctor."

"Do I?"

"It's a free country."

"Then I'd like you to get out of here, so I can finish my experiments."

Denkins laughed, but the sound was not pleasant. "You know, Dr. Lang, I don't appreciate your attitude. In fact, I have enough here to shut you down."

David remembered little of what occurred over the next two days. He could recall only vaguely the order to seize the animals; the police removing cages of rats; Inspector Denkins giving him a list of infractions and telling him that he had forty-eight hours to correct them or else he would be shut down permanently; the cancellation of all of his surgeries and appointments; the repeated exhortations to Denkins not to harm the rats; the forty-eight sleepless hours that he spent correcting the violations; the appearance that he made afterward at the Department of Animal Welfare, with the document necessary to reclaim the animals; Denkins informing him that he was too late, that his time had already expired, and that the fifty rats—on which thousands of dollars and hundreds of hours of effort had been spent, because they held the key to the mystery of the nervous system—had just been transferred to a downtown facility to be destroyed by lethal injection.

"Then I'll pick up the animals at the downtown facility right now, before they're destroyed."

"You can't do that, Doctor."

"Why not?"

"Because Downtown won't give the animals to anyone without our authorization."

"Then call the people downtown and tell them to give the animals to me."

"I can't do that."

"Why not?"

"Because your time expired, and the paperwork was already processed. Downtown has to follow the orders on the paperwork."

"Then get the paperwork back and change it."

"I can't."

"Why not?"

"There's no provision for doing that." Denkins shrugged helplessly.

"If you seized the animals to protect them, then why are you going to kill them?"

"Those are the rules," Denkins replied tonelessly, his listless eyes a bland contrast to his polka-dotted bow tie.

"Then why not destroy them *after* I finish my experiment?"

"But, Doctor, there's no provision for doing that."

David argued the matter with the inspector's superiors, but to no avail. He had to return to the hospital without the animals. For the rest of the day, he performed his work with the same ruthless precision that was as much a part of him as his signature, but without the quiet excitement that had always colored his manner. He was like a computer performing prodigious feats by rote, without the pride, ambition, and joy of a human engine. That evening he stared out the window of his office, watching a winter storm sweep through the street below. The blizzard reduced the normal buzz of traffic to the plaintive screech of a few skidding wheels. The lively dots of people always speckling the pavement at dusk had disappeared, but for a few shivering bundles huddled against doorways, waiting for buses that would not come. He stood motionless at his window, as if he, too, were waiting for something that would not arrive. There were articles to read, papers to write, brain scans to study, sketches to draw, notes to record, but he could not summon the energy to peel his weary eyes from the frozen glass.

He left his office and wandered in the snow, having no desire to go home, to eat, or even to join the reddened faces behind the frosted tavern windows along his path. No activity interested him, not even the act of pulling up his collar to fend off the cold. He drifted as aimlessly as the branches that the wind pulled off the trees and tossed across the desolate streets.

There was a growing scarcity of research animals, making the rats that he had lost irreplaceable. Except for a few cats, he had no other research animals and no hopes of obtaining them—at a time when he needed many more to make progress! His years of work seemed as futile as the car wheels spinning on the icy streets beside him—he could not find traction on a road that led to success, to achievement, to triumph. Then beyond the white brush strokes of snow, he spotted a flashing sign announcing a new production at the Taylor Theater. The sign brazenly proclaimed the existence of that which he thought impossible: *Triumph*. Was the marquee right, or was he? He walked to the theater. The billboard of the show's star suggested a universe in which defeat did not exist. Looking at the proud posture and immense gaiety of the young dancer on the poster, he decided that there was, after all, something he wanted to do. He bought a ticket to the show.

That night he watched a production that took liberties—with nothing less than the story of the creation of mankind. Where actual legend told of woes and miseries irrevocably unleashed on the human race, *Triumph* told of its salvation. That evening David discovered a magical presence that made victory as certain as the sunrise: Nicole Hudson.

When he left the theater, David no longer felt the biting cold. The warm cone of the spotlight seemed to cover him, sealing him from the elements. For the first time in months, his passion for his work was rekindled. Something of immense importance was possible to him, and every fiber in his body burned for it. Then he remembered the unfocused eyes of Inspector Daryl Denkins. Could he surrender his solemn quest, David wondered, not to a noble enemy whom he would fight proudly at the barricade but to a defender of . . . rodents?

The hour was late and the streets were deserted that stormy night. It was easy to return to the hospital for his car, gather cages from the lab, drive to the unguarded animal holding facility in a deserted area by the waterfront, break in through a window, find—to his utter relief!—that his rats had not yet been destroyed, and take some of them and leave the rest, so as not to arouse suspicion. He opened the cages of other animals, scribbled across the wall in crayon *Liberate the animals and cage the people—that's what the world deserves*, smashed the windows, returned to the lab, and worked feverishly through the night. Then as the sun rose after the storm with bold red rays across a new blue sky, he learned that his procedure worked. It worked! For the first time in seven years, success!

Because violent groups of simple vandals or political activists were common, David was not a glaring suspect. Because he had released all of the animals posing no danger, the action did not seem targeted at the rats. And because most of the animals had declined liberation to remain inside the heated facility on such a forbidding night, many of the rats were found there the next morning, lending more credence to David's innocence.

After completing his experiments, David incinerated the rats he'd taken back, destroying the incriminating evidence. With the storm officially closing the laboratory building, no one was present to notice David's activities. He was questioned but not charged with the break-in.

David thought that he should feel relieved to be out of danger—but was he? A greater threat seemed to appear, one that he would have to guard against constantly, for when he'd smashed the windows at the animal center, he'd done so with more . . . diligence . . . than was necessary—with more blows, more shattered glass, and far more ardor than required. Standing amidst the havoc he had created, David Lang had laughed in exultation and deliverance. He had laughed so heartily that he almost forgot to escape.

The next day, through the marvels of horticulture, while the ground lay covered with snow, David sent Nicole daffodils. "Pandora sprinkled me with hope," he wrote in the first of many unsigned letters.

After that night, he would attend Nicole's show whenever his discouragement returned with such tenacity that he could find no other remedy. He always saw her performance alone, as if she were his special secret. The next day he would send flowers accompanied by an unsigned letter. The more he wrote, the more he needed to write. He could not burden his wife, Marie, with his problems when she . . . did not seem to understand. Thus, Nicole became his confidante. He welcomed anonymity; it freed him to express his greatest desires and deepest anguish. To be unknown was to be unencumbered.

He never intended to meet Nicole. He disliked the frivolity of the artists he had met, so he did not expect to like Nicole. He thought his fascination with her was a fantasy. But that was before he saw the thing that astonished him—the solemnity of her face gazing at him from across the street.

Stop it! he ordered himself. Nicole was dangerous. The perverse inspiration with which she imbued him would lead to his demise. He took his worst chances after seeing her show. And most disturbing of all, he did his most brilliant work when he flirted with the impossible, when he attempted to rewrite his fate his own way, and to hell with any one else's script.

Stop it! he ordered himself again. He opened a desk drawer and removed a playbill he kept with Nicole's radiant face on the cover. He tore the pages in half and tossed them in the trash.

Then he heard a knock on his door.

"Yes?"

"Doctor, your first patient has arrived."

"Thank you," he said cheerlessly, rising to begin work.

In a nearby building that was a landmark of the Broadway stage, Tony from Regal Flowers delivered a package to Nicole Hudson's dressing room and collected his bounty. She found the expected envelope tucked in the wrapping, tore it open, and read:

Dear Nicole,

Did you know that the most exotic orchid grows only on top of the tallest tree in the rain forest? From that height, its petals are nourished by the sun, never bruised by the dirt or swallowed by the weeds. Is it wrong to want to reach the brightest flower in the jungle? Is it wrong to climb higher and higher, lured by its unusual beauty?

It wasn't the dizzying height, the searing heat, or the jagged bark that could make me turn back, not when the treasure was so rare. But when creatures too base to seek their own prizes shoot poisoned darts at me, I begin to lose my footing and I can feel myself slipping.

I once believed that the race was to the swift and the battle to the strong. But that was long ago. Now I know that the race is to the turtle and the battle to the sloth. Why is it that weeds can overrun flowers? Yesterday I couldn't break loose from the underbrush that entangled me.

But that was before I saw your show last night, before I saw your body leaping through the air, celebrating the supreme glory of your own existence. That was before I felt the warm wave of your laughter flowing from the stage and lifting me in its crest. Last night you poured before me a different world, a cloudless kingdom where one could climb clear up to the sun. The bright vision of you splashed against my tarnished dreams until they shined again.

For a few magic hours last night, your vibrant spirit lured me away from my despair until I rose so high I could smell the orchids.

She looked for a signature but knew she would find none.

Under the gift-wrapping was a crystal bowl containing two dozen of the most exotic orchids she had ever seen. Their translucent velvet petals soaked the room with color and fragrance. Nicole closed her eyes, inhaled a symphony of sweet perfumes, and envisioned the Phantom's face.

Soon she took her place onstage, waiting for the curtain to rise. *Will he be watching?* she wondered. *This is for you,* she told the lingering presence in her mind. *Today I'll dance especially for you.* Later, when climbing to Prometheus on the desolate cliff, she thought of the proud, lonely figure outside the flower shop. Was he chained, too, and could she set him free?

6

Unnecessary Treatment

A headlamp beamed on a hole being drilled. Although the tool's deafening noise seemed suitable for riveting bolts into concrete, the user's sensitive hands were boring a hole into the base of a young woman's skull so that she could become pregnant and lead a normal life. A desire for children had brought her and her husband to David, who discovered that a tumor on the woman's pituitary gland was causing a hormonal imbalance and preventing conception.

The pressure building inside David's own skull that week—the burning anger after his meeting with Dr. Cook and her research committee, followed by wild thoughts of quitting medicine—subsided when he entered Riverview Hospital's surgical suite. The OR was both the tranquilizer that calmed him and the stimulant that excited him. With unblinking eyes, he began an absorbing task within a unique brain.

In a complex, interlocking chain—from the surgeon who operated to the resident who assisted to the scrub nurse who supplied the instruments to the circulating nurse who tended the patient to the anesthesiologist who kept the patient breathing to the scalpel making the incision to the drill cutting the bone to the microscope enlarging a tiny work field to the instruments removing the tumor to the stitches closing the incision—every person and object would play a vital role in removing a pea-size tumor on a grape-size gland so that a young woman could bear children and be healthy.

David had decided to reach the little structure at the base of the brain that was known as the master gland by operating through the patient's upper lip and sinuses. This approach, which penetrated the base of the skull, spared the patient a craniotomy and pulling on delicate brain tissue; however, operating through the sinuses shrank the surgeon's area of vision from a large cavern atop the skull to a long, narrow passageway through the mouth.

In choosing his route, David counted on a device called a mobile scanner, which could be wheeled into the operating room to provide instant, sophisticated images of the body. The mobile scanner was particularly valuable to neurosurgeons in checking their positions and progress and in ensuring the complete removal of tumors in spots difficult to see. The tumor David tackled that morning would normally have required an intracranial operation. With the mobile scanner, however, David could do the job via the sinus route. At a critical point in the procedure, he ordered the device to be brought in.

A technician wheeled the equipment into the OR. With movements as routinized as brushing their teeth, the operating team silently stepped back from the patient to accommodate the instrument.

A voice broke the calm: "One minute, please." It belonged to a man wearing small glasses above his surgical mask and holding a large clipboard against his scrubs. The man had followed the technician in. "I'm Inspector Norwood of CareFree. A request to use the mobile scanner in this surgery was denied. It was found to be unnecessary treatment."

On hearing this, the technician backed his machine away from the patient while the OR team returned to the operating table, again in silence, as if this, too, were the expected.

David's headlamp crossed the room to shine impolitely on the eyeglasses of the inspector. "There *will* be a scan done, now," said the surgeon.

Again the technician moved the machine toward the patient and the OR team backed away.

"Dr. Lang, let's not have any unpleasantness this morning. You know that as an inspector of surgery for CareFree, I must ensure compliance. Whenever I observe you surgeons directly, costs drop and the hospital meets its budget. I'm here for your benefit, Doctor, so you won't have a hard time later with the review board," Inspector Norwood said with strained politeness.

"So I'll have a hard time later," replied David. "Right now, I'll have the scan."

"Preauthorization was denied. As the inspector, I say the scanner will not be used."

Like a movie reel played in forward and reverse, the technician and machine backed away from the patient while the OR team moved toward her once again.

"As the surgeon, I say the scanner *will* be used."

The players finally stopped and waited, freezing the scene in a still frame.

"And I say it will not be!" Inspector Norwood's voice puffed from his mask, steaming the lenses above it.

"When did you go to medical school?"

"That's irrelevant."

"Shall I wake the patient and see if she thinks it's irrelevant?"

"CareFree hasn't authorized the mobile scanner." Inspector Norwood squinted in the spotlight still rudely hitting his eyes.

"CareFree isn't doing the surgery—I am."

"Studies show that using expensive technology is often just a frivolous indulgence of the doctor."

"So I'm frivolous. The scan will be done."

"The scan is unnecessary!"

"Something in here is unnecessary, but it's not the scan."

The two argued across the operating table, whereas the limp body between them had no comment.

"Excuse me," resident Tom Bentley interjected. "Two weeks ago, a patient skipped town before a postop brain scan could be taken that CareFree approved." He glanced at the inspector hopefully. "Maybe we could swap that one for this one."

"Or the ER patient who died this morning before we ran images," said one of the nurses. "Those pictures would have been for the cervical spine, but maybe that's close enough—"

"I'm not making any bargains." Inspector Norwood raised his hand for silence. "The technician must leave, and the operation must resume without the pictures."

"And without the surgeon. Are you prepared to finish the job, Inspector?" asked David.

"Are you threatening a strike, Doctor? You know that's illegal. Doesn't your conscience tell you to stay and work?"

"As the state orders me to? Isn't there a name for that?"

The inspector sighed tolerantly, waving his hand to dismiss the matter. "Whoever said anything about ordering anybody? Really! The other surgeons are cooperating voluntarily, without any unpleasantness."

"You mean after you threatened to slap them with fines?" David asked.

"Of course, if you've gotten yourself into a bind and can't see where you are without a film, perhaps your resident can help." Inspector Norwood glanced at Bentley.

David's eyes glazed past the official to a vision of their own. The surgeon observed himself clinically, as if he were the patient. He noted pressure building as his blood seemed to hit a clogged artery, the same pressure that he had felt when he struggled to save Eileen Miller, when he faced the committee halting his research, when many other blockages occurred. *The condition seems incurable; the patient should learn to live with it,* he thought. *Or should he?*

"Think of how much you're costing the system, Doctor. We need to conserve medical resources by eliminating unnecessary things we're better off without," said the inspector.

"Do you know what a surgeon does to unnecessary things we're better off without?" David replied.

The headlight went dark, its cord pulled from its power source, as David grabbed a scalpel from the equipment tray and lunged toward the inspector. A collective gasp was heard from the others. Clutching the inspector's shirt, the surgeon pushed him through the swinging doors of the OR and into the hallway, the knife aimed at the man's throat.

"Now get away from me, and don't come into my OR again," he said quietly.

Inspector Norwood's clipboard shook. With the coldness of his attacker more frightening than any rage, the official slowly stepped back, and then found the trembling snarl that had become his voice.

"You'll hear about this, Doctor! You'll see which of us will be cut down to size!"

As the incredulous surgical team watched the incident through the windows on the OR doors, the inspector stormed down the hall. David scrubbed again and donned a new gown and gloves. The technician took the image. The OR team resumed its positions. And the surgery proceeded—all in silence, as if this incident, too, were now to be taken in stride.

When David's staff left the office that day, he yearned to do the same. Since dawn, he had energetically handled his surgeries, hospital rounds, and office appointments. Now, facing a desk full of papers, he suddenly felt drained. Medicine had always been the seductress in his life, one to whom he had been untiringly faithful. Why had he lately found it difficult to clear his desk?

He sat in an office that was a library. Mahogany bookcases filled with musty medical volumes lined the walls. The worn arms of a leather chair testified to thousands of patients seen, scores of papers written, and years of study by the chair's owner. A plastic replica of the human brain rested on a shelf. From the wall, a portrait of history's first neurosurgeon smiled approvingly.

A photo on the desk displayed a rare medical anomaly: twin boys, aged two, joined at the head. A more recent picture showed the boys as normal four-year-olds, two years after David had separated them in a landmark surgery. Before coming to David, the children's parents had traveled from their home in Europe to consult with neurosurgeons around the world, all of whom had agreed that separating their sons was impossible. A glance at the photo of the healthy, smiling four-year-olds, who had become his adopted nephews, brought David a moment's pleasure. It vanished when his eyes dropped to the small mountain of documents that his staff had left for him.

He grabbed the first form, regarding permission for early admission, which was attached to the chart folder of Carla Adams, a patient scheduled for surgery. Because of her medical history, David wanted her admitted to the hospital the day before, instead of the morning of, her operation, as a precaution. The early admission fell outside of CareFree's range of norms, so David had to write a report justifying the action. He glanced at his watch. To provide the information would take thirty minutes. Should he forget the precaution or write the report? What were his chances of getting approval? He did not know. He set the form aside; he would return to it later.

Next in the stack was a letter from the Quality Assurance Review Board of

Riverview Hospital, a consulting group hired by CareFree to evaluate how attending physicians used the hospital's services. The letter asked David to explain why he had kept a Mr. Muldoon, who had developed a postoperative complication, in the hospital four days longer than was customary after the patient's surgery. David paused again. Another half hour to write this reply. If he ignored the letter, he would be fined. If he replied and the review board overruled his judgment, he would be fined anyway. If he challenged the fine, he would have to present his case at a hearing, costing him more in lost time than the fine itself. David sighed. He set this form aside also; he would return to it later.

He glanced at the remaining papers. There was an authorization to perform additional testing for an upcoming case similar to the one he had just encountered, a tumor at the base of the brain that could be evacuated via the sinus route, if use of the mobile scanner was permitted. To use the device, he had to request permission by completing the form. After the morning's incident in the OR, he could guess the response. He crushed the document into a ball and slammed it into the wastebasket. To save the agency the cost of the test, he would do the craniotomy, which would be more expensive—and riskier for the patient!

Next was a claim that David had filed concerning a Mr. Harrington. CareFree returned the claim because David had failed to enter a diagnosis. He could make no diagnosis without performing more tests. However, CareFree required a diagnosis before it would allow more tests on Mr. Harrington. David sighed again. The man who made split-second decisions in surgery could not determine what to do now. He set this form aside also.

At the bottom of the stack, he spotted a large envelope that he had been eagerly awaiting. It contained brain scans that he had ordered for a patient. David permitted himself to peek at the scans, just glimpse, promising himself that he would return to the paperwork at once. He guiltily clipped the crisp films to a view box behind his desk and gazed at a colorful web of blood vessels from the patient's brain. His fatigue vanished as the swirling vessels cast a red net over his face, trapping him in their mysteries. In a moment there were no authorizations, no forms, no letters, only an unusual vascular problem in a brain that intrigued him. Could he find a solution? For the next thirty minutes he studied the films for the answer.

He did not hear the footsteps advancing to the opened door of his office or the first knock.

"Dr. Lang, I need to speak to you. . . . Dr. Lang?"

Pulling his eyes from a galaxy away, he looked up at a pale pink suit containing the dark-haired, bespectacled Pamela Varner, a CareFree administrator.

"Now's not a good time. Please make an appointment through my secretary." He turned back to the view box.

"But, Doctor, if I have to wait, then the payment we owe you will be delayed. I can't authorize it until we discuss some things."

He swiveled his chair around to face her. "What is it?" he asked tiredly.

She pulled a chair close to the desk and sat, crossing her legs comfortably as if preparing for a lengthy visit. Looking at him above glasses resting low on her nose, she opened a folder from her briefcase and began: "Blake Otis had a simple case of back discomfort."

"You mean the Blake Otis who couldn't get out of bed without searing pain?"

"His general physician didn't think a visit to the neurosurgeon was necessary, only physical therapy. But Mr. Otis walks into your office—without authorization from his general doc—and next thing we know, he's in the OR."

"I thought everyone was entitled to treatment."

"Of course everyone's entitled to treatment."

"Well?"

"Treatment according to the guidelines, Doctor."

"But not according to the patient's problem and wishes?"

"His general physician prescribed physical therapy."

"His spinal cord images showed a ruptured disk. After my surgery to remove it, Mr. Otis could tie his shoelaces for the first time in years."

"But, Doctor, you have a moral and legal obligation to the general physician."

"But not to the patient?"

"We were willing to hear your side on this one. I sent my case manager to see you, but you refused to talk to him." She sighed. "It's his job to determine if treatment is necessary. Surely you can't object to us wanting to spend the taxpayers' money wisely."

"By sending a clerk with no medical degree to second-guess me? How is that wise?"

"Wise or not, that one cost you four thousand dollars."

He said nothing. She read the next document.

"Then there's the case of Sammy Sullivan. Here's someone who *was* sent to you by his general physician. He was entitled to your services, but you threw him out of your office, didn't you, Doctor?"

"If he had gone into cardiac arrest, I'm not sure I could have forced myself to save him."

"But this patient was *entitled* to your services."

"Even though he was rude to me and my receptionist? Even though I'd bet you never found anything wrong with him because he had a history of hypochondriacal behavior?"

He smiled at the momentary flush reddening her face, an admission that he was right.

"Even though he's filing a discrimination suit against you, Doctor?"

David's smile vanished. Pamela Varner's eyes widened subtly in victory.

"Whether you like him or not, Sammy Sullivan is still entitled to treatment."

"But Blake Otis isn't?"

"Two thousand for refusing treatment."

She selected another document from her stack. "You expect us to pay extra for twelve hours of surgery to remove a meningioma from John Rittenhouse's brain?"

"So?"

"So our statistical studies brought the cost for those surgeries *down*, not *up*."

"What does a statistical study have to do with John Rittenhouse?"

"You know we pay on the *average* cost, Dr. Lang. I can reimburse you for six hours of surgery, not twelve."

"But after six hours, the tumor wasn't completely removed. It would have grown back."

"That's not the point."

"It's not the point whether the patient lives ten years or thirty?"

"Your fellow surgeons are cooperating with us on *reducing* their time in surgery. There are courses on how to do that. Maybe you should take one."

His eyes flashed in anger, but he reminded himself that Pamela Varner was not the appropriate object for a strong feeling of any kind.

"If that's it, Ms. Varner, you will excuse me."

"There's also the case of Denton Moore. When you operated on his herniated disk, you also removed a tumor near the surgical site."

"So?"

"So we can't pay for two different surgical procedures during one operation. You know we stopped doing that after the scandal with surgeons padding their bills with extra procedures they never performed."

"You mean the scandal that began after you cut the surgeons' pay?"

"Compensation models are established by another department, so I can't help you there. Regarding Denton Moore, I need to know if you want to be paid for the tumor or the disk."

"And how do I get paid for both?"

"That's explained in the practice guidelines, Dr. Lang. You'd have to perform separate operations on different days."

"But I thought I needed to *reduce* the time I spent in surgery."

She had no retort. He smiled bitterly.

He rose, walked to the door, and held it for her. "Now, you will excuse me."

She gathered her papers and walked toward him, her face somber, her voice low. "And don't think the whole agency hasn't heard about the incident with Inspector Norwood this morning in the OR. We know about that one, all right!"

"You should also know that I'm not above treating a woman the same way."

"You hand-picked the right case to terrorize an inspector. You were clever, I'll give you that."

"What do you mean?" he asked blankly.

"I mean your patient with the pituitary tumor being the niece of Senator Wayne Carlton."

"What?"

"I called you about that case last week and told you her connections."

"That's right! You did, didn't you?" The relief in his voice confessed how much the incident had worried him.

"Could you really have forgotten the only thing that saved your skin?" she blurted out involuntarily. "I've seen licenses pulled for much less."

For an unguarded moment, she saw his face tighten in fear.

"Dr. Lang, for your own sake, you'd better change your ways. You're going too far. With all due respect, you're uncivilized, you're dangerous, you're a menace to society."

"Funny, I was thinking the same thing about you."

7

The Last Chance

The ball pounded the racquetball court with the blasts of a shotgun. Two heads—one with black hair, one with blond—followed it. Two lean bodies cornered it, and two tanned arms raised racquets to slam it. The players reveled in a violent release of energy that seemed more like a need than a pleasure. The game, a Sunday-morning ritual, ended that particular day with the dark-haired man scoring the winning point.

"Since when do you smile when I beat you?" David Lang asked his brother as the two ran dry towels over sweat-drenched heads and arms.

"On a day when nothing could go wrong in the world," replied Randall Lang, the president of Riverview Hospital.

Their faces still held the boyish good looks of their childhood, except for the loss of innocence in the eyes. David's had grown more cautious; his brother's, more suspicious. However, that day Randall Lang's face beamed with an exuberance that David had not seen in years.

"You're unusually happy today, Randy." David's voice held surprise and pleasure at the change in the man two years his junior.

"Actually, I have some pretty exciting news to tell you," Randy said with a grin, as he followed David through the clear plastic door of the court.

"Oh?"

"In fact, I couldn't wait to finish the game so we could talk. That's why I let you win."

"Yeah, sure you did."

"Let's go to my place."

They walked soundlessly down a carpeted corridor to the locker room of the Oak Hills Athletic Club, with Randy affectionately throwing an arm over his brother's shoulder.

David relaxed in a beige leather chair facing a teak desk, looking comfortable in his brother's home office. Lemony walls, light wood furniture, and a large-leafed philodendron gave the room an airy feel. Randy stood outside the door of the second-floor office, calling to his wife from the balcony.

"Say, Beth, do we have any champagne?"

"I think so. Why?" A sweet voice rose from the floor below.

"We have something to celebrate. Come and join us."

"We do?" asked David.

Minutes later Randy's attractive, redheaded wife appeared with a champagne bottle on ice and three crystal glasses.

"Now what do we have to celebrate?" David asked, as he hugged Beth in greeting.

"The end of your frustration, brother."

"The end?"

"Yes."

"What are you two talking about?" Beth asked.

Randy popped the cork with a flourish and filled the glasses. "I propose a toast," he said, standing behind his desk in the sun-filled office, his arm around his wife. "To the completion of David's research and to the medical breakthrough of the century!"

"To David!" Beth smiled warmly, raising her glass to him.

Randy clicked his glass against Beth's, and the civilized chime of resonating crystal filled the room. The object of their salute, however, did not smile or touch his glass as the couple drank.

"Won't you cheer for a worthy cause, brother?"

"The BOM just denied me permission to do any more animal studies."

"We'll see about that," said Randy, reaching for his briefcase.

Sensing that the two men were beginning a meeting, Beth quietly slipped out the door.

"There's a loophole," continued Randy.

"What?"

"You know, of course, that John Carter won't be returning to work after his stroke. His resignation as our chief of neurosurgery is effective the last day of this month."

"So?"

"I discovered something interesting." Randy settled in his chair. "Shortly before his stroke, Carter received a generous research grant from the BOM. He got it because he's the head of our neurosurgery department and we're the main teaching facility in that discipline for West Side University Medical School. Carter received permission to establish a lab, to experiment on animals, and to employ research fellows."

"So how does that concern me?"

"The hospital can transfer Carter's grant to the next chief of neurosurgery." Randy pulled a paper out of his briefcase. "This letter from the BOM outlines the terms of the research." He slid the paper to his brother.

David read a description of the abundance of animals permitted to John Carter, the money for laboratories and fellows, and the criteria for the grant, which fit his own project. David stared at the paper for a long moment after he had finished reading. Finally, he pushed it back across the desk to Randy, his hand moving slowly, as if forcing a heavy weight.

"Don't ask what you're going to ask me, Randy, because I can't do it," he whispered painfully.

"Why not?"

"You know why."

"I'm offering a starving man a truckload of steaks."

"No."

"David, you'll have all the animals you need and a crop of postgraduate fellows falling out of the trees like apples to assist you. Another year is all you'll need. I know you'll work day and night, you'll answer all the remaining questions you have, you'll polish your new procedure and be ready for human trials—before you have a chance to regret your decision to accept this opportunity."

"I can't."

"And while you're completing the animal studies, things could change. What if Mack Burrow loses the election and becomes a pimple on the nose of history? What if more hospitals fold and the people finally get fed up? What if the new governor is forced to abandon CareFree?"

"Then he'll invent FearFree or TearFree."

"But what if they're finally forced to leave us alone? Then the way will be clear for our Institute for Neurological Research and Surgery. Have you forgotten the dream we've had since high school?" Randy leaned over the desk excitedly, trying to engage David, who sat back, crossing his arms skeptically against his chest. "Once such an institute is free to turn a profit, Riverview's board of directors will fund it, and if they don't, we'll find other investors who'll want to make a fortune. Leave that to me. With you as medical director and me as president, how can we fail? David, you'll have patients begging for your new treatment; you'll have doctors to train; you'll have a research lab; you'll have a dozen other projects you'll want to start—"

"Randy, please!"

"The world will have a momentous medical breakthrough, your new treatment, which will launch the Institute for Neurological Research and Surgery. And I . . . I'll get to leap out of bed every day, rushing to get to work, because I'll have a hundred ideas that I'll want to try, that I'll be *free* to try. My work will be a story of progress and success, instead of . . ."—his eyes dropped—"well . . . never mind."

"I know you're unhappy," David said sadly.

Randy ignored the comment. "With all that's still possible, why won't you accept the opportunity I'm throwing at you?"

"Because in order to get the grant, I'd have to replace John Carter as the new department head, and that thought should scare you, not make you want to throw a party." He gestured to the champagne bottle. "Besides, I'd never be accepted."

"With your clinical record, the surgeons *will* accept you in the chief's post," said Randy with conviction. "Oh, there'll be some griping because some of them want the job, but that kind of politics can be handled. And although you're young for the position at thirty-seven, your accomplishments, especially the separation of the twins, will silence any objections."

"But the board of directors would never approve of my other record, the one I have with CareFree. And they'd be smart not to, so let's drop the matter."

"Believe it or not, David, the board is open to considering our star bank robber as its next chief of police."

"Then you must be twisting their minds out of whack."

"I've already been . . . well, campaigning on this. . . . I didn't tell you, but—"

"I don't want you campaigning for me! It's too risky for you."

"Nevertheless, I can get the board to approve you. Because I worked as a medical researcher before switching to hospital administration, I have the pull to recommend a clinical appointment."

"Does the board now endorse surgeons knifing inspectors?"

"They don't know about that, and they won't find out. The BOM doesn't want Senator Carlton getting curious about what really goes on. His niece is one patient who can get anything her doctor wants."

"I still wouldn't be approved by the board. You'd have to be blackmailing the members."

"If I had anything on them, I would," Randy said, smiling. "Actually, almost everyone on the board owes me a favor or two, and now's my time to cash in. There's just one condition you'd have to agree to. You'd have to address the board personally and assure them—*convince* them—that you have reformed. You must be very persuasive when you tell them that you'll comply with the practice parameters, that you'll never receive another fine from the BOM, and that you'll conduct yourself in a way that will not embarrass the board or compromise the hospital."

"No."

"The board will approve you, David, if you promise to obey CareFree's rules."

"No."

"Then how will you complete your experiments? You've already applied to every agency that deals with science, medicine, education, or research, and they've all turned you down. So what's left? Are you going to throw away seven years of experiments—seven years of your life—and abandon your dream?"

Randy's blue eyes stared across the desk at David's green ones.

"This is your last chance, David. If your promise to the board is compelling, they'll trust you."

"Will you, brother? Will you trust me?"

Randy knew what David meant. A tinge of worry shaded the administrator's face.

"I've heard you say many times that you need to keep your job until the kids are through with college."

Randy and his wife had three gifted children whose artistic and scholarly talents were nurtured through special lessons and private schooling and whose college tuitions were looming. Both parents worked; however, Randy's job provided the larger income to support the children's futures.

"Now you want to walk a tightrope with me," David continued. "What are you going to tell your kids—*my* two nieces and nephew—if I pull you down with me when I crash?"

"You can't allow that, David. For your own sake, you can't . . . crash."

"I don't want you running any fan clubs for me. In fact, I'd feel a lot better if you joined my critics."

"For the sake of your research, for your career, for everything you love, for our dream, for Pete's sake, David, give in! You can't fight them; they're too strong. You have to *compromise*."

David had no reply.

"Please, David, accept this opportunity and learn to do things differently. Before you see a patient, be sure you're allowed to. Before you order tests, get approval. Before you admit a patient, study the rules. Before you drill a hole in somebody's skull, read the guidelines. Before you make adjustments, ask. Learn to hit the ball on your knees. You can't wallop it over the fence. The game doesn't exist on that scale anymore. Either you play by the new rules or spend your career in the dugout. Damn it, brother, I'm offering you a chance to run around the bases! Won't you be smart and accept it?"

David stared across the desk at his own features framed in blond hair, but it was not Randy that he was seeing. Two sights forced their way into his awareness: He remembered the first rats that he had operated on unsuccessfully seven years ago, when he had nothing more than a hunch to try, and he saw the final cats that he had operated on just months ago, proving at last that his hunch was right and leaving him with a burning desire to operate on a hundred more animals, a hundred at once, at that very moment, because he could not sleep or eat or even wait until the next morning to unravel the amazing puzzle that had held him spellbound for seven years. But he had no clearance to proceed, only a roadblock to frustrate him.

"David." His brother's whisper was like a hidden voice from his own consciousness. "I know you want to accept. Couldn't you find a way?"

David pushed aside the glass containing his untouched champagne. "No, Randy, I can't. Besides, my brother would despise me if I did."

That night a strong wind hissed through the fragrant shrubs of a garden, warning of a thunderstorm. The gust blew through opened French doors and into a lit study. David sat at his desk, the pages of a notebook crackling in the wind. He kept a collection of notes and drawings of his surgeries. Like the pages of a detective thriller, his entries chronicled the absorbing dramas of his life: the tales of diagnosis, treatment, and results. That night in his home, he sketched the brain of Eileen Miller, the patient he had saved when his wife was attending the banquet for the governor. He drew the woman's brain as he had first seen it—distorted, swollen, wild with blood; then he drew it again as he had left it—calm, clean, restored.

He began writing his notes: "A subdural hemorrhage in the posterior fossa—" But his mind kept wandering to his conversation with Randy, as it had all day. Against his will, his mind was searching for a way to accept the unacceptable. *No*, he told himself, forcing his attention back to his task.

He raised his head when he heard footsteps approaching. He saw Marie standing at his half-opened door, wearing a silk dressing gown and high-heeled slippers. The scent of her perfume floated through the air as she entered the room. She took a seat facing him, the rich tan of her slender legs a provocative contrast to her white silk robe. He looked at her with the purity of a monk.

"How long are you going to be angry, David?"

"She almost died, Marie."

"It wasn't my fault."

"You were her doctor."

"Eileen Miller only said she had a headache. She didn't think to tell me that a baseball hit her on the head."

"Why didn't *you* think? Why didn't you ask? Why didn't you take a better history?"

"I can't send every patient who has headaches for a brain scan, David. No one can fault me for that—except you, of course."

"You probably didn't spend more than five minutes with her, so you could zip on to the next poor slob."

"Why don't you try understanding for a change, instead of launching one of your self-righteous attacks?"

"All hell was breaking loose in her head. Were you waiting for a coma before you did anything?"

"You always have to be right, don't you? Hindsight is great!"

"It's not hindsight, Marie. Anticoagulants, trauma, and bleeding paint a picture any med student would see."

"Any med student would also know that migraines explain headaches much more often than hemorrhages."

"Not in Eileen Miller's case. She had a head injury!" He could feel his voice rising.

"Why can't you leave me alone? You always have to find fault!"

"You treated a migraine headache that she didn't have and missed a cerebral hemorrhage that nearly killed her. Don't you find fault with yourself?"

"Everybody misjudges a patient occasionally. Even you, David."

"It's not occasionally with you. What about Charles McIntyre?"

"Are you going to throw that in my face again?"

"You sent him for physical therapy, which he could have had till doomsday without correcting the weakness in his legs. If he hadn't crawled into my office and I hadn't removed the ruptured disk fragment pressing on his spinal cord, your patient, who's normal today, could have become a paraplegic."

"I did what I could. I spent hours preparing his case for quality assurance review, but the committee wouldn't approve a referral to a neurosurgeon. They wanted to try physical therapy first."

"So you did what a committee that never met your patient told you to do. But was it *right*?"

"You did what they told you *not* to do. You operated on him without authorization, and instead of getting paid, you got fined. Was that right, David?"

He did not know why he wanted to press on, to convince Marie, when an inner voice warned him that it was futile. "Was it right to tell Helen Pennington that she, too, had migraines, when her headaches and temporary paralysis resulted from a blocked carotid artery about to cause a stroke?"

Marie's face reddened. "Sometimes migraines *can* cause temporary paralysis. Was it right to examine *my* patient without my permission? Was it right to rush her to the hospital, to demand that the technicians test without authorization? Was it right to throw a temper tantrum, to do the damn test yourself, then to rush her to surgery to open the artery without consulting anyone, without asking, without explaining your case to the certifications officer?"

"Was the main artery to her brain ninety-eight percent blocked or not?"

"There has to be a better way to make your point."

"Was Helen Pennington going to have a massive stroke at any minute or not?"

"Why do you have to make enemies everywhere you go?"

"Was it right to save her life or not?"

"Was it right to embarrass me with your hotheaded attitude, with your un-civilized behavior, with the way you practice medicine?"

"The way *I* practice embarrasses *you?*"

"What would you have me do, David? Become a misfit, too?"

"Those patients of yours needed surgery, Marie, not aspirins and sweet words."

"But my hands were tied! Their treatment was fixed by the guidelines."

"But is it *right*, Marie?" he asked quietly.

"Is it right to perform those surgeries without permission?"

"I got permission—from the patients."

"A lot of good that did you!" she laughed mirthlessly. "Tell me if you got paid!"

He did not answer.

"In fact, *you* paid the state. And you're lucky that fines are the worst penalty you've gotten so far. It's bad enough that you're destroying your ca-reer, but now you want to drag me down, too. You want me to practice the way you do, to ignore the rules, to do unapproved tests, to make unautho-rized referrals, to stick my neck out. Soon you'll be paying out more in fines than you're getting from surgery. Then who will pay the bills? Who's paying most of them now?"

He had no answer.

"David, I'm doing the best I can. It's not as if I have a choice in the matter. Do you think I do?"

A wave of guilt overpowered him. It was true, wasn't it? She had no real choice, did she?

"It's hard for me. I'm under a lot of pressure. You can't imagine!"

He knew there were demands on her. Surely she did not like the situation any more than he did. How could he blame her for the way she bore the unbearable? What did he want from her, anyway?

"Why are you making things worse for me?" she asked, echoing his thoughts. "You're so protective of your brother. You want Randy to walk a straight line and never break the rules or get in trouble. Then why do you want *me* to?"

It was true, he had to admit to himself. But an inner voice warned him that somehow Marie and Randy were different.

"Your demands on me aren't fair, David."

It was true, he thought; he was not being fair. He was causing the heated ar-guments burning a hole through their marriage. He wondered about the strange circuit of anger and guilt that he could not break. He rubbed his eyes, as if try-ing to erase the bloody image of Eileen Miller.

"All right, Marie," he said softly. "I understand that you didn't have a choice."

"There, that's better now," she whispered calmly.

The wind filled the curtains of the French doors, blowing them into the room like starched white sails. Reaching her robe, the gentle breeze lifted it to reveal more of her legs. She rose and walked behind his chair. Sweet scents from the garden mixed with her perfume. She threw her arms around him, her hands touching his chest, her face leaning over him, her mouth brushing his hair. She had always been drawn to the tall, muscular body, the striking features, and the subtle sensuality of the man who was her husband. She wanted him in a way that went beyond the raw need that his body stirred in hers. She somehow wanted to unleash in him a feeling that he could not control, to see him helplessly in her power, even if just for a few convulsive moments, as a kind of victory over him, over something in him that she could not reach.

"David," she whispered, "let's have a drink on the porch and watch the storm."

She sat on the desk, facing him. She waited for the signs she knew well—eager eyes that traveled over her, exquisitely sensitive hands that caressed her, a warm mouth that covered hers. She saw none of them.

"I just want to finish my work and go to sleep."

"In the guest room again?" she stood up abruptly. "Maybe the trouble with our marriage isn't what I'm doing in my office, but—"

"If that's all, Marie—"

"How long can you hold a grudge? Don't you want to do something for pleasure?"

"I am," he said, and gestured to the journal, lifting his pen to resume his work.

Instead of leaving, Marie returned to her seat, circling the desk slowly, as if trying to dissipate her anger. "Actually, David, I wanted to talk to you about something else—about John Carter's post being up for grabs."

So that explained her visit, he realized. Surely she had not come to discuss Eileen Miller, a subject that she had avoided all weekend.

"I think that being chief of neurosurgery at Riverview will be very good for you. It'll put your career back on track, and that'll help us get along better. If you want John Carter's position, surely Randy can pull strings to get you approved."

"It would allow me to finish my research, but—"

"Your research? Are you still chasing that windmill?"

"Isn't that why you mentioned John Carter's post?"

"What does that have to do with your research?"

"Carter has permission from the BOM to do animal research. That permission would transfer to his successor."

"Oh," she said disappointedly.

"When you said the director's post would put my career back on track, didn't you mean it would enable me to finish my experiments?"

"God, no, David! Your research only spells more trouble for us, more controversy. I meant that if you became chief of neurosurgery, you'd be forced to do things differently. You couldn't continue to be at war with everybody. And I wouldn't have to cringe every time your name cropped up in one of my committee meetings."

He looked away, losing interest in the conversation.

"David, my career is booming. I don't want you to drag me down; I want you to be more like me."

A hot rush of anger hit his face. "You mean you want me to be incompetent?"

She jumped up, her hands on her hips, her mouth twisted. "How dare you? Maybe *you're* the one who's incompetent. Maybe you shouldn't practice medicine at all. Maybe we'd both be better off if you opened a hardware store in Brooklyn!"

"That's it!" he cried, leaping out of his chair, his eyes looking through Marie to an image of their own.

"What are you talking about?"

"Why didn't I think of it?"

"Think of what? Where are you going?"

He did not seem to hear her. The pages of the journal brushed shut as he left the room.

❧　　❧　　❧

The wind had grown more menacing by the time David's car hit the graveled driveway of his brother's nearby house. A gust stirred the loose pebbles into a hissing gray funnel. A hanging pot of geraniums swung wildly from the porch. A streak of nearby lightning threw a jagged beam on the tall silhouette of Randy, who was waiting on the porch after receiving his brother's call from the car.

"I thought of a way I could accept the director's job." David called in the darkness as he got out of the car.

"How?" Randy asked, approaching.

"I'll stop practicing medicine for a year or so. Not entirely, but I'll drastically restrict my surgeries to those I'm sure the inspectors will allow. There has to be a way to take only the easy cases, the ones without controversies or complications to drive up the costs and the fines. Other surgeons do it all the time. I'll shuffle the paperwork, run the department, and focus on the lab work. The less I see of the OR, the better off I'll be."

"But, if you stop accepting the hard cases . . . who will take them?"

David had no reply.

Randy stared vacantly into the distance, his voice low. "What will happen to those troublesome patients . . . the really sick ones that no one wants anymore?"

David's head dropped slowly, his eyes blank, his mouth grim. "I can't be the chief of neurosurgery if I don't stop doing neurosurgery."

A roar of thunder seemed to underscore the remark. Their hair flew wildly in the wind, but their eyes met and held steady.

"Okay, David, then it's settled." Randy smiled, but there was no joy in it.

"Not quite. If you want to help me, I'll accept your backing for the director's post. I'm prepared to make the necessary promise to the board and to keep it. But there's one condition. You have to make a promise to me, a solemn vow."

"What?"

"If something unforeseen happens and I get in trouble with the hospital, you must promise to abandon me. You must publicly withdraw your support and denounce me. And you must do it wholeheartedly, so the board will believe you. I absolutely insist. I want your word on that."

"David, really—"

"You intend to keep your job for a long time, don't you? I've heard you promise your family that they can count on you. Then promise me what I ask."

"But I also want to help you. For my own sake, I want you to finish your research, so we can lay the groundwork for our new institute. It's not a sacrifice to back you, David. It's one of the few things I want to do, so I'm prepared to take a risk, too."

"I can't allow that. You have to promise that if I screw up, you'll throw me to the wolves, you'll recommend my dismissal as director, you'll even revoke my staff privileges if you have to—"

"David, come on. I'd have to betray my own mind—"

"Then forget the whole thing. I have a feeling we're better off dropping this crazy idea." David squeezed his brother's shoulders affectionately, and then turned to go.

"All right, David, all right! I'll agree."

"Shake on it," David demanded.

He held out his hand to Randy. Lightning that seemed alarmingly close flashed against his outstretched palm. Randy extended his hand to grasp his brother's. With the first drops of rain splattering over them, the two shook hands.

"I promise, brother. I'll do what you ask."

"If I get in trouble, you'll denounce me."

"It would be like denouncing myself—"

"I want you to say it—and mean it," insisted David.

"Okay, if you get in trouble, I'll denounce you. But don't make it come to that, you hear?"

"I'll try my best."

The rain quickly became a downpour. The brothers did not seem to notice the liquid needles striking their faces and soaking their shirts. The two figures with the same tall frame and steady eyes held their firm handshake.

❧ 8 ❧
Payment Due

The sun still hung high in the summer sky when David's staff quit for the day, leaving him with the familiar mound of paperwork. Two ribbons of light, from windows flanking a bookcase, streamed through the transparent curtains and crossed the earth-toned carpet to converge on David's face. As he sat at his desk, he resisted the temptation to close the blinds, savoring the only contact he would have that day with the outdoors.

He thought of the impending appointment as department head and of his promise to his brother to be a model doctor. His great passion, his career, once inextricably linked to his performance at an operating table, now depended more on how he handled the documents on his desk. He wondered how he could make split-second decisions in the OR, and then have his mind frozen by a pile of papers. He vowed once more to be a model doctor, to handle every document.

The first one involved Bobby Norton, an architect with acute back pain. David had applied for permission to operate on the young man. While awaiting a reply, David was prescribing large doses of narcotics for Bobby. The medication was necessary to relieve the patient's pain—and sufficient to trigger an official inquiry.

He read a certified letter from the Board of Medical Examiners, the agency that controlled his license, questioning the quantity of narcotics prescribed for Bobby, requesting the patient's records, and directing David to appear at a meeting. By the way, the letter added, David could bring an attorney. The surgeon stared in bewilderment at the paper. Because of the medication, Bobby could work for the first time in years, and he had landed a job with an architectural firm. The surgeon knew of many cases in which patients in acute pain did not become addicted to the narcotic he was prescribing in the same dosages that normal people did. Bobby showed no signs of being an addict. He kept his appointments, read architectural books in the waiting room, and asked intelligent questions. According to his wife, for the first time in years Bobby was happy. In David's judgment, his prescriptions were necessary and properly monitored.

Bobby had an appointment the next day. David would need to prescribe more narcotics. If he did, his problem with the Board of Medical Examiners would worsen. If he did not, Bobby would be unable to work. David sighed. The preservation of his license seemed to require that Bobby Norton lose his job and live in pain. Of course, he thought, if he could have operated without waiting for certification, the prescriptions would have been unnecessary! He set the letter aside. He would call his lawyer in the morning.

He reached for the next paper in the stack but could not summon the energy to lift it. His eyes drifted to the photos on his desk of Artur and Bernard, the conjoined twins whom he had separated. Because they were foreign citizens, they had been exempt from the state's entitlement programs, giving David complete control over their treatment. Their attached brains had shared the same circulatory system. In separating the boys, David had to untangle a complex network of blood vessels flowing through an oblong double brain in the most bizarre pattern that he—or anyone else—had ever seen. David remembered studying the two brains sharing the same blood, trying to decide which vessel to give to Artur, which to Bernard. If he rerouted this artery to Artur's brain, could Bernard survive? If he gave that vein to Bernard, could Artur survive? The twins seemed to be so intricately linked that separation would kill them.

He remembered the remarkable harmony of movement that the brothers displayed as they played in his office before the surgery, their attached heads pulled to the side, allowing four nimble feet to run along the floor. Their enduring awareness of each other reminded David of the childhood ritual of pricking one's finger to mingle one's blood with a friend's, creating a spiritual bond as well as a blood tie.

Had he ever experienced that kind of intimacy with anyone? He thought of Randy—and felt a rush of guilt. Shouldn't he have thought of Marie instead? Wasn't a greater bond possible between husband and wife than between brothers? What stopped his blood from mixing with Marie's?

He had met her when she was a medical student and he a young surgeon who taught and conducted research at the university. Just as she was now, Marie was beautiful then, her comely features dominated by arresting brown eyes that flashed with a keen intelligence. At the time, David had a grant to employ a few students as assistants in the lab, among them, Marie. She worked diligently, her efforts extending beyond her meager pay. Because of her parents' modest means, Marie worked at various jobs to support herself through medical school, a hardship that David, a doctor's son, never had to endure. She did not complain to him of her struggle. She possessed so strong a love for medicine, he concluded, that it made the years of study and deprivation worthwhile. He thought that in Marie he had found a soul mate.

A year later, they married. Now he wondered about something more puzzling than any physical fibers in the brain: the threads of character in the wife he wanted to understand.

Through adolescence, Marie had a talent and a passion for singing opera. David never understood why she had given it up after years of rigorous study. According to her mother, Marie loved opera but suffered from the jeers of other teenagers. When she practiced at home, her classmates would stand outside her window mocking the sounds so peculiar to their ears. Humiliated, Marie would stop singing. At an annual recital in her high school, Marie performed arias from famous operas. Afterward her classmates nicknamed her the "Warrior," after a horn-helmeted character that Marie had portrayed from a Wagnerian opera. The next year Marie declined to sing in the recital. Although even the most homely girls in her class had dates for the high school prom, no one asked the Warrior. The intricate musical compositions and grand themes of opera isolated her from other teenagers interested in rock music and video games. The artist in Marie, yearning to sing on the stages of the world, seemed to be at war with the teenager in Marie, seeking acceptance from her peers. On the night of the prom, Marie cried in her room. "I feel like a freak!" she told her mother.

When she entered college, Marie no longer feared being a freak. She gave up opera and with it, the simple joy of singing its haunting melodies. Instead, she focused on her social life—joining a sorority and dating. Her nickname became "Party Girl." For her college prom, her mother recalled, Marie had her pick of dates.

Years later, when David offered to buy season tickets to the opera, he could not understand why Marie refused. Then one of Marie's high school friends, a fellow opera student who had become a famous tenor, sent her tickets to his performance. However, Marie unexpectedly contracted a headache and could not attend. She did not play opera music around the house, which also puzzled David. The opera seemed to be a reminder of something painful that Marie wanted to forget.

With her keen intelligence, Marie acquired another interest during college. She enjoyed science and subsequently entered medical school. There she was drawn to cardiology. Dates with David were punctuated with her exuberant descriptions of the remarkable organ that was the center of the circulatory system and, judging by her exciting narratives, the center of the universe itself. One semester she was troubled by a course she took on future trends in medicine. She learned that the climate in medicine was changing, and the shift disturbed her. In one class, a prominent guest speaker declared: "Our health care system has been controlled for too long by high-powered specialists, using expensive technology and commanding exorbitant salaries. Society is now crying uncle, demanding a return to the simpler times when feeling under the weather meant seeing the reliable family doctor, who was also a neighbor and advisor." Other speakers concurred, warning the young healers: "Specialists, who are financially draining the system, will play a diminished role in the future." Marie began to lose sleep; her anxiety increased; she became tired and irritable. A new injury seemed to aggravate an old wound. Would she again be an outsider in a world made by others?

Tormented, she asked David for advice on what field of medicine she should enter. "Do what you love. Cardiology, of course," he said simply. Marie chose family medicine. She apparently did not want to lose favor again. Afterward, she complained about school and procrastinated. Her grades dropped to the minimum required to graduate. She no longer spoke of her career with the same enthusiasm. David felt as if a spark had been extinguished.

Then came the malpractice suit. Marie had vaccinated hundreds of children without incident. The inoculations protected the children from disease and were a requirement for attending school. As with most drugs, vaccines can cause side effects in the rare individual. The parents of such an individual sued Marie for millions, charging that her injection caused convulsions in their child. They won the case.

In a bitter battle taking months of preparation and days of court appearances, Marie was vilified beyond her ability to comprehend. She insisted, and David agreed, that she had given an acceptable standard of care, but the verdict did not seem to rest on that. According to the judge, "the risk of erroneous decision is tolerable when compared with the state's powerful interest in protecting the patient's safety." Who was an erroneous decision tolerable to? David wondered, as Marie cried inconsolably in his arms after the verdict.

From then on, Marie became hesitant about her work. She seemed to agonize over cases, fearful of making decisions. To help bolster her confidence, David bought her the *Taft Encyclopedia of Family Medicine*, an authoritative work in her field. However, when she was unsure of herself, Marie did not open the volumes. Instead, she called other doctors to seek reassurance. She seemed to take comfort in building personal relationships with politically savvy colleagues. She served on the governmental affairs council of the local medical association, and she attended influential parties. She abandoned her fledgling solo office to join a group. And she developed a fondness for committee work.

Doctors have formed groups since the beginning of medicine. David, too, attended meetings to share information and to collaborate. However, he wondered about the committees Marie joined, for they were not created by doctors but were forced on them by the outside. Marie's cost-containment committee challenged doctors' billings; her physicians' review group contested doctors' decisions; her laboratory committee imposed fines on scientists. By what standard did Marie's committees operate? When Marie had a questionable case, she would call a friend from one of her committees for advice. As a result of her contacts, Marie never was called to task for lengthy hospitals stays, excessive testing, or immoderate use of specialists. With a warm place reserved at the insiders' hearth, she was never turned away in the cold as David so frequently was.

When CareFree was established by Governor Burrow, Marie complained, just as the other doctors did. But after reading the practice guidelines, which prescribed to doctors the approved treatment for every disorder, Marie declared that the restrictions were "not so bad." Rather than taking away something sacred, David thought, the new system apparently gave Marie something comforting.

Stop it! David ordered himself. General practitioners were under enormous pressure. Weren't he and Randy also forced to do things they loathed? Why criticize Marie? Was her behavior questionable or merely a practical necessity?

Thoughts of Marie persisted as he gazed absently at the photos of Artur and Bernard. He could not untangle the threads of Marie's character; the winding vessels in the brains of the twins had been easier to unravel.

Then he heard footsteps approaching his half-opened door.

"Hello, Dr. Lang," said Pamela Varner.

"Kindly talk to my secretary tomorrow."

"I'll have no choice but to delay your payments until we talk."

He put aside his papers, wondering why she always insisted on seeing him personally and why she grinned coyly when she succeeded in forcing his attention.

"If you're here about Amy Washington's surgery, I wrote a composition for your certifications officer, who gave me a passing grade," David said, referring to a case they had discussed previously.

"That one flies. I'm here about another matter."

She paused, as if wishing to be prodded, but David waited quietly. He wondered why his dealings with Pamela Varner seemed to be some kind of contest.

"Eileen Miller," she said finally.

His eyes widened as if the case held a special interest to him. "What about Eileen Miller?"

"I can't pay you for her surgery."

"What?"

"Are you aware that your treatment wasn't warranted by the general physician's diagnosis?"

"I'm aware that the patient would have died without my treatment."

"I'm not disputing that. I'm talking about our new rule."

"And I'm talking about Eileen Miller's life."

"Doctor, we agree that the patient should receive the best care. The new rule was made to ensure that. It's designed to prevent people from flooding the ER to see specialists when their general practitioners haven't authorize a referral. You know the drill. A guy gets an earache, and the general doctor gives him eardrops. But the patient's not satisfied with that. He wants to see a *specialist*. So he goes to the ER, where he has all of the specialists and their tests at his disposal. Unfortunately, people abuse the system," she complained. "How can we give them their right to medical care when they do things they have no right to do?"

"What does that have to do with Eileen Miller?"

"We can't waste taxpayers' money whenever a patient wants to see multiple doctors about the same problem. Under our new rule, if a patient goes to the ER for the *same* condition that his general doctor treated within the last ten days, we'll pay only the amount allowed for the original diagnosis. In this case, Eileen Miller's husband filled out the new ER admitting form. 'What is the problem?' it asked. 'Migraine headaches,' Mr. Miller wrote. 'Was the patient treated for the same problem within the last ten days by a general practitioner?' the form asked. 'Yes,' Eileen's husband replied."

"So?"

"So that treatment falls within the fee we pay the general doctor's group practice for having the patient on its roster, and nothing more."

"But Eileen didn't have a migraine—she had a massive brain hemorrhage."

"If you had waited until ten days after the general doctor's visit—"

"If I had waited ten minutes longer, Eileen Miller wouldn't be here."

"Then the primary physician has to change the original diagnosis."

"But the brain scan shows the hemorrhage, so who cares what anybody diagnoses?"

"Our computer cares, Doctor. The diagnosis has to be changed in our records. But only the general practitioner can make that change, because it involves the *original* diagnosis, which, I explained, is the only thing we'll pay on now. This was described in last week's BOM bulletin."

She paused, as if waiting to hear an excuse or apology, but none was forthcoming.

"Eileen Miller's original diagnosis can be amended, but the form to do that still requires the general doctor's signature. Do you understand now, Dr. Lang?"

"I understand that Eileen Miller had a hemorrhage and needed surgery."

"Yes, of course. But our payment has to coincide with the diagnosis, and that diagnosis has to be confirmed by the other doctor involved."

"But I was the only doctor involved."

"You may *think* you were the only doctor who counted, but we can't agree. A second physician should collaborate with the first one and agree on treatment. We can't pay over and over for the same case each time the patient feels like seeing another doctor. Perhaps you surgeons might learn to consider other viewpoints."

"But if it weren't for my viewpoint, Eileen Miller would be dead."

She shrugged her shoulders. "Dr. Lang, we're not disputing your actions; we're only asking you to work within the system. Our new rule has decreased ER use by thirty percent," she said proudly, "and that's good for the people."

"What people?"

"The public."

"You mean the people who aren't Eileen Miller?"

"You can, of course, challenge our ruling on that surgery. Just appear before the Appeals Committee and explain your position. If you give the new system a chance, you might find us quite reasonable."

"If you're reasonable, then redo your red tape, so I can get paid for the Miller case."

"I can't."

"Why not?"

"That case is closed unless you appeal it."

"Why?"

"I did what I could, but I found no way to pay you."

"What did you do?"

"I asked Eileen Miller's general doctor if she would amend her original diagnosis from migraines to a head injury, which matches your story. Then we could enter a correction and pay you for the surgery."

"And?"

"The general doctor, *your wife*, refused to do it." She smiled contemptuously. Her eyes followed him as he sprang from his chair. "Dr. Lang, I'm not finished! Where are you going?"

A patient in the waiting room of a nearby medical office looked up curiously when a man in a doctor's coat stormed in.

"Where's Marie?" David almost shouted as he slid open a plastic partition at the front desk to peer at a startled receptionist.

Without waiting for an answer, he rushed through a door into the clinical area. The late hour had reduced the traffic in the back corridors of the group practice to a few weary doctors entering and leaving compartments along a maze of numbered cubbyholes. He found his wife alone in her office.

"If you're so proud of how you treated Eileen Miller, why can't you admit it for the record?"

"Quiet! The whole office will hear you!" she whispered angrily, shutting the door behind him. "What do you want me to do? Admit to a misdiagnosis in the patient's record? Please, David, be reasonable. Out of the thousands of cases I handle, I can't get every one right."

"Then handle fewer cases so you *can* get them right."

His eyes caught on something disturbing—a shiny pin on the lapel of her white jacket.

"I did what I could. It wasn't my fault!"

"Then why can't the record state that you misdiagnosed the problem, so I can get paid?"

"What if the Millers get curious? What if they request the patient's records and discover my admission in writing to the misdiagnosis? What if they hold me responsible for not acting sooner? What if they hire an attorney to bury me in court? I couldn't live through that! Not again!"

David's eyes landed on the gold pin on her lapel, inscribed *Distinguished Caregiver.*

"You don't care if I'm disgraced. Do you, David?"

"That pin disgraces you! It's letting you lie to yourself!" he said harshly.

She lowered her head sadly and did not reply. He watched the red-chocolate folds of her hair flow over her face. She looked younger and more vulnerable, the way he remembered her when they had first met. He wondered if she were hurt by his remark. His voice softened with a tone from their past, as if he were trying to recapture something—and someone—whom he had once valued.

"Marie, you're paying a terrible price for that pin, aren't you?"

Her eyes seemed to widen in fear, staring through the carpet to a disturbing image of their own.

"Marie," he continued softly, "you're upset, aren't you?"

"I'm . . . tired, that's all," she said unconvincingly. For an unguarded minute, her confidence vanished and her face looked troubled. "I sometimes feel I don't know what to do. I don't trust myself to decide. It torments me at times."

He recalled the frightened student who had sought his help years ago in choosing a field of medicine. "That pin is pressuring you to make some questionable decisions, isn't it?"

"Why, no, that's not true, David. I'm a good doctor." Her voice did not share the sentiment of her words; it trembled.

"Marie, I think you're upset, and I think it's because that pin is putting your patients in . . . danger."

"Danger?" she repeated, tasting the bitter word but not spitting it out.

A buzz from the phone interrupted them.

Marie pressed a button. "Yes?"

The receptionist's voice sounded through a speaker. "I'm ready to leave now, Dr. Lang, so I want to remind you of your photography shoot at eight tomorrow morning for the new recruiting ad. Marketing is in a rush for that ad, so they can place it in the national trade magazines in September."

The owners of Marie's group practice had chosen her as the ideal doctor to represent them in their campaign to attract new physicians, an assignment Marie coveted as a stepping-stone to a partnership.

"Yes. Thank you, Sally." The uncertainty in Marie's voice was vanishing. "You can tell our marketing people that I'll be there."

She turned to David. With the speed of a door slamming on an intruder coming too close, she snapped her hair back into place and her eyes once again narrowed in anger.

"Did you say I put patients in danger? How dare you? I'm a good doctor. Everyone thinks so but you! It's your reproaches that upset me, that's all. If I hadn't earned this pin, then which one of us could pay the bills?"

Her words silenced him.

"How much are you making after paying your fines?"

He had no reply.

"I'm trying to be practical. One of us has to be. I'm pleading with you not to make trouble with the Miller case. That wouldn't accomplish anything, would it? Please, David, forget it."

His head dropped, and with it, his spirits. The person whom he was seeking from a more innocent past had eluded him. Her anguish seemed to be dissipating, he noticed. He wondered if she had intentionally summoned her new ally, the one that was appearing more and more frequently to silence him and to end their arguments: his growing sense of guilt.

"Please, David, be flexible."

He whispered tiredly, "All right, Marie. You win."

"You won't dispute the case and force me to change my diagnosis?"

"No."

"Now that's better, isn't it?" She smiled.

He felt an exhaustion strange to him, as if a wound were draining his blood, not in one great hemorrhage, but more slowly and painfully, drop by drop. He could recall only vaguely the boundless energy with which he had started his career and the exciting world of medicine that he had expected to find. Far more vivid were the loose flesh of the inspector in the OR, the incessant knocking on his door by Pamela Varner, the whining of Marie, and the other jabs pricking his skin.

"Why don't you come home early tonight, David? I'll help you with your speech for the board of directors' meeting tomorrow, the speech that will make *my husband* the chief of neurosurgery!"

David did not go home early that evening or prepare his speech. He went to the Taylor Theater to watch Nicole Hudson dance.

❧9❧

The Threat and the Promise

Although it was a sunny day in Albany, vapors were rising from the hot summer ground to sully the blue sky with strands of dusty gray. Within hours, the harmless dark wisps could grow into menacing storm clouds whose pressure could be released only by the violence of a thunderstorm.

A limousine ascended a road that swirled through a grove of sugar maples to the top of a small hill. There the car stopped at an imposing white structure with classic Doric columns: the governor's mansion. The secretary of medicine emerged from the vehicle, waving to reporters gathered at the entrance. The ready greeting—partly humble, partly patronizing—gave him the air of a next-door neighbor who was also a diplomat.

As he was escorted to a meeting with Governor Burrow and his aides, the secretary felt a quiet excitement at passing a gallery of oil paintings of New York's governors. The leaders graced both sides of a wood-paneled walkway, arranged in a procession from the first colonial magistrates to the current holder of the state's highest office, Malcolm Burrow. The secretary walked through the display with an authoritative air befitting the mansion's proprietor rather than its visitor. He permitted himself a moment's furtive hope that the suspicions concerning the lieutenant governor would be proven true. Then he would likely emerge as Burrow's running mate in the upcoming election. After serving a term as lieutenant governor, he could achieve the post that put the personages around him on canvas. He had come a long way, the contented look on his face seemed to say. How much further could he go? the ambitious eyes seemed to ask as they noted the empty space on the wall next to Burrow, the spot awaiting his successor.

The secretary's father had been a manufacturer of kitchen gadgets, his mother a tireless volunteer for charity. Although his father's work had made possible all of the family's possessions, the children's education, the employment of one hundred workers, the products enjoyed by countless customers, and tax revenue in the millions, his mother was the one whom everyone had admired as a "good person." When his father died, the local newspaper ran a small announcement on the obituaries page. When his mother died, the same paper ran a two-page spread. The son was influenced by both parents. In choosing a career, he sought to combine the profitability of business with something that would bring him more esteem in the eyes of others. Medicine seemed fitting. When he started his medical career, the popular television shows, movies, and novels portrayed doctors as heroes. Patients were appreciative and news reporters respectful of the highly skilled, small-business entrepreneur who was the American doctor.

He was a good doctor who performed untold heroic acts to save patients. He restarted stopped hearts and forced air into dead lungs. Early in his career he enjoyed filling his study with mementos of his achievements: a scrapbook of thank-you notes from patients, an announcement of his appointment as a clinical department head of a hospital, a picture of him performing surgery, a magazine interview about one of his cases. He was proud of being a doctor and pleased with the rewards it brought him. He bought a new home, a luxury car, and a mink coat for his wife.

But over time, public opinion about medicine changed. A more recent movie depicted a cardiologist murdering patients in order to sell their organs on the black market. A novel portrayed patients given fatal drugs in a get-rich-quick scheme contrived by doctors and pharmaceutical executives.

"Medicine is tainted by the profit motive. The public must be protected from doctors lining their pockets at the expense of the sick," was the battle cry of ambitious politicians who enacted laws claiming to revamp medicine to serve the public good.

The secretary was caught off guard when the climate for medicine changed. His profession was somehow in crisis, and he had caused it. People no longer paid him homage. He felt a growing sense of guilt about his work. When a patient, Bob Martin, whose life he had saved, bought a new sports car instead of paying for his medical treatment, the secretary hired a collection agency. Bob Martin, adopting a helpless air and claiming poverty as an excuse, contacted the press to complain about his doctor's bill collector. To the secretary's dismay, the local newspaper, hungry for a cause célèbre, ran Martin's story as a Sunday feature. It portrayed the secretary as a villain who gouged the disadvantaged while he lived in luxury. This started a biting public attack that the secretary found unbearable. The curious stares by colleagues, the questioning eyes of patients, and the lowered heads of neighbors avoiding him had the dark power of an impending storm. Thus, he ran for cover. He thought that somehow he was wrong, so he stopped trying to collect his fee, and the waters of his life calmed.

When a local agitator, Charles Fox, and his group, Earthlings for a Simple Planet, vandalized the secretary's experimental laboratory, alleging that his research was polluting the environment with noxious chemicals, the secretary sued them. But he did not fight for long. The press depicted him as a monster whose self-serving experiments recklessly introduced hazardous material into the air and water. People reading the media accounts shunned him. His alma mater withdrew a speaking invitation that it had extended to him; friends excluded him from a golf meet; patients canceled appointments. Although the Earthlings' accusations were false, the secretary, capitulating to public pressure, dropped the lawsuit and abandoned his research. He was afraid to oppose people claiming to protect the planet.

Events like these changed the secretary. He came to believe that he was too selfish in loving medicine and profiting from it. Over the years, the topsoil of his life eroded, leading him to plant a new crop. The kinds of mementos that he collected changed. They no longer marked achievements from his medical practice but from other activities gaining in importance to him: a hat from a charity fair at which he manned a hot dog stand, a newspaper clipping about him giving money to a poor person, a photo of him sweeping trash from the street in a campaign to help the city's garbage collectors. The secretary included among his new souvenirs a framed thank-you note from a family whose dog he had rescued from a ditch, while he omitted an impassioned letter of gratitude from an executive whose life he had saved in the hospital—and who had paid a handsome fee.

He sold his luxury car for a jeep, asked his wife to wear a wool coat instead of a mink, and canceled a major remodeling of his house. He gave up his medical practice for what he considered a more public-spirited role. He became president of the state's medical association, where he made political contacts. Ultimately, he was appointed to head the state's Bureau of Medicine and to administer the governor's new program, CareFree. The post of secretary of medicine lifted his guilt. CareFree was a kind of atonement.

When asked to describe his job, the secretary would say humbly, "I work for the people." Gradually, the luxury car, the mink coat, and the home remodeling returned to his life, along with an arsenal of new treats: the limousine, the extravagant parties he threw, the hobnobbing with the prestigious, the entourage of press, the celebrity status. No one seemed critical of his posh lifestyle now, because he worked for the people.

One morning a week, he opened his office to any citizens wanting to discuss their medical problems and their difficulties with the system. One afternoon a week, he conducted hearings against those whom he called "medical delinquents," the doctors who broke the rules. The press hailed him as medicine's savior.

With the lieutenant governor and other officials under investigation for accepting costly gifts from contractors awarded government projects, the governor's administration was wounded. Burrow needed a running mate untouched by political scandal. Should the heat on the lieutenant governor increase, the secretary would likely be chosen. As he approached the meeting room, the secretary's ready grin, authoritative gait, and impeccable grooming suggested that he could win the public's confidence for the office he so ardently sought.

But after a life of duty, was he happy? he sometimes wondered. He had married a woman, since deceased, whose social aplomb was an asset to his career. Although he had felt many positive emotions toward her, passion was not one of them. He had bought a house suitable for entertaining, but it lacked the grounds needed for his favorite hobby, gardening. He played golf with the influential, but he really enjoyed fishing. He worked as a bureaucrat, but he loved medicine. He basked in the glory of his position; however, on the rare occasions when he was alone, he was gripped by an inexplicable sadness. His life seemed colorless in his kaleidoscope.

There was, however, one bright spot on the gray landscape of his inner life. He had two children, and although he loved them both, he favored one of them, who idolized him and shared his interest in the same field of medicine from an early age. Watching that child grow up was the thrill of his life. The child's first words, first trip to school, first graduation were the golden milestones of contentment etched in his memories. These remembrances formed a locked room in the open house that was his life, a place not to be shared with the world but cherished in privacy.

"This way, Mr. Secretary," said the escort, opening the double doors to a meeting room whose antique mahogany table, tapestried walls, and old paintings were reminiscent of a time when colonial statesmen met to adopt a new government. The formality of the room seemed to clash with the rolled sleeves, crumpled shirts, and loosened ties of the people gathering there.

With the air of an executive whose boardroom was the world, the secretary greeted his colleagues. His linen suit, custom-made by a London tailor, his well-styled white hair, and his Italian leather attaché case added dignity to the gathering. When all had assembled, twelve advisors sat around the oblong conference table, with the governor and the secretary at opposite ends. The table resembled a boat with oarsmen lining the sides and officers at the bow and stern.

Burrow drank from a coffee mug bearing his picture and the inscription *Back Mack for governor*. The governor's actual face showed no trace of the smile dominating the mug. He often seemed to shift masks from comedy to tragedy, with the former reserved for public consumption and the latter, more natural, face for private.

"Good morning, Warren. You look awfully starched today, considering the heat and humidity," said the governor, with a faint tinge of mockery in his tone.

"Good morning, Governor. I'm pleased if my appearance matches the dignity of the meeting I'm honored to attend," said the secretary, feeling complimented.

A thump of Burrow's feet was the only response as he put them on the antique table, leaving the secretary to gape at a hole forming on the sole of one shoe. Malcolm Burrow knew that he and the man whom he might choose for his running mate were different. The media described his secretary of medicine as "respectable," "honorable," and "a pillar of the community," but it characterized him as "cagey," "crafty," and "shrewd." The governor's staff expunged the expletives from their language in the presence of the secretary but allowed their speech to flow uncensored before their boss. And Malcolm Burrow knew—not as a conscious identification but more as a hound sniffs food—that somehow these differences made the secretary suitable to be both his running mate and the object of his gibes.

"What time is your press conference, Warren?" Burrow asked.

"It's at three."

"Then let's get busy, folks. In three hours Warren's giving the media his report on CareFree, so we've got to figure out how he'll answer the rumors. We've got tough problems to face and big decisions to make, so let's focus on the important things: the polls and the media." He turned to one of his advisors, a young, energetic man sitting at the edge of his chair.

"You've been dropping in the polls since the kickback scandal broke. Yesterday you dipped two points behind your opponent, Governor," said the young man. "The people think they're worse off now than four years ago, and the program they're griping about is CareFree."

"The press next," said the governor irritably.

An attractive female advisor held a newspaper. "This morning the *Globe* ran an editorial with the headline 'CareFree or CareLess?'" She lowered the eyeglasses resting atop her head and read aloud: "'Barely two years after its ceremonious beginning, the governor's pet project, CareFree, is rumored to be bankrupt. Reliable sources say that the demand for health care, which was expected to increase slightly when the state took over medicine, has actually doubled and is still climbing.

"'While the public clamors for care, there's a growing scarcity of providers. This year a record number of doctors quit, enrollment in medical schools dropped, and long-established hospitals closed their doors.

"'We suspect that CareFree may cause the governor's demise on election day, unless a tonic is administered now to treat the ailing program. In his news conference this afternoon, will the secretary of medicine announce an elixir for CareFree? Or is it too late for remedies? Will we be wise to break our legs and have our strokes before CareFree's budget springs a fatal leak? Perhaps the time has come for someone new to steer the ship of state.'"

When the advisor dropped the paper and looked up, the only smile she saw in the room was imprinted on a coffee mug.

"Those reports are vicious lies spread by my enemies," said the governor, springing to his feet and pacing. "CareFree bankrupt? That's preposterous!"

"It's absurd!" said an advisor.

"It's ridiculous!" said another.

"It's outrageous!" said a third.

"It's true," said the white-haired man with the starched shirt.

All heads turned to him.

"The situation is worse than the media guessed. Our budget *is* going to run out," said the secretary.

"*After* the election?" the governor asked hopefully.

"Before."

No one disputed the secretary's words—or seemed surprised.

Burrow's voice shrieked. "Something's gone wrong, and we've got to fix it."

"I prepared a financial report on our expenditures," said the secretary, reaching into his briefcase for a stack of spiral-bound documents and distributing copies to everyone.

The governor rolled up his copy and slapped it against the table. "CareFree can't go belly-up!"

"Let's hit Washington," someone said. "They bailed us out before."

"Forget it. They contributed all they're going to. We're making history with a landmark program, and Washington's leaving us to rot," griped Burrow. He paced restlessly, waving his rolled copy of the report at the group. "Let's analyze this baby line by line and throw out everything unessential."

Twelve heads bowed to study the report.

"We mustn't allow anything new," said someone to Burrow's right. "No new hospitals, wings, pavilions, or treatment centers. More facilities mean more billings, and we can't pay them."

The others nodded in agreement.

"Here's something for the scrap heap," declared the woman who had read the newspaper column. "On page two, I see that one district is adding two thousand hospital beds, but they already have more beds per capita than any other district in the state. Let's ax this now."

"But that's Waterbee's district," said the governor, glancing at his report. "Don't anybody scratch that!"

"Oh, right, I forgot."

Bill Waterbee was an influential congressman who had broken ranks with the opposing party to back CareFree.

"Keep looking," Burrow said, tapping a finger on the table. "Watch for expensive equipment like scanners. No facility can buy one without our authorization, and we're not giving it."

"Page seven shows that Nassau County is getting two new scanners," said a woman who had been a business consultant. "This report indicates it already has more scanners per capita than any other county. Let's scrap that acquisition."

"Sure, Helen! Scrap Louie Marcone and watch me end up on the trash heap, too."

"Sorry, Mack, I forgot about Louie."

Nassau County was home to the largest manufacturing plant in the state and the seat of a powerful union headed by Louis Marcone, a man Burrow wooed the way a casino courts a high roller.

"Keep looking, folks," the governor continued. "We've gotta trim the residency programs, so we limit the number of new surgeons. They cost a fortune, and only a small percentage of people need them."

"Here on page eight, the budgets of Galen College of Medicine and its residency program were increased. Let's cut them," said another aide.

"But remember last March?" someone replied. "We were free-falling in the ratings over Galen."

"Oh, of course," the first aide said apologetically.

The previous March, the community served by Galen College Hospital staged a massive demonstration to protest the state's rejection of their plan for a new cancer facility, and the governor's approval rating plummeted until the BOM finally consented.

"Keep looking! Let's curb medical research," Burrow continued. "That's the easiest thing to cut. Because people don't have the benefit of it yet, they don't know what they're missing."

"Governor," remarked an advisor, "page ten shows we're shelling out millions on research to cure baldness. Let's cut this."

"Are you crazy, Chuck?" replied a voice from across the room. "Last week in Manhattan the applause meters jumped off the scale when the governor announced CareFree's research project to cure baldness."

"Oh, that's right. Damn!" Chuck responded, leafing through the report to find something else.

"You people want to cut things that are necessary! Let's look for something we don't need," said Burrow.

"What about the ten million dollars for education? Let's scratch that."

"CareFree needs education, Norma. We need seminars, videos, booklets, TV spots, and counselors to explain to people what the new system is and why it's good," said the governor.

"And we always gain in the polls after we blitz a community with an education program," someone added.

"Then let's get rid of the fluff—the free checkups, free contact lenses, free nutritional counseling, and free vitamins. These programs bleed us dry, and they couldn't be essential," said another aide.

"They're more essential than anything else. The majority of folks are healthy. They need some benefit from the taxes they pump into CareFree, something to remember on election day. I need to *increase* what you're calling fluff," said the governor.

"Besides, those programs are Buddy's turf," another voice added.

Buddy Terkins, New York City's director of community affairs, was an outspoken supporter of Burrow, and Buddy had a following.

"Maybe we can eliminate some bureaucrats, Governor," said another aide. "We now have as many bureaucrats as we do doctors."

"Then where's the progress?" asked Burrow, as he stopped pacing to stare at the aide. "We need the bureaucrats to run things because they're unselfish and impervious to personal gain."

"Then let's raise taxes," said a young advisor just out of college.

The governor laughed. "Glen here thinks it's simple. All I have to do is raise taxes . . . when I promised for four years to cut them? When I'm committed to cutting them? When my opponent smears me every day for not cutting them—and you're telling me to *raise* them?" the governor bellowed.

The young man fidgeted. "It was just a thought," he whispered.

"Keep looking!" Burrow ordered. But no one replied. Glen's flushed face seemed to silence the rest. "How much time do we have, Warren, before things get . . . out of hand?"

"If we continue spending the way we have been, CareFree won't be able to meet its payroll in three weeks."

"Three weeks!" gasped the governor, his forehead wet, his face white. "Our employees will strike. The doctors will join them. We'll have demonstrations, violence, chaos! The media will cremate me. It'll be the end of my political career!" Burrow sagged into his chair with a thump, his shoulders slouched, his jaw dropped. "We're in a goddamn fix. I can't cut the programs; I promised to expand them. I can't raise taxes; I promised to lower them. What am I going to do?" "Warren, help me," he pleaded. "Do you know what to do?"

Everyone turned to the white-haired man who had been silent through the discussion.

"Yes, Mack, I do." The secretary's calm voice was a cool salve on the governor's frazzled nerves. "But first I want to explain some actions of my agency that were mentioned here, actions that would be embarrassing to me if they were misconstrued," said the secretary. "Some of you may wonder why my agency seems to have dispensed favors and given preferential treatment to some people over others for political gain."

"Nobody wonders about that, Warren. Everybody here knows how politics works," said Burrow.

"Two years ago when I became head of the BOM, I vowed to place no concern over the public interest, so I want to explain, as a matter of principle, why my agency seems to be acting arbitrarily and playing favorites left and right."

The governor glanced at his watch. "Let's not waste time, Warren. Everybody knows we have to scratch a few backs to get ours scratched."

The secretary continued. "I assure you that I am still dedicated to upholding my sacred trust to serve the public. However, I realize that for CareFree to survive, our party must win in November. Therefore, any measures we take to win votes are noble actions for a worthy cause, rather than arbitrary abuses of power for political gain. A noble end sometimes requires, well . . . practical means."

Burrow snickered. "Folks, I think you'll find that Warren hits the ball just like everybody else, only he does it from his high horse."

The advisors silently turned their heads back and forth, from the governor to the secretary, as if watching a tennis match.

"I blame the doctors for our troubles," the secretary continued. "They want the old way back. They don't follow the rules. They drive up the costs. They give us a hundred excuses why they can't comply and why we should make exceptions. Their stubbornness requires continually more inspectors and rules to police them. Regulators and red tape consume *half* the budget. But if the doctors cooperated, we wouldn't need *any* bureaucrats. If the doctors complied voluntarily, because they were just as enlightened as we are, we wouldn't need the inspectors and paper trails to keep them in line. Can we permit this subversive behavior by a group privileged to serve the public?"

"No, Warren, we can't!" cried the governor, galvanized. The anger building inside him like an overheating radiator seemed to find a vent. "You've put your hands on the problem. We've got our great program threatened, my political future collapsing, and the people thrown into a crisis—by what? A few individuals with special skills who think they can hold the rest of us hostage. And for what? So they can have a few fancy cars in their garages? Is that why the people have to go without the services they need?" He snarled. "I won't stand for it. We need to hit the doctors over the head."

"Forgive me, Governor, but while we agree on the cause of the problem, I must reject your solution as, well, barbaric."

"Just what do you mean by that?" snapped the governor.

"We need to impress on the doctors their social responsibility," said the secretary.

"We need to show the doctors who's boss," said the governor.

"We need to enlighten them about their moral obligations."

"We need to rein them in."

"We need to tell them to stop breaching our rules. We need to tell them *emphatically*."

"*Emphatically?*" the governor asked, puzzled.

"Yes, emphatically."

A coffee-mug grin was forming on the governor's face as he studied the secretary.

"We've been too lenient, Mack. When the doctors disregard the rules, we fine them a few thousand dollars, which for many of them isn't enough of a deterrent. The arrogant ones pay the fines and commit the same offenses again. We have the power to be tougher. We can suspend them, revoke their licenses,"—his voice lowered—"or even throw some of them in jail."

The governor clasped his hands behind his head and leaned back in his chair, as if basking in the noonday sun. "Perhaps I was too quick to question your approach, Warren."

"I disagree with you, Mack, when you say that we have to hit the doctors over the head. With all due respect, I loathe such uncivilized behavior, if you will forgive me."

"Oh, I do, Warren, I do."

"Rather than instill fear in the providers by resorting to the force of the state, we must raise their consciousness so that they look beyond their personal interests to the common good. The cooperation and compliance of the doctors will save us millions of dollars and will save the soul of CareFree. I believe that the only thing that can save us is the doctors' acceptance."

"Warren, I now see your point," said the governor, his face beaming. He looked like someone pleased to be getting what he wanted, even if under a different name.

"At my press conference this afternoon, I'll tell the doctors that they must meet their social obligations, which means they must cooperate, sacrifice . . . and obey."

All signs of suspicion vanished from the governor's face. He smiled at the white-haired gentleman with the regal bearing. "Warren, I think you have the *perfect* solution."

The tall shade trees on the lawn of the state capitol strained to resist the gusts bending them to the breaking point. The secretary of medicine faced reporters at the steps of the stone building, his well-groomed white hair being jostled by the wind. The state and national flags draping his outdoor podium flapped loudly in the turbulent air. The secretary eyed the mounting storm clouds, for he had planned not only to hold his press conference outdoors but also to travel afterward from Albany to New York City for an important dinner engagement.

"Mr. Secretary, would you like to move the conference indoors?" an aide asked.

"Why, no. We shouldn't let a few dark clouds scare us."

The secretary reassured New Yorkers that CareFree would triumph because it was a noble plan. His thick white hair brightened the darkening scene like a beacon atop a lighthouse. His impassioned voice sparked hope.

After his introductory remarks, the secretary delivered his message: "Fees paid to hospitals and doctors will be reduced by fifteen percent in order to meet CareFree's temporary financial challenges, which the providers themselves have caused with actions that were self-serving rather than public-spirited."

He felt a sudden jolt at the sight of a young man joining the crowd that had gathered. The man, who was a wearing a doctor's white coat, had probably wandered over from a nearby hospital. A disturbing image of himself as a young doctor under siege flashed through the secretary's mind. Was he now the Bob Martin and Charles Fox in the life of the physician before him, making unfair accusations that everyone would believe and that the doctor would be helpless to combat? His mind slammed a door on the unwelcome thought before it could gain a foothold. Another, more comforting idea hurried to replace it: He reminded himself that he was working for a noble cause—the good of the people. Thus, his actions were justified.

He continued his speech with added vigor. "CareFree guarantees everyone the right to medical care. The doctors have a duty to provide that care, and I have an obligation to see that they do. If any doctor flagrantly and willfully violates the law, I will personally impose stringent consequences. We cannot permit lawlessness. I will uphold the rules so that the public can receive all the benefits of CareFree."

Lightning flashed in the distance. It was soon to strike closer.

The same dismal sky blanketed Manhattan that afternoon, subduing its glorious cityscape to a cluster of black shadows in gray space. Inside the executive offices of Riverview Hospital, the board of directors was meeting to elect a chief of neurosurgery. The group had invited David Lang to address them prior to their private deliberations and vote. In their pinstriped suits, they sat on swivel chairs around a glass-topped conference table, listening to hospital administrator Randall Lang enumerate David's credentials. To the board, the surgeon, who sat beside his brother, appeared calm. Only Randy could detect the troubled look in David's eyes, which made him decide that it would be better if his brother spoke as little as possible.

David reminded himself of how close he was to unveiling the secret of healing that the nervous system had so cleverly hidden. In time, he would heal, too. He warned himself that if he gave his word, he would have to honor it. For as long as he could remember, he had viewed a promise as a sacred commandment never to be broken. He reassured himself that there was no reason to feel uneasy. Hadn't he already taken the necessary steps to keep his vow? He had begun to curtail his practice. He had hired an additional secretary whose sole job was to ensure his compliance with CareFree. He had resolved to enter and leave his office from a back door that bypassed the waiting room, to avoid contact with unauthorized patients attempting to see him. And he had cleared his desk! He had taken steps to bring himself closer to CareFree and to distance himself from the growing number of desperate patients who somehow managed to find him.

He wished the meeting were over. His head was beginning to ache. He wanted to be happy at the prospect of completing his research, but he could feel nothing. The vision of a young dancer swept across his memory, and with it the special joy of a free spirit. But he must not think of that particular image—of a free spirit—at this meeting. He forced his mind to concentrate on the simple task at hand. He would be asked to give his word, and he would do so. Then he would steadfastly stick to his plan and keep his promise. By virtue of this one vow, he could complete his years of research and resolve questions left unanswered through the centuries.

The sound of Randy's notes dropping onto the table forced David's attention back to the meeting.

"Now that I've enumerated David Lang's qualifications for the director's post, I'll pause for your comments and questions," said Randy.

"David's clinical qualifications are unquestionable," said the chief of staff, an aging man with tired eyes. "But Randall, you haven't mentioned his research, which I understand would be supported in the chief's post." He turned to David. "We know you're working on a new surgical treatment for nerve repair. What are the chances you'll succeed?"

As David opened his mouth, about to indicate the great promise of his work, Randy jumped in, faster and louder. "Don't worry, Sam. When you consider the scientists who've tried over the years, and they had unlimited access to animals, what could possibly come of David's paltry efforts? He'll putter around the lab with the research fellows, but what can we expect from a few modest studies of such a massive problem?"

David flashed Randy an angry look too subtle for anyone else to detect, and Randy sent David an apologetic shoulder shrug. Randy had neglected to tell David that the board was expecting him to fail.

"So let me allay your fears," Randy continued, the undertone of bitterness detectable only by his brother, "and assure you that the prospect of trail-blazing a cure to one of medicine's greatest problems is unlikely."

The treasurer, a big man with sagging shoulders, turned to David. "In the old days when we operated like a corner grocery, being inundated with customers wanting a new product would have shot profits through the roof. Oh, yes! Your new treatment would've been like finding a mother lode—*back then*. But times have changed." He shrugged his shoulders indifferently. "Whether that's good or bad isn't for me to say. As a businessman, my job is to adapt to changing conditions, not question them. So, I emphasize, Dr. Lang, that today an onslaught of additional patients needing costly procedures could trigger a financial catastrophe for the hospital. *If* CareFree accepted your new treatment and paid us enough to perform it here, fine. But that's a big *if*. What if Care-

Free accepted your procedure but assigned too low a fee to the hospital for your patients? What if CareFree set our fee so low that we had to provide your treatment at a loss?" The others nodded in agreement. "We must avoid that risk at all costs!"

"Dr. Lang's new procedure would treat very sick patients," commented another board member. "There could be expensive complications that CareFree would never have anticipated in fixing our fee. And, of course, once they put on their price tag, we'd be stuck with it for everybody who had the treatment. Where would we be then?"

"I understand," said David.

"I'm sure you wouldn't want to cause the financial ruin of this hospital, Dr. Lang," said the vice chairman.

"I wouldn't," David replied.

Charles Hodgeman, the chairman of the board, cleared his throat thunderously. He was a husky man with thinning hair and an intimidating voice. "Aside from the research angle, I'm concerned about Dr. Lang's shaky compliance record with CareFree."

The others quickly nodded their agreement.

"Let me be blunt, Dr. Lang," Hodgeman continued. "CareFree is here to stay, like it or not. I'm a realist, so I accept the conditions of doing business in this age. I want to know whether you're a realist, too. Because if you should get in hot water with CareFree, you could pull Riverview down with you. If unlawful practices were performed here, we could lose our accreditation. The BOM could close us down in a heartbeat, and they'd be damn glad to do it, too—it'd help their budget. That's why I want your personal guarantee that you won't act like a loose cannon."

David rose, his proud bearing and steady eyes evoking confidence, despite the board's skepticism.

"Ladies and gentlemen, what you're saying about me is true, and you're justified in being concerned. I have resisted CareFree because I believe that medicine is a private matter between a doctor and patient, and none of the state's business. However, I realize that I can no longer survive in medicine with this viewpoint. For the sake of my career, I have resolved to comply with the rules fully. I am determined to be a . . . model . . . CareFree . . . doctor. I give you my . . . promise."

Because the only response was a conspicuous silence and a few eyebrows raised skeptically, Randy thought it prudent to provide an additional incentive: "You know that other hospitals in the city have closed because they couldn't survive the rising costs of compliance, coupled with the reduction in their fees by CareFree. Riverview Hospital *has* survived, and many of you have personally thanked me for that. If Riverview is to remain viable, I need to work even harder in the future. Having key people in important positions helps me sleep at night, and my sleeping habits should be of concern to the board, if Riverview is not to fall the way of Memorial, Columbus, East River Medical—"

"All right, Randall, you've made your point," said the chairman. "But we must avoid at all costs any misguided idealism. We want realists who know how to play the ga—"

He paused at the sudden entrance of an aide.

"Excuse me," said the man, handing papers to Randy and the chairman. "A message from CareFree just came for Mr. Hodgeman and Dr. Randall Lang for their immediate attention."

The chairman frowned as he read the correspondence. "This is pretty bad," he declared to the others. "CareFree has just announced a *fifteen-percent cut* in our fees . . ."

The others gasped.

". . . and they're warning the medical profession that there will be hell to pay for those who don't comply with the rules."

"The bastards! This isn't fair!" Randy blurted out involuntarily, his eyes burning with indignation.

The chairman shrugged his shoulders, his eyes as dull as the ashes of a fire long extinguished. "Fairness is irrelevant. It's a policy we'll have to live with somehow, so there's no use getting angry," he said flatly, turning to Randy. "I want you to inform our clinicians immediately of CareFree's statement. Then I want you to devise ways to monitor their activities more closely. We need stricter controls. We need to look at the way these doctors get access to radiology, to imaging, to surgery, to anything they want. We need more internal forms, procedures, approvals, and protocols. We need to hire more administrative staff to curtail the doctors' activities. We have to show CareFree that we can police ourselves, so they'll let us remain a free enterprise."

"I'll take care of it, Charles," Randy replied, pocketing the notice. "Now what about the matter at hand?"

"Oh, yes, the matter of catapulting medicine into the next century," the chairman said, snickering.

"The matter of providing me with peace of mind, so I can figure out how we can take a hit for fifteen percent and still not go belly-up," Randy replied.

The chairman stared at the inflexible face of his administrator and the unreadable face of the surgeon. "Dr. Lang, reassure us again, please. Do we have your *solemn promise* that you will do nothing in the OR that hasn't been approved, certified, permitted, authorized, and endorsed by CareFree?"

David saw pages he could not tear from his memory. He saw seven years of careful experiments, painstaking records, tedious analyses. He saw a dream that kept him alive more than the air he breathed.

"Mr. Hodgeman, you have my word of honor. I promise to do only what is permitted. I swear I will obey the rules."

✤ 10 ✤

On Shaky Ground

"Am I interrupting?" The blond head of Randall Lang appeared at the door of David Lang's office.

"Come in," said David.

The surgeon was at his desk, dutifully tending to the day's crop of documents, which had sprouted like new weeds just when he thought that he had cleared them all.

"You made it, David! You're our new chief of neurosurgery. The announcement will come tomorrow."

"Thank you," David said, standing up.

The two men of the same height and features, one in a business suit and the other in a doctor's coat, shook hands across the desk.

"Now that CareFree is tightening the torture rack for the heretics, you didn't reform a minute too soon."

"I suppose," said David, walking around the desk toward his brother.

"The day you see a sign over the entrance to a building that reads 'Institute for Neurological Research and Surgery,' you'll know you did the right thing."

"I hope so."

"Picture the staff, the laboratories, the surgical suites," Randy said excitedly, his face raised and his arms outstretched, as if standing before a temple. "Picture yourself as the medical director and me as the administrator! We opened the first door to that goal today. Once everybody sees what a failure CareFree is, nothing will stand in our way."

"I don't know," said David, his gaze drifting out the window, the gray sky reflecting in his eyes. "I sometimes wonder what makes CareFree possible. It doesn't seem to be a concern with success or failure."

"If the system doesn't collapse, I'll get that institute anyway. I'll find a way, so help me!"

"How? By selling our souls?"

"Don't think that."

"Haven't we already?"

"We're doing what we must. What recourse do we have?"

David had no reply.

"Hi, guys!" His wife appeared at the door, a swirl of auburn hair swinging above her white doctor's coat, a narrow border of brown skirt showing beneath it. "What happened at the board meeting today? I'm dying to know!"

"The board has approved your husband as our chief of neurosurgery."

"Wonderful!"

Marie flung her arms around David's shoulders and kissed him. His arms remained at rest, his face expressionless.

"Don't look so glum, honey. You'd think you were voted chief of funerals." She turned to Randy. "It might take David time to get used to respectability. But I think he'll like it. I think we're about to see a *new* David."

"Yes, a new David, a brilliant surgeon who conducts medical experiments and makes revolutionary discoveries," Randy replied.

"A new David who's finally accepted among the city's top doctors. I'm so proud to be the director's wife!"

David said nothing.

"I knew you'd make it. I already made dinner arrangements to celebrate," Marie continued.

David was planning to work late that evening, but felt he owed Marie her celebration. "Okay," he said, forcing a smile.

"By the way, David, I invited someone to join us tonight."

"Oh, who?"

"It's a surprise, but I think you'll be pleased," she smiled gaily, her arm around his shoulder. "The *new* David will be pleased."

Her smile froze at a sudden tension in his body. He heard before the others the staccato footsteps approaching his office and recognized their urgent tempo. He turned to the door a moment before his secretary appeared there.

"Dr. Lang, you're wanted in the ER. There was an explosion nearby that damaged several buildings. The police think it was caused by a gas leak. About two hundred people are injured. The ambulances are arriving!"

"Oh, dear!" Marie's words hit the back of the man who was already out the door.

The healers and the wounded crammed the ER. Doctors and nurses came from wherever they were when they heard the news. They arrived in white coats, in hospital scrubs, in business clothes, in tennis shorts, in sundresses. They came to tend to the bundles of bloody clothing and burnt flesh arriving on stretchers.

Beyond the swinging doors of the ER, David heard sirens wailing and glimpsed ambulances gridlocked on the ramp. Beyond the swinging doors on the opposite side, he saw the waiting room being transformed into a makeshift ward by the infusion of white clinical uniforms, linen, and bandages. His wife and others were gathering there to assist the injured.

Under the glaring fluorescent lights of the ER, at a command post of work spaces behind high counters, nurses were making a flurry of phone calls—to search for more stretchers, to locate rooms for new admissions, to alert Surgery to impending cases. Phones rang plaintively, computer screens flashed, pagers buzzed, monitors beeped, respirators whooshed, and all the time, the wounded moaned.

White-coated doctors flew to meet blue-clad rescue workers bringing in the victims. Doctors examined the wounded while keeping stride with the rolling stretchers. Staff members in hospital scrubs questioned the victims, jabbed them with needles, wiped blood from their faces, and held their hands. When all of the beds were occupied, rescuers left the injured on stretchers, on chairs, or on the floor, so they could return to the ramp for a new load. Hospital workers stepped over an obstacle course of wounded flesh.

Glass-enclosed rooms with life-support equipment received the most serious cases:

"He's unconscious."

"Her pressure's crashing."

"He's bleeding out on us."

The steady hands and sure voices of the healers brought calm to chaos:

"Let's get a chest film."

"Start a second IV."

"Sir, can you hear me? Where does it hurt?"

"He needs a chest tube."

"Call the OR. Tell them we're on our way up with a ruptured spleen."

"This woman's in labor. Call OB."

"This guy just stopped breathing. Call Respiratory."

And, as a sheet was pulled over a victim's face, "Call the morgue."

David arrived galvanized for work. "Where was the accident?" he asked a passing doctor.

"Don't know."

Rescuers clustered around a gurney coming into the ER. A blue-tinged body lay motionless on the stretcher. One rescuer was pressing both fists against the victim's chest. Another was pumping air through a rubber bag into the patient's lungs. A third had his fingers on the victim's pulse. A fourth held an IV solution that was dripping into the patient's arm. A fifth steered the gurney, with the whole entourage careening to the left or right with every turn.

"Male in full arrest. No vital signs," said one of the rescuers.

David joined the retinue, following the gurney into one of the rooms.

"This is Mr. Reiner. He's fifty years old. When we found him at the explosion site, he was complaining of chest pains. He arrested on the way over," a rescuer explained.

With the personnel who normally handle such situations already engaged, David took charge. He examined the patient, directing the rescuers to assist:

"Check his airway. . . . Position the monitor leads. . . . Start a DT4 drip. . . . Get a cardiologist in here."

Wires, patches, and tubes soon connected Mr. Reiner to the room's equipment. Buttons flashed, monitors brightened, numbers flickered on electronic screens, and beeps sounded. David had made the room come alive. Could he do the same for the patient? His eyes turned to the monitor, shaking his head in disapproval of the graph traversing the green screen. He tried chest compressions, electric currents, drugs, every remedy he knew.

"Still no pulse," reported one of the nurses who had joined him.

He repeated the maneuvers.

"Still no pulse, Doctor."

He tried the maneuvers again. With each effort, David's eyes returned to the stubborn monitor until, finally, the green screen relented, presenting a more pleasing picture.

"I have a pulse," the nurse uttered at last.

After a few minutes, Mr. Reiner slowly opened his eyes. David explained what had happened and assured the patient that a cardiologist would arrive to continue his treatment. Mr. Reiner grasped David's hand in relief and gratitude. As a pink glow began to color the victim's face, a smile warmed the doctor's features; life seemed to have returned to both men. David had done what he did for a living. Nothing more could ever fascinate him; nothing less could sustain him.

He placed a comforting hand on Mr. Reiner's arm. Mr. Reiner placed two weak hands over David's one and squeezed with all the strength he could summon, his eyes containing the whole of his relief and gratitude. David held his glance and smiled in answer. The same current that had jolted Mr. Reiner's heart seemed to charge David's own face with exhilaration.

He'd never understood why people said that doctors should derive no selfish reward from the care they provide. He felt the most glorious sense of pride from saving someone's life, and he could not make the grueling effort that medicine required without fervently loving his work. He knew the world meant that he could love his profession and derive spiritual fulfillment from it but that he should not love making money from it.

"Doctors must work for the good of others because they possess special skills that are critically needed by society," his teachers had said.

Was he supposed to offer people the ultimate value, their very health and existence, yet not desire a financial reward for his services the way in which the provider of a house, a car, or a swimming pool would? Because their services are *more* valuable than those offered by others, are doctors to be prohibited from setting the terms of their own compensation? Are doctors to be punished because they offer so much? Because they are . . . good?

"Unless restrained, a doctor will work for selfish gain, not for the patient's welfare," the politicians had said.

Did this mean that harming his patients benefited him, or harming himself benefited them? If he received all the value from his work and the patient derived none, didn't that make him a thief? If the patient received all the value and he derived none, didn't that make him a slave? Was his only choice between robbery and slavery? He had always believed that what was good for his patients was good for him. If he were gifted, then his patients would thrive and his career would prosper. If he were incompetent, then his patients would suffer and his career, as well as his supreme pride in his own being, would be destroyed. What perversion linked his self-interest to his patients' detriment, and their self-interest to his own destruction? Wasn't that the premise behind his oath to the board? Wasn't treating his patients leading to his own demise, and wasn't he vowing to compromise treatment to save his career? While he monitored Mr. Reiner, a voice inside him asked why it was necessary to make such a promise to the board.

Mr. Reiner, now breathing on his own, whispered, "Everything was fine when . . . I heard . . . a loud bang. . . . The floor . . . rumbled, the chandeliers . . . shook, people screamed. I felt . . . a sharp pain that . . ."—the victim breathed laboriously—". . . scared the hell out of me."

"Take it easy," a nurse warned, as she helped him out of his clothing and into a hospital gown.

By this time, a cardiologist had entered the room. David briefed him, and then headed for the door.

"The stage buckled," Mr. Reiner continued.

David stopped. "The stage? What stage?"

"The stage." Mr. Reiner grew pale. "I was in . . . a . . . theater."

"What theater?" David moved close to the man but received no response. The man's eyes were closing eyes and his head was drooping.

"Blood pressure's falling!" cried a nurse.

"Respiration's becoming shallow!" said another.

"We're losing him."

"Get out of the way, Doctor," the cardiologist ordered, shoving David aside, giving directions to the nurses, and springing into action.

"Where was the accident?" David asked the group at large, but no one responded.

He lifted a large plastic bag in which the nurse had placed the man's clothing, and he reached inside the shirt pocket. There he found something that made him gasp—a ticket stub to Nicole Hudson's show.

In an instant, he ran into the corridor. He hunted for Nicole in the rooms containing the seriously injured. To his relief, she was not there. He searched among victims in the other beds. Again, he did not find Nicole. Suddenly, he stopped. An attendant was wheeling a gurney holding the slim lines of a woman's body under a sheet that covered her completely—including her face. He ran toward the delicate, oblong form, knocking the gurney off course. He pulled the sheet down—and saw the ghastly blue tinge of death on the face of an old woman.

The attendant was startled. "Hey! What's the matter, Doctor? Are you okay?"

"Are there any more . . . fatalities?"

"One more, DOA, at the end of the hallway," the attendant pointed to a stretcher with a body under a white sheet. "She was a young blond. You could tell she was pretty before her skull got smashed. What a shame!"

David grimly walked down the long corridor. Was he to regret for the rest of his life that he had not approached Nicole at the flower shop? he wondered. She had sought him; he had run away. Walking down the stark white hallway, he was suddenly aware of how brief life was. He wondered whether he was treating his own precious days with the proper reverence or wasting irreplaceable time on matters that only brought him grief. He reached for a white sheet over a cold body. A patch of golden hair froze his features into a solid block of pain. With a trembling hand, he lifted the sheet. He winced at the pulverized pulp that was once a living brain. But hope beat wildly inside him again, for the stony eyes he closed were not Nicole's.

He scanned the adjoining radiology unit, peering into cubicles where patients were being X-rayed. He found a room that he had to enter.

"Stop! The machine's on! You know better than that, Doctor," a technician exclaimed from behind a partition.

David rushed to a man wearing stage makeup who was lying on the table. The patient was the dancer who played Prometheus.

"What happened?" David placed a sympathetic hand on his shoulder.

"Broken . . . ribs . . . they think." The dancer flinched in pain.

"What happened to Nicole?"

"Who're you?"

"I'm her doctor."

"Don't . . . know," the dancer struggled. Every word seemed to unleash a searing pain.

"Where was she when the explosion occurred?"

"Nicole was . . . on . . . the cliff with me," the patient whispered.

The technician approached. "We need to take another picture," she said, repositioning the machine.

"A loud boom . . . like a bomb . . . shook the stage. A light . . . fell on me," the dancer continued.

"What happened to Nicole?"

"She fell . . . off the cliff. . . . I called to her."

"What did she say?"

"Nothing."

"What do you mean nothing?"

"She was . . ." The man winced.

"She was what?"

"Owww, it hurts!" The man grimaced.

"Easy, now—we're almost through," said the technician, as she adjusted the man's position.

"Nicole was what?"

The task of breathing presented an agonizing struggle for the patient. He gasped for air, then moaned at the pain that the act caused.

David's voice was sympathetic, but he persisted. "You called to Nicole, and she said nothing because she was—what?"

"Out."

It was David's turn to gasp. "She was . . . unconscious?"

"Yes."

"Where is she?"

"Ambulances came. People . . . carried us out. . . . I don't know."

David's white coat swung like a cape behind him as he flew to the ramp, skirting stretchers and colliding with people. He breathed stifling, humid air heavy with gas fumes and vomit but had no time to notice. Nicole was in trouble, and he needed to find her! He scanned the victims being carried from the ambulances. No Nicole. Then another ambulance arrived. He flung its rear door open and peered into the long tunnel. On his right he saw victims sitting on an overcrowded bench, their bandages seeping blood, their bodies sweating. On the left, his eyes caught a patch of gold as bright as a field of sunflowers.

She lay on a stretcher in the truck, still wearing her stage makeup and sheer costume, her voluminous straw hair pulled around her like a blanket, her eyes closed. She might have resembled a princess in repose—except for the purple bruises and swelling across her forehead, the blood dripping from her nose, the raccoonlike black circles under her eyes, the red-stained bandages over lacerations on her arms, the IV line attached to her wrist. Her head was at the front of the vehicle. Without waiting for the others to exit, David climbed over the protesting tangle of bodies on the bench.

"Nicole! Can you hear me?"

There was no reply.

He worked quickly, aided by equipment in the truck. Her airway was clear; she was breathing on her own; her blood pressure and pulse were steady. Her skin color was pink, a sign of oxygen in her bloodstream. Her body responded to stimuli when he performed a few simple tests. She had fallen on her face and broken her nose, he surmised. He would take her inside and run brain scans. Her warm breath on his hands reassured him.

He removed a penlight from his pocket. She was alive; her vital signs were good; she was not deeply unconscious. He opened one of her eyelids. She could awaken at any moment and flash a radiant smile at him. Then they would both laugh at their two peculiar meetings in recent weeks, one in an ambulance and the other outside a flower shop. He aimed the penlight into her eye, expecting her to awaken, to recognize him and smile. Then he could forget the sickening fear he never had to—

Sweat suddenly beaded his forehead. He stared incredulously at her serene face. He slowly opened her other lid and shone the little light into that eye. He shook his head in denial and repeated the test on both eyes. Then he gasped. He was confronted by two tiny demons that did not respond to light. Instead of constricting as they were supposed to, they remained fixed, dilated . . . lifeless. The demons were Nicole's pupils.

He pulled his feverish face to within inches of her composed features. Her eyes were cold and blank. His were filled with fear.

Just then the dainty head began to move. The eyelids blinked. Nicole was awakening.

"It's dark. Very dark," she said, her eyes wide open.

Trembling, David cast the penlight directly into one eye, then the other.

"I . . . I can't . . . see . . . anything," she whispered. Then her face fell to the side and her eyes closed once again.

❧ 11 ❧
The Diagnosis

David Lang pushed his unconscious patient to Imaging at an alarming speed. He was oblivious to the curious looks of the people he passed and to the gurney wheels that squealed in protest around the corners. A brain scan in the ER had indicated a fracture at the base of Nicole's skull. He urgently needed to run another kind of scan, one that would reveal soft tissue, to learn more about Nicole's condition. Traveling with his precious cargo through a maze of pastel corridors streaked with a myriad of black-lettered signs, he considered the possible causes of his patient's condition. With every hypothesis, the corrective measure that he would take flashed instantly in his mind, as if healing were synonymous with injury.

Having detected no direct trauma to Nicole's eyes, David suspected that a behind-the-scenes culprit was responsible for Nicole's blindness, the prime mover in the magnificent production called vision—the optic nerve. Although sight seems to occur in the eyes the way a play occurs onstage, it's directed behind the scenes, as is any great performance. The optic nerve carries impulses from the eye to recesses at the back of the brain, transforming stimuli from the outside world into sensations grasped by our minds in the unique phenomenon called sight. By enabling humans and other animals to see, the optic nerve allows Earth's creatures to discover the world outside of themselves. Fitting with its vital function, this nerve belongs to that elite corps of tissue comprising the central nervous system.

As if the brain were concerned with the disastrous effect of injury to its precious optic nerve, it produces two, one emanating from each eye, with each able to bear the entire burden of vision should its twin die unexpectedly. The two optic nerves are protected from simultaneous injury when separated, but in their travels from the front to the back of the brain, they intersect, charting a course that resembles a large **X**. This means that despite nature's careful duplication, an injury at the crossing point could harm both visual fields. To make matters worse, the delicate nerves travel along a dangerous route right by their intersection. There they lie on top of something as thin as fine crystal, the delicate sinus bones that line the nasal cavity and form the base of the skull. Nicole had sustained a fracture in that area, and the gauze that David had just placed under her nose was already darkening with blood.

David had asked an ophthalmologist to meet him in Imaging to examine Nicole's scans. The eye surgeon, a trim, handsome man in his fifties with a kind face and an engaging smile, was waiting when David arrived.

"What've you got there, David?"

"A fall on the forehead from a distance of about twelve feet. The patient momentarily regained consciousness, reporting a total loss of vision. Both pupils are nonreactive to light, and she has a skull-base fracture."

The ophthalmologist shined his pocket light on the stagnant blue pools that were Nicole's eyes. "Let's take a look," he said, his smile vanishing.

The imaging room was dark and bare, as if staged for a mystery. A spotlight on the ceiling beamed a cone of light on the room's lone furnishing, a pale-gray machine with a narrow sliding table at its mouth. The sleeping Nicole was to take center stage. The two men lifted her onto the table and positioned her head by the arched opening. The white sheet draping her body hung from both sides of the table, concealing the support so that she seemed suspended in space. The only soft touch in the stark setting was eighteen inches of lustrous gold hair, disobediently tumbling off the table, despite David's attempts to restrain the tresses for a ride into the machine.

A monitor hung by Nicole's side, its wires attached to sensors on her skin. David frequently glanced at the electronic charts and numbers, reading her heart rate, pulse, and respirations. He mentally rehearsed the scene that he would direct should the metal box sound an alarm.

After positioning Nicole, the surgeons stepped into the adjoining control room to watch her through a large window. A technician sat in the darkened room by a computer console and monitor. The operator activated a command that sent Nicole's head slowly into the mouth of the machine. The ophthalmic surgeon settled into a chair next to the technician. David, too troubled to sit, paced restlessly behind the men, his black hair blending with the dark walls, his face reflecting the ghastly gray of the monitor.

The scanner was an advanced model that would pass a harmless substance through Nicole's lovely head, providing exquisitely detailed pictures of her brain to transform ignorance into knowledge and to rescue David from the worst fear of all—the unknown. The machine would endow him with a superhuman power, like the childhood legend who could see through walls. He was thankful that he could spare Nicole the ordeal of exploratory brain surgery in which her skull would be opened by a surgeon as blind, in a way, as she, not knowing in advance the nature, extent, or location of the injury. In a few minutes the remarkable block of metal, his oracle, would enlighten him.

The machine hummed its electronic tune, and the screen displayed its first picture, an overview of Nicole's brain. David examined the artistlike rendering. The machine produced images that distinguished tissues, bones, and vessels with a fine precision.

"Let's get cuts through the sinus and the sella turcica," David directed the technician, "so we can see the pathway of the optic nerves."

The technician played a sonatina on the keyboard. The machine hummed. A new image appeared. The two surgeons leaned over the screen, gray hair next to black. While Nicole lay unconscious, the doctors scrutinized an overhead view of her brain sliced horizontally at the floor of the skull. Nicole's eyes were prominent white orbs. The trail of the optic nerves extended from each eye, tracing the familiar wide X across the brain. The fragile sinus bones that formed the cranial floor under the nerves were a contrasting hue. But the pattern of the bones and nerves was not a smooth one. An abnormality appeared just before the intersection of the nerves.

"Look, there's a disruption of the nerves in the optic canal," said the ophthalmologist.

"Magnify that," David murmured almost inaudibly, too absorbed in thought to raise his voice.

While the technician played the keyboard, David wondered what mystery the next frame would reveal. What was the cause of the disruption they were seeing? Would there be a hemorrhage in the optic nerves from blood vessels ruptured in the fall? He could stop the bleeding and restore vision. Would hematomas—blood clots—be pressing on the optic nerves, blocking their function? He could remove the clots and restore vision. Would he find that edema—swelling—of the nerves was impeding their work? He could reduce the swelling and restore vision. Would the fracture on the floor of the skull have caused bone to press against the taut nerves in the optic canal? He could decompress the fragile nerves and thereby restore vision. He could and he would because he most desperately had to restore vision.

He leaned closer to the monitor. The technician pressed buttons. The machine hummed and vibrated. The next picture flashing on the screen cast a dark shadow across David's face. He gasped.

"Oh, no!" the ophthalmologist cried.

David's body stiffened behind the two men. He stared through the window at Nicole suspended in space. He knew the diagnosis. The image on the screen told him everything that the ophthalmologist would now say. The older doctor remained deeply engrossed in the brain scan, unaware that David's hands had left the table, just as his eyes had left the screen and his thoughts had left the room.

"Oh, the poor thing! What a pity!" exclaimed the eye surgeon.

David did not see an object of pity. Under the folds of the thin sheet, he saw the exciting vitality of Nicole's body, the striking pattern of taut lines and graceful curves, the flesh that was firm and supple. He saw a figure carved by a loving sculptor who masterfully mixed strength with softness to create beauty.

He thought of an ancient statue that he had seen of a goddess with wings, a statue that had stood on the prow of a ship as a symbol of victory. The sculptor had captured the deity descending onto the ship, with one foot touching the prow, the other still in flight. The eight-foot-high marble lady moved against a gusting head wind palpable in the fullness of her wings, the zesty swing of her robe behind her, the thrust of her body forward. The flowing drapery of her robe revealed the vibrant sensuality of a woman's body. Sea-soaked and windswept, the voluminous garment clung to the front of her body like a transparent film, encircling her breasts, stretching against her taut stomach, highlighting the long lines of her legs. The statue's pose revealed her spirit. Her arrogant thrust forward and visible delight at the touch of the sea and wind was more than a call to victory—it was an exaltation of victory, a triumph not merely over an enemy at sea but the triumph of the human spirit celebrated in the soaring body of a goddess with wings. The graceful movement of the stone lady had reminded David of a dancer. The statue had no head; it had been lost in the rubble of centuries. At that moment in the imaging room, David envisioned the winged goddess with Nicole's radiant face.

The ophthalmologist continued to study the scan. "The fracture of the sphenoid bone did the damage. It must have hit with some force, because it cut right through the dura."

The dura mater, Latin for "hard mother," is the outer membrane covering the spinal cord and brain. The dura forms sheaths around the optic nerves.

"With the dura cut," the ophthalmologist continued, "you can see the injury to the nerves. What a tragedy!"

The eye surgeon's final word was like a heavy weight on the goddess's ship. David knew that such ballast would not sink the marble lady. One sweep of her giant wings would cast the unwanted load out to sea. Was tragedy to be Nicole's fate, he wondered—and his own? Could he abandon her to defeat, pain, and misery? Or could he change her destiny to that of the stone goddess—to triumph?

The ophthalmologist rose from his chair and turned to face his younger colleague, pulling David's thoughts back into the room.

"There's nothing you can do, David. A fragment dislodged from the fractured bone on the cranial floor and transected the optic nerves. They're both completely severed. The situation is hopeless. She'll never see again."

David did not reply.

"You know as well as I do, David, that the optic nerve is identical to the white matter of the brain; therefore, it's incapable of regeneration."

"Do I?"

The floor, the walls, and the fluorescent-lighted ceiling of Nicole's hospital room were devoid of color. Outside the window, David observed a lively blue jay fluttering in a willow-green tree, performing its early evening grooming. The little bird's world was bright, but Nicole's was dark, he thought absently, sitting on the bed, watching her. She was still unconscious but was stirring and about to awaken. He found it ironic to be bringing her news that her sight had vanished, when she had sparked his own existence with such a vibrant light. Although he sat right next to her, his still pose, his furrowed brow, and his pensive gaze distanced him, as if he were pulled away by an inner conflict.

She stretched her arms, tossed her head, and opened her eyes. She blinked, at first dazed, then with a growing sense of her new condition. The sublime tranquility of sleep vanished, and a cry of horror formed on her lips. She reached up to touch her eyes.

He gently pulled her hands down to her waist and held them in his own. He watched her sympathetically, his focus seeming to return to the room, as if he had resolved the matter tugging at him.

"Don't rub your eyes, Nicole. I'm afraid it won't help."

"I . . . I can't see! I can't see!"

"I know." He squeezed her hands. "You're in a hospital. There was an explosion. Do you remember falling?"

"Yes, yes, I fell!"

She was trembling. She tossed restlessly, fighting off the grogginess, struggling to regain full awareness. She tried to sit up, but he gently pushed her shoulders back against the bed.

"Not so fast—you've had quite a fall."

The muscles that moved her eyes were unaffected by the injury, so they continued to focus with an eerie vitality.

"I'm a neurosurgeon—David Lang."

"What's wrong with my eyes?"

"You've had an injury."

"Why can't I see, Doctor?" The voice—and the fear in it—were growing stronger.

He hesitated.

For the first time, David had to be coaxed by a patient. "If you want to be kind, you'll just tell me straight."

"You fell on your face and broke your nose. A bone fragment got loose and . . . pierced the optic nerves. I'm afraid they're . . . severed, Nicole. That's why you can't see."

"And . . . what does that mean?"

He felt her hands become wet and icy.

"In the past, that meant that you . . ."—his voice dropped—"would not see . . . again."

"Oh, no! That can't be! This is the end of me! I want to die! Help me to die, Doctor! *I want to die!*"

Her hands broke away from his and pulled at her hair. She cried furiously, convulsively, interminably. Her immense capacity for joy was matched by the violence of her anguish. Each cry was like a knife slashing his skin. He waited, as if caught in a storm that had to run its course. Her tears soaked the lustrous hair around her face until the strands became dark, straight, and coarse. Then she seemed to remember something that stopped her cries abruptly. "What did you mean when you said 'in the past'?"

"There's a new procedure that might help you."

A hint of hope colored her face.

"I hasten to add that it's experimental. It's never been tested on a human before and the animal research is incomplete, so I can make no claims about its outcome. But this procedure has been tried on some laboratory animals, and it has regenerated severed tissue like that of your optic nerves and restored lost function."

Her eyes retained a haunting intelligence.

"It would require two brain surgeries, Nicole, and since it's unproven in humans, it's hard to say what the chances are that it will help you. I'd say they're slim."

"What are my chances without it?"

His voice softened. "Your brain scans clearly show that the nerves are completely severed. Unfortunately, they just don't repair themselves."

"And there is no other treatment?"

"I'm afraid not."

"Then the procedure you mention is my only chance?"

"Which is why I offered it."

"Doctor, I would try this new treatment even if my chances of dying from it were ninety-five percent."

"I wouldn't. If I thought there was a serious risk to your life, I wouldn't operate. I have no evidence that the new procedure is any more dangerous than many other brain surgeries. That's why, while you were unconscious, I thought this thing over and decided to offer the treatment, even though it's experimental. However, I must stress that there are risks inherent in brain surgery, which I'll explain and which you should consider seriously."

Her voice broke as she tried to speak. "The risk to my life is this . . . horrible injury. I feel helpless. I'm scared . . . very scared."

He thought it useless to try to convince her that she could live with total, permanent blindness. He shared her desperate desire for a cure. Wasn't that why he had become a doctor—and why he was about to do the unthinkable?

"You see, Doctor, I have something I do—my work—that means . . . so very much to me. I couldn't do it . . . blind. But it's more than that. I've never been . . . helpless. I've always been on my own, able to look after myself. I'd risk everything to save the one thing I . . . I couldn't live without. Can you understand that, Doctor?"

"Yes."

The solemnity of his voice encouraged her to say more.

"Life would mean nothing to me if I couldn't be . . . *free*. Do you know what I mean?"

"Oh, yes."

"I'd take a terrible chance, gladly, for the one thing I . . . mustn't give up. Can you see what I'm up against?"

"Clearly."

"So you know why I'm most desperately interested in this procedure . . . why I'm . . . most . . . desperate."

"I do."

"Who's the world expert on this treatment? I want only the best person to help me."

"I am."

"I believe you."

Nicole liked confidence. For the first time since her injury, she smiled.

He asked her questions and checked her neurological condition, satisfying himself that she displayed no other impairments. Then he described her injury, indicating the function of the optic nerves and tracing with her fingers on her head their path through the brain. He also explained the risks of brain surgery.

She was alert, listening, asking questions, digesting every word. The knowledge that he gave her was strong medicine for allaying her fears and for restoring a sense of control, even in her desperate situation. This strange new voice with no face, this frame in her mind with no picture, had the power to calm her.

He spoke of the problems of nerve repair and of the treatment that he had devised to overcome them.

"The reason that severed nerves don't repair themselves," he explained, "is that they have no capacity to regenerate as broken bones do, coupled with the fact that unwanted scar tissue grows at the sight of the lesion and further impedes the nerves' function."

He explained how his procedure stimulated the nerves to grow with his newly discovered embryonic growth protein, and how he could stop the scar interference with another new compound, the scar inhibitor. He told her that the two jobs had to be done in separate surgeries, spaced three months apart, because the two drugs did not work together. She asked questions and he clarified points, until he felt certain that she understood.

"During the time between the surgeries, you should regain some primitive vision, Nicole, but only up to a point. You'll perceive light, then motion, maybe even color. Because the scar tissue is also growing, it's unlikely that your vision will advance to the stage of distinguishing objects. Then you'll reach a point at which the rudimentary vision you've regained will begin to diminish, as the growing scar interferes with the growing nerves. I must stress that the timing of the second surgery is *critical*, Nicole."

She nodded her head, listening intently.

"We must wait until the nerves regenerate; however, we must not wait until all remnants of your new vision are lost. If that happens, based on my animal experiments, you'll never regain your sight. So, you'll need to be available for the second surgery at exactly the right time."

"Of course, Doctor."

"And I don't want to raise false hopes because I can make no promises of success."

"I understand."

"If we proceed with the treatment, I don't want to delay. We have our best chance if I operate immediately; otherwise the nerve ends will start to recede and scar will form quickly, causing complications for me. I don't even want to wait until tomorrow. But I must be sure I've given you enough time to make your decision."

"I've already made it. I want you to go ahead."

"Don't you want to discuss the matter with someone?"

"Who?"

"Someone close to you."

"No one's close to me," she said without self-pity.

"Don't you want to talk to your family?"

"I have no family," she said simply, as someone else might say, "I have no red dresses."

"How about the people you love?"

"I don't love anyone."

"Don't you want to consult with someone?"

"Why?"

"To help you in thinking about the matter."

"Why would I need help?"

"Nicole, I'm trying to assure myself that I have your consent, given to me with full knowledge and careful deliberation."

"You have."

Her confident tone convinced him. "All right, but there's one more thing."

"Yes?"

"The surgery is illegal."

"What?"

"It's illegal. The state prohibits me from doing it and you from having it."

"How could that be?"

"It is."

"But then how could you operate?"

"I'm not worried about how I can operate. That's not why I raised the issue."

"But won't you get in trouble?"

"I'm not worried about getting in trouble. That's not why I raised the issue."

"Doctor, I'll sign any papers you wish. I'll free you from liability. We'll get witnesses. I'll swear I begged you to do it—"

"I'm not worried about my liability."

"I'll pay you any amount you ask. I'll pay you triple your fee—"

"I'm not worried about the money. I just want you to know that the government prohibits what I'm about to do in the name of protecting you from me. I mention it in case the state's edict matters to you."

"It doesn't."

"Then I'll see you in surgery." He squeezed her hands, and then headed toward the door.

"Doctor, wait!"

He walked back to her side.

"I'm . . . afraid."

"Of what?"

She began to cry.

"What's the matter, Nicole? Are you having second thoughts?"

"Oh, no! But I'm afraid you will. If the surgery's against the law, why . . . why should you . . ."

Weak and short of breath, she tried to raise herself. Her arm swept the space around her to find him, to reach out to him. He gently pushed her down.

"You'll change your mind, Doctor!" she cried, her eyes filled with terror. "You'll back down!"

He buried two trembling hands in his own larger, steadier ones. "Don't be afraid, Nicole. I give you my word that I'll operate. You have my solemn promise."

He shuddered in the knowledge that this was the *second* sacred oath he was swearing that day. He reprimanded himself for having made the first one. He detested people who broke their promises. He accused himself of being a liar, but somehow he did not feel ashamed. *Lack of remorse is further proof of depravity*, he thought, but somehow he did not care. He told himself that he had no right to perform a procedure disapproved of by the governing body of the hospital. Wasn't he about to violate someone's property just as surely as hurling a rock through a shopkeeper's window? But was it the board of directors that was against his procedure? He remembered the tired flesh and weary faces around the conference table that afternoon. He thought of wooden figures pulled by a presence offstage, invisible to the casual viewer. The notion of choice seemed as preposterous to the board as it was to a herd of penned sheep. Was he to sacrifice the irreplaceable treasure that was Nicole's life and spirit for the sake of honor owed to . . . puppets? Was that integrity? If it was, he would have none of it!

But what of the honor owed to someone else, he wondered, someone whose presence had tormented him from the moment that he diagnosed Nicole's injury? He shut his eyes painfully against the knowledge that he was about to betray the one man whom he had no capacity to hurt. When he opened his eyes, he saw the one woman whom he had no capacity to refuse.

"I won't back down, Nicole. I won't let anything or anyone stop me. You have my solemn promise."

The corridor and nurse's station outside of Nicole's room were abandoned that evening. David walked along the lonely halls in the eerie silence, wondering where the staff had gone. He encountered them in a small room, hovering around a copy machine, whispering nervously as they grabbed sheets of a document being printed.

"What's going on?" he asked.

"Have you seen the new statement of policy?" a nurse replied.

"The what?"

"The new crack-down by CareFree. Copies are being sent to everybody. Here, take this one."

The document that David read was titled "A Statement of Policy for All Clinical Personnel from the Director of Medicine of Riverview Hospital."

You are hereby notified that CareFree aims to eliminate all violations of its policies and to achieve full compliance. As you know, Riverview Hospital is committed to following the regulations to the letter of the law. If circumstances have allowed exceptions in the past, you are hereby forewarned that there must be strict adherence starting immediately. This statement of policy summarizes the steps that you need to take in order to ensure your total compliance with the CareFree program. We expect your utmost cooperation.

David skipped past other information to a paragraph titled "Surgeons."

Surgeons must obtain prior written authorization from CareFree before performing any operation. The doctor must submit diagnostic test results and patient records to the hospital's Surgical Authorization Committee (SAC), which will relay the case to CareFree's Surgical Advisory Department (SAD) to determine if the procedure is necessary. Then SAD will advise SAC of its decision. If SAD is closed, then SAC, staffed twenty-four hours a day, will determine for the physician whether the surgery should be performed.

The last sentence of the order was capitalized:

UNDER NO CIRCUMSTANCES WILL AN OPERATING ROOM BE ASSIGNED TO A SURGEON WHO HAS NOT OBTAINED PRIOR WRITTEN PERMISSION TO PERFORM THE PROCE- DURE FROM SAD OR SAC.

No one noticed that the serene look of radiant purpose, an afterglow from his moments with Nicole, had vanished from David Lang's face.

✖12✖

The Treatment

A pair of white swinging doors sliced the third floor of Riverview Hospital. *No Admittance* was stenciled across them in bold black letters. Beyond the doors was the Department of Surgery. Before them stood a small, circular stand resembling a guard's post. David approached the high-countered station, which was manned by a petite nurse in blue scrubs, her hair tucked in a surgical cap, her eyes large in her hairless face. Among the duties of those staffing "the desk," as the post was known, was assigning operating rooms to surgeons.

"MaryAnn, I need a neurosurgical suite for an emergency case I'm bringing up."

"Do you have a procedure code?"

"I have an injured patient."

"Does the patient have an employee certificate, a student voucher, a senior citizen card, or a handicapped number?"

"She has a head trauma."

"But how did she get here, Dr. Lang? Did she join a worker's cooperative? Is she an unwed mother? Did she register at a CareFree district office?"

"She fell from a stage."

"Does the patient need a regular case number or a supplemental rider?"

"She needs surgery."

"You need to show me written authorization."

"I need to operate."

"Someone has to *allow* you to operate. Did you get permission from CareFree's Surgical Advisory Department or from the hospital's Surgical Authorization Committee?"

"I got permission from the patient."

"Dr. Lang, I need notice that the procedure is necessary."

"*I* give you notice; it's necessary."

"I need authorization from SAD or SAC."

"MaryAnn, how many times have we gone through this? You advise me of what I have to do, and I advise you that I have been so advised. You did your job. Now, I must have a room!"

"How can you ask on today of all days?"

"How can you refuse on this case of all cases?"

"Have you carefully examined the new statement of policy?"

"I carefully examined the patient."

"I'm sorry, Doctor."

He leaned wearily on the counter and placed his hands over her forearm, his voice pleading, his eyes desperate.

"MaryAnn, I'll take full responsibility. You won't get in trouble. Haven't I always protected you? And I'll never ask again. Just this one last time. It would be so helpful if I didn't have to go to . . . anyone else."

"Doctor, I can't, so please don't ask!"

"MaryAnn, it's a little silly, isn't it, that I should have to plead with you, the clerks, the secretaries, and the man in the moon every time I have to work? This case is such a small thing for the hospital. We do thousands of operations. How many bullets have I pulled out of the skulls of thugs, robbers, and murderers? And how many of them have cursed me for saving their rotten lives? MaryAnn, if you only knew how happy someone would be if I did this one surgery, someone who wants so much to live. Isn't it *right* that she should have a chance, too?"

MaryAnn fidgeted. "I don't know what's right or wrong anymore. I just follow the rules."

"If you could save someone from a life of misery by doing one small thing, isn't that what we're here for? Wouldn't that make you happy?"

"Nothing makes me happy! I'm getting to hate this job! I'm sorry, Dr. Lang, but I can't give you a room without authorization. Not anymore."

He released his hands from her forearm, surprised to see the red marks that they left. He rubbed the arm as if to erase the hurt that he had caused, then he grabbed the phone on the counter. His hand hesitated on the headpiece for a long moment before he lifted it and dialed.

"Randall Lang," said a voice through the wires.

"Randy, I . . . have to speak to you."

"What's wrong, pal?"

"I have a problem."

"What is it?"

"Can you come to Surgery? I'm at the desk."

"I'm on my way."

Randy soon sprang from the elevator, his shirtsleeves rolled, his jacket left behind in his haste. "What's up, David?"

"I have a trauma case from the explosion this afternoon. The optic nerves are completely severed, resulting in permanent, total blindness. The patient is a perfect candidate for nerve regeneration—"

"I hope you're not thinking the unthinkable—"

"I called CareFree to explain the situation, and . . . and . . ."

"And?"

David was rendered speechless by eyes looking into his with unconditional trust. But he could still hear Nicole screaming that she wanted to die.

"I got permission to try the surgery."

"From whom?"

"From the secretary of medicine."

"You called *him*?" Randy asked incredulously.

"Yes."

"And how did he react to hearing from you?"

"We had a nice chat."

"And you asked him if you could try your new surgery?"

"That's right."

"And he said yes?"

"He did."

"You mean he didn't tell you to wait until all the infected hangnails were cured? He didn't lecture you on how his hands are too clean to pull any strings? He didn't give you a song and dance about the public interest?"

"He said my surgery was in the public interest."

Randy laughed with an exuberance that blew David back to a time when that hearty sound was as much a part of his day as the sunrise. He realized how much he had missed the joy that had vanished from his brother's voice in recent years.

"You mean it was that simple, David? You asked our Great Civic Leader, and he said yes?"

"That's right."

"Well, I'll be damned! Congratulations, pal!" Randy raised his arms to embrace his brother, but David stepped back.

"I . . . uh . . . called him after his staff had left for the day. He gave me his consent verbally and said he'd send written approval in the morning." He gestured to MaryAnn at the counter. "If you could—"

"Of course. No problem. You'll have the operating room and the surgical staff you need."

"And I want no interruptions. No press, no cameras, no audience. Don't tell anyone what I'm doing until tomorrow morning. No one must know!"

"Of course."

"And don't tell Marie!"

"Whatever you say."

Randy's beaming face seemed ready to agree to anything.

"David, I never dreamed that tomorrow I would not only be announcing your appointment as chief of neurosurgery"—Randy was too excited to notice David's head turn away—"but also this historic experiment for medicine and for you!"

"Yeah, well, I really need to get ready—"

"Tomorrow you'll be a hero, brother! And I'll be one, too, because I backed you. After you left the board meeting today, I told those zombies that I would stake my reputation on you, that you would bring honor to Riverview Hospital, that you would become a medical legend—"

"Stop it! Please!"

Randy threw his sandy blond head back and laughed. "Don't look so grim. You'll need to get used to compliments. And me, too! My salary is up for review this month. I suppose I'll have to accept a fat raise. It'll come in handy with Michelle's tuition, Victoria's ice skating competition, and Stephen's piano training. Just wait till I tell my kids that their uncle's talent has made their father look good and given their futures a boost." He was talking to a bent head and closed eyes. He threw his arm around David's shoulders. "What's the matter, brother? You look so pale and . . . upset."

"I've got to go," David whispered, his eyes fixed to the ground.

"Of course! Leave the desk to me. Go and do what only you can do."

David's eyes seemed like two lead weights that he could barely raise to meet Randy's trusting gaze. "I can't refuse! Not for anything or anyone. Not even for you!"

The exit door creaked as David disappeared down the stairwell, escaping Randy's curious gaze.

When he entered OR 6 at 7:30 that evening, the only visible features on David Lang's face were his eyes, two green lasers between a cap and mask. His blue scrubs outlined the broad shoulders, long legs, and trim waist of a body poised for action. When the three members of his OR team had assembled, he announced loudly that he had obtained permission from the BOM to perform a new procedure. By the formality of his statement, he intended to leave no doubt that he had lied to the others; therefore, they could not be held responsible for his action. The only other person whom David had involved, a surgeon to set Nicole's broken nose, would not arrive until the next morning, after the neurosurgery was completed.

Attempting to second-guess the people wielding power over him and his patient had wracked his body with anxiety. Now that the arrangements were made and he felt certain that he could protect the others in the room from punishment for his deed, he wanted only to focus on the task ahead. The tension inside him was like an alien creature needing to be curbed before he could enter the shrine that was Nicole's brain.

He clipped the patient's brain scans to the view box on the wall. As he examined the films, the stress began draining from his body, as if the OR possessed the power to heal him, too. From a distance, his casual pose, with arms crossed and weight shifted to one leg, suggested someone waiting for a bus to the country. However, a closer look revealed that his eyes were riveted to the images with an unusual intensity. He soon forgot the people around him, the room, and the world, his thoughts buried in the scans. He calculated precisely where he would cut the skull and how he would reach the nerves. He mentally rehearsed how he would reattach the severed nerve ends and implant the capsules of the new drug that he had brought with him to the OR, the embryonic growth protein. He postulated the things that could go wrong in the minefield of tissue and how he would respond to each unexpected situation.

He noted the largest blood vessel of the brain, the carotid artery, alongside the optic nerves at the site of the lesions. The spot where he had to work touched the route of this major artery that brought blood to the brain. It was a vessel that he would have to avoid at every moment in the hours ahead. To slip just once and nick that artery could swallow his work field in a sea of red for an unspeakable few minutes, ending in total, final stillness. He studied the path of the giant snakelike artery curling through Nicole's brain, dwarfing all other vessels to the size of worms. He ordered himself not to permit a moment's lapse in which he would lose sight of that artery, regardless of how tired he became. Then he mentally rehearsed what he would do if the unthinkable occurred.

Behind him, a nurse arranged sterile trays of shiny tools, including scalpels, scissors, tweezers, hooks, and clamps. Some devices seemed gross enough to cut concrete, whereas others seemed delicate enough to split hairs. A large microscope covered with sterile plastic waited in the corner for its cue to go onstage. The anesthesiologist placed potions on her cart, checked the equipment for monitoring the patient's vital signs, and readied the respirator. Instrument panels, foot pedals, gas lines, and suction devices were placed under huge overhead lights. The room was a setting of metal and plastic, with all props positioned around one central item—the narrow operating table. David rubbed his hands to ease the remaining tension in preparation for the tall task and sleepless night ahead.

Nicole Hudson could tell when her gurney reached an intersection in the hallway by the sudden breeze across her face. An attendant explained that he was wheeling her to the operating room. She thought it odd to be driven by someone else's power during the worst crisis of her life. Her reaction to adversity had always been to find a solution and to act, as if life were synonymous with an abiding effort to sustain it.

As the wheels of Nicole's gurney clattered in the dark hall of her awareness, she heard the sound of clapping in a dimmed theater long ago. She was six years old and attending her first ballet. She sat in the balcony with a group of children from St. Jude's Parish, their tickets the gift of a church benefactor.

The curtain rose on a gathering outside a palace. Fairies in bright costumes of transparent lace danced gaily through a garden. Smiling children swung baskets of just-picked flowers. The stage was a watercolor meadow, lovingly brushed with pastel pinks and powder blues. The child in the balcony stared in amazement at the enchanted garden. Unlike the parks she knew, this one contained no garbage, no beer cans, and no bums, only beautiful people dancing happily to music as sweet as the flowers.

A lively puff of white crinoline fluttered onto the stage. It was the dainty creature who was the guest of honor at the gathering—the princess of the palace. The people had come to celebrate her sixteenth birthday! The princess knew her real birth date, and it was such a special day that the villagers threw a party. The slender princess wore an ivory gown sprinkled with pearls that shimmered as she pirouetted. Nicole looked down at her own threadbare dungarees, wondering what it would feel like to wear a garment new to her—a dress, and one that sparkled.

The lighthearted strings in the orchestra gave way to percussion, sounding a new and frightening theme. A wicked witch entering the scene cast an evil spell on the princess. The king and queen rushed to aid their ailing daughter. Remarkably, the princess saw *both* of her parents at the same time! As the curse took effect, the princess fainted. She was caught by the caring arms of her mother. The little girl in the balcony was confused; she thought that it was the mother who fainted and the child who did the catching.

The princess fell into a deep sleep from the witch's curse. Concerned for her safety, the townspeople carried the maiden to the most remarkable bed—one that had a roof! A curtain of rich tapestry hung from the roof, so that the princess could play in her bed without anyone else watching. The thin form of her sleeping body made a small imprint on the sheet. Nicole had not minded her serape and meager accommodation in the hallway—until she saw the cozy bed that was a little house.

A forest grew around the palace as a hundred years passed. The princess still slept under the evil spell. Just when Nicole had lost hope of her being rescued, the orchestra played its most powerful music. A handsome prince dressed in white leaped onto the stage. He towered over the evil witch, turning faster and jumping higher, until he banished the wicked presence from the stage with his lively dancing.

The prince broke the evil spell and awakened the princess with . . . a kiss! He had no knives or fists to fling, just his courage and his kiss. The ballet ended with the prince and princess dancing. But *dancing* seemed too mild a word to explain the serene tangle of graceful leaps and tender caresses reflected in Nicole's unblinking eyes.

The child had no words to describe the prince; she only knew what he was not. The prince was not dirty, not stinking, not stumbling, not breaking things, not cursing, not hitting the princess. He performed none of the frightening acts of her mother's companions. The prince belonged to a world that she could not yet name, a world that she knew only by its immense grip on her.

After the music stopped, the child felt as if she, too, were waking from a magic spell. She was surprised to see the seats around her empty and the children from the parish lined up in the aisle. "Come on, little one, come on!" Sister Luke, their chaperone, was calling to her. The child finally rose to leave the theater, but she knew that she would return. That was the day that Nicole decided to become a dancer.

When she was a teenager, she played the role of the sleeping princess. She recalled the audience clapping enthusiastically as she took her bows. It was then that she discovered the words eluding her as a child, the words to describe the meaning of the ballet. As the audience clapped, Nicole realized that the dance of the prince and princess was a supreme celebration of themselves and of a world of beauty, joy, and goodness.

The clapping ended as the wheels of the gurney stopped.

"We're in the operating room," said her attendant.

She felt hands sliding her onto a narrow table. A sudden warmth on her face was the only indication she had of the overhead lights.

As a child, whenever her universe seemed to be collapsing, she would remember the music of her first ballet and the promise it held of a better world. She finally entered that world with the strength of her one abiding ally: her ruthless will to fight for her dream, whatever the struggle. But in her current battle, she would have to do something harder than fight; she would have to step aside. It seemed odd to relinquish the stage, and with it, her fate, to the performance of another. This time she heard two sounds calling her: the music of her first ballet and—

"Where have you been, Nicole? I was beginning to think you made another engagement for the evening."

The Voice was somewhere in the room. It was not the things the Voice had said that gave her hope. The words of the Voice were grim: There were no guarantees; the treatment was experimental; her chances were slim; the odds were against her. However, the tone of the Voice was another matter. When it spoke of the animal experiments, the newly discovered growth protein, the outmoded beliefs about nerve repair, and the possibilities for the future, then the Voice possessed the same vigor as the music of the prince.

"Are you ready to be a medical experiment?" The Voice bore no trace of gloom; it seemed to be coming from a ballroom, asking her to dance.

"I'll do better than your animals, Doctor, you'll see. They didn't want their nerves repaired as much as I do."

"And you'll keep your vital signs steady. That's *your* part of the bargain."

"My vital signs have always been steady."

He clasped her hand in his. "You're not afraid anymore, are you?"

"No."

"That's quite a change from before."

"I trust your voice."

He squeezed her hand.

"And you're not afraid, either. Are you, Doctor?"

"Why, no. But I am indignant. Those optic nerves of yours can't just up and quit, not without a fight. And may the best man win."

She laughed softly, and the sound of it made him want to battle a hundred optic nerves, one hundred against one!

She heard the first tone of regret when he touched her hair. "You remember we mentioned—"

"It'll grow back."

"I was going to say that to you."

She laughed again—a mere little puff of air expelled from her lips, a sound that he could make an occupation of evoking.

"Are you ready to go to sleep, now, Nicole?"

"Yes."

"I should be waking you sometime tomorrow morning, maybe not in time for breakfast, but surely before noon."

"There's no hurry. I once played the role of a princess who slept for a hundred years."

"So, you think I'm that slow, do you? Well, I'll show you. I'll wake you while you're still young and . . . beautiful."

She smiled in his direction. It was the radiant smile of someone who believed in miracles.

He nodded to the anesthesiologist waiting at the side of the table. She placed a mask over the patient's face. "Nicole, breathe deeply, dear."

Nicole was clutching David's hand. In an instant, her fingers loosened. She felt her hand slip away, and with it, the last, faint melody of the ballet.

David scrubbed his hands at the sink outside of OR 6. Two doctors passed, talking about a case. A nurse asked someone for an instrument. A technician discussed an X ray. An intern quoted a baseball score. David heard nothing. He envisioned two long, fragile nerves, each containing a million fibers within the width of a child's thumbnail. He thought of how he would realign and reattach the fine tissue, then implant the growth protein in the timed-release capsules. Tonight he would call nature back for an encore of the acclaimed performance that had played in Nicole's brain before birth, when her nervous system had grown with abandon.

The operating room was as quiet as the ether in space, except for the beep of Nicole's heartbeat on the monitor. David's body was completely covered in garments, except for the one feature left exposed: his eyes. They scanned the room that was both his battlefield and his altar. Three people were ready to follow his cues. The life of the slim form under the blue surgical cloth was in his hands. He was about to do something that he wanted desperately to do, had trained for years to do, and most gloriously believed was right to do. His eyes found their target on a shaved head covered with a brown antiseptic ointment and positioned firmly in a frame. The tension, pain, and anger had vanished from his body. He felt nothing but an arrogant self-confidence at the prospect of opening that skull. His eyes did not move from the bare head. They would remain fixed on their target through the long night.

"Scalpel, please."

At 6:30 the next morning, while David was still operating, word of the revolutionary surgery in OR 6 was spreading to the hospital staff members arriving for work. The anesthesiologist told her boyfriend, a cardiologist, when she stepped out to speak to him. The circulating nurse told a friend whom she met at the autoclave. The surgeon who had arrived to set Nicole's broken nose told a resident at the scrub sink. The resident phoned his sister, a television news editor.

At 7:00, when Randy Lang arrived for work, reporters were waiting. Having just called the OR, he knew that David was completing the operation, so he confirmed the rumors about the experimental surgery.

"Can you comment on how this new procedure can come on the heels of the secretary of medicine's crackdown on the doctors?" asked one reporter. "We've heard that the treatment uses untested drugs and—"

"I'm glad you asked," replied Randy, "and please mention this in your reports: The new surgery performed at Riverview Hospital was done with the knowledge and consent of the secretary of medicine himself. The surgeon personally received the secretary's permission last evening."

At 7:30, while the secretary of medicine was eating breakfast in his Manhattan penthouse, the phone rang. He alternated between working from an office at the state capital in Albany and another in Manhattan, keeping residences at both locations. Before he could speak, the caller railed at him.

"What the hell do you mean by this double-cross, Warren?"

"Why, Governor, what are you talking about?"

"Have you seen the news this morning?"

"Not yet. I was just having breakfast. Are you talking about the gas explosion?"

"That was *yesterday's* news, Warren. How do you expect to make the big leagues if you don't check the news before you pee in the morning? I'm talking about an experimental surgery performed last night in Manhattan! What's its price tag and how many people are gonna clamor for it?"

"What?"

"And you authorized it! Right after you made your little speech about strict adherence to the rules, about sacrifices, about stringent controls over surgeries—you caved in! Every reporter in the state will be laughing at us. What are you gonna do with the doctors now, when they know they can walk all over you?"

"I didn't authorize any new surgery. I don't know anything about it."

"Come on! The surgeon said you *personally* approved it."

"I most certainly did not authorize any new surgical procedure."

"He says you did."

"He's a liar."

The voice on the line paused, and then sounded calmer, even cheerful. "Can I quote you on that, Warren?"

"Certainly, Mack. Tell the press, as I will myself, that I have given no doctor permission to do any new surgical procedure and that performing an experimental operation not authorized by CareFree is an endangerment to the public welfare."

"And you won't make any exceptions?"

"Of course not! I stand by my word."

"Then I can count on you to take the course of action you discussed yesterday? You know, the matter of . . . severe punishment?"

"The guy is automatically suspended as a CareFree provider, which means he can't work in New York, and no other state will license him after my censure. Then we'll review the case and decide on appropriate measures. We need to set an example, so the other doctors will know we mean business. Imagine forging ahead before we've reviewed the safety and effectiveness of his procedure! He's unscrupulous."

"I'm glad we agree, Warren."

"By the way, who is he?"

"David Lang."

The secretary of medicine gasped.

❖13❖
The Morning After

The August sun already hung high in the sky, and the operating rooms were busy with a full roster of morning surgeries when a nurse wheeled Nicole into the recovery room. A red-eyed man in hospital scrubs leaned over the frail patient with the bandaged head.

"Nicole, can you hear me?"

Her head throbbed beneath what felt like a turban. She opened her eyes but saw nothing. From a distant place, she heard the Voice calling her.

"It's over, Nicole."

She tried to reply, but the body that she daily pushed to its limit struggled to find its voice.

"Can you hear me?"

"Yes," she whispered.

"Squeeze my hand." Two fingers tapped her limp hand. "Come on, squeeze."

Drifting in a fog between sleep and wakefulness, she forced her five limp fingers around the two intruding ones and softly pressed.

"Very good!"

The Voice was pleased, she thought dimly.

"Now the other hand. Squeeze."

Continuing to pester her when she wanted only to sleep, the two big fingers rapped on her other hand. Again five weary fingers made the journey around the two persistent ones to give a little tug.

"Excellent! Now wiggle your toes."

Ten toes flexed.

"Outstanding!"

The Voice seemed pleased with the strangest of things.

"The nerves are reattached and the growth protein is in place, Nicole."

"This . . . means . . . I might . . . ?"

"It means you have a chance. We won't know until after the second surgery."

"How did . . . it . . . go?"

"Very well! You kept your vital signs steady, and I finished in less than a hundred years. I'm pleased with both of us."

She felt the warmth of his hands covering one of hers.

He held her hand still, but what he really wanted was to pull her up to dance. He thought of his first hopeless experiments seven years ago, of the lonely nights spent in a dingy lab, of the countless failures over the many years when he had nothing to kindle his dream but his own stubborn vision of what might be. Then he thought of the past night in the OR, of how he worked smoothly, precisely—almost effortlessly, were it not for the seven years of honing his efforts so that he could experience the most glorious moment of his career.

"The procedure worked exactly as I had hoped," he continued, his voice sounding as fresh as daybreak to her, his puffy eyes and unshaven face hidden from her view. "Everything went just—" He suddenly lost his voice when a figure appeared at the doorway. "—fine," he finished an octave lower, staring at the block of ice that was his brother's face.

Nicole felt his fingers tighten over her hand. Something seemed to be wrong.

"I heard footsteps," she whispered. "Who is it?"

Neither man answered.

"Who's there?" she repeated uneasily.

"It's someone I have to talk to, Nicole, so I'll let you rest."

The cheerful tone of the Voice had vanished, and a disturbing thought seeped into the fog that was her mind. "Did you . . . get in . . . trouble?"

"The operation went smoothly; neither one of us got in trouble."

"I mean . . . the . . . law."

He hesitated because the face staring at him from the doorway now looked like a portrait drawn by an enraged artist.

"Doctor . . ." She pulled his hand toward her, crimping the IV drip and setting off an alarm that startled her.

A nurse approached to assist. "Easy, Nicole. Don't bend your arm, or it will kink the IV. Just move within the limits it allows."

"Doctor . . . tell me! Are you in . . . any . . . danger—" A cry broke her voice.

"Don't worry, Nicole. I'm sure everything's fine." David patted her hand and forced a laugh, while Randy's violent eyes swept over the tender scene like a raging storm. "Now you must forget I mentioned that matter."

"Okay." She smiled peacefully, ignoring her instinct that all was not right with the Voice.

His words were the only beacon in the black ether around her. Her smile was the only ray of sunlight that would shine on him that day.

"So everything's fine?" Randy tried to whisper, but his voice threatened to roar. "I see you lie to your patients, too!"

David hastily grabbed Randy's arm to push him out of Nicole's earshot. The two walked into the doctors' lounge. With the staff engaged in the morning's surgeries, the brothers were alone in a room resembling the lobby of an inn after its guests had checked out, with plastic coffee cups littering the side tables and half-read newspapers tossed on the couches. Although he had not slept all night or eaten anything since the previous day's lunch, David did not sit but stood straight, the way a convict faces a firing squad. Randy paced back and forth before him like a sentry.

"Yes, pal, everything's just fine! Word of the surgery got out at dawn. I told the reporters that you had the *personal permission* of the secretary of medicine. He heard the news and hit the roof. That's how I found out that my brother is a liar—I and the rest of the city."

Randy paused to stare at David indignantly.

"I'm sorry, brother," David said quietly, closing his eyes against an unbearable pain.

"CareFree suspended you as a provider, so the hospitals in this state are closed to you. Of course, the Riverview board revoked your staff privileges. Because you're not licensed in any other state, you're grounded."

"I see."

"You can kiss the director's post good-bye. In the words of our chairman, he wouldn't appoint you to chief of broom closets now."

Randy continued to pace like an armed guard in front of the accused man in blue scrubs.

"Just this morning—what a coincidence!—CareFree denied Radiology permission to fix our Model 409 scanner, even though it just needs a routine repair that's never been refused before. And the BOM decided that *all* the medical practices of this hospital are questionable, so every patient chart for the last year must be examined in a massive audit, costing six figures—with the hospital footing the bill." He stopped pacing. "By the way, how did the surgery go?"

"Very well."

"So what are the chances she'll see again?"

"Ten percent."

"You're lying again, brother. Your face tells me better."

"That's *not* to be repeated to the patient."

"It's irrelevant because you can't finish the job."

David sighed tiredly. "Is there anything else?"

"Your wife switched to using her maiden name. She's having her stationery redone."

"I see. Anything else?"

Randy decided to omit from the litany the fact that his son, Stephen, an honor student, was suspended from school that morning for punching a classmate who called his uncle a butcher.

"The hospital's project to reopen the Stanton Pavilion has been stopped. Just this morning—another coincidence!—the Commission for Environmental Protection found that a rare species of striped-tailed squirrel is living alongside the old building. It seems that our plans to reopen will endanger the critter's survival, so bye-bye to the Stanton Pavilion, and bye-bye to you, pal, because you're the most endangered critter of all!"

"Anything else?"

"The chairman of the board gave me an ultimatum: Either I publicly denounce you or I find another job."

"Certainly you'll denounce me! I insist. We have a deal. You promised."

"Why did you lie to me, David?"

"You know why."

"Did you ever lie to me before?"

"No."

"How could you lie to your brother?"

"I didn't lie to my brother. I lied to the president of this hospital, who must enforce laws that would have condemned my patient to a life of misery."

"So instead you condemned yourself to a life of misery."

"But I didn't feel miserable. Last night in the OR, I felt happier than I've felt in years." His head dropped. "Except about what I'm doing to you."

"And what about to *you*, David? You'll never see an OR again unless you're wheeled in on a stretcher! You lost the only chance you had to complete your research. Think of it! Seven years of your life down the drain. But that's not all. You pushed the wrong buttons at the wrong time. You flung the rulebook in their faces; now they have to make good on their threats. And if the patient dies, you'll be charged with manslaughter."

"Nicole won't die!"

"Regardless, what you did was an act of wanton self-destruction. You ruined your career. You're going to be kicked out of medicine. And you did this on the eve of an appointment that would've led to the completion of your research and raised you to the pinnacle of your profession. Why on Earth did you do it?" Randy raised his arms, as if looking to heaven for the answer. "Why?"

"Because it was right."

Randy burst out laughing. "Are you crazy? You did it because it was right? Where the hell do you see right in the world around you, pal? Would right take money from your patient to pay for other people's treatments while hers is denied? And on the occasion of your greatest effort, would right want me—as your brother and as the president of this hospital—to plan your funeral instead of your parade? Would right allow Mack Burrow, who couldn't cure an infected pimple, to be throwing the ball for medicine while you're fetching it? If he really wanted to help people as he claims, wouldn't right demand that he nurture your talent instead of stifle it?

"You did something because it was right, David, but that's the surest way to be destroyed. If you and your patient can do whatever you please, then what do we need the governor and his program for? If you are right, it means CareFree is wrong. Do you think they'll let you get away with that? Do you think they'll exonerate you for the thing you did because of the ridiculous reason you give—because it was right?"

"I don't care what they do."

"But they run the world, brother."

"They may run the world, but they don't run me, and I won't let them destroy my patient."

"Then you should have been more cunning, David. You can't come out against them so flagrantly. You have to treat them with respect. You have to cooperate. And then you have to sneak in 'right' when they're not looking. And above all, you mustn't let them know how much right means to you, and that you'd risk everything for it. They don't like intensity. Impassioned people are difficult to control.

"So you have to grovel a little. Do you think that's demeaning? What's the alternative? Either you bruise your knees or you get flattened by a steamroller. Nothing gets done today without coming to terms with them. You have to *compromise*."

"What compromise do you recommend? That I fix Nicole's nerves so she can see, but only on Mondays, Wednesdays, and Fridays?"

"What I recommend has no bearing on your life. There's only one man who can save you now—if he dares. So that's a question you'd best ask *him*."

David's body stiffened. The serene glow lingering in his eyes from the successful surgery had vanished, leaving only the dark stare of a secret pain. The change in David did not escape the man who knew his face better than anyone.

"What's the matter, David? Did you think we could avoid dealing with him?"

"What did he say?"

"He hasn't made a public statement—not yet. But he called me. Oh, man! He's madder than you or I have ever seen him. He gave two orders, one for you and the other for me. He said that you were to march over to his Manhattan office as soon as you finished the surgery."

"Okay." David seemed ready to comply with the order as he walked across the surgeons' lounge to the door of the locker room.

"You don't want to hear this, David, but he's going to throw you to the lions, and I don't know how to stop him."

"You're not going to stop him! This is between him and me, and you're to stay out of it. You must outshout the hospital board in repudiating me. You must publicly denounce me in the most scathing terms. And you must disown me as your brother. You promised you would! I insist you keep your word! That's the only thing you can do to help me live with the fact that I had to perform this surgery in your hospital."

Against his will, the molten anger drained from Randy's face. "I think you'd best be on your way," he said quietly.

David was halfway through the door when he stopped. "By the way, what was the other order, the one he gave to you?"

"He ordered me to keep all news from reaching you while you were still in the OR, so nothing would upset you during the surgery."

❧14❧
The Outlaw

When David left the hospital at noon to hail a cab, he noticed that the storm of the previous day had given way to a heat wave. He stepped off the sidewalk, the sun-baked tar in the street feeling sticky under his shoes. To his dismay, every taxi that passed contained limp passengers seeking reprieve from the punishing summer weather. Removing his suit jacket, he resigned himself to walking across town to the Manhattan office of the secretary of medicine. He joined the lunch crowd of damp bodies drifting through the steam room that was Manhattan, his sole source of pleasure becoming an occasional blast of cold air escaping from the door of an air-conditioned shop. Although David had just showered and dressed, the city was already rumpling his starched shirt and sapping what little was left of his energy.

He paused to hear a news bulletin from a street vendor's radio: "A spokesman for the mayor announced that yesterday's explosion in the theater district is being investigated. The blast injured two hundred people and damaged several buildings. Faulty piping found in the debris may have caused a gas leak that triggered the blast. The Bowing Construction Company, which installed the pipes as part of a government contract, has already been under investigation for making illicit payments to high-level officials, allegedly including the lieutenant governor, in exchange for obtaining public projects. In other news, CareFree suspended a Manhattan surgeon for operating on Nicole Hudson, the dancer injured in yesterday's explosion. The agency charges that the doctor's treatment was untested and unsafe for humans."

David wondered if the oppressive climate in the city would stifle him and his patient. No, he vowed, it would not smother Nicole. CareFree might take medicine away from him, he thought, but there was something that no one could ever seize: the meaning of Nicole's surgery as the most glorious act of his life. The operation gave her hope where none had existed, and it gave him a thrill unequaled in his career. Her treatment was the culmination not only of his seven years of research but also of everything he had ever wanted for as long as he could remember. His life was like a symphony begun in his childhood and still rising to its most thrilling movements.

As he walked along, breathing the stagnant vapors of Manhattan in August, long-forgotten events flashed before him. He admonished himself for looking back, feeling that the present should concern him, but the stubborn intruders that were his memories refused to be dismissed. In some way he had to acknowledge them, for they were the signposts on the journey that had led him to Nicole's surgery.

He had grown up in the residential community of Oak Hills, New York. From his earliest recollections, his childhood had been divided into two different worlds. The first and overwhelmingly larger sphere included his mother and most other people. He remembered having to accompany his mother on gatherings with her friends, as well as on trips to the health club, the beauty salon, and the department stores—all of which left him with a lasting distaste for shopping and small talk.

Mrs. Lang had enrolled her elder son in special instructions of all kinds, such as piano lessons, acrobatics, and horseback riding, but David had dodged the classes imposed on him.

"I'm giving you wonderful opportunities, David," Mrs. Lang would remind her recalcitrant son.

"Who says they're wonderful?" he would reply.

"I do."

"Then why don't *you* play the piano?"

"Don't talk back to me, young man!"

David derived little more from these experiences than boredom.

School was of marginal interest to the boy. He was a bright student, but despite his mother's urgings, he declined to join clubs or teams. One teacher described what she called the boy's aloofness: "David does what is required scholastically but gives nothing of himself to anyone."

"Including me," Mrs. Lang added sadly.

However, there was another world in which David traveled that emitted a light bright enough to eclipse the rest of his universe. To David, this realm was more spellbinding than the greatest adventure story or the fastest roller coaster. It contained no policemen, firemen, sports champions, movie idols, or other typical heroes of young boys, only one solitary figure who performed superhuman feats as a matter of quiet routine. This was the world of the young neurosurgeon who was David's father.

David could pinpoint no moment in his life when he chose to become a doctor, because he could not recall ever desiring anything else. As immediate as his own heartbeat, the world of medicine was a continuous driving force within him from the beginning.

At age six, he was riding in the family car when his father stopped on the highway to aid the victim of an automobile accident. The unconscious man had no pulse or respiration. To David's horror, the man's flesh was turning blue. Kneeling on a patch of grass on the side of the road, the victim's wife and young daughter cried in fear. Before that day, death to David had been merely an event in the movies. As he trembled in the chill evening, he realized how terrible that same encounter would be in real life. He watched his father work fiercely, compressing the man's chest and breathing into his mouth, but to no avail. The unfortunate man remained limp and cold. The stunned mother clutched her daughter, dreading the worst. David's father worked relentlessly, until his voice finally broke through the gloom with four whispered words: "I have a pulse." A flush of pink returned to the man's face. Pride brightened David's features as he gazed in awe at the hero of his childhood.

The next week in school, David's teacher asked the students to describe the most exciting moment they had ever experienced. His classmates could think only of the movies, recounting horror stories, murder scenes, car chases, and fist-fights from the screen. But David chose to relate the real-life drama at the accident site, which he described as "bringing a dead man back to life."

When he was eight, his father gave him a plastic replica of the human brain, explaining its removable parts and their functions. The brain immediately became David's favorite toy. However, Mrs. Lang did not share her son's enthusiasm when she found the four subdivisions of the cerebrum drawn with a black marker on the hair of her six-year-old son, Randall. She had to wash his blond hair repeatedly until the black writing faded. Despite David's apology and offer to wash Randall's hair, Mrs. Lang insisted that the brain be thrown in the garbage—until Dr. Lang rescued it. "At least David didn't shave Randall's head, dear. Besides, the frontal, temporal, parietal, and occipital lobes were perfectly placed—and spelled!—so the boy deserves some credit."

That same plastic brain later accompanied David to medical school and then to his office, where he employed it in countless discussions with patients. When the well-worn brain finally reached retirement, David gave it a distinguished spot in a lighted cabinet, displayed as others would exhibit a museum piece.

Mrs. Lang's anger flared again on the day when David's collie died of old age—and the boy dissected it. David's explanation was simple: He loved the dog, but considering that it was dead, he wanted to see what was inside it.

Aghast, Mrs. Lang complained to her husband: "You grew up to be a doctor, but you didn't do revolting things like dissecting your own pet, did you?"

"I wasn't as gifted as David."

Later that year, Dr. Lang took his son to the animal laboratory where he conducted experiments. "If the boy's intent on dissecting animals, he should at least do it properly," said the father. In the lab, David watched with marble-faced attention while his father dissected a rat.

The next year, Dr. Lang took his son to the pathology department of Oak Hills Hospital.

"This is crazy," protested Mrs. Lang. "Nobody takes a ten-year-old kid to a morgue."

"We're going to the pathology department."

That morning David watched his father's friend, a pathologist, perform an autopsy on a human body. That afternoon David missed a classmate's birthday party to stay in his room, filling a sketchpad with drawings of body parts as if they were carburetors and gas tanks. To his mother's dismay, he hung the gruesome pictures on the wall like artwork.

More events followed that embarrassed Mrs. Lang, such as the time when she was entertaining the wife of a congressman and a cow's eye from David's dissecting kit slipped out of his pocket and onto her silver serving tray.

When David was eleven, his father took him to the operating room. With the patient's permission, the boy watched his first human surgery. Dr. Lang explained the procedure: "Today, I'm going to clip an aneurysm in the patient's brain. An aneurysm is a weakness in an artery that causes it to stretch like a balloon from the pressure of the blood running through it. This weak point is dangerous because it can burst like a balloon stretched too thin, causing a hemorrhage, which can kill the patient. Today I'm going to choke off the aneurysm with a metal clip around its neck, so blood will never again run into it and threaten the patient."

Dr. Lang lifted the small body dressed in baggy hospital scrubs so that David could see the diagnostic films on the view box.

"Yesterday, this aneurysm burst, but the patient's life was spared when the natural coagulating action of the blood temporarily sealed the tear with a clot. The patient passed out and was rushed to the hospital, where I examined him. Today's surgery is urgent, because a second rupture is possible and could be fatal. In order to clip the aneurysm before the artery bursts again, I need to clear away the blood clot. You see, I have to remove the clot in order to get to the aneurysm, but removing the clot increases the risk of the aneurysm's bursting before I'm in a position to clip it. So that's the challenge we face, son."

The predicament rendered David speechless; however, his father spoke in the matter-of-fact manner of a farmer talking about the need to clear a field.

A nurse wrapped the boy in a sterile gown winding twice around his slim body. With his arms tucked underneath, he looked more like a mummy than a would-be doctor. To raise his height, the nurse helped him onto a small platform positioned next to his father. He was forbidden to move his feet or arms or to do anything more than breathe, which was difficult through the oversize mask engulfing his small face.

The boy watched his father and a resident enter a brain swollen and red from the patient's hemorrhage. The two men used a suction device to evacuate the coagulated blood, piece by tiny piece, the way a vacuum cleaner picks up trash. The process was slow, tedious, and uneventful, until the small bulge of the aneurysm, covered with clot, came into view. As the resident tried to suck up more of the clot, the dreaded thing happened: the aneurysm burst.

A sea of blood suddenly and furiously filled the brain and splashed onto the floor. The men worked feverishly to suck off the blood, but it was gushing too forcefully to clear the field.

"Blood pressure's dropping," reported the anesthesiologist. "One hundred . . . ninety . . . eighty . . . sixty."

"Give me a temporary clip," Dr. Lang said calmly. "We have to cut off the main trunk of the artery."

David watched his father clip a large artery, an act that stopped the bleeding at once.

"We've got four minutes to find the aneurysm and clip it. Keep track of the time," said Dr. Lang.

To stop the hemorrhage, Dr. Lang had cut off the blood supply to the patient's brain, a state that could not continue for more than four minutes without permanent brain damage. David watched his father work quickly to trace the path of the artery and to uncover the neck of the aneurysm.

"Thirty seconds . . . sixty seconds," said the nurse who was counting. A deadly silence and palpable tension gripped the OR.

"I found the neck of the aneurysm," his father reported. "Let's try a straight clip."

"Ninety seconds . . . two minutes."

The scrub nurse handed Dr. Lang the desired clip. Although it sealed off the aneurysm, the clip also hit the main part of the artery, which meant it would interfere with the blood supply, so that clip had to be removed.

"Let's try a clip curving downward," Dr. Lang said. The scrub nurse gave him the requested clip.

"Two minutes thirty seconds."

The clip curving downward pinched off the aneurysm, but it pinched a vital function of the brain as well, so that clip also could not be used. Dr. Lang removed it.

"Three minutes fifteen seconds."

"Let's try a clip curving upward," said Dr. Lang.

After picking up the proper clip from her tray, the scrub nurse dropped it on the floor. She gasped.

"Three minutes thirty seconds."

"It's all right." Dr. Lang tried to calm her. "We still have time."

The scrub nurse searched for another of the same kind of clip on her tray.

"Three minutes forty seconds."

She gave the clip to Dr. Lang. He applied it. The clip sealed off the neck of the aneurysm. He checked to see that no other structures of the brain were impaired by it.

"This one works. Now give me a clip remover for the temporary clip on the main trunk," said Dr. Lang. He had to take away the clip from the main section of the artery to restart the blood supply to the brain.

"Three minutes fifty seconds."

There were a variety of clip removers on the instrument tray. The scrub nurse reached for one.

"Not that one," said Dr. Lang.

The nurse reached for another clip remover, which Dr. Lang approved.

"Four minutes."

Dr. Lang removed the temporary clip that he had placed on the main trunk of the artery four minutes earlier. Blood charged through the brain once again. The permanent clip on the aneurysm, which would remain in the patient's brain, held firm; there was no hemorrhage.

"This patient's going to be all right," Dr. Lang announced. The OR team collectively sighed.

The small witness to this event forgot his physical discomfort and even his very existence in the chilling four minutes that held him spellbound. When the crisis was over, he wanted to jump and cheer; however, he confined himself to a breathless "Wow" uttered from beneath his mask. That day the boy wrapped in a surgical gown discarded the clothing of childhood. Never again would he be content playing juvenile games after entering an arena in which life and death themselves were battling. No toy could ever again interest him after he had seen the intricate vessels, nerves, and convolutions of the stubbornly palpating human brain in its indomitable struggle for survival.

If he wanted a life's work that demanded the skill of splitting the atom, the precision of a bombardier, and the daring of a tightrope walker, David knew the only work that could qualify. At age eleven, *he knew*. As he gazed up at his father with a smile that was a salute, the father knew, too. He winked at the child in answer.

Walking to the Manhattan offices of the New York Bureau of Medicine, David was gripped by a sudden longing for the man in the OR who had winked at him on that final day of his childhood. He reproached himself, feeling it was silly for a grown man in a time of crisis to wish for his father. However, that presence in his life was inextricably linked to his career and to the meaning of Nicole's surgery.

He approached an old brick building with a plaque above its entrance that read *To serve the public interest above all other concerns—this is the noble work of medicine.*

The quotation was attributed to the secretary of medicine. David stared at the inscription long after reading the words. The man who had made that statement was the man he loathed more than any other, the man who wanted to destroy him and Nicole.

He took the elevator to the top floor of the building. Horizontal strips of wood-paneled walls converged on a varnished oak door at the end of the hall. He walked down the narrow corridor that seemed like the dead end of a one-way street. The man he was about to see was armed and dangerous, he warned himself. He must not be caught off guard.

The woman sitting at the desk of the outer office had been a nurse for the secretary during the years in which he had practiced medicine before accepting his current post. Involuntarily, she began to smile at the man entering the office, as if greeting an old acquaintance. She suppressed the impulse on seeing the solemnity of the visitor's face.

"He's waiting for you, David." She gestured to the door of the inner office.

The visitor reached the door. For a long moment, the knob seemed too heavy to turn, and then he disappeared inside.

The room's proprietor was standing by a window and vacantly staring out, absorbed in thought. David looked at the man whom he had not seen in two years, since the day he had denounced him for accepting the post of secretary of medicine and vowed never to speak to him again. The eyes of the two men filled with venom, but their voices sounded oddly, jarringly too soft.

"Hello, Father."

"Sit down, David."

❀15❀
The Law

$\mathbf{M}$rs. Lang seemed to have played no part in the birth of her firstborn, David. The tall, slim lines, high cheekbones, and stunning green eyes made the resemblance between Dr. Warren Lang and his son astonishing. Even the silky hair was identical in both men, except that the father's was bleached white by an added generation. When Warren's hair was black, David was sometimes mistaken for him. "Mind you, we have our differences," Warren would proudly say to those remarking on their likeness. "I'm the *good* surgeon of the family, but David's the *great* one."

After studying each other for an awkward moment, both men averted their eyes as if to ignore the stubborn resemblance forcing itself on their consciousness. David surveyed the office, surprised at its power to disturb him. The room was a marked departure from the medical office of the man who used to be his father. At thirteen, David had lovingly sketched that sacred place and then hung the drawing in his room to dream about the future. Gone from the new office were the copious medical diplomas and certificates that David remembered; in their place were pictures of Warren waving a campaign banner at a political rally, making a speech from a podium thick with microphones, and shaking hands with a powerful politician. Gone were the massive bookcases of medical volumes, replaced by the present room's only reading material, a stack of news magazines spread over a coffee table.

The desk of Dr. Warren Lang the surgeon had held only items essential to medicine—a replica of the brain, a clinical journal, a patient's chart. The desk of Secretary Lang was cluttered with newspaper clippings about CareFree, portraits from a photography session, a party invitation, a silver plate from an awards dinner. A tall vase on the desk contained a floral arrangement from a medical society that wooed him, its card reading: "With heartfelt appreciation for the rousing speech you gave at our banquet." The display featured two-foot-high gladiolas balanced precariously in the narrow vase. Like the tottering profession that gifted them, thought David. Only one personal object had been permitted on the desk of Warren Lang the surgeon. David's eyes involuntarily searched for—and found—it: a photograph of him at eleven, wrapped in a sterile gown on the day when he saw his first surgery. It was the only object surviving the radical transformation from the surgeon's to the secretary's office.

"You've gone too far!" Warren broke the uncomfortable silence. "You're disgracing me! I don't care what happens to you now, David. I must treat you like any other official matter I handle—all in a day's work."

David did not remember when he had last drunk anything, and he was per-spiring too much from his walk—two facts that suddenly struck him when the room swirled, then turned black. The next thing he remembered was sitting in a chair with the concerned eyes of Warren and his secretary peering at him. His fa-ther was loosening his tie, unbuttoning his shirt, wiping his forehead with a cool, wet handkerchief.

"Doris, he's been in surgery all night, and you know how David works. He probably hasn't eaten or slept in who knows how long! And his shirt is soaked." He poured a glass of water from a pitcher on his desk.

"Here, drink this, you crazy kid!"

David drank eagerly.

"Do you realize it's ninety-five degrees outside? What'd you do, walk here? You look like hell!"

"That will do."

"Doris, would you get David a quart of orange juice? He's not moving from that chair until he drinks it!"

David recovered enough strength to abort Warren's attempt to check his pulse. Doris soon produced a container of juice, then left the men alone, as David sipped the liquid. The fluids brought a warm glow back to David's pallid face, but his eyes remained cold and unyielding.

"No one else must be punished for what I did. Everyone else is innocent. Randy knew *nothing* about this, so call off your mad dogs, Father."

"How dare you? I don't know what you're talking about."

"How could you not know?"

"Know what?"

"That your staff's out for blood, Randy's blood, goddamn them! They're denying approvals and levying charges on the hospital just to flex their muscles. Do you consider your public served by vengeance against the innocent?"

"You're accusing my agency of misuse of power. Where's your proof?"

"The very existence of this institution is proof enough."

"We'll not go into that again. That's beside the point."

"That *is* the point."

"The point is that you will discontinue your nerve-repair treatment at once!"

"I will not."

"And because you unintentionally broke the law—"

"I *intentionally* broke the law."

"—you will apologize to the governor."

"It's none of the governor's business what I do in the OR."

"Overcome by grief for the patient's unfortunate condition, you had an overzealous moment in which you didn't think clearly."

"I thought very clearly."

"Is your new procedure the same one that you were working on when I saw you last?"

"It is."

"Then it requires a second surgery, doesn't it?"

"It does."

"You will *not* perform it." Warren stood towering above David in the chair, pointing a threatening finger at him.

"At minimum, I'd have to be dead not to perform the second surgery."

"The patient's health won't be jeopardized by discontinuing the treatment. The nerves will remain damaged, and that's that."

"And her life will remain in shambles."

"You've got to admit you made a mistake and retreat. That's the only way I can save you."

"Then don't save me."

"What?"

"Use some pretense or other to lift my suspension. Then look the other way until I finish the second surgery. Tie this matter up in a committee, assign a task force to study me, or do whatever it is you do here. Only stall the matter until after the second operation. Then do what you please to me."

"Cutting that patient again would be like cutting your own throat."

"Why should saving my patient lead to my own destruction?"

"You have no idea of the hot water you're in, David, so don't argue. You must discontinue the treatment."

"Why?"

"Because we made budget cuts. We had to! I issued an edict. I had to! With the rumors about my running for lieutenant governor, every reporter from here to Niagara Falls is watching me. I can't break the rules for my own son. That would be completely arbitrary."

"Any more arbitrary than the other decisions made by this institution?"

"You don't understand. Right now there are other priorities that are more pressing than nerve repair."

"Not for my patient, there aren't."

"There are the more pressing needs of the public, David."

"Like what? Does somebody in Brooklyn need a gallbladder removed? Does somebody in Buffalo need a tonsillectomy? Or maybe some poor guy in Ithaca is waiting for your blessing to have a heart bypass. What must my patient do to win a door prize, too?"

Warren noticed the absence of something in David's face that disturbed him—the admiration that face had once held for him was gone.

"I understand that the patient is a dancer, Nicole Hudson."

"Yes."

"Fortunately, she's not very famous, and not a senator's daughter or congressman's wife. You're lucky, David. You could've been damned if you did and damned if you didn't continue the treatment."

David smiled bitterly. "Why? Are some people more in the public interest than others?"

Warren walked behind the desk and paced nervously. "Never mind. You don't understand the practical expediencies necessary to advance the cause of social justice."

"Like selling my patient down the river? Is that what you call a practical expediency? And what type of justice would it advance?"

"It would save your hide, for one thing."

"Why should my survival require the demise of my patient?"

"Let's not say 'demise,' David, really. Your patient could end up very well off indeed. She'll sue the daylights out of you. That's for sure. But your insurance company will pay, and Nicole Hudson will receive a staggering settlement for being subjected to an unauthorized surgery. She'll be able to buy a condo in the city, a house in the country, a yacht to dock by the house, a plane to land on the yacht, a husband to fly the plane. She'll be rich. She'll be powerful—"

"She'll be blind."

Warren shrugged helplessly as he sank into his chair.

"Years ago, that would have bothered you," said David, facing him across the desk.

"If there were no other concerns, you know how I'd feel about this, son. Why, nerve regeneration is the most exciting thing to happen in medicine in decades! The implications are tremendous." For a moment Warren's face looked younger, his eyes livelier. "It could virtually wipe out paralysis as an aftermath of trauma!"

David saw an animated figure with black hair sitting in an office that was a shrine. That figure had patiently and lovingly shared with him the exciting secrets of the human brain.

"However, if CareFree hasn't tested and approved the new procedure, it can't be justified. But tell me about it anyway, David. And don't leave out anything!"

Warren relaxed in his chair, as if ready to hear a bedtime story. Dark lines of puzzlement cut David's forehead. For an unguarded moment, his face lost its anger, showing only the naked innocence of his childhood.

"Father, I don't understand you anymore," he whispered painfully.

"I wouldn't hurt you for anything, son."

"How can you sit in this office and say you won't hurt me?"

"How can I *not* sit here? How can I pass up the chance to do something of such social and historic significance?"

Contempt replaced the innocence on David's face. He leaned back in his chair, sipped the juice, and began his tale.

"The patient, a twenty-three-year-old woman, fell from a height of about twelve feet, receiving a laceration of the lower forehead and multiple other bruises. She was unconscious and bleeding from the nose when admitted to the hospital. Despite no direct trauma to the eyes, both pupils were nonreactive to light. She regained consciousness for a moment and reported a total loss of vision."

As the secretary listened to the dispassionate speech of a doctor, the father heard the exuberant voice of a boy of nine. Warren remembered the day when he had traced a terrible odor in the house to David's room. There he found a homeless man named Ben who, David explained, had not brushed his teeth in years and so had growing over them an amazing black substance that intrigued the boy. David had brought Ben home to examine material from the man's malodorous mouth under his microscope. Warren recalled David's excitement at discovering a lively colony of creatures in the man's oral cavity. The father remembered wishing that his son would never lose his capacity to find such an immense thrill in the things he did.

"A brain scan revealed a fracture in the sphenoid bone. Images through the sinus and sella turcica showed a disruption of the optic nerves in the canal, where fragments from the sphenoid bone had sprung up from the base of the skull to pierce the meningeal sheaths and transect both optic nerves. Because of the laceration of the sheaths, the lesions of the underlying nerves were exposed clearly on magnification; thus, their transections could be diagnosed prior to surgery."

Warren Lang looked at the calm face of a doctor, but what he saw was the enthusiasm of a young boy. David at thirteen was displaying an instrument that he had made. Warren had been offered a post in San Francisco and considered moving his family there. With the aid of a science book, David had built a seismograph to measure earthquakes, in preparation for living in San Francisco. He had taken matters into his own hands, the father recalled proudly.

"When the patient later regained consciousness, she, of course, exhibited total bilateral loss of vision. You know as well as I do, Father, that without my intervention, the trauma to those nerves would have rapidly resulted in total atrophy and permanent, irreversible blindness."

"So you took matters into your own hands."

"I explained the surgical procedure, its experimental nature, and risks. The patient gave me her informed consent. Then I called Randy." David leaned forward in his seat, his eyes intense. "I told Randy I had your permission to operate. He believed me. Neither he nor the OR staff nor anyone else knew the surgery was illegal. I lied to everyone. Is that clear?"

"What happened in the OR?"

"I performed a pterional craniotomy. I reanastomized the nerve ends. Then I implanted at the lesion site of each nerve an embryonic growth protein, a substance I had discovered in lower mammals that's active prenatally but absent from the body after birth. I found that the embryonic growth protein plays a critical role in the formation of the central nervous system." David paused to sip the orange juice. "When I treated injured nerve with this new protein, it imparted to that tissue the most remarkable powers of regeneration."

If only I hadn't been so weak, the father said silently to the figure that still possessed the slim lines and wavy tangle of hair from his boyhood. *But, no, I let you have your way in matters where you were wrong. I taught you science, all right, but I was too lenient in another area.*

"I encased the nerve ends in a silicon sheath to fix the alignment and focus the medication. Then I placed my embryonic growth protein in a timed-release capsule that will dispense the medication directly to the lesion site of each nerve for three months."

You had no right to do what you did to my patient, Bob Martin, Warren scolded the slender boy of ten in his thoughts. *Even though Bob bought an extravagant new sports car a month after his surgery and didn't pay me my fee, and even though he blasted me to the local newspaper for sending a collection agency to get my money, the majority of people in Oak Hills took Bob's side, David.*

"The operation went smoothly, and the patient exhibited no neurological deficit after surgery."

I felt the disapproving stares of the entire community whenever I walked down the streets, Warren silently said to a face resembling his own. *I couldn't stand it, David. So I gave up trying to collect my fee from Bob. I learned my lesson from incidents like that, but I failed to teach you yours.*

"Now the second procedure involves the scar. I discovered a substance that inhibits scar tissue from forming at the lesion site. Unfortunately, the substance inhibits nerve growth as well, so it can't be introduced until the nerve has been completely regenerated." David looked calmer, the fascination with his subject overpowering his anger.

When you slashed the four tires on Bob's new car, I was shocked at the anger inside you, David. When you refused to pay for the tires with money you had saved from your odd jobs, when you hid that money so I wouldn't be able to find it, when you defied my order to pay Bob and told me I could beat you instead—what did I do? How could I beat you when you were the only one who had defended me? So I paid for the slashed tires myself, and you didn't learn your lesson about social responsibility.

"In the second operation, after I surgically remove the scar tissue that has formed, I aim to prevent any more scar from growing by injection of the scar inhibitor."

And you had no right to do what you did to Charles Fox, Warren silently admonished a boy of twelve with eyes too large for his small face. *When Charles Fox and his Earthlings for a Simple Planet vandalized my lab because they said my work polluted the environment, I was angry, too. I sued him, didn't I? But what was I to do after they publicly smeared me? What did it matter that their accusations were false? People believed I was wrong, and they made me feel guilty. The Simple Earthlings were entitled to their opinion, too, weren't they? How could I bring suit against people working for the good of the planet?*

"If everything goes well in the second surgery, I will free the regenerated optic nerves from scar interference and permit the permanent restoration of function."

The day I dropped the lawsuit against the Earthlings, you were supposed to be in school, David, not outside the courtroom waiting for Charles Fox. At twelve, you were too old to punch him in the stomach and kick him in the shins not once, but five times, before I could tear you away. Even though I reprimanded you, grounded you, and took away your allowance when you refused to apologize to Charles, I didn't force you to do it. How could I, David, when you were the only one who had taken my side? I was much too soft on you. And that's why you never learned about social obligations.

"However, if the scar tissue isn't removed and prevented from re-forming, it'll impede nerve function and the nerve repair will be futile. Therefore, I must impress on you the *absolute necessity* of the second surgery." David sat back in his chair. "So, that's the story, Father. You know that an injury of this nature had to be dealt with quickly and couldn't wait for committees or certifications. You also know that the people granting the approvals—your staff—are incompetent to evaluate my surgery, and the thought of them telling me what to do in the OR is ludicrous. If you really want to do something noble, you'll leave me and my patient free to handle this matter without interference."

David studied Warren's face. It looked as immovable as Nicole's pupils.

Finally, the secretary spoke: "Medically, you are right."

"The first word is superfluous."

"There are considerations beyond medicine in determining right and wrong."

"Like what?"

"Like this agency's obligation to protect the patient."

"From me?"

"From unscrupulous doctors. If you can do whatever you please, that means all doctors can do the same. Then how will the public be protected from unprincipled physicians?"

"How will substituting your edicts for our judgment improve our performance?"

"Even if I wanted to, I couldn't spend public funds on an unrecognized procedure."

"Because the procedure is experimental, I insist on waiving my fee and personally paying the hospital bills."

"You can't pay for anything! That's illegal."

"You mean charity is now outlawed?"

"Your charity would have the self-serving motive of advancing your pet project. The press would see that."

"Would I do better work if I had no interest in my projects and couldn't care less whether Nicole lived or died?"

"You'd do better work if you could hold on to your license!"

"If I'm not permitted to finance my own experiment, then my patient will gladly pay her own medical bills to keep the surgery out of the purview of CareFree."

"She can't pay! That's against the law. If we let patients pay with their own money, then we'll be back to the old corrupt system where only those who can afford it get treatment."

"You mean it's corrupt to pay for the services of others but right to expect them for nothing?"

"Your patient must not pay a single medical bill. CareFree *guarantees* care to her for free."

"But she doesn't want the care you're guaranteeing."

"Even if you could waive your charges, Randall's hospital couldn't take private money for its fees. Our charter would drop the hospital as a CareFree provider, and it would go out of business. So your patient's treatment *is* publicly funded— and has to be. That's the glory of CareFree. It sets people free from having to pay for their medical care."

"How is my patient set free if she no longer can decide for herself?"

"Did you let your brother decide for himself when you performed the surgery at his hospital?" Warren saw a break in the marble face. "When Randall loses his job, as he will if he's foolish enough to defend you, are you prepared to bankroll the development of his children's talents?"

"Don't blackmail me with threats against the innocent!" Lines of pain twisted a face that could not conceal them.

"And Marie told me you've been paying hefty fines to this agency. Because I insist that no staff member is to bend the rules for my family, I was never told about your fines, nor would I have intervened had I known. Because you would apparently be strapped to help Randall out, and he wouldn't accept money from you anyway, are you prepared to explain to his children why they will lose their futures?"

"Are *you* prepared to explain to your grandchildren why their futures are being jeopardized to further your own?"

"But David, I'm not acting for myself. I'm acting for the *people!*"

"What gives them the right to stop a treatment that I want to do and that my patient wants to have?"

"It's *you* who had no right to perform an operation against the interests of your brother and the hospital."

"Why would a hospital disapprove of a new procedure that could skyrocket its caseload? I could bring a lot of money into that hospital—if it was free to make money. You know what's behind the clash between me and the hospital"— his voice became low—"and between me and my brother."

"And what about your wife's feelings? She and I dined alone last night. Did you know that Marie had invited me to join you two for dinner? She thought you'd want to reconcile your differences with me. Instead, look what you've done."

"I never agreed to dine with a man who wants to poison me."

The color drained from Warren's face. "You know, when you were two years old, you used to cry every morning when I left for work. You gave your mother a terrible time because you wanted to be with only me. Now you show not the slightest remorse at the pain you're causing me and the rest of the family."

"Is that what I'm supposed to tell my patient, Father? That she has to grope in darkness for the rest of her life because members of my family are personally offended by her surgery?"

Warren's face grew taut. He leaned forward in his chair, pointing an accusing finger at David. "There are severe penalties for what you did. So choose: Either you give up this case, apologize to the governor and the public, and hope to hell I can save you even then, or keep up this brash defiance and get yourself kicked out of medicine and possibly thrown in jail. Those are the penalties. I have not only the power but also the moral obligation to enforce them."

"If you have a moral obligation to throw me in jail, then who's allowed to roam free? If science is outlawed, then what's legal?"

"Choose, David."

"A new discovery lands me in jail, but blind obedience to the whims of this institution sets me free. Is that the choice you're giving me?"

"I'm acutely aware of the value of your research. If you would only have patience and go through the proper channels, in time we would make allowances for you to conduct your experiments and test your procedure. I'm giving you a choice between professional suicide, public disgrace, and a possible prison sentence versus your research, your career, your success, and your freedom."

"Doing my work at a time determined by you, with your funds, in your labs, under your rules, with your inspectors breathing down my neck? Is that what you call my freedom? Let's drop the pretense, Father. What you really mean is that if I do what you want, then you might become the next lieutenant governor. Isn't that true? Everybody knows that the governor's reelection rests on the voters' confidence in CareFree. And everyone also knows that CareFree is a colossal failure. The governor needed a scapegoat to explain why just a few years of CareFree has wreaked havoc with medicine. That's why you made your budget cuts, blamed the doctors for the mess, and issued your threats. Now you have to make good on those threats. So you're ordering me to ignore the whole of my medical knowledge and chose a treatment that's best for you and your boss to win an election. And in some perverted attempt to delude yourself or me or both of us, you claim you're doing something noble. I call it an unspeakable corruption!"

"Your mother warned me that you would become antisocial, but I never listened. You were so bright, David, and the things you did gave you such immense pleasure that I couldn't force you to change your ways. I let you think only of yourself and your interests while you ignored the opinions others had about you. That's why today you can think only in the narrow terms of one doctor, one patient, and one case and you don't consider the effects of your actions on society as a whole."

"And how am I to know what effects my actions would have on society? That's where you come in, isn't it, Father? You've got us all strung out on some cosmic necklace threaded by you and your boss, so that slack for some of us means gagging for the rest. What effect could Nicole's surgery have on a man with a broken ankle in Saratoga Springs if she paid for the treatment with her own money? Why would he care if she bought a mink coat or an operation if her treatment didn't result in the curtailment of his own?"

But David realized that his argument, like rays deflected off an impenetrable surface, did not reach Warren.

"Choose, David. Either obey society's laws or become an outcast and an outlaw. I hope that as a healer and as my son, you will make the only choice that a man of character can make."

"I choose to have none of your kind of character and to be faithful to myself and my work. If that disgraces me, then so be it."

"Then you will get your punishment."

David sighed, raising his hands in surrender. "Father, I never pleaded a case to you. I never begged for a favor. But I'm begging now. I'll do whatever you want, only I must perform the second surgery on Nicole. After that, I'll plead guilty to all of your charges, I'll leave medicine, I'll go to jail, I'll accept any punishment you choose. If it meant anything to you that as a child I wanted to be with only you, that I cried when you left the house, that I learned to love medicine from you, that I idolized you, that I loved you not only as a father but also as the hero of my childhood, then grant me this one and only favor—in the name of something that was once precious to both of us. Please, Father. Tie this matter up in a committee, look the other way, stall it—only don't stop me until my work is done. Lift my suspension and make Riverview Hospital reinstate my staff privileges—just until I can do the second procedure. And don't punish Randy and the hospital, only me!" David closed his eyes painfully. "Please, Father."

The crusty features of Warren's face were softened in a sudden remolding, as if an astute sculptor had captured a hidden layer of his subject's soul. "David, I never imagined that I would be able to share my work with you. I really do love medicine. Watching that same spark ignite in you, too, has been the joy of my life. But I can't do what you're asking. I want to, but Mack Burrow is demanding your blood."

David's eyes widened with hope. "Do you really want to save me, Father? Do you really want to be the person I thought you were?"

"Yes."

"Then do it!" David leaned forward, his arms spread over the desk, a sudden spark of interest lighting his face. "Quit this despicable institution and come back to medicine. Exonerate me as your last official deed and be done with this dirty work! Would you, Dad, would you?"

"Son, I want to defend you, but not as an act *against* this institution. Not at all. I want to defend you because your work is of immense importance, not just to you or your patient but also to society. It's in the public interest."

David's hopes sunk in a pit of disappointment. "That's *not* the way to defend me! You can't take a majority vote on Nicole's life or on my work. May the public and its so-called interest be damned!"

"Okay, David. I won't appeal to your social conscience. Let's look at this matter in a purely personal way. After all, a man never does forget the . . . hero . . . of his childhood. I gave you, well, so much to admire as a kid, and now I'm giving you even more to be proud of."

David raised his eyebrows in utter incredulity. "Are you thinking that I could be proud of you for teaming up with Mack Burrow?"

"Forget him. He's just a means to my later becoming governor. You can admit it, son—aren't you really proud of all I've accomplished?"

David's mind echoed with Nicole's anguished cries of wanting to die. For what senseless purpose would she be condemned to suffer? he wondered. He envisioned Mack Burrow with his limousine, his mansion, his followers, his press.

"Give up this hopeless quest for my sake. Tell the truth, son. Wouldn't you rather have my love than my censure?"

"I'd rather be a bastard than be a son of yours."

Both men were shocked into silence. Warren could have forgiven David for saying what he had if it were a cry torn from him in rage. But the fact that David uttered it calmly, coldly, and with full intent was a cut from which Warren would bleed for the rest of his life.

As a substitute for a hurt too deep to reveal, Warren became livid. He rose to his feet, pounding his fists against the desk until the vase and its gladiolas shook furiously. "I'll not sanction lawlessness. You'll not perform that second surgery! The answer is no!"

David stood, his body thrusting forward, his hands on the desk, his voice hitting his father from a distance of inches. "I would perform that second surgery even if it meant your death."

"You're no son of mine! You're finished! When I get through with you, you'll never operate again, just as surely as if your hands were slashed!" Warren continued slamming his fist on the desk.

Without warning and dangerously close to where David's hands lay, the tall crystal vase shook from the force of Warren's pounding and came crashing down. A flurry of broken glass, scattered flowers, and splashing water hit the desk.

"Look out!" Warren shouted. He pulled David's hands away from the flying crystal an instant before it could cut him.

Both men froze, stunned by the action. Warren's hands grasped David's, the way one clutches a baby safely away from a fire. Trembling, Warren protectively pressed his son's hands to his chest, with David permitting the act.

"Son, your work is a noble vision. But CareFree is noble, too."

"They can't both be noble, Father."

"But how can they not be?"

David jerked his hands away. He stepped backward cautiously, as if retreating from an unknown menace too fearsome to turn his back on. Then he stopped, raised his right arm slowly, and pointed a trembling finger at Warren, his voice resonating through the room: "I told you two years ago when you accepted this post, and I'll tell you again now: One of us is going to destroy the other. Before this matter is over, one of us will be finished!"

❧ PART TWO ❧
Thunder

❧16❧

The Model Citizen

David sat on the front steps of his house watching a few smoky pink clouds on the horizon turn silver gray in the western sky. Though his body looked relaxed as he leaned on his elbows, his long legs sprawling down the wooden stairs, his eyes were intense and distant. When the lawn, a lush green carpet circling the porch and stretching to the pavement, darkened to the same slate hue as the street, he walked into the house and across the kitchen.

Marie, brewing tea at the stove, watched him heading for the garage. She was wrapped in a long robe and settled in for the evening.

"Going out again tonight, David?"

"I told you on Friday that I'd be tied up for a few nights."

"And today's Sunday, supposedly a day when husbands spend time with their wives."

He looked at her silently.

"I'm still in shock over what you did to your career—and to our lives—last Wednesday evening."

He said nothing.

"Where have you been every night since you got suspended? I know one place not on your travel log, and that's the OR. So tell me, David, how does a man pass the time after destroying his career?"

He thought that she had a right to know where he was going, but a deeper voice cautioned him to keep his business to himself. "There's something I need to do, but I'm afraid I can't discuss it."

"What might that be? Anesthetize yourself in a bar?"

"If you wish." He seemed pleased at her conclusion that he was drinking.

"I see you're dressed like a jewel thief again."

He was clad entirely in black—from sneakers to denim pants to polo shirt to baseball cap.

"Good night, Marie," he called, vanishing into the garage, his voice tinged with sadness.

Twenty minutes later, his car clattered off the metal bridge from Queens to the East Side of Manhattan. He saw few people on the streets with the hour growing late—a man walking his dog, a shopper entering a late-night grocery, a couple leaving an empty restaurant. Although he was headed west, he parked on the East Side and hailed a taxi.

David stepped into the backseat, his head lowered to avoid the driver's glance. His face had appeared in the press that week, and he did not want to be recognized. His youthful appearance did not suggest an experienced surgeon, and his most revealing feature, the unusually intelligent eyes, were hidden by the baseball cap pulled down to his brows.

The cab's radio was tuned to a newscast: "Today the mayor ordered an investigation into the explosion in Manhattan injuring two hundred people. The blast has been traced to a faulty gas pipeline. The Bowing Construction Company, which installed the pipeline, is already under suspicion in the recent kickback scheme involving high-level officials in the Burrow Administration. Sources indicate that the lieutenant governor may also be charged in the scandal. The governor denied any knowledge of the affair."

The cab driver raised his eyes to peer at David through the rearview mirror. "How do you like that?" he said, snickering.

"I don't particularly," said David, averting his eyes in an attempt to end the conversation.

But the cab driver pressed on as he drove into the livelier nightlife of the theater district. "You think the governor wouldn't take kickbacks?"

"I don't know—" David began, but his words suddenly froze.

Outside the window, workers were erecting a new billboard where a poster of Nicole had stood. The giant ad displayed the reopening date of *Triumph* with a twenty-foot-high picture of the new Pandora, touted to be "Broadway's latest dance sensation." He was grateful that Nicole could not see that particular sight.

As the cab crawled in traffic detoured because of the explosion, a new radio show began. "Good evening," a soothing voice droned, "I'm Adam Nutley, your Sunday night host for *The Week in Review*. Tonight our topic is medicine and the state. Can a doctor disregard government regulations and treat a patient as he pleases? Neurosurgeon David Lang apparently thinks so. This week his experimental nerve-repair surgery on dancer Nicole Hudson, who was blinded in the gas explosion, has raised a furor in the Burrow administration, as well as in his own family."

"That guy's finished," quipped the driver.

David did not listen to commentaries, as he knew they would have no bearing on his actions. He wanted to ask the driver to change the station but decided not to invite more looks through the rearview mirror.

"Here is what Dr. David Lang said in a news conference after the surgery," said Adam Nutley.

David heard an excerpt of his statement to the press. As he had only spoken a few words in the cab, the driver apparently did not recognize the voice over the radio as his.

"This surgery is a private matter between me and my patient. It's none of the governor's business what I do in the OR," said David over the airwaves.

"Dr. Lang was peppered by questions after his statement," continued the show's host. "Here are some of them."

"Dr. Lang," asked one reporter, "if this treatment is successful, do you stand to gain personally from it?"

"I do."

"Did you *really* use drugs that weren't approved?" asked another reporter incredulously.

"They *were* approved—by me."

"Did you perform a procedure that wasn't authorized?"

"It *was* authorized—by my patient."

"But Dr. Lang, how can you know that you're right?"

"How can a bureaucrat in Albany know better?"

Adam Nutley interjected: "And here is what Governor Burrow said about the surgery."

"My responsibility is to protect the patient," droned the governor through the static reception. "Here we have a doctor who bypassed the law, subjecting a helpless accident victim to an operation not approved through the proper regulatory channels and to drugs not authorized by the appropriate agencies. I will not see the public turned into guinea pigs for someone's reckless experiments."

"The issue," said Adam Nutley, "is complicated by the fact that the head of the Bureau of Medicine, Dr. Warren Lang, is the surgeon's father. The governor was asked if the doctor might get off easy, considering his connections."

"Absolutely not! The surgeon has already been suspended," said Governor Burrow. "Warren Lang's integrity is unimpeachable. I *know* he'll do what's right."

"What *is* right?" interjected Adam Nutley.

"Even his old man won't be able to bail him out," said the cabbie indifferently. "Not in an election year."

The taxi came to a standstill, waiting its turn to pass construction trucks and blocked lanes. David noticed an unusually vigorous effort by the city to repair the roads damaged by the explosion. Was that another sign of an approaching election? He wondered if he and Nicole would face ruin because someone wanted to win an election. They were the innocent, wanting nothing from anyone, only to be left alone, yet they were somehow in the way.

"We asked the state's foremost medical authorities for their views on Dr. Lang's experimental surgery," said the radio commentator. "First let's hear from the president of the New York Academy of Medicine."

"A doctor has an obligation to serve society," said a voice David recognized. "We repudiate brash, egotistical, lawbreaking actions by a physician, and we repudiate David Lang."

The announcer next introduced the head of the New York Alliance of Neurosurgeons. "Doctors seeking new techniques and discoveries must work within the system," said another voice David knew. "Lawlessness is unacceptable in bringing about social change, even if such change ultimately proves to be of great value."

David cracked the window of the cab, and the incessant whine of the city intruded. He felt a sickening knot in his stomach at the thought of the thousands of dollars in dues he had paid to the organizations whose leaders were just quoted, organizations whose alleged purpose was to protect doctors. He was not surprised at censure from members of his profession—only at the biting power it had to hurt him.

But the voices of New York's medical leaders were mere pinpricks compared to the next one piercing his ears, a voice stinging with bitterness: "The surgery performed by Dr. David Lang flies in the face of established medical beliefs about nerve regeneration," said his brother. "It also flies in the face of other established beliefs, ones that brought us Mack Burrow, the Bureau of Medicine, and CareFree. If we accepted Dr. Lang's brazen experiment, then we would have to challenge much more than our medical beliefs.

"If Dr. Lang can perform his work by his own judgment, then why do we need the Bureau of Medicine? If his patient is capable of—and better off—handling her own medical treatment, then why do we need CareFree? While Governor Burrow parades in the ornate robe of public benefactor, David Lang points his finger, saying the emperor isn't wearing any clothes.

"What would it mean if the emperor were naked? Think of the statutes, committees, and departments that would be useless. Think of the thousands of inspectors with nothing to inspect. Think of the unused tax money that could be refunded to the people. What a waste! This is why Dr. Lang's deed must not be forgiven. As the president of Riverview Hospital, I . . ."—the first crack appeared in the voice—". . . have no choice but to . . . denounce him."

Randy's statement reached a bowed head in the back of the cab. It was not the words that disturbed David but the pain in the voice uttering them.

"If this doctor wants a friend, he'd better get a dog," said the cabbie.

David knew that he had many supporters, but they could not risk their positions by speaking out publicly. They were the majority of his colleagues, who silently watched his plight with the sympathetic stares reserved for the condemned. Although David was officially suspended, his colleagues tacitly gave him as much control as possible. When he transferred his preoperative cases to other surgeons, they accepted the patients regretfully. In theory David also relinquished his postoperative cases. In practice, however, his colleagues looked the other way while he continued to monitor these patients. Such gestures of respect, David knew, would never be made known to the public.

"In the interest of presenting both sides of the issue, we interviewed an outspoken supporter of Dr. Lang, the president of Morgan Pharmaceuticals, Philip Morgan," said Adam Nutley. "He issued his statement on Thursday morning, immediately after the surgery."

David suppressed a gasp at the mention of his trusted friend and former college classmate who had risen from being a bench chemist to heading his own drug company. He did not know that Morgan had issued any statement regarding Nicole's surgery. David had thought of his friend only yesterday when Care-Free had announced the removal of three of Morgan's drugs from its formulary. The drugs were too expensive and an unnecessary duplication of other medications, the agency had claimed. The sudden action wiped out the firm's sales of those drugs in New York State, David knew. Now he was mortified to realize that the ban had come immediately after Morgan was foolish enough to have defended him.

The leather-tough voice of Phil Morgan bristled on the radio. "You can bet something's terribly wrong in the world when a top surgeon like David Lang has to take orders from a bureaucracy. Dr. Lang had the courage to do what we all dream of. Sure, we bicker among ourselves about the regulations, but then we smile politely and open our doors to the next inspector who drops by our office to look around, and it's all so pleasant. Undoubtedly, David Lang will be hanged, but somehow I think he's better off than the rest of us patsies."

David gasped audibly. The driver glanced through the rearview mirror to see two hands covering a lowered face.

"Are you okay, buddy?"

"Yes," the surgeon whispered.

Phil Morgan's banned drugs included an anesthetic used in David's surgeries. CareFree's quest to provide free medication within its troubled budget had resulted in the use of fewer and less-expensive products. What would happen to Phil's company? David wondered anxiously. Would it stop doing business in New York State, as other pharmaceutical firms already had?

"We contacted the secretary of medicine," said Adam Nutley, "but he declined to comment."

How do you like that?" asked the cabbie.

David did not reply.

"When the politicians bash this doctor, that don't mean anything. But when other doctors blast him and his own family won't stick up for him and his only friend is a drug-company exec, it makes you wonder."

"You can stop here."

With the cab barely halted, David paid the driver and jumped out. He walked a few blocks past the row of theaters to the Hudson River, its murky waters trembling in the moonlight, until he reached the sprawling campus of West Side University and its medical school. Few lights shone in the buildings that Sunday night, and no cars appeared in the campus parking lots. David met no one along the lamppost-lit road to the William Mead Research Center. There, medical investigators like him kept laboratories and performed animal studies. However, the other researchers, warmed by the mantle of respectability, worked by day; he prowled at night.

The oppressive humidity and dank smell of the river made David wish for a hearty rain. But the sky was clear. Where was the downpour, he wondered, to cleanse the muddy waters that he waded in? At the desolate entrance to the brick research building, a black cat crossed his path. The two creatures startled each other.

The wooden door creaked when David's key opened it. The empty halls amplified the thump of his footsteps. The plaintive wail of a restless laboratory animal was his only greeting. When he arrived at the small, windowless laboratory that he kept on the second floor, a digital clock beeped to signal the hour: 10:00. He locked the door, galvanized by the task at hand.

He examined three of five cats caged in his lab. He had operated on those three in the nights after Nicole's surgery. In each cat, he had simulated Nicole's injury by transecting the optic nerves; then he repaired them as he had in her case. After checking his recuperating feline patients, David created a sterile field on his lab counter, prepared his instruments, and readied the last two animals for the same surgery. His plan was to perform the second operation on each of the five cats prior to Nicole's next surgery. With his suspension, he did not know *how* he would complete Nicole's treatment, only that he would. Operating on the cats would help him to foresee any possible problems, thus better preparing him for her second procedure. He wished he could perform hundreds of animal experiments before reentering the sacred temple that was Nicole's brain.

However, five felines were the only animals he possessed—five precious cats! They were not yet registered with the authorities. David had obtained them after he had successfully performed the nerve-repair treatment on the spinal cords of other felines. He'd intended to experiment on the fresh cats but had failed to gain approval from the BOM. He'd considered trying to procure more animals from a shelter but could find no way to circumvent the probing applications. Although hundreds of local pound animals were euthanized weekly, the laws forbade their use in medical experiments. Why? he wondered, but he had no time to search for an answer. As David applied an anesthesia mask to a cat's face, he tried to forget the laws that he was breaking, to anesthetize himself to everything save the one performance that he must orchestrate flawlessly—Nicole's second surgery, with the dancer's fate resting on the outcome.

The surgeon had no permission from the state to conduct animal experiments. Performing two surgical procedures on the same animal, as he was plan-

ning, required a special permit. The feline operations were supposed to be performed in a surgical area, not at a lab bench, and with a licensed veterinarian
present. The animals were supposed to be housed in a special room under controlled conditions, not in a cage in a windowless lab. The litany of regulations he
was violating was lengthy. He tried not to think of the growing number of medical researchers who were targeted by hostile groups infiltrating their labs, accusing them of infractions, and masterminding their arrests on cruelty-to-animal
charges. He had witnessed the chilling sight of a colleague handcuffed and taken
away in a police car for lesser offenses.

According to the law, David was cruel and inhumane, yet he could never bear
to see an animal mistreated. He had always kept his animals well fed, clean, comfortable, and pain-free. Was *he* comfortable and pain-free? Was Nicole? What entity was charged with the prevention of cruelty to them? he wondered. The
sound of a sudden movement startled him, but it was only one of the cats stirring. He again focused on his work. Finally, he reached a point at which the laws,
the inspectors, the whole of his worries faded like a nightmare exposed to the
first rush of sunlight. David was inside a mammalian brain and fascinated with
its majestic geography. He did not hear the clock's hourly beep again until six the
next morning.

He had completed his surgeries on the fourth and fifth cats when he heard the
first voices in the hallway that Monday morning. While he was cleaning up,
someone knocked on his door.

"Yes?" He cautiously opened the door a sliver.

"Excuse me, Doctor."

David relaxed. It was only Gary, the supervisor of the janitorial crew. "My attendant left a note that you didn't want service on Thursday or Friday, so I came
this morning for the trash."

"Thanks, Gary, but I'd like to empty the garbage myself for the next few
weeks, until I let you know otherwise."

David's foot behind the door prevented it from opening wider and exposing
the animals. Gary glanced at him curiously. The surgeon smiled uneasily, hoping
the cats would remain silent.

"Okay, Gary?"

"Sure, Doctor. Just let me know when you want my people in there again."

"I will."

David finished his work, satisfied that no one else had seen him. It was early
enough to leave the building before the researchers arrived. He slipped out of the
lab and locked the door. Just then a hand grabbed his shoulder, startling him.

"What are you doing here, pal? And why are you so jumpy?" It was Randy.

"I had some cleaning up to do. What are *you* doing here?"

"I have a meeting in the building. How's Nicole?"

"Fine."

"Say, I'm glad I ran into you."

"What's up?"

"You know the old man hasn't issued any statements about you."

"I heard he has no comment."

"He's hesitating. No one knows what he'll do. I spoke to him yesterday, and I think he's mortified at the prospect of punishing you. Maybe he'll find a string to pull. That's why you need to be on your best behavior."

David thought he heard a cat stirring behind the door.

"Don't break any more laws, David. Don't even jaywalk. And maybe the old man will decide to rejoin the human race and save you. But you must be a *model citizen.*"

"I want you to stay out of this! You didn't denounce me enough. You weren't harsh enough—"

"If you don't have any sense, then do it for me, because I worry about you. Even though I have a squad ready to pounce on you if you so much as glance at the OR, there are lots of other rules you could break. Promise me you won't."

"You know my promises aren't worth much." David's head dropped painfully at the mention of the subject of promises.

"So make one that is. Promise you'll be a model citizen."

"Drop it."

"The old man's your only chance, so don't throw kerosene on the fire . . . or maybe you already have." Randy's eyes moved suspiciously to the lab door. "What are you doing here anyway? Cleaning up? At seven in the morning?"

David's eyes widened in panic as he noticed a ball of cat fur on his pants. Would Randy see it? Would he uncover a secret that he must not learn?

"Okay, okay! Damn you, brother," he whispered, his irritation softened by affection. "Don't worry about me. I'll try to be a . . . reasonably . . . model citizen."

❧ 17 ❧
A Light Extinguished

A few blocks from the university campus, the rising sun hit the east wing of Riverview Hospital, turning its rows of windows into sheets of sparkling crystal. Inside a glass panel midway up the tall structure, the still-pink rays of early morning light warmed the face and wrinkled the nose of a sleeping Nicole Hudson. She dreamed of dancing under a spotlight on the stage of a great hall, with her red ballet slippers brushing against a blond wood floor. Other dancers surrounded her in a kaleidoscope of costumes. As the sun's heat intensified in the hospital room, the patient grew warmer, began tossing, and finally awakened. She threw off the covers and opened her eyes. The face so untroubled in sleep suddenly lost its serenity, for the scene with her eyes open was blank. The precious sensation of a new day's sun was reduced to a few tiny beads of perspiration on her warm forehead.

Nicole resisted an impulse to close her eyes again and slip back into her dream world, the only place where she could experience vivid color and effortless movement. *What time is it?* she wondered, cautiously reaching for her bed stand. Her fingers gently touched a pitcher of water, then a box of candy, the whole of her concern aimed at not toppling— She was startled by something falling to the floor. *The plastic cups again,* she figured. Her groping hand reached a cool metal object, the talking clock her doctor had given her, and she pressed a button on it.

"Seven thirty-five," said the obliging clock.

She was thirsty, but how long would it take to find the cups? When she had dropped them yesterday, their retrieval had taken thirty minutes. Perhaps she wasn't thirsty after all. Today was Monday, the day her doctor said she could go home. *Home!* She mouthed the word longingly. With her roommate having been discharged the previous day and with the nurses usually busy, she wondered if she could walk to the bathroom without their assistance that morning. After five days, and with all of her secondary injuries virtually healed, she could surely travel four feet. The dancer feared venturing to the bathroom without the watchful eye of another, yet she was determined to make the treacherous journey. She had always relished being alone because it had meant being unencumbered, but now it meant something very different—being helpless and terrified.

She stood up, grabbling in the bedding for her silk robe. She had lost weight, she thought, tying the garment around a vanishing waist. She stopped herself in the act of reaching for the mane of hair that she always pulled to the outside after putting on clothing. In its place was coarse stubble on a still-tender scalp riveted with stitches. She swayed unsteadily. Was it the surgery that had sapped her energy, she wondered, or the constant strain of having to relearn the simplest tasks of living?

She stepped tentatively. With her arms outstretched and groping for obstructions, she felt very . . . blind. She stumbled over something on the floor. Getting down on all fours, she discovered it was the plastic cups. She reached behind her to toss them onto the bed, but it was not there. Pivoting, she tried again. And again. Finally, she located the bed and redirected herself toward the closet and bathroom. Although she yearned for the safety of crawling, she rejected the indignity of it, so she forced herself to her feet, trying to forget that a week ago she could fly across a stage.

She reached the closet, grabbing her clothes and overnight bag. A few steps away, she found the bathroom. Its confined space better matched the limits of her ability. Yet here, too, there were pitfalls. She'd forgotten her towel! Instead of making the pilgrimage back to the bed stand, she used paper towels. Then there were the cans of deodorant and hairspray. One she needed, but the other was a carryover from what seemed like an eon past, when she'd possessed hair to spray. Which was which? She sprayed both into the air so she could sniff them to decide. Uncertain of the color of lipstick she chose or the accuracy of her application, she wore it anyway, determined to resume her normal grooming. After changing into her street clothes, she made the dreaded trip back to her bed, tripping over a chair that seemed to threaten her life.

Nicole sat up in bed, waiting to hear the comforting voice of the only person who gave her hope—her doctor. Breakfast came first. An attendant placed it on her sliding table.

"Good morning, Nicole. How pretty you look. Are you going home today?" asked a passing nurse.

"I'm hoping to."

"How are you feeling?"

Nicole sensed the familiar undertone of pity evident in everyone who spoke to her.

"I'm fine!" she said with a smile, refusing to be the last act of a Greek tragedy.

"Would you like me to feed you breakfast, dear?"

"I'd like to try eating by myself."

"Let me slide this tray closer to you. Your toast is at twelve o'clock, your eggs are at six, sausage at nine. You've got milk and juice at two and three o'clock. And I'll put these plastic cups back on the bed stand. Is there anything else you need?"

"Yes, a TV or radio."

"You know the answer, honey. You've got CD players with music and movies.

"I want to hear the news. Can someone read me the newspaper?"

"You'll have to ask Dr. Lang."

Nicole had already argued with Dr. Lang about the ban he had imposed on her hearing the news.

"It's my job to handle the news. Your job right now is to get well," he had said.

"But I can't have you hiding things from me," she had insisted.

"Of course you'll learn everything, but will you give yourself a few days first? And will you let *me* tell you?"

Losing her ability to function had been so devastating that she acquiesced. But now she was ready to hear the news and would insist that Dr. Lang tell her.

"I'm going to check on the other patients, Nicole. Call if you need me," said the nurse.

"Thank you."

The smell of breakfast nauseated Nicole, yet she knew she needed food. Her plate was a mysterious landscape of hills and valleys on which her fork must somehow land. How tempting it was to discard the utensil and eat with her hands like an infant! She sighed. A week ago her life was filled with theater performances, television appearances, movie offers. Now the whole of her awareness was reduced to a toddler's world of learning to walk and eat. She might have to sink to the level of a toddler, she thought, but she was *not* going all the way down to the level of infant. She clung to her fork as to the last vestige of her dignity.

Her first attempt at spearing her food brought nothing to her mouth but the empty tines. Her second attempt brought a morsel of eggs. Success! Her third attempt brought too much food, spilling the eggs on her blouse. She fumbled for the water pitcher on her bed stand but hit something metallic that crashed to the floor. Damn! Was it the little talking clock she liked, the gift from her doctor? She removed pieces of egg from her silk blouse, and then wiped the area with a napkin. Was there a spot? She could not tell.

The difficulties of the morning proved too much for the dainty ballerina, who had dedicated her life to graceful, precise movements. She felt a familiar impulse of her childhood, a driving urge to run away from an intolerable situation. But she could not flee from the new, dark tunnel of her existence as she had fled from a series of foster homes. In desperate protest against helplessness and fear, the new trespassers in her life, she slid her food away and cried. The tears suddenly, violently gushed down her face.

When you grow up, you'll be in charge, little one. She heard the distant words of a voice from her childhood, the one reassuring message that had made her tumultuous younger years tolerable and filled the future with hope. Prior to her injury, the only other time she had felt so helpless and cried so inconsolably was when she was eight, clinging to the voluminous robe of Sister Luke at St. Jude's Parish. The nun had stroked the hair of Cathleen Hughes, who would later become Nicole Hudson, and whispered the simple words that were to sustain her through childhood: *When you grow up, you'll be in charge, little one.*

After her mother had left her on the steps of St. Jude's Parish, eight-year-old Cathleen Hughes had walked through the dimly lit chapel. She passed the old convent behind the church and entered an adjacent building where the nuns maintained a soup kitchen and daytime shelter for the homeless. There, amid the stench of the unwashed bodies and alcoholic breath of the shelter's inhabitants, the little girl found the person whom she was looking for, the person who had comforted her before, an elderly nun with a stern voice softened by caring eyes: Sister Luke.

"My mother left me here," the child said simply.

Scanning the shopping bag of clothing that the child carried with her, Sister Luke's eyes moistened. In the days that followed, the nun placed a bed and night-stand for the child in a small, windowless room that had served as a closet in the convent. The child soon developed a happy routine. She awoke, made her bed, did her assigned chores, attended school, took classes at Madame Maximova's School of Ballet, and then returned to the convent for more chores and bed. She was like a butterfly, a sweet presence that buzzed about, busy with its own affairs and careful not to disturb anyone, least it be shooed away.

When Cathleen's mother failed to appear after a few days, Sister Luke investigated. "Your mother moved away and left no forwarding address."

A calm face accepted the news. The child met abandonment with resourcefulness. She filled the vacancy left by her mother with the business of her life. She had an understanding with Sister Luke: Provided that she attended to school, religious services, and chores, she could do as she pleased with the rest of her time, which of course meant going to Madame Maximova's. For the first time, the child's life was undisturbed by the violent, unprovoked—and terribly frightening—rages of a troubled mother. Rather than being shattered by her mother's disappearance, the child seemed content with her new surroundings. She did not notice the austerity of the convent, only its serenity. She did not think of her unadorned room as gloomy, only as peaceful, even comfortable, compared with sleeping in the dirty vestibule of her mother's residence on nights when she had been locked out.

Cathleen somehow managed to avoid the emotional minefield that blasted the lives of untold thousands of other abandoned children. An uncanny self-sufficiency rescued her from helplessness. Her quiet, instinctive dislike for her mother kept her out of the quicksand that had so readily swallowed other children. In her own way, the child had abandoned the mother long before. From this came the mental armament that shaped her character and determined her future.

She did not pine for her mother's helpless screams and angry rages. She did not miss embraces never received. She did not yearn for the staggering creature who gave her nothing. And she did not blame herself for her mother's disappearance or agonize over whether the woman would come back. She was not crushed over losing a booby prize. Cathleen never spoke of her mother again. Only once did she intimate her feelings to Sister Luke: "When I play the sleeping princess in the ballet, I can have *her* mother and father." If two words could sum up the calm practicality with which Cathleen responded to her mother's disappearance, they would be *That's that.*

The fondness that she never felt for her mother stirred inside her for Sister Luke. "One day you're going to be a great ballerina, little one, like the dancers here," said the nun, on the day she gave Cathleen a book about the ballet. The child turned the pages of the treasured volume and stared in amazement at the stunning color photographs of ballerinas on stage. In a spontaneous, unprecedented burst of affection, she threw her arms around the nun and kissed her. In an equally uncharacteristic display, the austere Sister Luke embraced the child. The book's glossy cover soon became worn from the untold times that Cathleen held the volume under the old lamp by her bedside, read its majestic descriptions of famous ballets, lovingly studied every detail of its pictures, and dreamed of the future.

"I've tried everything to find your mother, little one. She's disappeared from the face of the Earth," declared Sister Luke one day. "I have no choice, you know; I have to report this to the authorities."

Cathleen did not understand what this meant or why it touched the nun's face with sadness, until the day when two officials from the Department of Child Welfare appeared in the church to take her away. St. Jude's Parish, it seemed, was not a facility for rearing children. It had no counselors, no program, no dormitory, no license—only a warm bed and a caring nun who permitted a child to dream. The tears Cathleen did not shed for her mother were unleashed in a fury that day. The two male officers employed all of their strength to pry the child's arms from their viselike grip around Sister Luke's waist.

"No, no!" the child screamed, twisting violently and kicking the officers who carried her away. Her shrieks roared through the huge, hollow inside of the church. "I don't want to go! Let me stay! Let me stay!"

The stern voice of Sister Luke quivered, too. "When you grow up, you'll be in charge, little one. You'll be a great ballerina, and you'll do as you please."

For the next five years, until at thirteen she assumed the name of Nicole Hudson and ran away to San Francisco, Cathleen lived more like a vagabond than ever before. She felt as if she were being shuffled from one train to another, all parked and going nowhere, in the vacant depot called foster care.

Cathleen's case irked the social workers because their placements did not stick. If she were sent too far from Madame Maximova's, she would invariably run away. Like a homing pigeon once fed on kindness, she would fly back to her sanctuary at St. Jude's for a temporary respite before being recaptured.

"We can apply for a special allowance for the foster family, so they can send you to dance lessons near the home," offered one caseworker. "We're only supposed to request special allowances for the handicapped, but let me talk to my supervisor." The special allowance never came. Cathleen was not handicapped, and there was no extra boost for the gifted.

Many families found her intolerable. She did not dawdle in conversation at the dinner table; she did not hug or kiss; she had no interest in television or children's games. "I don't like kids. They're boring," she declared at age ten. When she was not engaged in dancing or schoolwork, she would lose herself in the sweet mustiness of library shelves, devouring literature, especially plays, which swept her into the mysterious enchantment of the stage. While the other children in the household were listening to rock music or playing video games, Cathleen would be in her room reciting the lines of Lady Macbeth, Joan of Arc, or other great roles from the classics. She passionately mouthed lines only partly understood and liberally mispronounced, because she liked the sense they gave her of immensely important things occurring on the stage.

Cathleen was returned many times to the child welfare agency. Her folder was one of the thickest. It stated that she was withdrawn, antisocial, maladjusted. At some point she became legally eligible for adoption. Being an unusually beautiful child, with finely etched features, giant blue eyes, and luxurious, flowing blond hair, she piqued the interest of many families. However, once they became acquainted with her oddly distant manner, there were no takers at the auction.

When Cathleen was thirteen, something unprecedented occurred. The Flemings, an affluent Westchester family, offered her foster care specifically because of her interest in dancing. The Flemings thought that Cathleen would provide companionship for their own daughter, Rita, who also studied ballet. Besides, helping a needy child was "the Christian thing to do," said the stately teacher, Mr. Fleming, who was being considered by a prestigious private school for the post of headmaster. Cathleen did not mind Mr. Fleming's flaunting her at social gatherings and his associates' whispering about "that girl from the slums whom Fleming has so generously taken in," because she and Rita were allowed to attend dance classes in New York's finest studios.

Rita was shocked by the disciplined dance practice, the grueling hours, and the austere dedication of Cathleen. When Rita's feet hurt, she stopped practicing. When she received a phone call, she left the barre. When there were boys to meet, Rita skipped practice. She was revolted by Cathleen's battlefield-blistered feet. "Lighten up, girl. Dancing's not supposed to be a holy crusade," Rita said

to Cathleen one day. "So what if you get a step wrong? Why do you have to re-
peat it fifty times? You'll be burned out before you're fifteen."

Both girls auditioned for the leading role, a dancer's part, in their school's annual theatrical production. Cathleen, the superior dancer and actress, was chosen, and Rita became her understudy. Cathleen was thrilled. This would be her
first stage appearance! She loved the part and plunged herself into rehearsals. A
quiet excitement punctuated her formerly distant manner. She laughed at the
dinner table, volunteered to help Rita's younger brother with his homework, and
at bedtime even kissed the surprised Mrs. Fleming.

The girls said nothing to each other of the role, Cathleen out of sensitivity
for Rita's disappointment, Rita out of an unbearable resentment. In Cathleen's
absence, however, Miss Fleming threw a tantrum. If her parents had not taken
in that stray creature, Cathleen, their *real* daughter would have gotten the part!
In the week following the auditions, Rita could not eat, sleep, attend class, or
speak to her parents. Her life was in shambles. Mr. Fleming called Cathleen into
his study.

"We've provided you with an excellent opportunity, Cathleen, probably the
best you'll ever have, to live in a real home with a real family. We've shared our
blessings with you because you were needy." Mr. Fleming paused, expecting a
display of appreciation.

Cathleen waited silently, facing him across his desk.

"I think you know how much Rita would like to have the leading role in her
school play. Because she's part of your family now, I thought you might want to
do her a good turn by . . . stepping down."

"But I don't want to step down, Mr. Fleming. I was chosen for the part."

The dignified face flushed. "Look, Cathleen, without our generosity, you
would never have gotten into our school or known about our theater production.
We've given you so much. I'm suggesting one good deed from you to help someone who's treated you like a sister. It would build your character."

"But Mr. Fleming, how would it build my character to give Rita a part that
she wasn't chosen for?" Cathleen asked simply.

Mr. Fleming picked up a pencil and tapped it irritably. "We've grown so fond
of you, Cathleen. I'm sure you wouldn't want to be difficult." He looked at the
unmoved face before him and broke the pencil in half. "I mean, you wouldn't
want us to have to . . ."

"I'll save you the trouble of returning me to the agency like a broken toaster,
Mr. Fleming."

"What do you mean?"

"You'll see."

That night Cathleen ran away from the Flemings. She took one thousand dollars from a stash that Mrs. Fleming kept in a saucepan under the sink. That was how thirteen-year-old Cathleen Hughes purchased the one-way bus ticket to San Francisco and the phony driver's license of Nicole Hudson, the character she would play for the rest of her life. A year later in San Francisco, the newly created Nicole Hudson had a job, an apartment, a car, a checking account. In a package with no return address, mailed from New York by a co-worker vacationing there, Nicole returned the stolen money to the Flemings, with interest.

The thirteen-year-old's entry into adulthood was a headfirst dive. Having run away numerous times, she knew there were nationwide hotlines established to locate her. Computer screens across the country would display her picture. She was a thief, besides. If caught, she could be sent to a juvenile detention center or caged for five more years in foster care, until she turned eighteen. If she were stopped at this critical time when she needed rigorous training, her dream of becoming a professional dancer would be ruined. The child had to do what fugitives do: She had to lay low.

She obtained a job in a place that asked no questions—a gentlemen's club on the outskirts of town. Its management treated the state inspectors well enough so that they, too, found little to question. The adolescent's pay was excellent and the evening hours perfect for intensive dance training during the day. Although her ballerina's form did not fit the typical mold for the club, she managed to be more alluring than the other women with her own special assets—the sinewy dancer's legs, the cascading blond hair, and the remarkable sensuality of a superbly toned body that was grace itself. In the noisy, smoke-filled club, the serious ballerina became a stripper.

She would have done much more to keep her freedom, but fortunately for Nicole, no one else knew that. Her striking beauty and dazzling dance numbers were sufficient to draw hordes of customers to her stage, dropping money at her feet. She broke all of the club's rules: She did not smile, mingle with the crowd, or dance private numbers. However, her aloofness only intensified her customers' excitement. Even then her dancing held the rare and stunning harmony of the sensuous and the spiritual that would become her trademark. Because she acquired the largest following of all the girls, the management permitted her to do as she pleased. Hence, she was gaped at extensively but remained untouched. The sublime innocence of the princess, displayed by Nicole in her first leading role at age sixteen and in all of her roles thereafter, was real.

Nicole was not ashamed of her work, because during those years in San Francisco, when she was in charge, her dance training at last was unimpeded.

Now, as she lay in her hospital bed, the helpless prey of despair, she thought again of the last time that she had felt so utterly powerless, when at age eight, she was taken from her sanctuary at St. Jude's. She heard the distant echo of Sister

Luke's stern but caring voice: *When you grow up, you'll be in charge, little one. You'll be a great ballerina, and you'll do as you please.* She had come so far. She had blasted out of the railway yard that fenced her. But just as her long-awaited train had reached its starry destination, it had veered into a tunnel! She buried her face in her hands and cried.

18

The Phantom Returns

"Hey, what's the matter?"

The question floated to Nicole from somewhere in her hospital room. Over the desperate sound of her sobs, she recognized the voice of the man who could restore light to her life. She tried to compose herself.

"What is it, Nicole?" David covered her limp hand with two sympathetic ones.

"Something too trivial to involve you."

"Try me."

"It's nothing, really. I'm afraid I'm . . ." the pain still caught in her throat, "wearing . . . my breakfast."

He glanced at the food stain on her blouse. "Do you have anything else to wear besides your breakfast?"

"There's a sweatshirt in the closet."

He brought the item to her. She slipped it over her head while he protected the stitches from catching. Without hair, her features stood out in stark relief, like a stage without a backdrop, stripped of all but its essential elements. Her eyes had grown larger above the gaunt cheekbones, her nose more finely sculpted, her lips fuller. The startling beauty of her face held him.

"Thank you, Doctor."

"Feel better now?"

"Yes."

"After a few lessons with your teacher, Mrs. Trimbell, you'll be eating sushi and escargot."

She managed a weak smile.

"Meanwhile, I brought you this." He placed a large plastic cup in her hand.

She sipped what had become her principal nourishment since entering the hospital.

"Hmmm. Chocolate this morning. Thank you!" Nicole, who had never been ill, assumed that all neurosurgeons brought their patients milkshakes.

David examined the incision and asked how she was feeling. "You're doing fine. You can go home today."

Her face showed the first sign of eagerness since the surgery, a mere hint of her former radiance, yet the sight made him forget his sleepless night in the lab.

"I'll ask Mrs. Trimbell to pick you up." She heard the click of his opening cell phone and the sound of dialing.

Mrs. Adeline Trimbell was a retired scrub nurse whom David had introduced to Nicole. Before becoming a nurse Mrs. Trimbell had been a teacher of the blind. The stout, elderly widow was amenable to moving in with Nicole temporarily to assist her between the surgeries. When Mrs. Trimbell quoted her fee, the dancer was shocked at the modest amount.

"I'll have to pay you double that. There are lots of things I'll need you to do for me, and I don't want to feel as if I'm imposing."

"Don't worry, you won't be imposing," said Mrs. Trimbell, "because you'll be doing most of those things for yourself." The crusty voice bore no hint of pity.

"I think she'll do," Nicole had told David.

Hence, Mrs. Trimbell had moved into the guest room of Nicole's Manhattan condominium to become her teacher and companion.

"I have Mrs. Trimbell on the phone, Nicole. She's coming to take you home."

"Were my personal belongings brought home from my dressing room at the theater?" The show's producer had gently requested that Nicole remove her things.

"Mrs. Trimbell can hear you. She says your things were brought home."

"What about all of the old flower arrangements? Were they brought to my apartment undisturbed, as I specified?"

David stared at her intently while Mrs. Trimbell answered the question on the phone.

"Yes, Nicole," his voice softened, "the flowers were brought to your home."

"The wicker basket with the African lilies and the painted vase with the birds-of-paradise and the wooden box with the hyacinths—did they make it okay?"

"Yes," said David, repeating Mrs. Trimbell's answer. The tenderness in his voice was a caress. He had no idea that she had saved the withered flowers.

"And the lilies. I got them just before the accident. Are they still alive?"

Nicole heard murmurs from the phone.

"Mrs. Trimbell says the lilies are holding their own."

"Good!"

David drank in the sight of Nicole savoring his gifts. When she completed the inventory of her flower remnants, he ended the phone call.

"Doctor, there's one thing we must discuss. I want to know what's happened with the surgery. I mean, it was illegal. You're not in any trouble, are you?"

"Nothing I can't handle," he lied. His lawyer was burning the phone lines that morning, protesting his suspension. "I'm waiting for a phone call about the matter. I'll let you know as soon as I learn more and can tell you where we stand."

"You're sure you're going to tell me? Remember, you promised."

"We'll talk today. And don't worry. Okay?"

"Okay."

If she could have seen him, clad in jeans and a polo shirt on a Monday morning, with no patients to see, having just spent a sleepless night breaking more rules, she would have known that her suspicions were justified.

His squeeze of her hand was like a staccato note. That meant good-bye. During the week of her confinement, she had come to know this faceless man by the touch of his hand on hers. A long squeeze meant that he wanted to give her important instructions, and she was to pay attention. Two hands covering hers meant that he knew she was in pain and that he felt it also. A short squeeze meant that he was leaving and would return later. As he turned to go, she called to him.

"Doctor, there's one more thing."

"Yes?"

"Did anything come for me? A gift of some kind?"

"You know about the stuff on the windowsill, don't you? The fruit and candy?"

"Not the things from the theater people. I mean . . . well, I guess I shouldn't hope for it after what happened, but were there any . . . flowers?"

He suddenly realized whose gift she was seeking. "Why . . . yes, of course! A gift was addressed to you in care of me, so it came to my office by mistake. Flowers, I believe."

For one cloudless moment, the joy she exuded from the stage returned to Nicole's face. "Oh, Doctor! Could you possibly have them brought to me?"

"It's done, Nicole. I'll get them right now."

Another staccato squeeze of the hand, and David left to make a beeline for the nearest florist, brushing past Nicole's next visitor, her agent, Howard Morton.

"Hi, Nickie. How are you doing?" Morton kissed her cheek.

Nicole hated the funereal tone she had heard in her agent's voice since her accident.

"When the movers took your personal things from your dressing room, they forgot to take these. I figured you'd want them."

He placed in her hands her first ballet slippers. She recognized their touch.

"I *do* want them! Thank you." She hugged the shoes like an old friend.

There was an awkward pause. Morton seemed to have nothing more to say. He poured himself a cup of water and walked around the room.

"So is Darlene going to play Pandora, Howie?"

"Yes."

"But only until I have the second surgery and get my job back, right?"

Morton said nothing. He knew something Nicole did not. He knew that her doctor was suspended and that there was not going to be a second surgery.

"Howie, my injury is grossly exaggerated. I can actually see you pretty well." She looked to her right.

"Nickie, I'm on your left," he said sadly.

Without vision Nicole was discovering that sounds were more difficult to locate than she would have imagined. "Anyway, if I had to, I'm sure I could dance

Triumph with my *eyes closed.*" She emphasized the last two words, as if testing the waters.

"With twenty other dancers out there? Nickie, they're not going to put a guardrail on Mount Olymp—" He stopped abruptly, as if regretting his words.

"It's really a moot point, because after the second surgery I'll pass the eye test for a bomber pilot."

She sensed a forced cheerfulness in his laugh.

"How about my interview with Gloria Candrell? Have we gotten offers from that? Any movie roles or TV specials? I hope you're telling everyone that in three short months I'll be back."

"We'll see, Nickie." He did not want to mention that the calls about her had stopped. "Say, have you thought of writing a book about your accident? I could sell that."

"I want to dance, not write books!"

Another awkward pause. Then she heard a little thump that sounded like Morton's cup tossed into the wastebasket.

"Nickie, I really need to get to the office."

She fought the burning sensation in her eyes; she would not cry in front of Morton.

"I know you're discouraged, Howie, but you'd best be ready for my comeback." *You or another lucky agent*, she added to herself.

"Sure, honey," he said halfheartedly. "You take care. I'll call you, okay?" He hugged her.

As he left, she had the sinking feeling that she was not going to hear from Howard Morton again. Another person abandoning her! But there was someone she *could* count on, she thought, resting her head on the pillow and waiting for her flowers.

Soon the stale air of her hospital room was replaced with a luscious fragrance.

"I smell roses! They're roses, aren't they?" she cried, as David set a basket of blooms on her sliding table and wheeled it close to her.

"They *are* roses. Does that please you, Nicole?"

"Yes! Thank you for bringing them!"

She folded her long, limber legs tight against her torso, propped herself up in bed, and ran her cheek along cool, velvety petals. She caressed the blossoms, inhaled their perfume, listened to David's description of the ensemble, and sighed with delight.

"So they're a deep burgundy, like a vintage wine?" she said, echoing his account.

"Indeed."

"I know there's a letter somewhere."

David tucked one in the arrangement and pushed it toward her searching fingers.

"Here it is!" she cried, lovingly pressing the sealed envelope to her breast.

"Shall I read it to you?" His voice defied his will by uttering a question that he had resolved not to ask.

"Oh, no! Thank you for offering, Doctor, but I couldn't let you."

"Why not?" The rebel voice continued.

"Because this is personal, and, well, you're a man."

"I plead guilty to that."

"And because you're amused. I hear it in your voice," she admonished him. "I won't allow anyone to make light of this matter."

"I'll try to show the proper respect."

She rubbed the envelope between her long, graceful hands, then ran it against her cheek. "Actually, it would be nice hearing this letter read by a man's voice. Maybe I *could* let you. After all, even though you're a man, you're also my doctor."

"I'm sure that would make it okay."

"But I can tell you're still amused!" She frowned. "Maybe if I told you something about the sender . . ."

"It might put me in the proper frame of mind."

"Do you have time? I don't want to impose."

"I do, and you're not." The place where he spent his life was locked to him, so he indeed had time. "Go ahead, Nicole. I'm listening." He sat on the edge of the bed.

She leaned back against her pillow dreamily. "His name is the Flower Phantom."

"The what?" He suppressed a laugh, lest he be reprimanded again.

"That's what I call him. 'The Phantom' for short. Actually, I don't know his name. He sends me beautiful flowers and letters, but always anonymously."

"I see." The note of understanding in his two simple words encouraged her to continue.

"The Phantom seems intensely troubled by something. I don't know what it is, only that he came to my show many times to escape from it, and I somehow gave him hope." With the supreme grace that becomes instinct through a life of ballet, she brushed a weightless hand gently along the roses as she spoke, caressing them. "I think he has a great passion in his life, something he loves in the same way that I love dancing. But there are obstacles. I don't know what they are, only that they frustrate him to the brink of giving up this great force in his life. I worry about him, because if he gives it up and if it's like dancing is for me"— her face tightened in pain—"then there'd be nothing left of him."

He grabbed her hand. "Maybe he *won't* give up. And maybe he won't let *you* give up dancing, not ever, no matter what happens!"

"Maybe." He detected a lingering sadness beneath the hopeful smile that she managed. "You know, I once saw the Phantom."

"Did you?" The amusement in David's voice had vanished, replaced by a solemnity that beckoned her to continue.

"I bribed a florist's employee to call if someone bought me flowers. That's how I tracked him down. I wanted to tell him something and to ask him a question. But he ran away before I got the chance. I wonder if he'll ever reappear."

She plucked a rose from the collection and brought it to her face. She twirled it, inhaled it, pressed her lips against it.

"If I could have chosen a man among thousands to have written me those letters, I would have selected him. He was handsome. Oh, yes! But he was much more. There was an intensity about him that seemed to penetrate through me . . . to frighten me. I felt certain that the passion I sensed in him was real, and that he felt it not only for his dream but also . . . for me."

She hesitated, as if she had gone too far. She did not know that at that moment two penetrating eyes were dancing over her with the same ardor.

"I see, Nicole."

"Every day, I draw his likeness in my mind. I'm afraid that with my blindness, I'll lose the memory of his face."

"You won't lose his face, Nicole. It might be closer to you than you think." He took the envelope from her. She heard the crisp sound of paper tearing. "Let's see what this guy has to say for himself."

"Wait!" A sudden panic pushed her hand out to stop him.

"What is it?"

"I'm afraid that after my injury, he'll feel differently about me. My agent and the theater people now talk to me with a sickening tone of pity! I don't want that from the Phantom."

"Why would he feel any differently?"

"Because he's *normal*. He deserves a woman who matches him."

"Why do you think you wouldn't match him?"

"I thought I *could* match him before. Then, I could have offered him so much! But now, look at me," she said, shrugging. "Of course," she added, her voice brightening, "if the second surgery works . . ."

He squeezed her hand with the clasp that meant *Listen, this is important.* "Nicole, I want the second surgery to work more than I ever wanted anything. But it's *experimental*, and you mustn't count on it. I can't raise false hopes."

"But it does give me a chance—my *only* chance—doesn't it?"

"Yes."

"Then it's the thing I live for. I know you don't like that, Doctor, but it's true."

He had no reply; it was the thing he lived for, too.

"If the Phantom ever came for me as I am now, he'd have to play nursemaid to me in my blindness, helping me with this and that and getting me sweatshirts when I dirty myself."

"Do you know that blind people get quite adept at taking care of themselves? And that the people who care about them don't mind helping?"

"I would never want to depend on the Phantom that way, to cling to him like a barnacle. I'd pretend I hated him first, so he'd find someone else—"

"Nicole, Nicole," he gently admonished, "it sounds as if this poor guy would be so thrilled to be around you that he might not even notice your blindness."

"But how could he not be repelled by a . . . major . . . handicap?"

"Maybe other things are more important. If your dancing gives him the hope to fight for his dream, then it seems there's something about you that's more significant to him. After all, everybody has eyes, but how much do they see? Maybe you have a vision that nobody else around him has, a vision that's *still* within you, even though you don't know it."

Her eyes retained an eerie alertness as she considered his words. "I hadn't thought about that."

"Then think about it, you hear?"

She nodded.

"Now let's see what this friend of the floral industry has to say for himself." He unfolded the letter and read to her:

Dear Nicole,

When you fell, the light you hung in the room of my soul came crashing down. The joy that had so comfortably taken residence there was crushed. Your laughter, the bright décor that gave warmth to that stark place, suddenly vanished. I wanted to wring the neck of circumstance and storm the unjust court of chance, demanding they give you back to me.

If only I could find the key that locks you from your joy, Nicole, how fast I would reunite you two! I know you'll find that lost key. You used it to unlock the heavy door of my despair and flood my house with your sunlight. I want to hold a mirror to the radiance you poured into my world, so you can see your own sublime reflection.

I sent roses to honor the endless summer that once made its home on your sweet face and that yearns to return to its rightful place. The dainty rose comes from hearty stock. Its roots run deep to brave the harshest winter. You, too, will blossom again in a new spring.

He handed her the letter. She pressed it to her lips, then placed it under her pillow. She lay back, closing her eyes, savoring the words. He knew whom she was envisioning. Beyond his wildest imagining, the blind presence before him had the capacity to see the beauty in his words and the truth in his soul. This revelation was a new torture for him. He could not risk complications with this case, above all others, and that included emotional ones. He warned himself: The Phantom must remain just that.

She opened her eyes and glanced in the direction of the man she had come to like and trust. "Doctor, thank you for reading the letter—and for listening."

"But you haven't finished your story. You said that you tracked the Phantom down because you wanted to tell him something and to ask him a question. What did you want to tell him?"

"That we can't confine our dreams to the world we see on the stage."

"Is that what you think he's doing?"

"He writes with such yearning for the joy he finds in me and my show, as if that kind of happiness isn't possible in his actual life."

David's mind burned over visions of his thwarted research, his quarrels with his wife, his disappointment in his father, his unspeakable exile from the OR, and the wrenching prohibition against performing Nicole's next surgery. "Maybe happiness isn't possible to him, Nicole."

"I hope that can't be true."

"What about the *question* you were going to ask him?"

"I wanted to ask him why he wrote to me, but once I saw his face, I knew the answer."

"What do you mean?"

"It was obvious."

"What was?"

"The predatory way he looked at me. The reason he wrote was clear. That man wanted me."

"So you've got this poor guy's condition completely diagnosed, haven't you? Maybe he wouldn't appreciate being such an open book to you!"

"Why, Doctor, you're protecting him from me. Now *I'm* amused!"

Just then Nicole detected the faint smell of starch, her only awareness of a properly dressed doctor in a crisp white jacket who had entered the room.

"Good morning. My, what beautiful roses! I wish my husband would send *me* flowers like that," a female voice said gaily.

"What are you doing here?" snapped David.

"I came to meet Nicole."

The patient sensed uneasiness in the room.

"Nicole, this is my wife, Marie Lang. She's a doctor at the hospital."

Marie took the dancer's hand and held it. "Hello, Nicole."

"How do you do, Dr. Lang?"

"It's Dr. *Donnelly.* I use my maiden name." After Nicole's surgery, Marie had ordered business cards in her maiden name and changed the nameplate on her office door. "I'm a general physician. Every CareFree patient must have one. It seems that you hadn't chosen yours yet, Nicole, so the system selected one for you. Here I am."

"But your husband's my doctor." Nicole removed her hand from Marie's clasp.

"He's a *specialist*. I'm your *general doctor*. Now, how are you feeling, dear?"

Nicole could not see a clawed hand seizing Marie's upper arm. She only heard a tightly controlled voice say, "Would you excuse us, Nicole?"

David's grip held firm as he led Marie to a vacant conference room near the nurses' station.

"David, you're hurting me! Let me go!"

He pushed his wife into the room and closed the door.

"Why are you doing this, Marie?" He shoved her back.

She stumbled over a chair, almost falling. "I want the honor of treating the patient whose case is wrecking our marriage and launching your new career as a public enemy. Why are you pretending you're still her doctor when you can't prescribe an aspirin anymore?"

"If you so much as check her pulse, I'll show you what a public enemy I am when I beat you up. After *that* story hits the press, you'll have to change your name again!"

"David, did it occur to you that I was just trying to help? What if you need to prescribe a pill for this lovely medical experiment? With your suspension, you can't do that yourself. But now you can do it through me."

He thought he detected a faint, gloating smile. "I don't want you to be a clearinghouse for me to practice medicine."

"What choice do you have, David? I'm trying to help, and for that you insinuate that I'm not trustworthy enough to care for your ex-patient."

"You're not to go near Nicole. She's in *my* care—and mine alone!—until after the second surgery. Understood?"

"Okay, David, have it your way. But tell me, how can she be your patient when you don't have any more patients? And how can you talk about a second surgery when there's not going to be any?"

"The only way I won't do that second surgery is if I'm dead."

"You may well be." She sighed. "Talk to me, David. You can't destroy our lives without discussing it. You can't sleep in the guest room and pretend I don't exist."

"When you're making your bed with my enemies, where do you expect me to sleep?"

"When you're making enemies with the entire medical profession, who is left for me to make my bed with? Talk to me, David. Explain why you've got to impose your point of view on the whole system—"

"The system is imposing its point of view on me! That remark is typical of the way you see things, Marie. I can't talk to you anymore. All that's important to you is getting the acceptance of your little circles, but I'd have to betray myself to give you that. Once, I thought you understood the things that mattered to me. When you were a student and we worked in the lab together, you were different. What's happening to you?"

"You were different, too, David. You were *building* your career, not *destroying* it. Back then you were quite interested in making your bed with me. Remember?" She smiled coyly, her eyes canvassing the ceiling in reminiscence. "I was the envy of the nurse brigade. They all wanted you, but *I* had you."

"Is that why you married me, to have a trophy to display?" He looked at her curiously, as if pondering a puzzle that he wanted to solve.

"Every woman wants to be proud of her husband. And every father wants to be proud of his son." She lowered her voice and spoke more cautiously, as if treading on thin ice. "David, your father is devastated by what you did. Just when the governor is about to pick him for a running mate, you bring a scandal on him. Just when my group practice is about to offer me a partnership, you publicly embarrass me. Just when Randy sticks his neck out to back you—"

His brother's name brought the first lines of real pain to his face. "Let's leave Randy out of this litany of how inconvenient it was of Nicole to be blinded."

"David, please listen to reason. You can still rescue yourself and our marriage. Give up this case, apologize to your father and the governor, and maybe Warren can save you. He wants to, you know, but you have to give an inch, too."

The anger drained from his eyes, replaced by a ruthless calm that she found more disturbing. "Marie," he said softly, "how can you curry the favor of fools who, through some glitch of history, claim to hold power over you? How can you call what you're doing medicine?"

"They don't just *claim* to hold power. They really do. I learned to live with that fact. It's called survival."

"But you don't just give in to them *reluctantly*, the way most of us do. You're the first one to support the new system, which is like slapping my face, and yours, too. That's what drives me into the guest room—self-respect."

"I'm not slapping your face, David. You make everything so black and white. I'm just asking you to bide your time, inch in with the right people, and get in the good graces of your father. Then they'll let you do your research."

"You know what I think of that viewpoint."

"I know, I know! No one has the right to trespass on the shrine you built to yourself and your passion for medicine."

He suddenly wondered about something. "What's *your* passion, Marie? What do *you* live for?"

"Isn't trying to keep my head above water enough of a mission?" she said, her eyes as dull as ashes from a fire long extinguished.

He wondered if there were something in Marie's life that meant to her what the OR meant to him and what dancing meant to Nicole. He thought of the opera and of cardiology, two areas that had sparked Marie's spirit. But she had given them up long ago.

"It's hard for me, David. I have so many patients. I have to watch the rules and still try to practice good medicine. And now *my* salary has to support the two of us."

When his head dropped, a subtle satisfaction seemed to brighten her face, as if she were about to score the winning point in a bitter match.

"What would you have me do, David? Join you in your futile rebellion? Randy had to denounce you, and you're okay with that. But when I merely switch to my maiden name, so I can preserve my patient base and pay *our bills*, which I now have to shoulder alone, you slam me. Do you know how punishing it is when you commit a blatantly self-destructive act, then reproach me for not following you off the cliff?"

He told himself that she had no choice. Like Randy, she was forced to oppose him. In fairness to her, he must try to understand her point of view. Then why couldn't he bring himself to answer the pleading arms that she placed around his waist and the fragrant auburn hair that she swept across his chest?

"David, can't we resolve this? Tonight let's have a candlelight dinner and a bottle of wine." She looked up alluringly. "Then later, when you're relaxed," she whispered, "we can call Warren and try to work out a way to reinstate you. I know you're committed to this case, but there'll be so many more victims to help in the future. For their sake, you might have to retreat now and give up this one case—"

He threw her arms off him and walked out.

In a room flooded with sunlight, Nicole sipped her milkshake in darkness. She had a simple desire: to place the Phantom's letter, which she had tucked under her pillow, into her purse. That way she would not leave the precious document behind when she was discharged. But where in the small space that had become a horror chamber was her purse? In the closet near the door? In the cabinet near the window? When she tried to reach those mysterious places, she almost invariably stumbled, causing a commotion. She decided to wait until Mrs. Trimbell arrived.

Just then the air in her room was displaced by sweet cologne as someone entered. "Excuse me. May I presume you're Nicole Hudson?"

"I am, so you may presume it."

"How do you do?" The visitor took her limp hand, shaking it vigorously. "My, what lovely roses!"

He waited for a response, but Nicole said nothing. The forced cheerfulness of his voice reminded her of a salesman with lacquered hair.

"I'm Commissioner Wellington Ames of the CareFree Department of Disabilities, New York City Region," he said with a flourish. "I just had to come to see you, even though I'm quite busy, with *nine* agencies under my directorship." He dismissed the inconvenience with a laugh, for a case with media attention was to Ames what dessert was to other people. "In view of your unfortunate circumstance, I wanted to meet you myself, *personally*."

"Why?" she asked indifferently.

"To welcome you to our family."

"What?"

"To welcome you to the CareFree Home for the Blind for your twelve-week rehabilitation program, followed by vocational training, so you can reenter the workplace as a Braille computer operator. Our gentle guardianship is free, as a gift from CareFree to our blind," he said, like a proud owner. "And after you rejoin the workforce, we offer affordable housing in our apartment building for the blind. There you'll meet others with the same challenges you have who will warmly welcome you into their lives. There's a room for social gatherings, so our blind can enjoy the camaraderie of their brothers and sisters in a caring community."

"I'm not going to any institution, so please leave now!"

"Ms. Hudson, I'm here at the request of your physician."

"You could not possibly be here at the request of David Lang, my doctor, so please go."

Nicole heard the crisp sound of paper unfolding. "I have here in my pocket a message from Dr. David Lang, handwritten across the enrollment application that we issued for you. He indicated that you most emphatically were not going to the Home for the Blind."

"So there."

"However, Dr. Lang's orders are now invalid."

"What do you mean?"

Nicole's voice was rising, its anger a thin veneer over her mounting fear. First the appearance of Dr. Lang's wife made her worry that he no longer controlled her case, and now this unctuous man called Dr. Lang's orders invalid. The milkshake shook in her hand as a dusty memory stirred in her mind of a screaming, desperate child being carried away by strange men.

"I mean that Dr. Marie Donnelly asked me to enroll you. And between you and me, there's quite a waiting list to get in, so you would be most privileged to be accepted—"

"Get out now! I'm warning you!"

"Ms. Hudson, do you realize who I am?"

"I won't go with you, so get out!"

She heard a nun's distant voice trying to sooth her, but she was terrified. She was being carried off roughly, violently, against her will.

"Now, really—" Wellington Ames grabbed Nicole's arm to reassure her.

"Don't touch me!"

Feeling that she was a helpless creature about to be overpowered, she swung desperately and flung her milkshake at him. Then she managed to locate the water pitcher, which she also hurled in his direction. The gasp from her visitor made her certain that she had hit her target.

"My goodness! What nerve! How dare you, Ms. Hudson? We need someone here to restrain you!"

"Get out and leave me alone!"

"With pleasure! We would never accept such a rude creature—" The voice stopped abruptly.

Nicole wondered why the man was suddenly silent. She did not know that with her sudden motion, the Phantom's letter had dislodged from beneath her pillow and dropped to the floor. Attracted by the handwriting, Commissioner Ames picked up the letter and began reading. His stunned eyes made three stops: on the letter, on the roses they alluded to, and on the handwritten note by David Lang across the enrollment application for his institution. The Commissioner of Disabilities discovered a secret that the writer had not shared with anyone. Wellington Ames's heart pounded wildly. He knew that this case was a political hot potato for Governor Burrow, the man whose favor he most ardently courted. After all, nine agencies were not the limit of Ames's ambition.

Nicole lifted the tray containing her uneaten breakfast, ready to hurl it. "Take big marching footsteps as you go, Mr. Beef Wellington, so I can hear them fade away from me and never return. Understand?"

The commissioner, wearing a beard of chocolate milkshake, slipped the Phantom's letter into his pocket.

David Lang entered, surveying the drenched person before him. "Hey, what's going on here?"

Nicole sighed in relief at the sound of a voice that would fix everything. "I'm so glad you're here, Doctor! This is Mr. Wellington somebody, from an agency for the handicapped. He wants me to go to an institution for the blind to become a Braille computer operator and live with a bunch of strangers."

"May I presume that you're Dr. Lang?" asked Ames, wiping his face with a handkerchief and looking distastefully at David's casual attire.

"I am. And my patient is not going to any institution. She'll receive the training she needs in her home," said a voice of such confidence that Nicole felt safe in lowering her food tray.

"That's what you indicated in your note to me, didn't you, Dr. Lang? I mean, it was *you* who wrote this note across the application, wasn't it?" The commissioner smiled oddly as he showed David the form.

"Yes."

"However, Dr. Donnelly asked me to—"

"She's not on this case anymore."

"But the patient needs rehabilitation."

"As I explained in my note, she'll receive training to make her self-sufficient in the world of the sighted, not to make her a permanent dependent in a sheltered world of the blind, which your agency creates."

"Of all the nerve! If she doesn't come with me, there are forms that the doctor in charge must complete. Who might that be?"

"Leave now," said David.

"How very rude of you! I'm a CareFree commissioner!"

Nicole raised the tray again. David took it from her, the fear on her face causing his temper to rise.

"You're upsetting my patient, and I won't allow that!"

"No one talks to Wellington Ames that way!"

"Get out of here!"

"Dr. Lang, you will regret this incident!" With his face a casualty of Nicole's milkshake and his hair a victim of her water pitcher, the soggy commissioner left the room.

David grabbed Nicole's hand. "Are you okay?"

"Yes, of course." A calm had returned to her voice.

"I don't want him bothering you again. Let me get his forms signed, so everything is official."

"Thank you!"

With the staccato squeeze of her hand that meant he would return, David left.

Nicole lay in bed, relieved that her intruder had been sent away. But she felt the grip of another opponent, the fatigue that was sapping her energy since the surgery. Slowly, disturbing thoughts about why the commissioner had described her doctor's orders as invalid slid away, and she fell asleep.

❦   ❦   ❦

"Nicole . . . Nicole, dear . . ."

A voice that she recognized awakened the dancer. A hand reached for hers, but Nicole instinctively pulled away.

"Nicole, I'm here to help you, dear. I know you'll be able to make this very difficult adjustment, even to dance again in some safe way. I want to ensure that you have everything you need to get your life back on track."

"I need the second surgery."

"I'm afraid there isn't going to be a second surgery."

"What?" Nicole's voice was a gasp.

"Dr. Lang has been *suspended* for performing your first surgery."

"What?!"

"It was just a crude experiment, not ready for human trials. Dr. Lang is well intentioned, and he's tried so hard on your behalf. But he was suspended by CareFree, which means he's barred from performing surgery in New York State. For five days now, he's been contacting every colleague he knows, every person of any influence, trying to get licensed somewhere else. But with the adverse publicity from this case, no other state is willing to accept him. Unfortunately, brain surgery isn't something you can do in a garage. So you see, dear," the voice said, softening with regret, "there's nothing he can do for you now."

The white sheet that was Nicole's face stared into a black void of space. She could not find a voice to speak or a muscle able to move.

"I want to help, Nicole. That's why I know it's right to tell you the truth. You may have heard of Warren Lang, the head of the Bureau of Medicine. He's David's father."

Another gasp of astonishment.

"You might think that his father can save him, but because Warren is expected to be chosen as the governor's running mate, he's under intense public scrutiny. He can't bend the rules for his own son with the media watching him through a microscope on this case."

Nicole felt an urgent pounding inside her head, a terrible pressure that she had experienced many times as a child, but never before with such urgency. A tunnel was collapsing on her, and she had to escape.

"I want so much to help you, Nicole. Do you want to get away? Convalesce in a place far from this unpleasantness?"

David Lang's phone dangled limply from his hand. He sat in a hospital lobby with his head down and his eyes staring vacantly at a tear in the carpet. After he had completed the administrative tasks to free Nicole of Wellington Ames, his lawyer had called.

The attorney had explored every avenue but had found no way to get David reinstated as a CareFree doctor. He had contested the agency's action against David, the lawyer explained, but to no avail. The attorney then tried to have the matter settled through the judicial system, where an impartial jury, rather than a CareFree administrator, would decide the case, but that attempt also failed. And challenging the constitutionality of CareFree's action would take too long to be of help in Nicole Hudson's case. His lawyer patiently discussed the issues involved.

David had attempted to get licensed elsewhere, but his difficulties with CareFree made other states unwilling to accept his application. He had even looked abroad, although the standard of medicine there had dropped in recent years. Other countries had variants of programs like CareFree, only older and in more advanced stages of budget cuts and deterioration. Nevertheless, he contacted influential medical directors abroad, but news of his problems had spread internationally. His case was a political hotcake that no one wanted to touch. His procedure was also clinically contentious, with most physicians skeptical about the feasibility of nerve regeneration. Medicine, like other lines of work, had an entrenched majority that avoided controversial issues, whether political or professional.

Thus, David could do no more than obtain a hearing within CareFree on rescinding his suspension and allowing Nicole's second surgery. The decision that would determine his and Nicole's future rested with the agency—and the father—he denounced.

He would have to tell Nicole the situation. But how? He walked toward the elevator, choosing his words.

He arrived at Nicole's room to find it crowded with nurses and aides. A stout older woman approached him, her face grave.

"Dr. Lang, I'm so glad you're here!"

"Mrs. Trimbell, what's the matter?"

The woman, whose expression was as severe as the tight bun of black hair at her neck, pointed to the empty bed. "When I arrived, Nicole wasn't here. We checked the restrooms, the patients' lounge, the corridors, and the other rooms on the floor, but we can't find her. Nicole has disappeared!"

❧19❧
Abraham and Isaac

Morning coffee awaited the secretary of medicine as he stepped into his limousine. Exposing a starched sleeve and gold cuff link beneath an exquisitely tailored suit jacket, Warren Lang waved absently to onlookers outside his Albany residence on that first Monday in August. With the turbulent events of the past week robbing his face of its perennial smile, he looked like a statesman with weighty concerns.

"Are we going to the office, Mr. Secretary?" asked the chauffeur.

"Yes, then in the afternoon I'll be going to the governor's mansion."

Charges against the lieutenant governor had intensified after the explosion five days earlier in Manhattan. He and other officials were accused of accepting kickbacks from construction companies awarded government contracts, including the firm believed responsible for the accident injuring Nicole Hudson and others. The faulty gas piping apparently involved in that explosion had been installed as part of a government contract, rekindling the scandal in the headlines. Although the lieutenant governor maintained his innocence, he finally withdrew from the race amid mounting pressure.

Because he was the target of a time-consuming investigation, the beleaguered official announced, he had decided not to run in the upcoming election. Publicly, Governor Mack Burrow accepted the decision with regret and expressed confidence that his second in command would be cleared of all charges. Privately, however, it was Burrow who forced his running mate off the ticket.

In speeches given across the state, the governor distanced himself from the kickback scandal. "I will select a new running mate of the highest moral character who will serve the public good," he promised.

Now Burrow had summoned Warren for a meeting that could only concern two topics, one that the secretary wanted passionately to discuss and the other that he wanted just as fervently to avoid: the first, his running for lieutenant governor; the second, his son.

Furrows appeared like fault lines on Warren's ashen face, a sign that a quake could rock the stately countenance. Entering a large hall in the BOM's Albany headquarters, he brushed his concerns aside. All eyes in the packed room turned to him as he began his weekly meetings with citizens.

"An official must be accessible, not sequestered in an ivory tower," he often said. "It's my duty to keep my finger on the pulse of the people." Hence, one morning a week the secretary was available to anyone wishing to discuss a health issue with him, at five minutes per person. "This is our private chat," he would tell those who came. In actuality, the "private" interviews were conducted before a gallery of waiting people, as well as aides directing traffic, keeping time, recording the proceedings, and processing papers.

The press hailed Warren's chats. "We commend Secretary Lang's open-door policy. He sets a new standard for caring government that is responsive to the people," said an editorial in a leading newspaper. A photograph of Warren sympathetically patting the hand of a distraught citizen appeared on the cover of a national magazine, accompanied by a flattering story titled "New Directions for Medicine." A blowup of that same picture hung in the living room of the secretary's home.

That morning a young mother approached him tentatively, as one would hesitate before nobility. Warren rose from his table, shook the woman's hand, and offered her a seat with the magnanimity of an aristocrat opening his door to a commoner caught in the rain. The woman pleaded a case for her five-year-old son.

"You see, sir, my Willie has trouble swallowing and breathing because his tonsils are growing together. But our doctor can't remove them because Willie hasn't had five episodes of tonsillitis in one year. Poor Willie, who comes up shy on most things, had only four. The doctor wants to take his tonsils out, and my Willie is having a terrible time, not sleeping or eating right, but it's something about 'practice guidelines' that Willie's case doesn't meet." She stared reverently at Warren, her hands clasped together as if in prayer. "I was hoping you could help us, sir."

Warren seemed to bask in her supplication. "I think we can look at the matter."

The woman bounced in her seat. "Can you really, sir?"

"I'll send you to Case Review, where I'll direct a coordinator to determine if there are extenuating circumstances to warrant an exception for your Willie."

"Oh, thank you, sir!"

An aide hovering over them made a note. All cases had the same disposition. They were sent to Case Review for a second look. Because they came from the Secretary's Court, as the proceedings were called, the coordinators automatically honored Warren's requests. The publicity generated from these propitious outcomes made favorable news stories for CareFree.

Warren smiled generously and shook the woman's hand. A news photographer snapped a picture of him in his custom-tailored linen suit with the woman in her polyester dress.

"You look happy, like you just hit the jackpot, ma'am," the photographer commented.

A sudden fear eclipsed Warren's smile. He thought of David's haunting words from their last meeting: *What must my patient do to win a door prize, too?*

The next citizen approached Warren, an older man self-consciously shifting his weight.

"Excuse me for bothering you, Mr. Secretary, sir." He fidgeted nervously. "It's about my bum knee."

"It's no bother at all." The man's timidity was like a splash of cool water to refresh Warren's confidence. "Please have a seat. . . ."

For lunch, the secretary traveled by limousine to a restaurant where his favorite table, overlooking the duck pond, was reserved for him. A glass of Chardonnay was poured ten minutes prior to his arrival so that it would warm to the temperature he desired. Extra tomato wedges were placed on his salad, and his steak was cooked exactly medium rare, as he preferred, without his having to ask. The staff, honored by such an important patron, kept a careful record of his predilections.

Just as Warren was enjoying the chef's personal visit to his table to check on the meal, a tall man with black hair entered the restaurant, giving the secretary a start. The man resembled David, triggering a sudden guilt in Warren, who felt like a child caught stealing a cookie. David's image seemed to be following him, sprinkling salt over his sweet pleasures. The secretary was relieved to find that the man was not his son, although he could not explain why. His emotions were like lightning bolts that struck with sudden fury and vanished just as quickly.

Warren returned from lunch to perform what he considered another important duty of his office: conducting hearings against doctors who violated Care-Free's rules. A health care provider could appeal a judgment imposed by CareFree and thus obtain a hearing before an administrator. "A public official must be a role model for his staff," Warren had said during a television interview. "I conduct the physicians' hearings myself, as my schedule permits, to set an example of firm justice for my agency."

Doctors privately snickered at such remarks, for Secretary Lang was known to lean far more toward *firm* than *justice* in his decisions on their cases. No doctor in the state wanted Warren as a hearing administrator. The press, however, reacted differently. "The tireless Dr. Warren Lang sets a new standard for hands-on management," said a flattering article in a New York magazine. "He runs the huge Bureau of Medicine like a corner grocery store, rolling up his sleeves and jumping behind the counter to lead his staff, a practice more agency heads should adopt."

Warren held the hearings in a setting resembling a courtroom. Every BOM office in the state had such a chamber. The administrator deciding the case sat at a judge's bench. The defendant, often accompanied by a lawyer, sat at a table to the administrator's right, with a CareFree attorney at a table to the left and a podium in between. The public observed from rows of seats behind the tables.

That afternoon Warren sat on the judge's swivel chair in the hearing room. One aide adjusted the lighting to the level the secretary preferred. Another brought him a glass of artesian well water with two limes. Another laid the file for the first case before him. Dr. Lang scanned the document as dentist Sheldon Fein, a balding man whose direct eyes stared out of his gaunt face, approached the podium.

"Good afternoon, Dr. Fein," said Warren with cool cordiality. Gone was the grandfatherly warmth displayed earlier in the day toward patients.

"Good afternoon, Dr. Lang."

"The record shows you've been waiving the copayments that you're supposed to collect from your patients."

"Yes, I have."

"You admit to the charge, so we have no dispute, Dr. Fein."

"We have no dispute over what I did, but I have a great dispute over what your agency made of it. I mean, a ten-thousand-dollar fine! The copayments were my own fees. How can my failure to collect money owed to myself be a crime?"

"Why didn't you collect your fees?" Warren asked sternly.

"It would cost me more to collect the fees than they're worth. Nobody thinks they have to pay for anything anymore," the dentist said resentfully. "Because I'm waiving fees owed to me, why should your agency care?"

"Did it ever occur to you, Dr. Fein, that the purpose of the copayments is *not* to embellish your income but to restrict the public's demand for your services, and that by waiving those payments, you give patients no reason to exercise restraint on their visits to your office? Do you realize that you are encouraging extra treatment and driving up costs, which are straining the system?"

"I realize that the system is straining me!"

Warren's eyebrows arched at the impertinence. "The judgment stands." He closed Dr. Fein's folder and tossed it to an aide. "Next case, please."

The dentist's expression oscillated between shock and anger until the latter prevailed: "I'll speak to my lawyer about this!"

The next folder appeared before Warren, and the next body appeared before the podium—psychologist Diane Lutz, a petite woman in her fifties with gentle eyes and an intelligent face.

"Good afternoon, Dr. Lutz," said Warren, flipping through her folder.

"How do you do, Dr. Lang?"

"It says here that you knowingly entered a false diagnosis in order to be paid for unauthorized treatment. You said you were treating a man for depression, which *is* covered by CareFree, but you were really conducting marriage counseling for the man and his wife, which is *not* covered." Warren peered up from the papers. "The record shows that you collected thousands of dollars of taxpayers' money under false pretenses, Dr. Lutz," said Warren accusingly.

"But my patient's depression has caused the problems in his marriage. Last year when I started treating the couple, CareFree paid for their marriage counseling. This year it doesn't. But I'm still treating the same couple."

"So what's your point, Dr. Lutz?"

"I mean that I couldn't abandon my patients in the middle of treatment because CareFree changed its rules, could I? No matter what we want to call it, depression or marriage counseling, it's the same case."

"But it's a different diagnosis. You switched the diagnosis."

"But the pain is the same!"

"Excuse me?" Warren asked threateningly.

Dr. Lutz looked down timidly, and a subtle satisfaction glimmered on Warren's face, as if he had won some kind of battle.

"But Mr. Secretary, if I had dropped the case when marriage counseling was no longer covered, then couldn't I be charged with patient abandonment? That's an infraction, too, isn't it?"

"So instead you decided to be charged with fraud?"

The comely psychologist did not protest, which seemed to permit the secretary to soften his tone.

"Next time," he added kindly, "call our office if you have questions about diagnoses and changes in our coverage. After all, we're here to help you."

"Well, I . . . uh . . ."

"I think the fine is justified. Now do you have any other questions?"

"I guess not," Dr. Lutz said disappointedly.

The secretary looked pleased with the dispatching of Dr. Lutz and signaled to his assistant for the next case. His aide approached, but this time without a new file, whispering something in Warren's ear, as a distinguished gray-haired man approached the podium.

"Good afternoon," said Warren to the tall man in a business suit.

"Good afternoon, Dr. Lang. I'm Kenneth Viceroy, the director of cardiology at Pace Memorial Hospital."

"I understand that we have no case against you, Dr. Viceroy."

"That's right, and CareFree has *never* had a case against me or any member of my department. We pride ourselves on following the law." The surgeon raised his right hand to his heart as if taking an oath.

"So what brings you here today?"

"An urgent request. We've applied for CareFree's approval to perform heart transplants at Pace Memorial, and we're told it will take thirty days more to obtain authorization. Yesterday a patient was admitted who is an excellent candidate for a transplant. With Whittier Medical Center having closed last month, the nearest hospital that can perform this procedure is fifty miles away, and the patient is too unstable to be moved. I came to ask your permission to perform this surgery immediately, or the patient could die. You see, we'll be using the same transplant team that worked at Whittier before it closed."

"Dr. Viceroy, your group may perform the surgery—"

"Wonderful!"

"—when you have met your regulatory burden."

"Dr. Lang, really!"

"We have a responsibility to ensure public safety."

"I recognize that, of course. But everyone on our team has experience performing transplants safely. Isn't there anything you can do?"

"There are reasons for the laws we have. If we could take on face value everyone who stands here and says he's okay, then we wouldn't need any regulations, would we? We'll just let anyone who says he's okay loose on the public. Is that what you're advocating?"

"Of course not. But can't you expedite the approvals?"

"We can't cut corners with public safety."

"But if we don't operate, the patient could die!"

"But if we make an exception for you, then others who have pending applications will want us to do the same for them. This undermines our system, Dr. Viceroy. We have the lives of millions of patients to consider. That's why we must focus on a wider context than one individual patient, and we must follow the proper procedures."

"I respect those procedures, of course."

"Yet you want me to disregard them?"

"But in this case—"

"Especially in the case of a complex, risky operation such as yours, it's even more important to ensure that society is protected. I'm confident the public can count on you, Dr. Viceroy, to continue your commendable record of regulatory compliance."

The cardiologist bristled, about to disagree, when Warren dismissed him by calling the next case.

Later that afternoon, Warren's chauffeur drove him up the winding hill to the fragrant front garden of the governor's mansion. Disturbing thoughts of his last encounter with David lingered, marring the secretary's usual rush of excitement on visiting his ardently wished-for future home. On his way to Burrow's office, he walked through the picture gallery of governors, reaching the empty place on the wall beyond Burrow's portrait where the next governor's picture would hang. As was his habit, he visualized his own likeness in the spot. But instead of feeling his usual thrill, the aftertaste of his bitter meeting with David intruded to evoke a pervasive, unnamed guilt. His son's acrid words seemed to echo ominously through the hall: *Before this matter is over, one of us will be finished.*

Warren recalled the people he had encountered that day who gave his life legitimacy: the patients who revered him as their only hope; the restaurant staff members who treated him like royalty; the doctors who, despite their frustrations with the system, respectfully accepted his authority. With the endorsement of all these people, how could one man make him avert his eyes from the portraits like an impostor undeserving of greatness?

In the opulent Victorian parlor outside the governor's office, an aide offered Warren a seat. While waiting for his appointment, the secretary observed the Burrow administration in action. The governor's personal secretary was telephoning a candy shop in Glens Falls to order a specific kind of truffle that Burrow craved. A writer composing Burrow's memoirs worked at a computer. One advisor left the inner office and another entered it, while many others waited. Warren had never known the governor to be alone. Like favorite pets, Burrow's aides followed him everywhere—in his bedroom while he dressed, in his bathroom while he shaved. Burrow constantly called meetings with aides, then wasted hours of their time by making them wait to see him. The governor was never punctual, Warren thought irritably, feeling like a boy at the dentist's office. Burrow seemed to take a peculiar pleasure in having a throng of people queuing to see him.

Before being appointed to his current post and establishing a home in Albany, Warren was an advisor to the governor and a frequent overnight guest at the mansion. Burrow, an early riser, had an odd fear of being alone and a reputation for waking anyone available for companionship. Warren remembered the governor's early morning wanderings into his room to talk. The pajama-clad, aging, somewhat helpless looking Burrow jarred with the persona of the commanding politician, masterful at playing special-interest groups against each other. Burrow could persuade the unions to back a bill and big business not to oppose it, all the while creating a universe of obligations, favors, and fears that he used to run the state. Warren wondered why such a man could not bear loneliness.

"These are my *real* friends," Burrow once said, pointing to a wall of twenty monitors installed in his office. The electronic array glowed with television news broadcasts and public-opinion surveys. The first time Warren had seen the massive display, the governor had laughed at his surprise. "The media and the polls," Burrow said reverently of his wall of videos, as leaders from another age might have uttered the words *truth and justice*.

Burrow employed a giant remote control to navigate the wall, muting the sound until his picture appeared on a particular screen, at which time he would engage the volume on it. On particularly stressful days, he was known to unleash the sound on all monitors simultaneously, creating a cacophony to rival a department store's television showroom. "These screens are the secret to running the state," the governor would say. Another menagerie of monitors existed in his bedroom. When the governor traveled, a team of technicians installed screens in his hotel rooms. He could not live without them.

Mack Burrow needed people, thought Warren, yet encounters with the state's most powerful politician invariably ended in a soliloquy. At Burrow's frequent dinner parties, he was always the center of attention. Warren, who held the seat beside the governor at the table, once declined an invitation in order to attend his grandson's piano recital. At Burrow's next dinner, Warren was relegated to a seat farthest from the governor. The secretary never declined an invitation from Burrow again.

If another person ventured to make conversation at the dinner table, it would invariably remind Burrow of a story that *he* liked to tell—of his ancestors, his childhood, his military service. He related to Warren how the first Burrow to reach America died fighting alongside George Washington in the Revolutionary War. Later Warren learned that the Burrow clan had not emigrated to America until a century after the War of Independence. Warren could understand, if not condone, the governor's mendacity to gain political advantage. But why would Burrow lie when no practical result could be achieved?

"Political oratory is like storytelling," Burrow once told Warren. "More important than truth is the response of the audience." Burrow often omitted major sections of his prepared speeches to spend time shaking hands with the audience. "No idea is as powerful as a handshake," he would say.

Burrow kept what he called his "stable of consultants," the Ivy League professors who counseled him. Their presence provoked the cruder aspects of his nature—the swearing, the lewd jokes, and the biting nicknames that he coined for them, delivered in jest and expected to be taken as such. Professor Samuel Klink, who held the economics chair at a prestigious university, was called "Klunk." Professor Tournkey was "Turkey." Warren bristled at the thought of these academicians grinning obsequiously at Burrow's nicknames. What did they need from him, and what did he want from them? Warren wondered.

Burrow read newspapers voraciously and devoured biographies of powerful men. Warren recalled the governor's rage at reading a news story about a popular department store laying off fifty workers in a candy-making operation that it decided to farm out of state. "They call every day to check on the status of the permits they want for their new store," Burrow pouted, "but when they fire fifty workers, you think they'd have the decency to let me know first!" Burrow looked personally offended, the way he did when someone declined his dinner invitation.

Warren glanced at his watch. Burrow's secretary, catching his eye, gestured that he would be next. On her desk Warren saw the customary stack of presents kept within Burrow's reach. In prior administrations, gift-giving had been relegated to a staff member. However, Burrow elevated this function to one rivaling the greeting of foreign dignitaries. The governor took a personal interest in giving gifts to the people he encountered. His favorite memento was a framed, autographed picture of himself. Such photos, like religious icons, decorated homes and offices throughout the state, where they seemed to beg for a candle to be lit before them.

Burrow also loved giving electric toothbrushes with his name inscribed on them. "Why toothbrushes?" Warren once had the temerity to ask. "I want people to think of me first thing in the morning and last thing at night," Burrow replied. He would give a person the same gift repeatedly, each time expecting the receiver to display surprise and delight. Warren himself had received nine toothbrushes and a dozen photos.

The ritual of the gifts, Warren thought, went beyond mere generosity or even eccentricity to place people in a state of obligation and dependence. Was Warren himself in such a state? And was he, as David accused, placing millions of others in a state of dependence through the gifts bestowed by Carefree? A momentary fear gripped him, but he resisted its pull. *The idea is ridiculous*, he told himself. *No one but David would think so.* A shake of Warren's great white hair dismissed the matter.

Warren disapproved of Burrow's displays of power, ardently believing that *Governor Warren Lang* would rule better. He would be perfectly positioned to run for the state's highest post after serving a term as lieutenant governor. But that would entail Burrow's choosing him for a running mate. What price would Burrow demand for this greatest of gifts?

In the inner office beyond the closed mahogany door that Warren faced, the governor was having a meeting with his campaign manager, Casey Clark. The two watched a demonstration taking place outside the window. Several hundred victims of spinal cord injury held placards reading *Cure, Not Care*; *More Research on Nerve Repair*; *CareFree Must Cure Us.*

"This could spell trouble," said the governor, peering through the transparent curtain.

"The publicity could hurt us," replied Clark, standing beside him. The double-breasted suit with padded shoulders that the tall, well-built young campaign manager wore gave him an almost military authority beyond his years.

"Since this David Lang thing began, my office has gotten calls from one hospital after another wanting us to approve a new scanner, a new pavilion, new beds, a remodeling," the governor moaned, pacing nervously. "A heart surgeon called, asking to perform his experimental procedure. A cancer research group wants permission for its new treatment. And I received a petition from doctors trying to unionize."

"This thing could blow up," said Casey Clark, taking a seat on the arm of a sofa. "And the election is only thirteen weeks away."

"Some of these groups don't just want our funding for their pet causes," said the governor. "They're more brazen. They want to act outside of CareFree, collecting private fees from private patients, putting us back where we started! I thought this divisiveness was behind us. Now some hotshot reopens a can of worms that could harm CareFree!"

"And without CareFree, you have no big hook to reel in the voters in November, Governor."

"And no platform for Washington in two years—or whenever I decide to make my bid."

Because critics accused Burrow of seeking reelection in New York only as a springboard for the presidency in two years, the governor was promising to complete a full four-year term in Albany. His fervent ambitions for the next presidential race had to be kept secret, so inadvertent references to his running in two years were always amended.

"To compete on a national scale, Governor, you need a big new program to distinguish yourself," said the authoritative Clark, who was seven years out of college. His impassioned support of Burrow in the latter's first campaign for governor had landed the young devotee the job as campaign manager for the reelection.

"I *have* a program: CareFree National. We're going nationwide with CareFree in two years—or whenever I run."

"You'll solve a problem that's gripped the nation for decades. You'll accomplish what other great presidents only dreamed of. Every time they tried to launch full-scale national health care, they got knocked down. You'll be the one who succeeds. You'll have the accomplishment of CareFree in New York to ride on. What a brilliant platform, Governor! That's the ticket for our bid in two years—or whenever you decide to secure your rightful place in history." An almost religious zeal flickered on Clark's face.

"But the divisiveness has to stop. A dangerous anti-big-government sentiment gained ground with the kickback scandal. It could intensify with the case of Warren Lang's son and rock the boat at the wrong time. What am I going to do, Case?" The loose skin on Burrow's face was like wet concrete waiting to be shaped by a passing footprint.

"Let's look at the opinion polls," replied Clark.

Both men pulled chairs close to the oracle that they trusted to answer all questions: the wall. They sat before four rows of monitors that gave the quaint colonial office the look of an airport control tower.

"I had the opinion meters set up on screen sixteen," Clark said, clicking buttons on the remote to produce the desired program.

Clark's staff polled public opinion by playing videos of people in the news to a sampling of voters and measuring their reactions. The first video segment showed the lieutenant governor. The dial of the opinion meter, displayed below the speaker, swung into the red zone, indicating strong disapproval of the voters.

"That's a no-brainer," quipped the governor. "That's why he's history."

The next video segment showed the secretary of medicine giving a speech. The dial swung into the green zone of the meter, indicating strong approval.

"Everybody likes Uncle Warren," said Clark.

The governor nodded.

The next video segment showed the governor responding to a reporter's question about David Lang's surgery: "We support research as an initiative of Care-Free. We have plans to fund medical research projects, which you'll see unfolding in the weeks and months to come."

"What plans?" interjected Clark.

"I don't know," said the governor, his eyes following the fickle little dial on the screen.

"Regarding David Lang's unauthorized treatment," the governor continued on the video, "we need to hear from all sides. There are dangers in listening only to one disgruntled doctor. Our first and foremost concern is with ensuring the patient's safety."

The dial settled in the middle of the meter, registering neither approval nor disapproval.

"They don't know what to think," said the governor.

Clark echoed his sentiment. "The people are sitting on the fence on this."

In the next segment David Lang was talking to the press, his head high, his eyes guiltless and insolent: "It's none of the governor's business what I do in the OR. The only permission I need is from my patient."

The dial swung into the green zone, indicating approval.

"The ingrates!" cried the governor. "After all I did for them, the people like the hotshot over me!"

"But *he* doesn't know that, so let's not tell him. Besides, there's more." Clark fast-forwarded the video. "We polled another test group on the same topic. Watch this."

A loyal supporter of the governor was taped during a talk show: "David Lang has a history of fines, citations, and warnings from CareFree. His new treatment is unproven. Should he be allowed to disregard the proper channels and the body of medical opinion to do as he pleases?" said the attractive female.

The dial swayed into the green zone, indicating the voters' approval of this speaker's statement against David Lang.

"That's better," the governor said, sighing. "What's your take on this, Case?"

"The public is swaying like driftwood, not anchored to any viewpoint," said Clark, turning off the monitor. "You must pull them to your side."

Burrow nodded. "But with the kickback scandal, the public's trust for politicians is at a low. If *I* slam the hotshot, the people will look at me with raised eyebrows." He pursed his lips thoughtfully. "There's only one man who can stop him and have everyone accept it."

The governor walked to his desk and signaled his secretary to admit the next visitor.

"Leave this to me," Burrow added, winking at Clark.

The brass knob twisted and the mahogany door opened to admit Warren Lang.

As Clark left, the governor sat behind the desk with an air of renewed confidence, gesturing for Warren to sit before him.

"So what have you done, Warren?"

"About what, Mack?"

Burrow smiled wryly. "What topic do you suppose we're here to discuss?"

"What about it?"

Burrow's smile vanished. "Because you so grandly talk about not letting disloyal doctors break the rules, what are you doing to walk your talk and put a lid on your son?"

"He'll have a hearing. He's entitled to one."

"And in the meantime, he's suspended, right?"

"Well, yes, but I thought I might lift that." His tone was tentative, as if testing the waters. "Only provisionally, of course, while the case is pending—"

"Are you crazy? If you even consider sending him back to work, I'll have the Board of Medical Examiners pull his license. Because you have no control over the board, you'll be powerless to stop that. You have some nerve defending him! What about all the doctors you punish for lesser crimes? The press would *cremate* you if you dared lift the suspension."

Warren's eyes sunk to the floor. "But, Mack," he said timidly, "David's a brilliant surgeon. I wouldn't defend him if he were a quack. I'd throw the book at him."

"Are they quacks, those other doctors you throw the book at?"

Warren recalled the dentist, the psychologist, and the director of cardiology whom he'd ruled against that day. A thin line of perspiration darkened the collar of his custom-made shirt.

"What about your duty to the public, Warren? Forgot about that, did you?"

"But David's work is in the public interest. Society needs surgeons like him. Do you remember the conjoined twins he separated? That was a brilliant feat!"

"How many votes does that count for?"

"But, Mack, this is science!"

"That's right, science for the public interest."

"The public needs David's new treatment," said Warren.

"The public needs pills for its ulcers," answered Burrow.

"The public needs medical research."

"The public needs salves for its muscle aches."

"The public needs breakthroughs that carry mankind forward."

"The public needs a lot of things, Warren. But what it doesn't need is a doctor who thinks he's above the law. Where's your fiber, man? You have to set aside your own narrow interests for the sake of the greater good, which you so pompously refer to in all your speeches."

"I *am* concerned about the public." Warren leaped to the window and pulled back the lace curtain. "I'm sure you've seen the protesters out there. That's public opinion, Mack. The voice of democracy is on David's side!"

Burrow leaned back in his chair, folded his hands, and laughed, like a player holding the aces. "Your voice of democracy is clamoring for more state funding of research and more CareFree. How can you say the picketers are on your son's side, when the thing they want more of is me?"

Warren dropped the piece of curtain he had crumpled in his fist and slowly returned to his seat. "Okay, Mack, what would you have me do?" he whispered, defeated.

"Wasn't it *you* who said we were being too lenient with the doctors? That we needed to teach them a lesson?"

Warren's sigh was audible.

"Wasn't it *you* who just last week solemnly proclaimed," the governor contemptuously placed his hands over his heart, "that you would personally punish the medical delinquents who flagrantly and willfully break the law? Wasn't it *you* who said those things?"

Warren's face was a stark white sheet stripped of all emotion except fear. He strained to hold his voice steady. "Yes."

"Look at you trembling—the man of integrity! I want you to practice what you preach and publicly smack your son's face by giving him a hefty fine and a year's suspension. He'd better thank his lucky stars I'm not asking for his license this time. I don't want to appear heavy-handed; that could backfire on me. If he drops the matter of nerve repair until CareFree has the resources to allow it, he can keep his license."

"But what about the case he started? He needs to perform a second surgery."

"Oh, does he now?"

"For the patient's sake, he has to finish what he's started," Warren pleaded.

"He should have thought of the patient's sake before he began. Letting him continue would be like cutting my own throat."

"But, Mack, if you're worried about the patient's safety, I guarantee you that in David's hands—"

"Warren, you silly fool, wake up! It's us against them. I want you to make a test case of CareFree's power for all the doctors to see. And I believe this is also a test for *you*."

"For me?" Warren asked suspiciously. "What do you mean? I can't be involved in David's case. One of my administrators will hear it and render a decision. For me to influence the verdict would be a conflict of interest. It would be favoritism."

"Not if you found him guilty, it wouldn't."

"What are you talking about?" Warren whispered timidly. "What test do you have in mind for me?"

"*I'm* not testing you, Warren, *fate* is. It's as if fate brought you your greatest challenge to elevate your public stature right before holding your first elected office." The governor paused to see Warren's eyebrows arch. "I'm talking, of course, about the office of *lieutenant governor*."

The two words waltzed in the air around Warren.

"You do want the post that I'm considering you for, don't you, Warren?"

"Why, yes, Mack," Warren said breathlessly. "It would be the highest honor of my life!"

"There's real drama here, Warren, real press appeal. It's your historic moment. You pledged to uphold CareFree and punish the lawbreakers. Then right before the election, you hear a case of great importance that's captured media attention, a case involving your own son. You and only you can hear that case! And you prove that you're everything the public thinks you are, a man of integrity who practices what he preaches. You, the great leader, put aside your personal interests and make the right decision for the public. After all, it's an open-and-shut case. Your darling boy broke the law—flagrantly, willfully, arrogantly. You uphold it, even at the price of great personal suffering."

Warren stared at the wainscoting on the wall, seeing nothing.

"Everyone will sing your praises," the governor continued. "And with your exemplary leadership, I'll announce you as my running mate, and we'll ride to victory. Then in two years—or whenever I make my bid for the presidency—you will become the next *governor of New York*." Burrow paused to let the words perfume the room. "That's what I'm offering you, a place on my ticket and a page in history. All I ask is that you do what you've already vowed to do, uphold the law and protect CareFree from its enemies. If you stay true to your ideals, you'll grab the deed to immortality."

Warren's face held the rapture of someone being granted his greatest wish—and the fear of making a pact with the devil for it.

Burrow smiled contemptuously. "If anyone but your son had performed that illegal surgery, you'd throw the book at him. Now's your chance to be the man you claim to be. Remember the biblical story of Abraham? He was ready to cut the throat of his son Isaac for the sake of his moral ideal, and he became a better man for it. I expect you to be the same man Abraham was. The public expects it, too."

"But *God* demanded that sacrifice, Mack. Is that what CareFree does for you? Allows you to play God?"

Burrow laughed easily, like a consummate professional enjoying the work he does best. "Me, Warren? Who issued the edicts against the doctors? You know what they say about people in glass houses."

∞ 20 ∞
The Doctor and the Dancer

Nicole awoke after a long nap, her head sagging into an old pillow whose case smelled of fresh laundry. She had lain on a small cot merely to think quietly for a few minutes, but the fatigue of the day's events overtook her, and she had drifted into a sound sleep. *How long have I been out?* she wondered. She reached down to her purse by the bed and slipped her hand inside. It brushed against her first ballet slippers. Then she felt the envelope that had come with the Phantom's letter. She pulled the envelope out, wanting to hold the crisp page it contained and, with it, a moment of pleasure. But there was nothing inside! Where was the Phantom's letter? Her hand rummaged through the clutter in her purse, but she could feel no letter. She spilled the contents onto the bed and touched each item. Still no letter. Had she put it back in the envelope after David had read it to her? She thought not. Had she taken only the envelope from beneath her pillow in the hospital, leaving the letter behind? Later she would inquire.

Her hand touched a cold metal object that linked her to a hostile world—her cell phone. It also tied her to the man she must call. She had turned off the ringer when she lay down. Now she dialed a number to check her messages. Many had come while she was asleep. She played them and listened painfully to someone whom she had caused to suffer.

The first message contained a voice she barely recognized, stripped of all texture except anguish: "Nicole, it's David. We know you took your phone. Call and tell me you're okay. Tell me who and what frightened you, and let me help."

He left a phone number that she recognized; it was the number to his cell phone, which he had made her memorize in the first moments after her surgery.

There were other messages, all from the man who seemed as much her friend as her doctor. Although his behavior toward her had consistently been professional mixed with some friendliness, she felt an intimacy toward him that went beyond their dealings. Perhaps she was responding to the softness in his voice when he addressed her, a quality that she noticed was missing when he spoke to others. She warned herself that after what she knew, she could no longer lean on him. The thought of losing the man who was her only hope was too terrifying to conceive, yet letting him go was precisely what she must do.

Playing his last message, she sensed in his voice a tortured mix of caring and fear and the strain of trying to control them: "Nicole, I'm beginning to think that . . . maybe . . . you were . . . kidnapped. Let me know that you're okay and that you left of your own will. I won't try to force you to come back if you don't want to. Just let me know you're safe."

She held the phone for a long moment before she could stop shaking to dial. *Your mind's made up,* she lectured herself. *You know what you have to do. Be very formal, and don't feel anything. Just do it. After it's done, you can feel anything you want to, but not now.*

She dialed.

"Hello."

"David, I'm all right." For the first time, she found herself using his given name—despite her resolve to be formal.

A moment passed. "Nicole!" he finally said.

She had never heard her name sound like a hymn. "I was tired and fell asleep. I didn't mean to worry you."

"Forget that. Tell me again—you're okay?"

"I'm fine."

"Where are you?"

"In a safe place."

"Where?"

"I'm not saying."

"Why not?"

"People need to be alone sometimes, where no one can find them."

"Why did you run away?"

"Because—" Her voice broke, and there was nothing but the silent struggle of someone trying not to feel anything.

"I know you want to cry." The baritone voice seemed to caress her. "Let it out, Nicole. You'll feel better if you do."

"I need to be . . . tough," she said, more to herself than to him.

"The tough cry, too, you know."

"David, I'm not having the second surgery."

"Why not?" he asked, astonished.

"Is it true you were suspended by the state and can't practice medicine anymore?"

"So *that's* it. Who told you?"

"Is it true?"

"Yes. I could kick myself for not telling you sooner! I figured I'd get suspended when I offered you the surgery, so it came as no surprise to me." A hint of anger crept into the voice. "Who told you?"

"And your father's the head of CareFree, so this thing's splitting your family apart, too."

"My break with my father happened years ago and has nothing to do with you. If it weren't your case that brought me to an impasse with him, it would've been another."

"Then let it be another. I won't let you destroy your career over my case. If you think I could ever enjoy seeing again, knowing that—"

"You're wrong, Nicole," he said softly. "Your case isn't destroying my career. It gave me my greatest moment in the OR. It's what I've trained for since med school and dreamed about my entire life. Doing your surgery was like getting the lead role in a Broadway show."

"And then breaking your legs so you couldn't perform. Even if I allowed the second surgery, which I won't, you couldn't do it anyway. It's prohibited, isn't it?"

"If I'm alive, I'll do it. The only two things I need are your brain and mine. The rest are details I'll work out."

"But you'll lose your license if you do that surgery, won't you?"

"Maybe not. CareFree is going to have a hearing on the case."

"Oh?"

"Even though my father has . . . changed," he said painfully, "he was once a neurosurgeon. That work takes a different sort of person than he is now. When you're inside someone's brain, there are no public opinion polls to tell you what to do, no media to impress, no hands to shake. The brain doesn't wheel and deal with you, it doesn't accept your promises, and it's unforgiving of your mistakes. It's you and the best stuff you have against the forces of nature. My father once loved that kind of work—and he loved me. There was a different principle inside him than I see today."

"I'm sorry he let you down."

"I can't believe he could change so radically. Some remnant of his old self must still remain."

"Even if he were sympathetic, I heard his hands are tied."

"It seems you heard a lot of things."

"If your father's in the public eye because the governor's going to choose him for a running mate, how can he pull any strings?"

"Pulling strings is what he does for a living," David said contemptuously. "Won't you stick around, Nicole, to see what happens at the hearing?"

"The best way to save yourself is to drop this case now."

"Won't you give me a chance to do what I really want to do?"

"If that means to destroy yourself, no."

"I want to finish your treatment not as an act of self-destruction but as my greatest achievement."

"No!"

"When I performed your surgery, I was doing *my* work, *my* way, without having to give explanations, excuses, and apologies to people who get their kicks out of keeping me in line. I'm fed up with it! I want to fight it with your case, and I want you to let me."

"No!"

"You said that the Phantom mustn't confine his dreams to the world he sees on the stage. What about us, Nicole? Are you going to run away from your dream—and mine?"

"But I *helped* the Phantom. I didn't destroy him."

"Now help me. Fight with me for what we both want."

"David, you must give up my case."

"You worry about the Phantom giving up the driving force of his life, and if he does, you're afraid there'll be nothing left of him. Remember your own words?"

"That was different."

"Why? What would be left of me if I gave up my research and your case? What would be left of you if you let me give up your treatment?"

"Does my surgery mean that much to you?"

"More than you know." The words hung in the silence that followed, as he thought of all the things he could not say. "Surely you'd agree to the surgery if it were legal."

"Well, yes."

"The hearing could reverse the ruling against me. Won't you come back to learn the outcome and whether we can proceed legally?"

"But David—"

"No buts, Nicole. Come back, for the reasons I gave you."

She paused. He waited.

Finally, she whispered tentatively, "Okay."

She heard a sigh that was like a sudden release from a torture rack.

"But I'll let you operate *only* if it's legal. Is that clear?"

"Where are you? I'll pick you up." His voice was lighter.

"No. I can get home."

"You're newly blind and not yet trained to deal with it! It's *dangerous* to be on your own now! I'm picking you up."

"I'm afraid not. Try not to worry. 'Bye, David."

She hung up, leaving him to frown at the dead phone.

He was leaning against the brick balcony of Nicole's brownstone apartment, where he and Mrs. Trimbell had gone with a private detective, searching for clues to the dancer's whereabouts. The late afternoon sun was seeping between the leaves of a tree, dappling his body in lights and shadows as he resumed reading a report that he had been given by the detective. It was a background check that the investigator had run on a child named Cathleen Hughes. The investigator discovered that this child had run away at thirteen to become Nicole Hudson. That was how David learned about his patient's past—the abandonment by her father, the disappearance of her mother, her entry into foster care, the revolving door of faceless families, the countless episodes of running away, and the only statement from the child herself in the whole of the dry document: a persistent plea to be near Madame Maximova's School of Ballet. He lingered on the pages in silent tribute to the little swallow that had weathered many storms to reach its lofty perch.

David was waiting outside when a car turned onto Nicole's block, a tree-lined street with a row of brownstones on the West Side near the theater district. The vehicle, which bore an emblem reading "Reliable Car Service," stopped before him.

"Watch your head getting out," said David, opening the back door. He placed a protective hand over the head of the turban-clad beauty who smiled softly, almost sadly, on hearing his voice.

After escorting Nicole to the safety of the sidewalk, he approached the driver's window.

"How much do we owe you?" he asked the well-dressed young man.

"That's already taken care of."

"Where did you pick her up?"

"I'm sorry, sir, but we don't give out that information."

In his line of work David had learned never to make the same mistake twice. If Nicole were to vanish again, he wanted to be prepared. He flashed a hundred-dollar bill at the driver.

"Maybe you can make an exception this time for someone who's trying to help her."

"I'm sorry, sir. Ms. Hudson's a regular customer. We used to drive her to the theater all the time. You'll have to ask her."

The young man smiled cordially and pulled away, never looking twice at the bill in David's hand. The driver had scruples, which David did not appreciate! He walked to Nicole, squeezing her hands tightly against his chest in an expression of his immense relief at seeing her.

"Everyone going into your hospital room knew not to tell you the news. Who told you?"

"I'm not saying."

"Someone on the hospital staff?"

"I'm not saying."

"Someone from the theater?"

"David, please stop."

"Promise—swear to me!—you'll never pull that stunt again. Promise you'll talk to me first if you hear something frightening and give me a chance to explain."

"Promise you'll tell me the news as it happens, David."

"Don't let the news frighten you, Nicole. I'm not down yet. This is only the first round."

Tears swelled in the still-vibrant blue eyes dominating her face. "I can't believe this is happening! When I was a kid, a lot of things I didn't like were thrust upon me, and I was powerless to fight them. A nun named Sister Luke said that when I grew up, I would be in charge and could do as I pleased. I lived for the day when Sister Luke's words would come to pass." An inner pain furrowed her sublime face. "What do they want from us, David? Why can't they leave us alone?"

"If I knew the answer, I would understand my father—and all the others like him."

He curled her hand around his arm and walked a half step in front of her, past the gate of her brownstone, up the front steps, and to her third-floor apartment. She felt a heightened awareness of his body, as if he were leading her in a dance. When he walked, she walked. When he turned, she turned. He narrated the leisurely trip for her as they progressed:

"The sun is to the left of the garden. It's casting a long shadow of leaves and flowers over our path. We're stepping on the rosebush now." She laughed. He stopped walking. With the reflexes of a dancer, she stopped, too, instantly and gracefully. "We're at the steps, Nicole." He climbed up, and she rose effortlessly with him. "The sky is turning a deeper blue. The sun is reflecting off the tall buildings to the right, making their windows sparkle like hot metal. On the left, a few wispy clouds near the horizon are already tinted pink. It's going to be a pretty sunset."

She listened with a child's enchantment to the description that was a painting, and the world she could not see had never looked lovelier.

He escorted her into the neat, attractive apartment on the upper floor of the brownstone, explaining how he and Mrs. Trimbell had moved furniture out of the center of the rooms to prevent her from tripping. She touched things to get her bearings as they walked through the living room, dining area, ballet studio, master bedroom, and guest room.

After the tour, he faced her in the living room. "Mrs. Trimbell went for groceries. When she returns, I'd like to see you eat a big dinner."

She nodded, knowing she needed food. "Thank you, David . . ."—she put her hands to her heart—"more than I can say. I'm sorry I worried you." Her eyes had somehow hit the spot where his were, as if she were seeing him.

"I'm sorry you were frightened."

They stood facing each other for a silent stretch that seemed strangely comfortable to both of them.

"I want you to rest now," he said finally.

Tiring easily on her first day out of the hospital, she welcomed his guidance to the couch and limply sank into it. With dusk approaching, he turned on the lamp on the end table next to her. The large, translucent globe was on a dimmer switch. It came on faintly at first, then grew in intensity as he continued turning the knob. Nicole moved her head to the light.

He looked at her curiously. She stared intently at the globe from a foot away. He kneeled beside her and soundlessly turned the dimmer switch down until the light faded. Then he turned it up again, slowly. As the light reached full intensity, she cried, "I see light! David, I see light!"

He dimmed the light again.

"It's gone now," she said.

He raised the light once more.

"It's back!" She stared excitedly at the globe, her voice trembling. "You told me I would recover some of my sight before the scar tissue grew to obstruct it again. That's what's happening, isn't it?" The globe cast a golden glow over a childlike face of sheer delight. "The nerves are growing! The experiment's working!"

He gazed into her eyes with the excitement of Louis Pasteur at a moment of discovery. The thrill on his face swept away the anguish of the day and week. Finally, he found a voice that trembled as hers did.

"Hell, yes, Nicole! The experiment's working!"

In the weeks that followed, David tried to keep busy in his lonely office. He read medical journals, wrote notes for research papers, and attended to the animals hidden in his lab, the five cats that would receive the second surgery to repair their optic nerves prior to Nicole's operation.

He searched for a backup plan for performing Nicole's second surgery, should CareFree maintain its prohibition, but nothing materialized. He continued his efforts to become licensed in another state or country in time for the operation, but to no avail. The rejections of the licensing officials formed an impenetrable wall:

"We require a clean history of regulatory compliance. A doctor who breaks the law in one state is a poor risk in another."

"We check for legal cases pending or judgments against a doctor. We don't license those with a questionable record."

"Fill out the forms, and we'll let you know in six months. . . . No, I'm afraid we can't speed up the process." Nicole's second surgery had to be done in three months.

He explained his case to influential medical leaders, hoping to find one individual who would help. The answer he heard repeatedly was along the lines of "Unfortunately, Dr. Lang, there are considerations other than a distinguished clinical record, which you have, that make us unable to help you."

During those weeks following Nicole's surgery, David and his lawyer prepared for the hearing to repeal his suspension and to permit Nicole's treatment. Care-

Free set a date for the case in mid-September; however, the agency failed to name an administrator to hear it. Meanwhile, Governor Malcolm Burrow was conducting a search to find a suitable running mate, declaring that he would make a decision in the coming weeks: "I will choose a candidate of the highest integrity and character, someone impervious to personal gain, someone who will work for the public interest."

Sitting in his office, his hands idle, David tried to ignore the sound of turning pages amplified in the silence, the empty examining room beyond the door, and the unoccupied chairs in the waiting room. He tried to avoid looking at the hospital outside his window, where doctors in white coats walked briskly along the grounds, nurses attended patients, and ambulances whizzed by. He was in the midst of plenty, but his horn was empty. He could find no substance to fill the huge crater that had formed in his life. He covered his eyes to block the vision of the man who had ripped the OR from him and left in its place an empty pit.

A half-mile from David's office, another lonely figure fought a quiet battle with despair. Life to Nicole felt like a bare stage. Gone was her beloved theater and busy career. Gone were the continuous, refreshing visual delights that sweetened her existence—the joy of reading a book, seeing a garden, watching the sun sparkle on the buildings, perceiving her own appearance in a mirror, preparing a colorful salad. Gone, too, was the visual excitement of movement—of a bird flying, a child running, a tree swaying, a car passing. Gone was her ability to observe other people, to know their appearance, to root them to a specific location, to observe the facial expressions and body gestures that had enriched her communications. Her lively universe of sights, colors, objects, and motions had vanished, leaving a vast emptiness.

Then there were the endless, maddening inconveniences that magnified her helplessness. She could not write a check, read her mail, compose a letter, count money, shop, eat, or dress without assistance. There were the untold frustrations of trying to walk across a room without stumbling, the disorientation of moving about in the unknown. Her cathedral of reality had shattered into a few disembodied fragments within the immediate range of her touch. Her awareness of whole objects existing in a whole world crumbled, and with it, her proud sense of efficacy in that world.

There was the financial strain of losing her job. And the disruptions in her sleep caused by the inability to distinguish night from day. Gone was her glorious confidence in facing the world. In its place crept a pervasive anxiety about a barrage of mysterious sounds and objects. The unknown was the frightening, and her entire new world was unknown. To be awake was to be anxious.

After a life of relying on her own inner resources, Nicole felt the crushing loss of her privacy and independence. She who had opened the huge gate of achievement now needed assistance finding the bathroom door. The result was, inevitably, depression. Gone was the radiant face, the easy laughter, the childlike exuberance that colored her manner. Nicole mechanically received Mrs. Trimbell's guidance on eating, dressing, arranging household items, walking with a cane. Without excuses, complaints, or anger, the bewildered dancer practiced the simplest tasks, such as eating with a knife and fork. She tried, fumbled, and repeated the same actions countless times. Mrs. Trimbell patiently attempted to bring order and self-respect to the chaos and indignity of Nicole's new condition, while her student developed an austere acceptance of her predicament.

Cheerlessly, Nicole entered her studio, a bare room with a hardwood floor, wall of mirror and ballet barre, where she spent hours each day practicing. She was supposed to dance holding the barre. When she disregarded her doctor's instructions and ventured into the center of the room, every turn left her disoriented, discouraged, helpless.

There were, however, two sources of light in the dark chamber of her existence, two people whose glowing presence burned through her stoical indifference and rekindled her capacity for pleasure—her doctor and the Phantom.

David made an arrangement with Mrs. Trimbell in which he visited Nicole once a week, allowing the teacher time off. When he first appeared at her door, Nicole protested what she described as baby-sitting.

"I'm perfectly fine being by myself, David."

"I'm not," he replied.

"Do you mean that I need company, or that you do?"

"Both. I mean that I'm here because I want to be. Because I didn't come to monitor you clinically, you're of course free to throw me out."

"And if I don't, then it means you're here because *I* want you to be."

"That's right," he said, smiling.

"Then come," she said, finding his arm and drawing him in, "and tell me what the world looks like today."

Each time he visited, David chronicled the surroundings from the balcony of her apartment or from a nearby park they visited, lifting the gray clouds of Nicole's internal landscape and filling the scene with color. He spoke lavishly, as if giving words to the sights before them was as much a need for him as it was for her.

"The city looks as if a stage crew backlighted it tonight," he said one evening at dusk. He leaned against the brick border of her balcony. She stood beside him, her hand resting gently on his as he pointed to the sights. "The skyscrapers are dark gray columns silhouetted against a royal blue sky. Many lights from the windows dot the tall steel frames, defining them in the darkening sky. The buildings look serene and solid, like something you can count on. There's a point of light above the city, too, the first evening star in a cloudless sky."

"Where is it?"

"Right there," he pointed above them, with her hand over his.

She leaned her head back, drinking in the beauty of the world she saw through his eyes.

One day while they walked home from the park, to Nicole's delight, a thundercloud burst in a brief but violent summer storm. They took shelter under the canopy of a building.

"I like the rain. When it hits things, I'm aware of them," she said. "I hear the low, rumbling sound of the rain beating against the awning over our heads. And the rain has a higher pitch where it strikes the roofs of the cars," she observed with a childlike fascination. "I can hear the car wheels hissing against the wet pavement, and more drops seem to be landing on something to my left, maybe a windowsill."

"It *is* a windowsill. You have a good ear for the music of the rain, Nicole."

With the air suddenly cooled, he removed a light jacket that he wore and wrapped it around her. He held her in the warmth of his arm as she shivered in a thin blouse and shorts. Sprouts of blond hair barely covered her scalp, and a few freckles dotted her suntanned face, giving her a boyish, childlike look that pleased him.

"The sky is angry today," he said. "It's dense with ominous black clouds that have swallowed the tops of the buildings in fog. The city is dwarfed, robbed of its towering presence. And the sky also stripped the color away. Everything, from the buildings to the people to the pavement, is a different shade of gray. The sky, which is vapor, wants to swallow the steel, glass, and flesh that is the city."

She detected a tinge of bitterness. "David, that's something the Phantom would say."

"And what would you tell him?"

"I'd say that the city won't let anything swallow it, certainly not something as wishy-washy as the sky. I'd tell the Phantom that the city will prevail. Don't you think it will, David?"

She was shivering more now. Her enchantment with the rain had vanished, and the question she asked left a troubled look on her face. Instantly regretting his remarks, David tried to dismiss the gray clouds that were creeping into his thoughts—the upcoming hearing, the idle hands restless to work, the innocent life before him for whose sake *he* must prevail.

"You bet, Nicole," he said, his arm tightening around her in a reassuring squeeze. "The city will prevail."

Ignoring the forced cheerfulness in the voice whose shadings were becoming familiar to her, she told herself that he believed his words, and that she did, too.

When they returned to her apartment, David read Nicole a play from her voluminous collection of classical dramas.

"I love reading, and I love literature," she said of her library, which could rival any English professor's.

Afterward, she played music for him. The lighthearted spirit of her selections made him think of his work. He described the history and problems of nerve repair, speaking as if she, too, were a doctor, sparing no technical terms. Interrupting only to have him define the words she did not understand, Nicole listened with interest, her quick mind grasping everything.

Mrs. Trimbell returned to find David lying on the couch, talking about nerve regeneration. Nicole sat on an area rug facing him, her long legs stretched in a split with her elbows resting before her, a pose that only a ballerina could find comfortable. The two greeted Mrs. Trimbell absently, surprised to see her, unaware that an entire day had passed. Then they continued their conversation. Mrs. Trimbell soon became accustomed to feeling invisible.

The Flower Phantom made his presence felt during the six weeks between Nicole's homecoming and the hearing. His table occupied a prominent place in the living room. It held the dried remains of his flower arrangements. Nicole continued her search for the letter he had sent to her in the hospital, the one that was missing, but to no avail. The Phantom quickly obliged by sending another, along with a porcelain vase filled with fragrant white jasmine. Every week, a new arrangement followed, which served as the centerpiece on the dining-room table. David read the new letters as Nicole inhaled the scents of the luscious bouquets.

"The Phantom found out where I live," she remarked to David when she received the jasmine.

"So it seems."

"I wonder when he'll come to see me. He doesn't seem in any hurry," she complained.

"Why don't you give him a break?"

"Why do you take his side over your patient's? And why are you laughing? My affairs seem to amuse you."

"I'm sorry, really I am."

"But you're still laughing! The Phantom's probably waiting to see if I'll ever be normal again, and I don't blame him."

"Nicole," he said, the amusement tapering off, "maybe he has a pressing matter on his mind and can't step forward. When he does appear, you might give him a chance to explain. Maybe he would be thrilled to have you just as you are. Maybe you're absolutely perfect for him right now and you don't even know it."

❧ ❧ ❧

David arrived at Nicole's apartment one afternoon to hear a thump as he entered. He found her on the floor of her studio, in a leotard, her hands covering her face. She felt his comforting hand touch her shoulder.

"Are you okay, Nicole?"

"Yes," she mumbled through her hands, her voice heavy with despair.

"No one said it would be easy," he said sympathetically.

After he helped her to her feet, they stood still, holding hands, her bent head brushing his shoulder, a few tears dropping onto his shirt.

"I tried to turn and lost my balance."

"You'll get it. But right now you're supposed to be at the barre," he gently admonished. "You were nowhere near it."

"I know I disregarded your instructions. But I just wanted to dance one simple routine, free of any crutches. I almost had it! It was the first dance I do as Pandora, after the gods create me."

"That dance is too dangerous! I don't want you flying through the air now. If you fall—"

"I modified it to— Hey, do you know the number? Have you . . . seen . . . my show?"

"Yes."

She looked astonished, her tears drying. "How come you never mentioned that you saw my show?"

"It didn't seem . . . relevant."

"It's *very* relevant, David! What did you think of it?"

"I think the Phantom has good taste."

"That means you liked my show? Did you really?"

"Oh, yes."

The solemnity in his words made her forget her discouragement. They were still holding hands. She squeezed his.

"I want to try the dance again. And I want you to watch, if you'd like to."

"No! It's dangerous. I don't want you to—"

"Please try not to worry, David. I'll do what you don't like anyway when you're not here. But you *are* here, so would you like to . . . see me . . . dance . . . for you?"

She felt a sudden breathless excitement at offering herself to his eyes to watch. Without waiting for his answer, she walked to a sound system in the corner and began the music.

That was how David received a private showing of Pandora's first dance, which had held him spellbound since a desperate night the previous winter. He thought of that snowy evening when he had discovered Nicole Hudson. Armed with Pandora's hope, he had reclaimed his rats and completed the first successful nerve-repair experiments. Now, as she danced exclusively for him, *her* spirit reawakened. He saw in glorious close-up the qualities he had admired from the audience, the stunning mix of a disciplined, almost ascetic, skill with the exultation that was Nicole. She danced flawlessly, the pride of her achievement glowing on her face. When she finished, he approached her, a rush of afternoon sun from the window beaming across him.

"You're lovely, Nicole."

She stood facing him with her head lifted and her body pulled back. Although she avoided gestures underscoring her blindness, at that moment she urgently wanted to touch his face. She raised her hand to the features that she had never felt, but she did not complete the movement. She suddenly developed a strange fascination with her arm, shining in the sun's rays. She waved it from side to side. David stared intensely. He grasped her chin to hold her head still. Then he waved his arm before her. Nicole's eyes followed the movement from side to side. Then up and down. When his arm stopped waving, her eyes stopped, too.

"David!" she whispered incredulously. "I can see a dark shadow moving. It's your arm, isn't it? I can see your arm waving!"

On a cloudless day in September, David and Nicole sat in the park near her apartment, enjoying the delicious nip of the first fall air. Nicole's sight was improving. She could see light and motion from greater distances. The once-empty canvas of her perception now held shadings of gray masses that moved. The five cats in David's laboratory mirrored these improvements. The severed optic nerves were growing back. From his past experiments, David expected Nicole's limited vision to plateau and then to deteriorate as the scar tissue grew to impede the regenerated nerves. His experience with animals indicated that he must perform the second surgery to remove the scar tissue before Nicole lost her newfound vision entirely; otherwise, she would never see again.

Such were the matters on his mind that day, a week before the hearing, sitting with Nicole on the park bench. Her face was serenely calm as it caught the crisp fall breeze, her swanlike neck accentuated with a turtleneck sweater and short blond hair, her shapely legs outlined by her slacks. She felt contentment in his presence, in the rich baritone voice and warm hands that conveyed the thoughts and feelings of the man whose portrait was missing from her mind's collection. She also enjoyed the intimacy of their frequent moments of comfortable silence.

As if an inimical world suddenly asserted itself to choke the peaceful rhythm of their afternoon, a man in the park collapsed. Nicole heard screams for help and felt David spring from the bench to assist. Desperate cries from the man's frightened companions gave her a start: "He stopped breathing!" "Call an ambulance!" "He's turning blue!" After interminable minutes trying to revive the stricken man, David finally uttered two words that relieved everyone: "He's breathing." Nicole heard an ambulance siren, the wheels of a stretcher rolling along the pavement, her companion's voice describing the man's condition to the rescuers, and the scramble to lift the victim into the vehicle. Then the ambulance door slammed shut and the matter was over. Nicole heard voices growing fainter as the crowd that had gathered dispersed.

When David returned to her side, he described the incident the way another man would relate a boxing match, blow by blow. His words were punctuated by the excitement peculiar to him when he spoke of anything medical.

"You miss the hospital, don't you?" she asked when he had finished.

"Yes," he admitted.

For one painful moment, her eyes closed.

"I was an emergency medical technician when I was fifteen," he explained. "I lied about my age to get certified, but it was worth it. I got a real thrill from the fieldwork."

"And what happened?"

"I got caught."

"Did you get in trouble?"

"Oh, yes. I was charged with a crime. My father was furious. He grounded me, so I was a prisoner in my room. But later he backed down. You see, I had done good work, and he knew it. He couldn't punish me for long, so he got the charges against me dropped and gave me back my freedom."

"So now we're wondering if your father will be so kind as to give us back our lives, aren't we?" Her exquisite mouth frowned. "It's the thing I always hated most, having others decide for me. Sister Luke said that when I grew up, *I* would be in charge. Now—" Her voice caught in the tears she tried to contain.

She felt his hand tighten around hers. "I know," he said softly.

"What gives them the right?"

He had no answer.

"How can this be happening to us?"

"I want you to hang on for another week, until the hearing, and not let this torment you—"

He realized that Nicole was no longer listening. Her head was turned to a street vendor's cart next to their bench. She rose slowly from her seat, like a sleepwalker in a trance. Her eyes widened, then squinted, as if straining to . . . *perceive* something. David followed her, watching intently. Nicole placed her face up against a cluster of balloons that the vendor was selling. Her fingers lightly touched the colorful balls.

"They're balloons!" she exclaimed. She pressed one of them against her face. "This one's red." Then her fingers found another and pulled it to her face. "This one's blue." She repeated the action for another balloon in the cluster. "Yellow."

David grabbed her shoulders and stared into the amazing blue pools that were his experiment.

"I can see color! David, I can see color!"

They stood like two children, laughing in tribute to the great promise of life within them. David bought the cluster of balloons from the vendor and handed them to the radiant figure beside him. They linked arms in sheer delight, with the sound of their laughter filling the sunlit park.

"Pretty soon, I'll see you, David!"

"That should be interesting."

❦21❧
On Trial

The secretary of medicine slept fitfully in his Manhattan penthouse. Although he had taken sleeping pills the night before, Warren Lang lay awake for many hours. At the first light of dawn, tension finally gave way to exhaustion, and he dozed off. He dreamed that he was walking a large, unruly dog. The animal tugged at its leash, barking viciously. Warren struggled to hold the beast, but it broke loose. It moved menacingly toward a boy of about ten years old. The dog leaped up on its hind legs, towering over the frightened child. It jumped on the boy and pushed him to the ground. The terrified child screamed. Warren tried desperately to run to the boy and to cry for help, but his legs were paralyzed and his mouth was unable to utter a sound. With outstretched arms, the boy begged for assistance. Warren could only watch in horror as the salivating beast tore its sharp teeth into one of the small arms and the child screamed in pain. Warren awakened, sitting up in bed, his heart pounding and his body soaked in sweat. He sat trembling, head in hands, overcome by the lingering terror of a dream too real.

That day marked the seventh week since his elder son had performed the surgery on Nicole Hudson and the seventh week before the gubernatorial election. It was the week when Mack Burrow would announce his running mate. That overcast Wednesday in September was also the day of David's hearing before CareFree.

Too upset to eat, Warren skipped breakfast. When he left his apartment, he was dressed like the consummate executive. However, the dark circles under his eyes and the loose-fitting suit revealed the loss of sleep and appetite that had plagued him for the past seven weeks. He saw the sun reduced to a pale backlight on a cluster of clouds, making the sky a translucent, snowy gray. The secretary ignored the passersby who watched him enter a waiting limousine. No smiles, no waves, no drinking in his admirers like a fresh cup of coffee to give Warren a boost that dreary morning.

Climbing the steps of the Bureau of Medicine's Manhattan building, he read the inscription on the gold plaque dominating the entrance: *To serve the public interest above all other concerns—this is the noble work of medicine.* The quotation had his name etched under it.

He was a distinguished public figure but also a sleepless wreck. His son was a hero but also an outlaw. He was about to perform a noble act by his own quotation, but he felt only misery. As he entered the revolving door to the old brick building, his life was also whirling in an endless loop. He thought of the philosopher he had once read who said that reality consisted of an inherent conflict of opposites. What was right? What was wrong? Warren, the great moral leader, did not know.

He reached a wood-paneled chamber that was a former courtroom now used by CareFree to conduct hearings. The varnished oak floor and rich mahogany benches were suitable for a grand assembly where statesmen pursued just causes. Warren took his seat at the judge's bench to face a crowd of people. To his left was a witness stand and jury box. Before him were the defendant's and prosecutor's tables. Behind them was a balustrade, and beyond it, a gallery of witnesses and visitors. It was now Warren's task to explain to the packed room that this was not a trial and he was not a judge. The conflict of opposites.

His eyes scanned the reporters and onlookers in the gallery and the twelve people whom he had asked to sit in the jury box. He noticed the stunning young patient, Nicole Hudson, and her older female companion in the audience. He glanced to his left at CareFree's lawyer and, last, to his right at David, sitting with his attorney. CareFree had not announced the administrator for the hearing, and his son looked astonished to see him.

Warren greeted the gathering and explained the procedure. "This hearing will loosely resemble a trial, but with more flexibility for the free expression of all views. I have asked six distinguished community leaders and six medical professionals to act as my advisory panel." Warren pointed to the twelve people in the jury box. "This way the government, the community, and the clinicians can decide this case democratically. I will serve as the moderator to ensure the free flow of information, so the truth can be known and justice can be served."

He had options, he reminded himself. If the advisors exonerated David, then maybe the governor would relent. If they opted for punishment, then maybe David would relent. If they rendered an unacceptable decision, then he had the power as secretary to overrule them and to be the final authority on the matter. But what was acceptable? He could not decide. If only he could have *both* of his fervent wishes: the nomination for lieutenant governor *and* the rescue of David. The conflict of opposites.

Attorney Brian Harkness, a short, bespectacled man with a shrewd face that made him look older than his thirty-six years, presented CareFree's case against David. He described how the surgeon had disregarded the hospital rules and broken the law on the evening of Nicole Hudson's surgery.

"So that no one will think there were extenuating circumstances to excuse David Lang's infraction, I will demonstrate that his surgery was based on bogus research, that it represented an unwarranted use of public funds, and that it posed a danger to the patient," Harkness explained.

He called on neurosurgeons to describe from the witness stand the formidable problem of nerve regeneration. These experts testified that countless researchers through the centuries had tried unsuccessfully to regrow the tissue of the central nervous system. The unanimous opinion of the state's experts was that such nerve regeneration was impossible.

Harkness then asked a public-health spokeswoman to describe the shortage of medical resources and the imperative for doctors to use them prudently. Wasteful tests, unnecessary surgical procedures, and unauthorized hospital stays constituted a misuse of public funds that were urgently needed elsewhere, she testified.

Harkness produced regulatory officials to describe the laws controlling surgeries and medications. The witnesses stated that the surgical procedure and the drugs that David Lang had employed in his experimental treatment were unapproved by the government for use in humans and were therefore illegal. Harkness charged that the surgeon acted brashly, creating unsafe conditions for his patient.

David's lawyer, Russell Green, a tall man in his forties with a gentlemanly manner and intelligent, gunmetal eyes, answered the state's charges. Regarding the validity of the procedure, Green asked David to explain his research. Using a visual presentation from his laptop computer, the surgeon showed how he had repaired the severed spinal cords of cats. The state's medical witnesses then argued that the spinal cords of the animals had perhaps not been completely severed at the start of the treatment, thereby invalidating the results. This allegation, which implied carelessness or dishonesty in the experiment, made David bristle.

Regarding the misuse of public funds, Green displayed three checks written to Riverview Hospital, each sufficient to cover the experimental treatment. The checks were from David Lang, Nicole Hudson, and the producer of the show *Triumph,* each with an accompanying letter directing the hospital to use the money for the dancer's care. However, Green explained, the hospital was prohibited from cashing the checks. In the name of protecting the public against profiteers who make money off the sick, a hospital accepting private payment for treatment was automatically dropped as a CareFree provider and consequently forced out of business. This left the patient no choice but to rely on CareFree, which meant to use public funds for her medical care.

Regarding the issue of Nicole's safety, Green stressed that the patient was unharmed by the procedure. Indeed, a rudimentary vision was returning to Nicole. The state's experts countered that the patient could have had that rudimentary vision the entire time, and a technical argument ensued over the interpretation of Nicole's brain scan and her claim that she could not see anything before the surgery.

"Could I interrupt this erudite discussion, all of which is irrelevant?" a voice rang from the back of the courtroom. "I'm Randall Lang, the president of Riverview Hospital." Heads turned to watch the tall blond man whom David had banned from the hearing walk down the gallery to the railing. "I would like to address the court—oh, excuse me—the *hearing*," Randy said, bowing slightly to his father. "You know, I almost said 'Your Honor,' but then you're not a judge, are you, and that's not a jury, is it?" He pointed to Warren's advisors in the jury box. "And forgive me for mentioning it, but the defendant isn't exactly presumed innocent, is he?"

"He can't speak!" cried David, leaping from his seat to approach Warren's bench. "This matter doesn't concern him, and I won't allow him to speak!"

"It does, and I will," said Randy, walking forward to stand next to David.

Warren emitted the sigh of a father long resigned to having strong-willed children. "All right, Randall Lang, say your piece."

While David protested in vain to his father, Randy was sworn in. Declining the witness chair offered by the attendant, Randy remained standing before Warren and the courtroom. David had no choice but to return to the defendant's table.

"As the president of Riverview, I represent the owners of the hospital where Dr. David Lang performed the surgery in question. We're the *owners*, but we weren't invited to this little gathering that will determine what transpires in our hospital." He glanced derisively at Warren. "That's okay. We're not offended. We're used to being owners but not being able to buy bedsheets without clearing it through a regulator. We're not like the doctor and patient before you, who think they have rights. We know we have none. The public told us so when it elected Malcolm Burrow.

"We accept that. Why? Because we feel guilty. Why? Because we want to make a *profit* from treating the sick. Can you imagine? We go to school, learn a profession, get a job, take on the immense liability of running a hospital and overseeing complex, risky procedures performed on countless numbers of you, the public, to restore your health and save your lives—and we're supposed to lay this at your feet without an eye on our lifestyles, our families, our homes, our children's education, or our retirement. We're supposed to put forth gut-wrenching effort through decades of our lives without an eye on personal gain—only on unselfish devotion to you. Do *you* want to make money, as much as you can, from your chosen work?

"The people who now run medicine claim that they don't want to make money; they just want to take care of you. How touching! Let's examine what's happened to medicine since it was taken over by an institution without a financial motive. Look back, those of you who are old enough, to a time before Mack Burrow and his precursors trampled over medicine. Did profit keep you waiting for vital tests? Did profit keep beds out of service while you fainted in the ER? Did profit deny you needed surgeries? Did profit give you antiquated buildings, broken equipment, and lousy service? Did profit price you out of insurance when the actuaries, not the politicians, dictated how policies were written? Profit wouldn't dare treat you that way, because you'd take your business to competitors smart enough to serve you better.

"What is it they want, your benefactors who put us in the backseat and told you that our drive for money would crash the car? Are you, the patients, really in the driver's seat, as you've been told? We don't dare ask who's steering the car or where it's headed. We just do what we're told, and in exchange, we get to take the financial risk of owning an enterprise that we have no control over.

"If making health care a business is wrong, then why do you keep us around at all? Many Mack Burrows of the world took over the hospitals outright. So why is the mother of all relics, the private hospital, still here? Because *we* take the punches. Here's how it works. The state, your great savior, promises you free vaccines, free checkups, ten-dollar brain scans, or what have you. Then why not take Johnny to the doctor every time he gets the sniffles? Everyone loves a bargain, so the demand for health care skyrockets, and the state spends more than it ever imagined. What do our great leaders do now? Do they admit they made a mistake and cut their programs? Never! They blame us, the selfish profiteers, of course; and they cut our budgets, which only intensifies the crisis.

"And you, the magnificently clueless general public, don't see this. All you know is that no one answers our phones anymore, no nurses are available when you need a pill, and no doctor is around to set your broken leg. You see us treat you badly, and your knee-jerk response is: 'Those greedy hospitals. They're only out for money. What do they care if we die in their hallways.' Do you stop and ask yourselves why we would let you die in our hallways if we were out for money? If we manufactured shoes, would it be a wise decision to let our customers roam barefoot? But we're not permitted to make decisions anymore.

"Do you realize any of this? No. Do we tell you? No. Do you know that the only people who can treat you poorly and get away with it are those who *don't* make money from treating you? Frankly, they make more money from *not* treating you. When they collect the same taxes regardless, the way to make ends meet is to curtail service, not to render it. And you keep swimming into the current, clamoring for your Mack Burrows to pass more laws to tip our boat deeper into the water, while we're trying to haul you in."

Randy paced, throwing occasional, insolent glances at Warren. "You know, there's money and there's *money*, but your leaders paint it all black, regardless of how it's acquired. Someone who spends ten years after college learning to be a neurosurgeon, or someone like me, who runs a hospital, is a different sort of person than a bank robber. Our money is earned, not robbed. It comes from *giving* something, not *stealing* it, from giving you the supreme value of your health and life. What are the motives of those who tell you that a director of cardiology is as shady a character as a bank robber—because they both want money? Do you know what it does to the cardiologist to have you believe this? Why *do* you believe it?"

Randy threw his hands up, stopped his pacing, and turned to his father. "Every drowning creature has its swan song, so here's mine. Let's *compromise*. You keep your rulebooks, your inspectors, and all of medicine; only leave one small aspect free, an aspect that hasn't been born yet and that will never be born within CareFree. Lift the regulations concerning nerve repair, and a newly formed, privately funded Institute for Neurological Research and Surgery will be opened, ready to admit its first patient, Nicole Hudson, in time for her next surgery, and ready to allow David Lang to complete his research. We don't want a penny from the state! We know that he who pays the bills calls all the shots. We only want to be left alone, unencumbered by CareFree's rules. Do you think we need your inspectors to tell us to sterilize our needles? If we were negligent, we'd have the *real* law courts to answer to, as we should, and that's the patient's true protection. I'm asking you, Mr. Secretary, to stand aside and let a terrible thing called profit bring forth a glorious thing called a medical breakthrough."

Randy looked at his father, waiting for a reply.

"Mr. Secretary," said CareFree's attorney, Brian Harkness, "I don't think we can waste any more time on such an extraneous issue as the establishment of some kind of institution."

Warren nodded.

Randy grinned insolently. "It's *my* institution that's extraneous?"

"You've been heard, Dr. Lang," said Warren. "Now leave us to continue."

"Have I really been heard, Mr. Secretary?" For an unguarded moment, the mockery vanished from Randy's face. He looked more open and vulnerable, and his mouth seemed to tighten with the hidden pain of an old wound. "Have you ever really heard me?" he asked quietly. "Have you ever really known me?"

"Thank you, Dr. Lang, for sharing your thoughts with us," said Warren. "Now, Mr. Green will continue presenting his case."

Randy's eyes, still blazing from the passion of his plea, cooled when he saw only blank stares around him. An advisor in the jury box swatted a fly. Harkness read his notes. Warren evaded his eyes, looking down. Randy thought of a pile of ashes from which a phoenix would never rise. He turned to his brother to find the only eyes that met his squarely in silent salute. His glance lingered on David, acknowledging a bond that had always been theirs. Then Randy left the courtroom.

"I call the patient, Nicole Hudson," said David's lawyer, Russell Green.

Aided by Mrs. Trimbell, Nicole took the witness stand. Her clothes and makeup were tastefully understated, yet all eyes followed the arresting beauty that was a complete statement of its own. The boyishly cropped hair, the majestically high cheekbones, and the perfectly aligned features suggested a fashion model, whereas the tailored red suit, the tiny diamond earrings, and the small leather purse suggested a young executive. The midthigh length of the skirt defined the boundary where refinement bows to glamour.

Her face possessing a child's openness and a woman's self-assurance, Nicole addressed the gathering: "Everything good that ever happened to me stemmed from my own choice, not from others choosing for me. When I was six, I decided to become a dancer, and everything I've done since then has been geared to achieving that end. People tried to discourage me, but I listened to my own voice. As a result, I developed something precious in my life that has given me the greatest fulfillment I could ever imagine. All of that came from my own decisions about my own life.

"When I was eight, I was abandoned. I lived as a ward of the state, shuffled from one foster family to another until I ran away at thirteen. I had to run away because I was being completely controlled by others, hampering me to the point of desperation. When I left, I rescued my life and my future career. Running away was the best decision I ever made.

"I thought that this dreadful condition of total dependence was something to be endured because I was a child. The hope of one day being in charge of my own life sustained me through the worst moments of my childhood.

"Just when I achieved my goal and was certain that my days of helplessness were over, I received this terrible injury. Dr. Lang told me about his experimental procedure—that there were risks, that my chances were slim, that his animal research wasn't completed, that the procedure had never been tried on a human. He explained that the surgery was illegal and asked if the state's edict mattered to me. Lying in the hospital feeling half dead, I remember wondering how some alien thing called 'the state's edict' could presume to make a crucial decision about my life. I told Dr. Lang that I would want his surgery even if my chances of dying from it were ninety-five percent. I made my own choice, knowing everything I needed to know.

"Now, with Dr. Lang being suspended and with us pleading for permission to complete my treatment, I . . . feel as if I'm a . . . ward of the state . . . again." Her eyes grew more intense. Her voice, superbly steady until then, threatened to crack. Years of experience in fighting for herself made Nicole take a pause that restored her control. "This nightmare existence of having no choice, no will, no way to act has now come back to torture me. I *must* decide this issue for myself, and I *must* have the second surgery. I don't want other people to pay for my medical bills, nor do I want to pay for theirs. I want to stand alone, as a single person, to rise or fall at my own hand. I don't want decisions about *my* life made by others. I want out of this haunted house called CareFree that turns adults into helpless, frightened children."

Her voice rose to fill the room with an anger she could not contain. "And you must stop punishing my doctor for helping me. If you don't, I'll go on every talk show and speak to every newspaper. I'll tell the world how vicious you are. If you destroy me and my doctor, I'm going to make CareFree crumble at my feet!"

Nicole had disobeyed the instructions of David's attorney to be calm and respectful. David tried to dismiss the thoughts he was having about his patient, because his urgent desire to grab the little red suit and to rip it off her body had no place in a civilized meeting.

Harkness sprang up when his turn came. "Ms. Hudson, let me first say how extremely sorry I am about your injury."

He paused for Nicole to thank him for his concern, but she did not.

"I think it's understandable that you would be distraught, Ms. Hudson," he continued soothingly. "Wouldn't you say that under these trying circumstances, you are upset and perhaps not yourself?"

"I'd say I'm very much myself."

Harkness picked up a file from his table and skimmed through the documents inside. "You have quite a history, don't you, Ms. Hudson, of running away as a child and of being returned to the child welfare authorities by foster families? They tried to reach out to you, these records say, but you rebuked their attempts. You were described as being antisocial, uncommunicative, headstrong, disobedient, and maladjusted. This *is* your history, isn't it?"

"Yes, but how is that relevant to what we're discussing?"

"And when you ran away at the age of thirteen, with the blush of childhood on your cheeks, didn't you work illegally under an assumed name as, shall we say, an *entertainer* in a gentleman's club?"

"I was a stripper in a strip joint. But how is that relevant?"

"You were a problem child. You ran away from families that tried to give you a home. You became a stripper at the tender age of thirteen. Could one say that these decisions you boast about having made for yourself are of dubious distinction?"

Nicole smiled wryly. "Does that mean you can force better decisions on me? Better because they're made by you?"

"And through some iron-willed obsession that you had throughout your life, you studied, you succeeded, you became a star. Wouldn't you say that you now have the money, personally, to pay for these nerve-repair surgeries ten times over?"

"And if I didn't have the money, do you think I'd want you to decide for me? If I had no money, do you think I'd want to have no brain, too?"

"Answer the question, please."

"Yes, I have the money."

"You sit here and tell us you want no part of CareFree. That's fine for you to say, isn't it, Ms. Hudson, when you can buy the services of a personal heart transplant team if you wanted to? What about the people who can't afford medical treatment? If CareFree crumbled at your feet, as you'd like it to, what would you suggest we do with the people who depend on this program because they're disadvantaged?"

"More disadvantaged than I was?"

"But you rose above that, Ms. Hudson. You were one of the very few who beat the odds. What about the others who won't ever reach your level?"

"How do you think I rose? How do you think they would rise? I'm telling you from personal experience, the worst thing you can do for the disadvantaged is to keep feeding them like a mother bird that won't let her babies fledge. My blindness is . . . devastating . . . because it makes me dependent on others. Why would anyone want a self-imposed blindness? Basically, there's only you and the world, and you take your chances. That's the challenge—and the glory—of life, isn't it?"

"If I may remind you, the people of this state elected Governor Burrow democratically. The people *want* CareFree, Ms. Hudson. As a citizen, don't you feel an obligation to respect society's laws?"

"No, Mr. Harkness, I can't say that I feel an obligation to respect a law that's destroying me."

"All right, Ms. Hudson." Years of practice raised Harkness's voice to a high pitch of moral condemnation. "It's understandable, granted your history of antisocial behavior and fugitive activities, that you are rebellious and arrogant toward the law!" As David's attorney rose to object, Harkness sat down. "I have no more questions. Thank you, Ms. Hudson."

Nicole felt lost in a dark tunnel echoing with the shouts of Brian Harkness. She lowered her head and sighed as two familiar warm hands covered her cold ones.

"It's over, Nicole. No one's going to ask you any more questions," said the hushed voice that she needed to hear.

"David, I don't know how to talk to these people," she whispered. "They don't speak my language."

"The language you spoke was beautiful." She felt the familiar squeeze of hands telling her this moment was important. "Don't be afraid of them. Here, I'll help you down."

Attuned to the subtle movements of her guide, Nicole needed no verbal cues as David escorted her to the gallery. They looked not like a blind patient and a doctor but more like a young couple, arm in arm, strolling through a park.

When Nicole was seated, Warren nodded to David's attorney to continue.

"I call Dr. David Lang," said Green.

The man taking the witness stand did not look like an outlaw. The clean lines of the starched white shirt, silk tie, and deep green suit had an elegant simplicity. The suntanned face formed a bronze backdrop for the light green eyes that glowed like gemstones. The tall, trim form with the subtle waves of hair cropped closely around the face was serenely classic. The hands with the long, sensitive fingers looked exquisitely carved by a master sculptor. David leaned back in the chair and related his story.

"I broke the law because I can't work with CareFree in the OR with me. To diagnose an illness, to interpret a brain scan, to decide when to operate, to remove a tumor—all require that I analyze the case at hand and apply the sum of my medical knowledge to make a decision. It is profoundly important that I be able to think unencumbered, because a patient's life can rest on my actions.

"To treat a patient, I must examine the person, diagnose the problem, and determine how to fix it. Because the human body is complex, there are no pat answers—only countless combinations of symptoms, conditions, and treatment options. Medicine is not a connect-the-dots puzzle.

"With CareFree, the scientific inquiry I have to make stops. Instead of deciding what are the best tests to run in a particular case, I have to ask: What tests am I *allowed* to run? Someone behind a desk miles away who never met my patient will make that decision.

"Instead of asking what treatment is best in a given situation, with CareFree I have to ask: What treatment am I *allowed* to use? A clerk in an office and a book of regulations can override my judgment. That's what CareFree is—the incompetent ruling the competent, the faceless bureaucracy superseding the individual doctor and patient.

"If it takes an average of six hours to remove a certain kind of tumor, that's what CareFree bases my fee on. Because the human body doesn't confine itself to CareFree's surveys, you may have a tumor that will take me twelve hours to remove, but I'll get paid for only six. What do I do? Remove it completely and work for nothing? Or follow an utterly arbitrary ruling, quit after six hours, and leave you with a vestige of tumor that will regrow in ten years? CareFree rewards the short-term, the mediocre, the shoddy, the unconscientious and penalizes the doctors who are above average.

"With CareFree, instead of deciding what pill is best to prescribe, I have to ask: What pill am I *allowed* to prescribe? My judgment is superseded by an arbitrary third party. If you multiply this kind of humiliation by thousands of cases, and by the chronic fear doctors have of punishment if they break the rules, you'll know why the best ones are quitting medicine, and you'll also know why the American standard of care, once the finest in the world, is deteriorating. The doctors who survive, the ones who play by the rules, give up the thing that makes them good healers: their free, inquiring minds.

"CareFree's rules don't represent any judgment superior to mine—just the opposite. They represent political decisions and statistical averages that have nothing to do with your case. If you can't get the tests or the surgery you need for your condition, it means that your tax money went to buy something else for someone else. The state tells you it's giving you something for nothing, but there's no such thing. What CareFree really does is tax your money, which you can't spend as you choose, so the state can spend it—or not spend it—as it chooses. Not only are you still paying through taxes for your medical care, which is now grossly inflated by the cost of running a huge bureaucracy, but you're also paying a hidden and deadly price—the price of giving up your right to make your own medical decisions. He who pays the bill sets the terms; therefore, there's no method of improving CareFree so that you and I can be autonomous. Any variant of CareFree would be and always has been the same. So do you really want medicine to be 'free' of charge?

"No airline would ever have a clerk in an office miles away telling your pilot how to fly your plane. No hospital or doctor would ever give you cookbook medicine. None of us would give you a distant administrator to decide your treatment on the basis of a statistical average or on the basis of who's trading favors with whom among the politicians. Medicine and politics don't mix. Everyone in medicine knows this. CareFree is like an elephant in the house of medicine. We pretend it's not there, we walk around it, and we try not to get trampled.

"You, the public, seized medicine from the doctors and gave it to the politicians because you wanted your treatment to be free. It's *not* free. You want the providers to shun material rewards and to work primarily for your benefit. I reject that. I practice medicine because I love it. I help others, which gives me great satisfaction, but it's not the thing that can fuel a life's dedication to a grueling profession. I didn't endure the poverty and grind of med school and residency so that I could do a good turn for you without personal gain for me, and that includes material rewards beyond what I could achieve in a job not requiring ten post-college years of training.

"Besides controlling the material rewards that I obtain for my work, CareFree also controls something else that is vital to me and my patients. Nicole Hudson's case demonstrates the issue clearly. It's not about bogus research. I showed that I have grounds for the action I took. It's not about costs. Her surgery can be paid for without taxpayers' money. It's not about the patient's safety. The patient is doing fine. It's about one issue only: my judgment or CareFree's power?

"What's really on trial here? If you want to save not only my patient and me but also medicine itself, you must recognize that you can't straitjacket the doctors; you can't force us to serve you. If you build houses for a living, I don't have a right to march the state in to control your business so that you can provide me with a house for free. That would amount to holding you as my slave. You can't do that to the doctors. It's a fact that in the days when insurance was not controlled by the state, private policies—the good kind that didn't interfere with treatment decisions—were affordable. It's a fact that before the passage of licensing laws, lobbied for by the medical profession, there was a greater supply of doctors and auxiliary personnel, which kept fees low. And it's a fact that before the state's meddling, private charity abounded for those who couldn't pay. The freer, happier, and more prosperous the doctors were, the more generosity they showed to the needy. You tell me whether you'd be in a mood to give private charity after you performed twelve hours of surgery but got paid for only six.

"I tried to give charity to Nicole Hudson, but her treatment was prohibited by law, even though I charged no fee. You tell me the motives of your so-called benefactors who claim they want to help the unfortunate yet condemn a young woman at the pinnacle of her life to a future of misery. I say *CareFree* is on trial here, and I urge you to give it the sentence it deserves. Your own life may depend on your decision."

When he finished, David was looking at Warren.

"Thank you, Dr. Lang," said his attorney. Then Green nodded to Harkness, signaling that it was his turn.

"Dr. Lang," said Harkness, rising from his seat, "your dedication to medicine is admirable, I'm sure. However, from the information I have, it also seems as if you're dedicated to other things, as well. Is it true, Dr. Lang, that before Care-Free, your office pulled in several million dollars in billings each year?"

"Yes."

"So you admit you made a lot of money before CareFree pulled the plug on that?" roared Harkness accusingly.

"I did."

"Excuse me, Mr. Harkness," said Green, rising from his seat, "but why don't you also ask how many ball players, rock singers, company executives, and, yes, even lawyers, made more money than my client did? And how many lives did they save?"

"Mr. Secretary, this interruption is out of line!" Harkness cried indignantly.

"We're not bound by legal protocol here. I think Mr. Green can finish his point," said Warren.

Harkness looked astonished. Green, who was about to sit down, also seemed surprised at being permitted to proceed.

"And what about the years of schooling and residency in which Dr. Lang made little or no income?" Green continued. "And the overhead expenses for his loans, malpractice insurance, office rent, staff salaries—"

David contradicted his attorney. "Well, no, Russ. Even after I paid all the overhead, I still made a pretty good living."

David ignored the angry look his attorney flashed at him. Harkness beamed. With Green silenced by his own client, Harkness continued his questioning.

"And isn't it true, Dr. Lang, that you and your brother talked to private investors about creating a research center with venture capital, where you would test your ideas about nerve repair, ideas that the body of reputable scientists say are impossible?" Harkness's condemning tone made the deed sound terrible.

"That's right."

"And you talked to a pharmaceutical company about producing the drugs you discovered for nerve repair?"

"I did."

David had discussed the matter with his friend, pharmaceutical president Phil Morgan, whose company had several of its drugs removed from CareFree's formulary when Morgan defended David's surgery on Nicole.

"And if a company manufactured those drugs, you, as the discoverer, would collect royalties, would you not, Dr. Lang?"

"I would hope so; that was my intention."

"And if you could launch your research center and get your new drugs manufactured, you could make a great deal of money, couldn't you, Doctor?" Harkness bellowed reproachfully.

"Perhaps."

"And it would please you to make a lot of money, wouldn't it?"

"It would."

"Ah ha! So, in your overzealous drive to market your new products and to get as rich as you possibly could, you cut a few corners and ignored a few rules, didn't you? With wild dreams of fame and fortune whirling in your mind to cloud your medical judgment, you pushed a barely developed procedure and untested drugs on a helpless patient to serve as your personal guinea pig, didn't you?"

"That's absurd," said David quietly.

David's attorney raised his hand to object again, but Harkness prevailed for the final, biting word: "We'll let the jury decide how proper it is for a healer to be wheeling and dealing with drug company executives and venture capitalists and to be recklessly endangering his patients. I don't think I need to ask you any more questions, Dr. Lang, because your actions speak for themselves about your character! Thank you."

Looking pale and distraught, Warren called for the closing statements from both attorneys, and then dismissed the twelve advisors for deliberation. He adjourned the proceeding for two hours. Although it was one o'clock and he had skipped breakfast, he had no appetite for lunch. He retired to his office, staring vacantly out the window for two hours.

When he returned to the courtroom, it was filled. His advisors were already seated in the jury box, and David was staring at him from the defendant's table. Warren turned to the spokeswoman of the panel, who rose to face him.

"What have the advisors decided, Ms. Farley?"

"I'm afraid we're deadlocked, Mr. Secretary. Six of us strongly believe that you should lift Dr. Lang's suspension and allow Ms. Hudson's second operation. The other six of us feel just as strongly that Dr. Lang should receive the maximum suspension and fine for subjecting Ms. Hudson to an unauthorized procedure. Those six further believe that Dr. Lang should be barred from doing any nerve-repair surgery on humans until the animal experimentation is completed and the proper authorities have reviewed the findings and found the procedure safe. We think it would be useless to deliberate further. We have no dispute about the facts of the case, but we have a profound philosophical disagreement about the role of the state in medicine, and it doesn't appear likely that any of us will have a change of heart."

The spokeswoman looked timidly at the secretary, as he had a reputation for demanding that others fulfill their obligations. He had asked for a decision and the advisors had given him none. Would he order them to deliver a verdict that they found impossible to render? Surprisingly, Warren, looking tired and weak, only nodded.

"Thank you, Ms. Farley." Although his next words were addressed to the entire courtroom, he looked directly at David: "We'll adjourn until ten o'clock tomorrow morning. At that time I will give you my decision."

✤22✤
Trapped

An evening breeze stirred through the shade trees and flowed into the open windows. The warm air was like the last gasp of summer, thought David, sitting next to Nicole in her living room. In two days autumn would arrive, a time when the leaves would reach maturity, then die with grace and beauty. His eyes traced the svelte lines of his dainty companion, who wore silk slacks and a sweater. The short puffed sleeves of her outfit accentuated the thinness of her arms. Nicole was in the summer of her life, and he would permit nothing to cause her decline.

Mrs. Trimbell had retired to her room, exhausted from the trial that day. Nicole, resisting her own fatigue, turned on the television to scan the news stations, despite David's protest. The trial was the major story of the day, and the likely topic of discussion on the evening talk shows and news broadcasts.

"We proved our case today," Nicole said with radiant innocence. "Surly everyone will agree."

"Don't count on it."

She located a channel announcing the stories in the headlines: "Tomorrow Secretary of Medicine Warren Lang is expected to issue a decision in the case involving his son's experimental surgery on dancer Nicole Hudson," said the newscaster. "Sources in the Burrow Administration believe the verdict will affect the secretary's credibility as head of the BOM and his chances of running on the governor's ticket. We also have word that Governor Burrow will announce his running mate tomorrow. For more on this story, let's go to his campaign headquarters in Albany."

Nicole switched the channel to another news station. David felt as if he and his patient were about to be swallowed by a large shadow cast by a small man named Mack Burrow.

"Should CareFree be canned, as David Lang and Nicole Hudson suggested at their hearing today?" the host of a talk show asked a political analyst.

"We must respect the law and achieve social change within the system," said the analyst. "If we don't enforce CareFree's rules, we run the risk of anarchy."

"Doctors like David Lang should be reducing the spiraling costs of health care, not devising ways to spend more," said another analyst. "That's why the government must step in."

"But David Lang says that government interference caused the soaring demand and spiraling costs of health care in the first place," interjected the host.

"How we got where we are is irrelevant. What's important now is to prevent the problem from worsening, and only the government can do that."

Nicole once again changed the channel.

"Dr. David Lang and his patient Nicole Hudson today complained that Care-Free is too restrictive. How do you respond to that?" a reporter asked Assistant Secretary of Medicine Dr. Henrietta Richards.

"CareFree is an outstanding program with a distinguished record of helping people," replied Dr. Richards authoritatively.

"Then why have doctors left New York State in record numbers since the start of CareFree?"

"Oh, that's not the fault of CareFree but just the normal human reaction to *change*. Studies show that people don't accept change well at first." Dr. Richards smiled pleasantly. "But their resistance passes after an adjustment period."

"How about Dr. Lang's charge that the doctors can't decide for themselves how to handle cases?" asked the reporter.

"Our administrators always listen to the doctors' requests. A healthy exchange of opinions occurs constantly. CareFree shouldn't be viewed as *imposing* its views on the medical community but rather as *collaborating* with it."

With an angry snap of her finger on the remote, Nicole searched for a better channel.

"Should society allow its doctors to make a pile of money off the sick?" asked Miriam Bell, a talk-show hostess who had just signed a four-million-dollar contract with her television station.

"I believe that the profit motive is incompatible with the life of a healer," replied guest Ronald Wells, a lawyer whose recent defense of a football player in a rape trial brought him a fee of two million dollars.

"And bending the rules for family members is definitely a no-no for a public official," interjected another guest. "CareFree will have to punish David Lang, or else Warren Lang can kiss his political career good-bye."

David took the remote from Nicole's hand and muted the sound. She rubbed her eyes wearily.

"Let's not dwell on the news, Nicole."

She nodded.

"Mrs. Trimbell tells me you're sleeping fitfully and crying out in the night."

She sighed.

"What's wrong? Tell me."

"It's a nightmare I used to have as a child, at times when I felt . . . trapped. I was free of it for years . . . until recently."

"What's it about?" He took her hand.

Her face grew intense, as if troubled by an inner vision. "I dream that I'm in a big church and men are taking me away. I scream and try to break loose because I want to stay with a nun called Sister Luke, but they won't let me. It's the way I was carried off from a neighborhood parish as a child and placed in foster care."

"I see." David left her side to get a glass of water from the kitchen. He gave it to her, along with tablets from a bottle that he took from his pocket.

"Mrs. Trimbell called me this morning, concerned about you. So I brought these pills to help you sleep."

He sat on the couch next to her.

"I suppose I should take them. Thank you."

"Tonight I want you to forget about the trial and to think only about something that's pure pleasure."

She threw her head back wistfully. "I'll dream of the Phantom . . . naked."

His mind burned with wild thoughts of lifting the dainty bundle, carrying her into the bedroom, and making her dream a reality. She would have no nightmares then! Instead, he stood up abruptly, distancing himself from his temptation.

"Take the pills, will you, so I can get going?"

She swallowed the medicine, curious at the sudden brusqueness in his voice.

"I'll see you tomor—" he stopped, catching an image on the television screen. "What is it?"

"It's the commissioner for the blind. Remember the guy you decorated with your milkshake at the hospital? He's on TV with the governor," said David, engaging the sound. "He looks different now that he's dry."

"Today Wellington Ames, the commissioner of New York City's Department of Disabilities, was promoted by Governor Burrow to one of the most coveted posts in state government, director of the Department of Human Services," a reporter explained.

"During a lengthy search to fill the vacancy in Human Services, Commissioner Ames's fine work in New York City came to my attention," said Malcolm Burrow from a hotel podium. "It gives me great pleasure to award the director's post to a distinguished official who has an outstanding record of public service."

"It's a great honor to be appointed to this position," said Ames, standing next to Burrow. "I'll be working closely with the governor on important matters for the people of New York . . ."

Nicole recognized the voice of the official who had wanted to place her in a home for the blind. He was the man who had visited her in the hospital on the day that she had received the Phantom's roses, which was also the day that she had lost the Phantom's letter.

❧   ❧   ❧

In a quiet neighborhood on Manhattan's East Side, a man sat alone on the balcony of his penthouse. He glanced up at a misty sky and down at a deserted street. Dinner from a local restaurant lay untouched on a table. The evening was unusually quiet for the restless figure because it did not include a party, a banquet, a speaking engagement, a meeting, or a television appearance. Although he rarely thought of his wife, who had died several years ago, he missed her that night. He had canceled two engagements that evening—a trip to a shelter for the homeless and dinner at a posh restaurant. The conflict of opposites. For the first time that day, sitting alone in the darkness, he had no attendant to open his mail, to clear his food, to take his messages, or to keep his schedule. He felt revulsion at the thought of being around people and anxiety at the prospect of being alone. The conflict of opposites.

Nonsense! he told himself. He just had indigestion, which made him melancholy. The discomfort worsened when he walked into his study to read a document that he had asked his secretary to prepare for his signature. It was his decision to punish David with the maximum suspension and fine for his unauthorized nerve-repair surgery, thus curtailing further treatment of Nicole Hudson. It was a noble act that would save an enlightened program and only temporarily inhibit his son's career, he told himself. He wanted to sign it, yet he could not lift his pen to do so. He swallowed two antacid tablets to settle his stomach.

The doorbell rang. He answered it eagerly, relieved to have a moment's escape from the task at hand.

"Good evening, Mr. Secretary." Randall Lang bowed from the hallway.

The boyish tangle of blond hair looked as it always had, Warren observed, but the face of the child of his memory had lost its innocence. The once high-pitched voice that had called him Daddy was heavy with contempt.

"Come in, Randall."

The son followed his father through a granite foyer into the living room. There an array of personal photographs displayed on the walls caught Randy's attention.

"Now isn't this quaint? A gallery of your career," he said, examining the pictures. "Here you are, Mr. Secretary, among the new mommies holding their babies in the maternity ward." He removed the picture from the wall and waved it at Warren. "No doubt CareFree brought the little cherubs into the world. I think the boys should be named Warren and the girls, well . . . how about Wareena?" He returned the picture to its place and moved to the next one. "Now here's a nice shot. Mr. Secretary with a baseball cap, throwing out the first ball of the season. Wow! You've got to be important to do that! And look at this next pose. You're in a hard hat breaking ground for the new wing of Buffalo General Hospital. I hope you didn't get your French cuffs dirty. The hospital must've finally gotten through CareFree's labyrinth of permits and approvals. The man next to you must be the hospital administrator, because his spine looks bowed from groveling. Didn't that make you feel good, Mr. Secretary?"

"I know you despise me, Randall. What I don't know is why you came here."

The open contempt of his sons disturbed Warren. He wondered why he felt unsure of himself in the presence of something intractable within them.

"Excuse me for dallying over your photo gallery. It has special significance to me, because if my brother is destroyed tomorrow, it will have been to give you this wall."

Randy stood behind a leather chair, leaning his elbows on the high back. His smile was derisive, but his eyes seemed to hold a long-standing pain.

"You're wrong about me, son."

"Am I?"

"Why did you come here?"

"Why does anyone come to you? I guess I did it the wrong way. I should have invited you to dinner, poured expensive wine down your throat, and inclined my head in a perpetual bow. I should have filled your gut with the nourishment you thrive on. Then I should only hint, indicate, suggest . . . without ever naming my purpose blatantly. Innuendo is so civilized, honesty so crass. Forgive my lack of finesse, but the plain truth is that I came to make a deal."

The last word lingered in the room while Warren walked to an antique liquor cabinet. He poured cognac from a crystal flask into two snifters, handing one to Randy. The men sat in leather armchairs before a marble fireplace. Both drank rather than sipped.

"What kind of deal?" Warren asked suspiciously.

"Mack Burrow sends his goon squad to talk to me regularly. He wants the leading hospitals in key voting districts to support CareFree. He wants us to voluntarily educate the community by offering programs and seminars about the glories of CareFree. He calls this 'enlightening the public through the progressive vision of the providers.' I think in the old days they called it . . . propaganda."

"So?"

"So I'm ready to boost Burrow's campaign with a renowned hospital jumping on his bandwagon. He'll get lots of votes from converting a disbeliever like me. I'm willing to be born again."

Warren's hand stopped in midair, with cognac swaying in a suspended glass. "I don't suppose that your sudden enlightenment comes without strings attached."

"You can guess the only thing you have that I want."

Warren placed his drink on an end table. "Do you realize you just committed a crime?" he said sternly.

"If CareFree operates within the law, then I prefer to be a criminal." Randy emptied his glass.

"Do you further realize that you hurt me deeply?" Warren's face was becoming red-hot with anger. "You came here to wave a campaign favor in my face in exchange for exonerating David!" He sprang up to point his finger in Randy's face. "I'm insulted!"

"But *Burrow* is waving a campaign favor in your face, isn't he? He's dangling his big carrot, the lieutenant governorship, before your eyes in exchange for *convicting* David. So why should my offer offend?"

"How dare you think that I'm open to bribes? And on the question of my son! Who do you think you're talking to? Mack Burrow?" he blurted out involuntarily.

Randy laughed bitterly.

"All right, so now you know. I despise Mack. He's a crude man who loves power for power's sake."

"And yet you back him, you work for him, you want to be his running mate, and you believe in all the same causes he does. You allocate CareFree's resources in ways that win him votes, turning medicine into his personal servant. Forgive me, Your Excellency, but I see two soul mates."

"Stop those humiliating names you call me! I'm not out for power like Mack. I do what's right for the public. *My* motives are pure!"

"Ha!" Randy rose to his feet to stand eye to eye with Warren. "The only person I see who's doing anything right is somebody who never brags about how noble he is so that we mere mortals can revere him. The only person who's doing something right is doing it quietly. That's the person whose motives are pure, the person who has been steadfastly true to his patient, to his profession, and to himself. He doesn't look for 'little' people to keep down so that he can arrange their lives for them, because his goodness depends on their wretchedness. But *you* do. Your motives are *not* pure, Father!"

"How dare you? You're saying I'm some kind of monster who craves power. I don't! I just want to help people." Warren slumped down in his chair.

"Sure you do. You just want to help people, and that places you beyond reproach. You rub those words over your actions like slick ointment, so you can cover up your infected motives. Remember when you wanted to help our neighbor, Richie Haynes? When Richie was a starving writer and you performed back surgery on him for free, that was fine. You were a doctor, and he was a neighbor in need. But you didn't stop there. You were always over at his place, helping him fix the roof, paint the house, do things he couldn't afford to hire someone for. Do you think you were subtle when you wove your good deeds for Richie into every conversation you had with the neighbors? Were you really surprised, as you pretended to be, when someone called a newspaper to suggest a heartwarming story about a neurosurgeon who also repairs a patient's roof? You were so busy fawning over the reporter who covered the story that you didn't notice how embarrassed poor Richie was by the whole thing.

"Then when Richie sold his screenplay to Hollywood and made a bundle, you changed, didn't you? When Richie insisted on paying you for the surgery, why did you look so unhappy to receive his check? Why did you lose interest in Richie as soon as he made good for himself? You went to his place when he was a poor slob who depended on you, but you declined his invitations after he spent a fortune redecorating his place to entertain in style. You wanted him to stay needy so that you could get some kind of perverted kicks out of being his savior. Would you say your motives were pure?"

Randy poured himself another cognac. "I saw things like this all the time as a kid, and it was obvious that you were grandstanding. David was so mesmerized by you as a surgeon that he had a blind spot. While he worshipped you in the OR, I saw another side of you. When you took the post as head of the Bureau of Medicine, David was devastated, but I wasn't surprised."

Randy angrily swirled his cognac, spilling some on the rug. "If you destroy David tomorrow, I want you to know that someone understands the real nature of your action. Someone knows that you sold your soul for what you call a noble ideal but what is nothing more than the limousine you ride in, the attendants at your fingertips, the reporters who fawn over you, the hospital presidents who tremble in your presence, and the 'little people' who give you what you salivate for: superiority, supremacy . . . power. Don't you see that the same bug that bit Burrow has infected you?"

"Your picture of me is so black, Randall. Everybody gets a little thrill from the glitz and glamour of being a public figure. But I use my power to do good for people."

"What people? David and Nicole?"

"David, his patient, and all of us are part of a bigger picture that I, in my post, must consider." There was no hint of the fatherly affection that Randy recalled from a distant past. The stranger before him was the official Warren from the political podiums. "I want so much for you and David to understand that, to help me out here, to give a little!"

With an angry snap of his head Randy emptied his drink. "If you don't exonerate David, because you won't let go of this magic balloon you think will pull you to heaven," Randy said, staring into Warren's eyes, "then you'll lose *two* sons tomorrow, not one."

A cool draft from the hallway hit Warren's flushed face as Randy left. The agony over signing the document in his study intensified. He fought the temptation to switch on the television. The talk shows would feature pundits offering him advice. But he was the leader whom people turned to for guidance. Why did he turn to the talk shows? He found it demeaning to consult them, yet unbearable not to know what they said about him. The conflict of opposites. He sat in the silent living room for a while, brooding.

Then the doorbell rang again.

"Mack!" Warren said, opening the door in astonishment.

"Hello, Warren. I hope I'm not interrupting."

"Why, no. I'm just surprised to see you. Come in."

"I'm staying in Manhattan tonight, so I thought I'd swing by and maybe get offered a drink." *Swinging by*, for Mack, meant having a limousine and bodyguards covering half of Warren's block. Yet no one had entered with him.

"Of course. Cognac?"

"Sure."

Warren nervously poured two cognacs. The governor had never come to his apartment before, nor did Burrow go anywhere without an entourage of aides. His purpose was apparently too important to discuss by telephone and too private for anyone to overhear.

"I figured you'd also be in Manhattan tonight because of the hearing."

"Yes." Warren handed Burrow a drink.

The governor's tie was loose, his hair disheveled, and his paunch bulging from an open suit jacket. Without a podium and a cheering crowd, he looked like a simple, tired, middle-aged man.

"I wondered what you were up to with that jury you appointed. I thought you were going to do things differently than we had discussed. But it's turning out better this way. There's suspense building, Warren. People are riveted to the hearing and speculating on what you'll do. Tomorrow morning you'll announce your decision, and tomorrow afternoon I'll announce my running mate. Yup, there's real drama in this."

The men sat in armchairs, facing each other across a coffee table. The fireplace along the wall made a cozy setting for a chat.

"So what's your verdict?" Burrow asked pleasantly.

Seven weeks of insomnia marked Warren's eyes with dark rings and his gaunt features with a ghostlike pallor. "I haven't completely committed myself yet," he said in the tone of one selecting a coffin.

Burrow's smile vanished. "You mean you're *still wavering?*" he asked incredulously.

"It's not that easy, Mack! David's work is brilliant, and his patient is a young woman fighting for a normal life. How can we turn our backs on that?" Warren whined like a child asking one last time for permission to do something forbidden. "That can backfire for you at the polls."

"Not if he doesn't succeed in curing her!" the governor blurted out involuntarily.

"If David were disreputable or negligent or a disgrace to his profession, it would be so easy to punish him. I wouldn't blink an eye."

"I have news for you, Warren," Burrow said slowly, in measured tones. "Your son *is* a disgrace to his profession, which is why you *will* punish him tomorrow."

"What?! That's nonsense!"

"I was hoping I could spare you this." Burrow pulled a paper from his vest pocket. His voice sounded reluctant, yet he offered the document eagerly. "I thought your integrity would lead you to the right decision, but I see how much I can count on that! Read this, and you'll find the justification you need to make the right choice."

Warren began reading to himself a letter written in a flowing script that was familiar to him: *Dear Nicole, when you fell, the light you hung in the room of my soul came crashing down . . .*

Warren was gripped by the words.

I want to hold a mirror to the radiance you poured into my world . . .

For an unguarded moment, Warren felt not like the head of an agency but merely like a father discovering a new aspect of his son. He thought that he should be outraged by the impropriety of the letter, but he could only marvel at the tender sentiment and the beauty of its expression. Warren read in awe, like a spectator of a feat beyond his capacity.

I sent roses to honor the endless summer that once made its home on your sweet face . . .

The way fresh waters sometimes stir murky streams, the letter momentarily roused Warren. It cleared the sediment on his soul, unearthing a tiny gem long buried—the dream of romance and adventure that he had sometimes entertained in his youth. He recalled Nicole's proud manner and passionate assertions about her own existence, and three words came to Warren in response to the thing he had just learned: *But of course.*

Reading the letter, he seemed to be an intruder on something sacred in another man's life. A thought struck him with horror. Was he not now making a far greater intrusion on the lives of these two people?

"That's a copy. I have the original, of course," said Burrow. "Three experts inform me that among your son's many talents is an unusually distinctive handwriting. So they can prove he wrote that letter even though it's unsigned."

"How did you get this, Mack?"

"A public-spirited person brought it to me when the patient apparently let it slip from her hands in the hospital. It was near a bouquet of roses that she had received from her lover, your son. You say he's a good doctor. I say he's a lousy adulterer. He is married, isn't he?"

"I'm sure you already checked that out."

Burrow smiled. "Did you realize that he knew the patient before the operation?"

"Regardless, the medical treatment was sound."

"Warren, I'm shocked! If Romeo were anybody but your son, you'd see that this letter makes our case perfectly against the doctors. The public needs us to protect them from unscrupulous practices by doctors, like this shameful conduct by your son. Because you can't see the nose on your face, let me explain the obvious: Your married son was having an affair with a showgirl. She was injured. He was distraught over her accident; he says in his letter that he'd do anything to make her feel better. So in a moment of passion, he makes a desperate attempt to rescue his girlfriend by pushing on her an experimental procedure before it's ready. He's her lover and he's a surgeon, so she believes anything he tells her. He takes advantage of that fact to get her consent to an unlawful brain surgery.

"I thought your son had a following, and I couldn't press too hard on him. I thought people would perceive a certain honesty in him that could arouse sympathy. But now I know better. Do you think that in light of this letter anybody is going to utter a peep when I pull his license?"

"You can't touch his license! You can't make this public! We need to ask David about the letter. Maybe there's a more innocent explanation."

"What difference does it make?" Burrow shrugged his shoulders. "The letter, along with the charges that I just indicated, will suffice for a strong case against him, regardless of his excuses."

"But isn't it important to know the truth before jumping to conclusions?"

Burrow laughed. "The truth is that he broke the law! You make me sick, Warren, with your philosophy, you noble causes, your high-class act. You're like a wax model that looks good in a display box but melts in the heat. Now here's your choice, and I don't care what you pick, because I win either way." Burrow's voice was part thunder, part mockery. "You can exonerate your son, in which case this letter will leak out, causing a public scandal that will cost him his license. I haven't announced you as my running mate, so it's no problem for me. If you exonerate him, I will publicly express my disapproval of your decision and choose another candidate. When the letter hits the press, I'll be proven right and you'll be forced to resign."

Warren gasped, his mouth agape in the undignified pose of someone fighting for his life.

"Or you can punish your son with the maximum suspension and fine, putting a lid on his new treatment. After he cools his heels for a year, he can practice again, this time in a humbler frame of mind. So what's the problem with this? The public hails you as the honorable leader you claim to be. The doctors learn that they can't walk all over us. Your son has another shot at continuing his work in the future. The patient sues and becomes filthy rich with a huge malpractice judgment paid by your son's insurance company. Your son finds a new girlfriend. . . . And I announce you as my running mate."

The last sentence brought a tinge of hope to Warren's face.

"And we ride to victory on your great moment, Warren. You're Abraham, the man of integrity who sacrificed his personal interest in order to serve a higher good."

Warren tried to forget the words just uttered by the previous visitor about a slick ointment that covered tainted motives.

Burrow rose, pacing restlessly, his weariness gone. "Warren, I need this election. I must maintain the momentum that's going to catapult me to the presidency. I'll be the leader of three hundred million people and the most powerful man in the world!" Burrow's face burned with excitement. "Do you think I'm gonna let a hotshot doctor and his Broadway cupcake grind my career to a halt? Do you see what I mean, man?"

"My sons would say you're blackmailing me to win an election."

"I see it differently. I have a duty to bring this letter to your attention because it's relevant to a case you're evaluating. You need to control your son before you can hope to control an entire state. If you don't put a lid on him, you can say good-bye to your place in history."

Warren sat quietly for a long moment, contemplating the situation, while Burrow sipped his cognac patiently. Then the secretary rose from his chair with the resolve of someone who had reached a decision. Excusing himself, he went into his study and made a copy of the document that his staff had prepared for his signature. It was so much easier to act now, he thought, to do what he really wanted—no, not *wanted*, but felt was his *duty*—to do . . . for the *public*, of course. But now there was no more conflict, because the act that he would perform for the people was also the act that would save David. He at last had full justification for doing the . . . right thing. Even his sons could not challenge his actions in light of the new information just revealed to him. Warren brought the papers to Burrow.

"Mack, today I wrote this decision, which punishes David. I have two copies, which I can sign. One of these documents I'll bring with me to the trial tomorrow, and the other I can give to you now . . . in exchange for David's original letter to Nicole."

Burrow smiled in sheer delight. "Now you're learning, Warren!"

"This isn't what you think it is, Mack. I'm not signing this document to buy a political post from you. I could never do that! I'm acting to save the career of a brilliant surgeon and to do what's right for the people."

Burrow grinned mockingly. Warren eagerly handed him the papers but evasively looked away. "The people need David's skills. Protecting him from scandal and preserving his license is in the public interest."

"Whatever you say, Warren, my friend." Burrow laughed derisively.

Warren signed both copies of the document while Burrow summoned an aide to bring him a confidential folder containing David's original letter. Soon a noble exchange of papers between two honorable officials was completed.

❧ 23 ❧

The Final Verdict

For the first time in weeks, Warren slept soundly and awoke refreshed. A gourmet meal service arrived with his breakfast, which he devoured. The dark rings around his eyes had lightened and a pink color had returned to his gaunt cheeks. When he arrived at the brick building of the Bureau of Medicine, he lifted his head to the gold inscription above the door, as if catching sparks from a power source: *To serve the public interest above all other concerns—this is the noble work of medicine.*

Inside the crowded hearing room, David and his lawyer sat at one table, Care-Free's attorney at the other. The reporters and onlookers were in the same places as on the previous day. Only the young patient was missing. When David had telephoned Nicole's apartment earlier that morning, he learned that she had not yet awakened, doubtless the result of his sleeping pills and her exhaustion. He had asked Mrs. Trimbell not to wake her; instead, he would visit her after the hearing to relay the verdict.

"She'll be angry if she misses court," Mrs. Trimbell had warned.

"Blame it on me," David had replied.

When his father appeared at the judge's bench and called the meeting to order, David rose to hear his sentence.

Warren had subdued the warring factions in his mind so that his voice was calm and confident. "Dr. Lang, you are a gifted surgeon. Your research is excellent. However, you have broken the law, and you must be held accountable. I have no choice but to fine you twenty-five thousand dollars and to suspend you for one year."

A murmur rolled through the spectators. David gasped in horror.

"You may return to medicine after your suspension and enjoy many productive years of practice," Warren continued. "We encourage you to pursue your research at that time through the proper channels. Your work is a noble vision, Dr. Lang, but CareFree is noble, too. We must combine the two for the public good. This is why you are prohibited from performing any more unauthorized surgeries. And for the patient's safety, you must discontinue treatment in the case in question."

David's voice was an outcry of anger and hurt: "I *will* complete the case I started, Mr. Secretary."

Warren's voice faltered. He looked taken aback. "Dr. Lang, I expected that once the sentence was official, for the sake of your future, you would resign yourself to it. You have many years left to practice and thousands of cases to treat. I hope your love of medicine will prevail and help you to accept this fair decision!"

"I *don't* accept it." David's voice reverberated through the courtroom. He pointed his finger at Warren. "But it does set me free. I can say anything I please now, because I have nothing to lose. I'm going to expose CareFree so that everyone will know how arbitrary and corrupt it is. I damn your institution and I damn *you* as irrevocably evil!"

He stomped angrily out of the hushed courtroom, the echo of his steps reverberating in Warren's ears.

When the secretary reached his office on the twelfth floor, he vanished behind closed doors to tackle his most important assignment: composing the acceptance speech for his nomination as lieutenant governor. There was no time to spare, he told himself, bracing for a whirlwind seven weeks of campaigning.

He resisted the temptation to ask for his messages until completing the task at hand. He eagerly expected congratulations on his courageous decision from across the state and even from Washington. The secretary of the National Department of Health Services would surely call, and perhaps even the president himself. After Burrow's announcement of his running mate, there would likely be a banquet and a late-night party. He sprang from his seat to check his adjacent closet and dressing room, relieved to find a favorite outfit, a linen suit handmade by a tailor in southern France, ready for him if he found no time to change at home. He had best keep multiple suits handy in his house, his penthouse apartment, and his offices to meet the demands of the campaign. There would be strategy sessions, speeches, rallies, magazine interviews, television appearances, photography shoots. He felt a rush of excitement unequalled in his life.

His door opened a crack.

"Dr. Lang, I'm sorry to interrupt—"

"Doris, come in, my dear! Can you schedule my barber and manicurist to stop by tomorrow?"

"Yes, of course. The reason I—"

"And could you arrange to have two of my tuxedos sent from my Albany home to my Manhattan condo?"

"Yes. Now I have—"

"And I'll need more dress shirts. Can you telephone my tailor?"

"Dr. Lang, the governor wants to see you *right away*."

"Oh, yes, of course!" Warren smiled broadly.

"He's at his suite in the Rutledge Hotel."

Warren leaped from his chair with the energy of a sprinter at a track meet. He opened his closet door so he could look in a mirror to straighten his tie and smooth his hair. "I may get stranded with the governor for lunch and a press conference, Doris, so don't be surprised if I'm gone for a while." He winked at her with a boyish exuberance.

"Of course, Dr. Lang. Your driver is waiting outside."

Warren inhaled the splendor that was the private parlor of the governor's suite at the Rutledge Hotel. A crystal chandelier hanging from a gold-leaf ceiling rested like a bejeweled crown over the antique furnishings. He entered with the spry gait of a prince called to the palace for his coronation. Smiling broadly, he approached the governor, his hand extended for a robust handshake. Burrow raised a limp hand to oblige halfheartedly, then gestured to a seat on the sofa.

"Have you heard the news?" Burrow said crossly as he sat in an armchair opposite Warren.

"You mean the news of my decision at the trial?" Warren said cheerfully, expecting to be congratulated.

"That news is two hours old! You're always a step behind, aren't you?" Burrow snapped. "I mean the announcement by *Insight*, the most popular news show on national prime-time television, that your son will appear in a special segment called 'A Critical Look at CareFree'!"

"He's grounded, Mack. He's just letting off steam. He'll get over it."

"You silly fool, he's gonna open a can of worms, and just weeks before the election! You were supposed to put a lid on him, damn it!"

"I did. He's handcuffed. He can't operate."

"What about his mouth?"

"I did exactly what you said to do. Now, I was hoping to discuss . . . our campaign."

"You mean *my* campaign." Burrow folded his arms sternly.

"What?!" Warren whispered incredulously. "What do you mean, Mack?"

"I'm rethinking my choice for lieutenant governor."

"*What?!* How could you? I acted honorably. We had a deal! I'm expecting my name on the ballot!"

"Our deal was that you'd put a lid on your son. I can't pick a lieutenant governor whose son is waging a crusade against me. He'd get tremendous news coverage if his father were on my ticket. His gripes against CareFree could dominate the campaign. I can't have that."

Warren's face was a white oval of naked fear. "Mack! What did I buy for signing that document last night?"

"You bought his license, man. You got the love letter, so he keeps his license."

"What about the . . . lieutenant governor's . . . post? You were ready to choose me. It's the . . . dream . . . of my life. I've sacrificed everything for it!"

The desperate plea failed to register on Burrow's indifferent face. He walked to an antique desk in the room and removed two documents from a delicate drawer of carved wood. "There's plan A and plan B." He held a document in each hand. "In my right hand is a speech announcing you as my running mate. In my left is a speech in which I announce that the state comptroller will be my running mate instead. If you can't deliver the goods, I'll go with plan B."

"But you said that if I punished my son, the press would hail me as a man of integrity who puts aside personal motives to serve a higher good, and that's what you needed. You offered me a deed to immortality. You said we'd ride to victory on my great moment."

"But you didn't have a great moment. The news reports are mixed. Your son is a loose cannon, threatening to blast CareFree. The press is wondering what secrets he knows and what dirt will come out."

"But Mack, I still chose *you* over my son!" Warren rose from his seat to plead his case before Burrow. "Remember Abraham and Isaac? God rewarded Abraham for his loyalty. You can't double-cross me!"

"I expected you to crush your son. You tied his hands but not his mouth. Having you on the ticket now will embarrass me and help him get massive media exposure as the son of my running mate."

Burrow surveyed the trembling body before him that moments ago held dignity, and even he felt sickened at the transformation. He sighed. "Okay, Warren, I'll give you one final chance." He glanced at his watch. "It's noon. My press conference is at three. You have a couple of hours to talk sense into your son. If you can get him to cancel his appearance on *Insight* and call off his crusade by two-thirty, you're in. That's the best I can do."

The secretary's limousine stopped in front of the medical building next door to Riverview Hospital. Warren composed himself before entering. He traveled a familiar path to a simple wooden door with a translucent glass window, a place laden with memories. Black letters on the glass announced *David Lang, MD, Neurosurgeon.* Warren recalled his immense pride on opening that door for the first time, when David had begun his practice. Back then the father had entered with the brisk walk of a welcomed visitor. Now he almost tiptoed.

By virtue of CareFree's decree, the bustling office of his memory was now a ghost town. The front desk and waiting area were lifeless. He walked further, past a dormant examining room to the half-opened door of an office. Sounds from a radio floated into the corridor, with an announcer introducing a sonata.

He knocked gently. "David?"

David had learned from Mrs. Trimbell that his exhausted patient was still sleeping. He was awaiting a call from the nurse to tell him that Nicole awakened, at which time he would visit her to relate the outcome of the trial.

"What are you doing here?" David looked up from a newspaper spread open on his desk. Blank eyes and a toneless voice did not offer Warren the benefit of anger.

"I want to explain why I had to do what I did today. May I please come in?"

"No." The face that used to brighten whenever Warren entered a room was expressionless.

Warren cautiously opened the door wider while remaining outside. "I had to punish you for your own good, to save your license. Yes, I saved your license today! I want you to know that."

Warren stepped in gently and waited to be offered a seat. The offer did not come, so he remained standing.

"There was a beautiful letter that you wrote to Nicole. It was unsigned, but in your handwriting."

"How would you know about that?"

"Mack Burrow had it."

A faint raise of the eyebrows was the only response Warren received.

"I don't know how Mack got it."

"I do." David's mind made two stops: on the letter's disappearance the day Commissioner Wellington Ames had visited Nicole in the hospital, and on the news report the previous evening of the promotion Ames had received from Burrow.

"That letter could be very damaging to you."

"Why?"

"Because Mack was going to leak it to the press!"

"So?" The son looked at his father blankly.

"David, really," Warren admonished gently. "You know it's improper to be having an affair with a patient, especially in such a controversial case. Mack was going to make a scandal out of it that would have cost you your license. By threatening to leak the letter, he forced me to punish you, and I gave in to save your career. You're suspended for a year, but you still have your license, thanks to *me*!"

Warren waited for words of gratitude but heard only the sonata on the radio. "Well, David?"

"I'm not having an affair with my patient. She doesn't know who sent her the letter. I admired her from a distance and wrote to her anonymously. That's all. There's no scandal to threaten my license." David frowned thoughtfully. "If your decision to punish me was based on that letter, then why didn't you ask me about it beforehand?"

"But Mack was going to say there was a scandal. With his smear campaign—"

"The truth is my defense. Let him say what he pleases."

"But he could make the letter public!"

"So let him."

"But the letter would hurt Marie. Surely you'd want to spare her feelings."

"Not really."

"I can get that letter back to you, so it will never be made public." Warren acted as if Burrow still had the letter.

David looked at his father suspiciously.

Warren eagerly pulled a chair up to his son's desk and sat facing him. "All you have to do is cancel your appearance on *Insight,* and I can get that letter into your hands. You can save yourself from a smear campaign run by expert mudslingers!"

David burst out laughing. "And what will *you* get, Mr. Secretary? Is this the last hoop for you to jump through to become Mack the Blackmailer's running mate? Forget it." The amusement in his laugh never reached his eyes.

"I'm only thinking of you!"

"Then why didn't you ask me about the letter and find out the truth before making your decision?"

Warren looked away from eyes that were too intelligent. David leaned back, cocking his head as if contemplating a puzzle.

"The letter is innocuous. I'm not having an affair. I could probably demonstrate the truth if I had to. Why were you so . . . quick to . . ." The son studied the pathetic, fidgeting entity that used to be his idol. "You were *eager* to accept Burrow's accusations, weren't you?"

"That's not true!"

"Because you *wanted* to punish me, and the letter gave you grounds. That must be it." David's expression changed from grappling with a problem to solving it. "You wanted to punish me so that you could please Burrow and get on his ticket. It might have been hard to keep from yourself the knowledge that you sold Nicole and me down the river to get your nomination. But with the letter, you could tell yourself that you punished me for my own good, to save my license and spare me from a scandal."

"That's not the way it was!"

David eyes narrowed as if he was piecing the rest of the puzzle together. "And if you made a deal with your boss to punish me in exchange for the letter, then you'd have it yourself. You would have *bought* the letter with your decision against me. I'll bet you *do* have it!"

"But . . . but . . . David . . . " The thought of the letter in the drawer of his study choked Warren's denial.

"I guess you didn't do enough to please your boss, so he sent you out to squeeze the noose around my neck tighter. And you obliged. Tell me, Mr. Secretary, if CareFree is as great as you and your boss say it is, then why are you two scared silly of me talking about it on television?"

The sonata on the radio ended, leaving the question to linger in the silence. Warren was too petrified to say more, David too revolted.

Just then the radio announcer reviewed the day's news: "Today Governor Burrow will announce his running mate for the gubernatorial election. Sources are now doubtful that he will choose Secretary of Medicine Warren Lang, once the leading contender, because of the secretary's ongoing family disputes. The charges of corruption that his son made against CareFree are said to be an embarrassment to the governor."

"So that's it," David said with certainty. "Burrow is about to spit you out. You need to shut my mouth, so I won't cause 'family disputes' or make embarrassing 'charges of corruption' to keep you off Burrow's slate. So you're blackmailing me with a letter that you yourself already have and could burn if you were really concerned about it hurting me. I'll tell Nicole that I won't appear on TV to fight for her surgery after all. I decided to let her rot in a world of darkness so that my ex-father can practice his new line of work: lying, blackmail, backstabbing, and abuse of power."

Warren's face twisted into a soundless scream. He had found no welcome in Burrow's parlor, only disapprobation. He now found only contempt in the office of a son who had once given him the only hero worship that he had ever known.

"But David, you make me sound terrible. It's not like that. I just try to help people." Warren was unconvincing, even to himself. "I was the hero of your childhood. Don't you want to patch things up between us?"

"You never were the man I thought you were," David said quietly, as if talking to himself. "You enjoyed medicine for a while, but you never loved it the way I do. You craved something else more than medicine, more than me . . . more than anything. I was wrong about you."

"I don't crave . . . what Mack does! I couldn't stand to be like him. It can't be true. You're just being difficult. Why won't you try to make up with me?" Warren cried desperately. "I'm losing everything!"

"So you want Nicole and me to lose everything instead. Get out of here."

"But—"

"No buts. Just go."

David walked to the door, politely holding the knob the way he would for a salesman overstaying his visit. Two terrified eyes looked into two unyielding ones, and Warren knew that he had lost forever David's admiration, the greatest gift that anyone had ever given him.

The secretary walked into the building next door, tracing another familiar path, this one to the glass and chrome executive offices of Riverview Hospital. An inner voice, cultivated over years as a public official, recited lines for him automatically: He was furthering a noble cause; therefore, it was permissible to bend the truth on occasion. However, he could no longer remember a cause other than his own political ambition.

After being refused admittance, Warren pushed his way past a receptionist into the office of his other son. The father expected to be thrown out, but Randy remained seated at his desk, as if the intruder were not worth the effort of evicting.

Warren pleaded the same case: He wanted to protect David's license from a scandal cooked up by Burrow. Would Randall help save his brother by convincing him not to speak against CareFree on television?

"No," Randy said flatly.

"David trusts you. You're the only one who can save him from a terrible scandal that will cost him his license."

"No."

"Don't you want to save David?"

"By collaborating with his enemies?"

"But this is for a worthy cause, Randall."

"Your only cause is you and Burrow."

"Won't you hear me out?"

"No."

"But the situation is urgent!"

"No."

"Once I'm elected, I can help you and David."

"Get out."

Warren felt as significant as a fly on the wall.

Frantic with fear, he returned to the limousine. He had only one option left. If it worked, he could not only win a place on the governor's ticket but also make amends with his sons, he told himself. "The Rutledge Hotel, please," he directed the chauffeur.

Moments later, Warren beseeched the governor in his parlor suite. "Mack, the only way to stop David from talking on television is to allow him to finish Nicole's treatment."

"We closed that door, Warren," Burrow said impatiently.

"But David doesn't care about anything else, not even his license."

"He's grounded and stays grounded."

"We can find a loophole for him to appeal the case, Mack. Then we can reinstate him and allow the new treatment because it's in the public interest. David's on the verge of a medical breakthrough, and the public needs new discoveries. CareFree must support these efforts."

"Warren, you tire me," Burrow said, sitting at the antique desk in the expansive room, reading his messages and glancing at the newspaper headlines while Warren stood over him, pleading for his life. "The public needs a lot of things. You decided what they needed seven weeks ago when you told me you couldn't make your payroll, and you told the doctors they had to limit their tests and treatments. How can you blatantly contradict yourself?"

"But you contradict yourself all the time, Mack. I mean, you change your mind on issues constantly. So we can say that I changed my mind. The public interest lies in new treatments and cures."

"The public interest lies in limiting treatment, so we can meet CareFree's payroll."

"The public interest lies in nerve repair, Mack."

"The public interest lies in vaccinations for kids."

"The public interest lies in crossing new frontiers."

"The public interest lies in keeping up with our old frontiers."

"The public interest lies in David's work!"

Burrow smiled slyly, like a card player holding the better hand. "Warren, you silly man. Don't you know that human desires and needs are unlimited? Is it good to cure baldness? Yes. Is it good for mommies to rest in the hospital after having their babies? Yes. Is it good for people to get expensive brain scans every time they bang their heads, just to be safe? Yes. Is nerve repair good? Is it better than curing cancer? Better than fixing bad hearts? Better than kidney transplants?"

"David's research has to have a place in all that. You can't decide it doesn't, Mack."

"Grow up, man! I *do* decide. The public elects me to decide these things. Right now I've got to win in November, otherwise there won't be any CareFree, so it's definitely in the public interest for me to get votes. And that's not gonna happen if we cave in to the doctors. Your son broke the law, and you clipped his wings. If we backed down now, the press would cremate you for favoritism. I can't have *another* running mate embroiled in scandal. Case closed."

"But, Mack, listen to yourself. All you're saying is that David acted against *you* and will make it harder for you to win. But he didn't do anything against the *public*."

"I stand for the public! An act against Mack Burrow is an act against the people!" Burrow roared angrily. Then his voice lowered to a whisper, as if sharing a secret: "*The public interest is me, Warren.* Haven't you figured that out yet? *The public interest is me!*"

Warren looked dumbfounded, like an animal frozen in the sudden glare of approaching headlights. "You mean," he said, his voice trembling, "that there is no . . . noble cause. There's only . . . you?" The headlights were closer, larger, blinding.

Burrow's sagging face came alive. The immense power he wielded burst from his towering voice. "That's the glory, man! Great leaders make an impact on their times. We alter the course of history!" His hand was raised in a fist, his eyes wild with excitement.

Warren was shaking, his voice a mere whisper. "Are you telling me, Mack, that I sacrificed the gifted surgeon who is my son for the sake of *your* interests . . . for . . . *you*? I thought that I was working for something greater than us, something noble. But now you're telling me that the public interest is only you—it's whatever you want, your wishes, your . . . arbitrary . . . whims."

"It's your whims, too, Warren. Don't forget that," Burrow said shrewdly. "We've been over this ground before, man." He glanced at his watch. "I'll have to figure out how to deal with your son myself from now on. I've got a press conference, so if you'll excuse me . . ."

He rose from his desk and reached into the drawer. He examined two different documents and selected one.

"What did you choose, Mack? Plan A or plan B?" Warren asked timidly, his white hair disheveled, his imported suit rumpled, his face unable to capture its former dignity. His eyes held the fixed stare of a patient dreading a terminal diagnosis.

"I'm afraid it's plan B, Warren." Feeling slightly sympathetic, Burrow tapped him on the shoulder consolingly and left the room.

⊱   ⊱   ⊱

Warren listlessly returned to his office, like a man who had nothing better to do.

Doris followed him to his desk, standing over him with her notepad. "Senator Tibald and Congressman Ederly called. *National Weekly* wants to interview you." She peered up from her glasses, "Dr. Lang? Are you listening?"

"No," said Warren indifferently.

"Shall I come back later?"

"If you wish."

"Dr. Lang, are you feeling all right? Can I get you anything?"

"No," he said despondently. "And I don't want to see anyone."

"But people to whom you granted appointments are waiting."

"All right. Show them in."

A succession of citizens paraded into Warren's office to plead their cases to the person who held their future in his hands.

An older man with a cane was Warren's first visitor. "Mr. Secretary, I pay four times the taxes my neighbor does. Four times! How come he got a liver transplant when I can't get dialysis? What makes his liver more important than my kidneys? They say I'm too old to qualify for dialysis. I'm only sixty-two, not too old to pay taxes for other people's treatment!"

Warren's next visitor was a woman in her fifties. "I'm on a waiting list for heart bypass surgery. I'm told there are no beds, but I passed a ward of empty beds in my hospital. It's something about exceeding their budget, so the hospital took beds out of service. Does this make sense?"

Then a woman in her forties entered. "I was able to get a screening test for lung cancer in one day. But now that I learned I have cancer, I have to wait three months for surgery. Three months! My neighbor's kid just had an operation on his knee, so he can play sports. My husband is not an enlightened man, Dr. Lang. He doesn't understand why the boy's knee got priority over my lungs. I'm afraid he's going to bash in the child's other knee!"

How could he decide these cases? Warren wondered, terrified at the answer flashing in his mind. He heard the echo of David's voice: *What must my patient do to win a door prize, too?* And the snicker of another man who had said: *It's your whims, too, Warren.*

Then a hospital administrator arrived: "Why has Coleridge Hospital been denied a request to repair its only brain scanner? We're a small hospital, Dr. Lang, but we've always prided ourselves on our modern technology. We've never been without a scanner, and Hudson Hospital just got two approved. Why them and not us?"

Another hospital administrator followed that visitor. "Why can't Mercy Hospital charge higher fees than Jefferson Memorial? Mercy is in a more expensive area, with higher mortgage, taxes, and other expenses. How can you expect us to charge the same rates as a hospital with half the overhead?"

The gratification that Warren had once felt in deciding the matters before him now turned to revulsion. He recalled Randy's haunting words: *You don't see that the same bug that bit Burrow has infected you?*

Warren no longer felt a thrill from granting favors, refusing requests, being the one who decides the fate of millions. When the person with the last appointment left, he picked up his picture of eleven-year-old David, wrapped in a surgical gown, watching his first operation. Warren observed the eagerness on the boy's face. Then he thought of himself flying in a private plane, sipping whiskey with windbags at political meetings, and seeing his picture on the cover of *National Weekly*. He thought of the faceless doctors who had only a fraction of the talent of the boy in the picture, the doctors who would attend the right parties, say the right things, and mingle with the right people. They would get the grants and the positions of importance, he knew. Warren closed his eyes against a deadly question forcing itself on him: Who would have made that possible?

He placed David's picture in his pocket and opened the door. "I'm going home, Doris. I don't feel well."

"But Dr. Lang, your department heads are arriving for a meeting with you." She spoke to the back of his head as he quietly left.

When Warren arrived at his apartment, he removed the photographs hanging in his living room, leaving a dotted black line of bare hooks across the almond-colored walls. On one of the hooks, he hung the picture of David as a boy. Then he poured himself a drink and sat facing the little photo. He thumbed through a large scrapbook stuffed with news clippings and magazine articles. Years ago he had filled the book with stories of David's surgery to separate the conjoined twins. He paused over a picture of David in scrubs after the landmark operation. His son looked weary from the ordeal, but his head was tilted upward and his eyes filled with the most profound pride that Warren had ever seen. He glanced at the boy of eleven in the OR, beaming at him from the wall. He saw the pride of the surgeon contained in the face of the boy, and the childlike excitement of the boy in the face of the surgeon. Then Warren left the room to enter his study. He returned with David's love letter and lit a match to it.

The father spoke to the eleven-year-old boy in the picture:

"You and Randall were right about me. I bragged about doing things for the public interest, but I was never concerned with real, individual people. I gave things to some people at the expense of others, prompted only by my political ambitions. Oh, yes, I admit it! I destroyed you, David, not for any noble cause but just so I could be Burrow's running mate and grasp the most exciting thing I've ever experienced, the thing I breathe for. The true nature of my acts was never real to me until your case. I knew that the *means* used by Burrow—and me—were corrupt, but I didn't know that the *end* . . . that there was no noble end, only a string of . . . injustices . . . I committed toward other men's children, and now toward my own son as well. But the most shocking thing of all to me is that even knowing this, I'd still give anything to stand with Burrow on the steps of the capitol, and I'm devastated by losing my most passionate dream. To lose you and Randall on top of that is too much. There was a time when I did love medicine and you, and I see that I was happy then. Now there's no going back . . . and no . . . going . . . forward."

As Governor Burrow stood at a podium at the Rutledge Hotel, announcing the state comptroller as his running mate, there was a commotion on the street outside of Warren's high-rise condominium. Someone had fallen from a balcony. A white head of hair lay crushed against the black pavement.

✤ PART THREE ✤
Hope

❧24❧

A Colorless Day

As Warren Lang pronounced his verdict in the courtroom, Nicole Hudson slept. She had awakened during the night, and, exhausted from her recent bouts of sleeplessness and fearing the return of her nightmares, she had taken more sleeping pills, exceeding David's prescribed dosage. Mrs. Trimbell had followed David's advice and let her sleep through the trial. Hence, the ballerina rested as soundly as the princess of her childhood ballet. However, unlike the princess, Nicole was awakened not by the pleasantness of a kiss but rather by the ring of her cell phone. She groped for it on the nightstand.

"Hello," she said groggily.

"Hello, Nicole, dear. Do you know who this is?"

Nicole recoiled at the voice. "I don't want to talk to you."

"I called to tell you how terribly sorry I am."

"About what?"

"You mean you don't know, dear?"

Nicole tapped the talking clock on her night table. It was three-thirty in the afternoon! She sat up abruptly. "What are you talking about?"

"You sound as if you're just getting up. How very thoughtful of your doctor to let you sleep through everything. I'm talking about the news everyone knows but you, dear."

The voice paused teasingly, as if wanting to be prodded. Nicole did not oblige but waited silently.

"This morning your doctor was suspended for a year, fined twenty-five thousand dollars, and prohibited from continuing your treatment. He must comply or lose his license and never practice medicine again."

The caller could not hear the gasp Nicole suppressed or see the phone trembling in her hand.

"And I'm afraid there's more, Nicole. Are you still there, dear?"

It took the whole of Nicole's effort to whisper two steady words: "Go on."

"Warren Lang fell from his balcony and was pronounced dead."

By six o'clock that evening, Nicole had slipped two of David's sleeping pills into Mrs. Trimbell's coffee, and the hardy woman had fallen asleep. The distraught ballerina called for a car and, aided by her cane, left the apartment to wait for her ride. Someone observed her from a vehicle parked down the street: David. He had been returning from the hospital where he had identified his father's body and met with family members. As he had been wondering how to tell Nicole the terrible news of the day, she appeared at the entrance of her building carrying a suitcase. The shock of the verdict and the horror of his father's demise had unnerved him. The sight of Nicole running away again made him livid. He would teach her a lesson, so she would never pull this stunt again. Those events were what led a doctor to frighten a blind person.

He pulled his car up to her building and got out. Hearing the slam of the door, Nicole opened the locked gate of her residence.

"Is that you, Mike?" she said.

David shoved his way through the gate. He pinned her arms behind her and gripped both of her wrists with one hand. He gagged her mouth with the other, suppressing cries of pain and fear. He dragged her into the bushes lining the verdant entrance. Hidden by tall shrubs, he pushed her into the side of the building and pressed his body against her. She felt cold bricks scraping her back and a warm body squeezing her chest and thighs. Her sightless eyes saw terror. Sandwiched between the building and the body, Nicole's desperate efforts to scream, to pull away, to kick, to scratch were fruitless against his iron grip. She was horrified.

"You crazy kid! It would be so simple to hurt you!" he said at last.

"David!" she murmured through his hand. At the sound of his voice, the fight drained from her body. She stood limp in the arms of a man she had no capacity to fear. He eased his grip on her.

"You scared me to death! And you hurt me! David, how could you?"

"No one saw me. You couldn't identify me. I could rob you, rape you, murder you!" He shouted angrily, shaking her by the shoulders.

Hands still trembling from her scare curled around his neck. She felt firm muscles through his thin shirt. "You loved him. From the way you spoke of him, I know he once meant a great deal to you, David."

"Goddamn it, you were running away again!"

"You loved him for all he once gave you."

"You could've been hurt!"

"And you're horrified by what he did to you and to himself."

He sighed painfully, his anger yielding to grief. "Yes," he whispered, his arms wrapped around her, his head buried in her neck, his lungs breathing the maddening scent of her perfume. She held him close, consoling her assailant.

"You loved him before he changed," she whispered.

"I did."

"And he loved you."

"He did."

Her arms tightened against a shuddering pain that left him speechless. For a long moment that was a memorial to something sacred, he held her tightly in what had become their first embrace. Finally, his body steadied and he lifted his head.

"David, I'm . . . devastated . . . by what happened today . . . by the way I'm wrecking your life."

"You mustn't think that. You're the only thing *not* wrecking my life."

"But I . . . my case . . . killed your father."

"My father . . ." He paused painfully, his voice unsteady. ". . . thought he was drinking the nectar of the gods, but it turned out to be poison. He learned that men don't need gods after all; it's the gods who need men. That's what killed my father."

Hearing a car approach, he released her, gently brushed some twigs from her hair, and straightened her clothes. She submitted to his grooming, the feel of his body still lingering on hers. He took her hand and led her out of the bushes. He in a wrinkled suit, his tie loosened and hair disheveled from the day's harrowing activities, she in wool slacks and sweater, still dazed from his attack, they walked the few steps to the gate enclosing her building.

"Ms. Hudson? It's Mike from Reliable Car Service," said a man at the gate.

David recognized the young driver who had previously refused a tip. "Ms. Hudson won't be needing your services after all. She's not going anywhere."

The driver paused for Nicole's confirmation.

"I'm sorry, Mike, but I've had a change in plans," she said. "I'm not going any-where . . . tonight."

With the side of David's body touching hers, she could feel him turn to her sharply on the last word.

"No problem. Have a good evening," said Mike.

When the driver left, David grabbed her by the arms, his anger returning. "Why were you running away?"

"CareFree ruled against us. You can't do the second surgery, so the case is closed."

"I promised you from the beginning that I'd do the surgery. I never said it would be legal."

"And I never said I'd let you destroy your career by operating illegally. But you're crazy. You'll knock me out and drag me to this surgery. And you'll lose your license! That's why I have to run away."

"Do you think you're doing me a favor by keeping me in medicine today? Why would I want to practice under CareFree? It destroyed my father, and it's destroying . . . someone else . . . in my life. I'm not going to let it take you." He lifted her hands to his chest. "Nicole," he whispered excitedly, "I'm in a bind. I can't raise false hopes. But if your surgery's a success, no one will dare touch me! I ardently want to take this chance. It's more than your surgery. It's what medi-cine means to me: my work and my life out of anyone else's grip. Do you know what you convey to the audience when you dance and why people love your show? You're their dream of a boundless freedom. That's what real medicine means to me, with its endless secrets to explore and discoveries to make. I don't want to *dream* about it. I want to *do* it."

"You once said that you saw my show."

"Yes."

"Did you feel those things, watching me? A . . . boundless freedom?"

"I know why the Phantom needs you. He needs you desperately, you know."

"David," she said, her voice trembling, "I'm in a bind, also. To save myself, I risk destroying you. And to save you, I destroy myself."

"Don't let them pit us against each other. Think of the surgery as helping me to fulfill my dream. Will you?"

She had no reply.

He squeezed her hands and pulled them tight against his chest. "Nicole, the timing of the second surgery is *critical*. You must be around when it's time. *Swear* that you won't run away."

She lowered her head, weighing the matter, then looked up. "Swear that you won't do the surgery illegally."

He dropped her hands disappointedly. "Let's go upstairs."

Knowing every subtlety of his moves, she folded her cane, preferring to walk with his guidance exclusively. As he carried her suitcase, she tucked her hand under his arm and used her finely honed awareness of his body to lead her.

They opened the door of her apartment to loud, rhythmic snoring from an alcove off the kitchen. The unconscious Mrs. Trimbell was slumped on an armchair with her legs spread open ignobly.

"What did you do to her?" asked David.

"What do you mean?" Nicole replied innocently.

David grabbed the bottle of sleeping pills that he had left in the kitchen and counted them. "Never mind. I know the answer."

They walked into the living room, where a nippy breeze from the balcony signaled the approach of autumn. The wind swayed through a bouquet of balloons. Since Nicole had first perceived color, David had kept her supplied with bright bundles of balloons, which she fastened to the end table and gazed at by the lamplight.

"Okay, you win for now," said David, facing her. "We'll try to find a way to do your surgery legally. We have about six weeks before I need to operate. Let's blitz the media and attempt to muster popular support. The election is in seven weeks, so Burrow will be highly sensitive to public opinion. I've already scheduled an appearance on *Insight*. My father's . . ."—his voice broke painfully— "fall . . . could damage Burrow. We'll try to pressure him to permit the surgery. How's that for a plan?"

"Perfect!"

"I don't know about that. The public is drifting. They may like our ideas momentarily, but then they'll be afraid of losing their so-called entitlements and clamor for Burrow to stay in power. We can't fix our course on driftwood."

"But we have to *try* to reach the public, David."

"We can try. And it'll keep you from running away. But if that doesn't work, we're back to my plan."

"We'll discuss it."

"By the way," he asked, the anger creeping back into his voice, "who told you the news?"

She did not respond.

"I called Mrs. Trimbell before I came here. She said you hadn't listened to the news yet, and she wouldn't let you hear it from anyone but me. Did someone call you?"

"I'm not saying."

The day's tragic events had sapped his emotions. He felt impatient with an opposing will as strong as his own. He grabbed her by the arms and shook her. "Was it the same person who frightened you in the hospital and made you run away then?"

"David, you're hurting me."

"Someone's frightening you. I want to know who it is!"

"I'm not saying."

She pressed her hands against his chest, pushing free of his grip. The force of her movement threw her back a step, tangling her in the balloons. She lost her balance and almost fell over the lamp on the end table. David steadied her.

"Easy now," he said more calmly. With darkness approaching, he switched the lamp on. "Are you okay?"

Nicole was not listening. She was looking at the balloons, holding them against her face, one by one, with the lamp under them.

"David," she said fearfully. "They're all gray. These beautiful balloons . . . have turned . . . gray. I can't see the colors anymore."

✣25✣
Close Friends

"Wigged out" was the way the governor's staff described Malcolm Burrow on the last Monday of September. Although he had gained weight, Burrow scolded his tailor when his new suit would not button. Although he had jerked his head during a haircut, Burrow roared at his barber for nipping his ear. Although he had arrived an hour late for a scheduled luncheon, he reprimanded his chef for serving overcooked chicken. The governor had been acutely wigged out since his approval ratings had plummeted after Warren's death the preceding week. "Damn you, Warren," he mumbled to himself whenever he saw the decedent's picture on television.

In public, however, Burrow lamented: "I was shocked and saddened to learn of Warren Lang's untimely accident. He was a noble man who gave unceasingly of himself to serve the public interest. His passing is a terrible loss."

The coroner found that Warren had suffered a heart attack, but he could not ascertain whether it occurred first and caused the fall or whether the fall came first and precipitated the coronary. The governor's press secretary gave the administration's interpretation: "Last Thursday afternoon, the secretary of medicine felt ill and left his office early to rest at home. It appears that he was on his balcony when he suffered a heart attack, causing him to lose his balance and fall."

David Lang explained the sequence of events differently. "My father jumped because he was driven to desperation from being double-crossed," he told the press.

"Who was double-crossing your father?" questioned a reporter.

"Ask the governor."

That Monday afternoon, campaign manager Casey Clark discussed the political implications of the tragic event with Burrow at the governor's mansion.

"When Warren died, your rating fell *ten* points! People are uneasy. Sixty-two percent of those polled believe David Lang's charge that you double-crossed his father and drove him to desperation," said Casey, pacing on the Oriental carpet in Burrow's office. "People are wondering what dirt the hotshot will have on you and CareFree when he appears on *Insight* next Sunday. And remember how the opinion meters registered approval when the guy spoke for himself about his own cause?"

Burrow slammed his fist onto the mahogany desk and swore, shaking his droopy jowls. He stood up, rolled his morning newspaper, and clubbed the desk with it in cadence with his words: "I've got six weeks to the election, goddammit! What am I gonna do?"

Burrow beseeched his young devotee for help the way the ancients had consulted their soothsayers.

Clark stopped pacing, the lace curtain of the window making a white frame around his dark suit. "The way I look at it, insanity means repeating the same behavior and expecting different results."

"I've got to do something different. But what?"

"David Lang must be stopped."

"I've got to shut his trap. But how?"

"There's the carrot and the stick, but you already tried the stick."

Burrow bristled. "That leaves us with the carrot—his new surgery. But I can't cave in on that."

Clark's questioning face seemed not to agree.

"I can't, Case. I won't!" The governor pouted, his bottom lip protruding petulantly, his shoulders slouching, his hands in his pockets nervously jiggling his keys.

"Let's not say *cave in*, Governor. Remember, a tragedy occurred. You may want to intervene in a special circumstance, as an act of mercy."

The governor's keys stopped rattling. His face brightened with the only radiance it knew: that of finding a crafty scheme. "That might play."

"It will. And you'll position yourself as the friend of science. The doctors and the people want research. It's in CareFree's charter to support that. What better time to create an institute for medical research than when the issue is hot and we can get maximum press impact?"

The governor stood in the center of the room, waving his hands as if on a podium. "Mack Burrow, friend of science, hears the voice of the people and announces a new initiative, a way for medical researchers to breeze through the regulatory process and gain speedy approvals."

"Scientists can apply, and friend of science Mack Burrow will ensure that noteworthy projects bypass red tape and get quick approvals from the state," added Clark.

"In the same spirit that an intervention was made for Abraham in the Bible, I will intervene for another man who put a higher good before his own. I'll lift the suspension on Secretary Lang's son so that he can apply, too."

"And when he does, we'll push his application through. If his new treatment is successful, you'll be the hero for making it happen. If it's not, he still was fined twenty-five thousand dollars and suspended for two months, so no one can say he got off easy. You're covered both ways."

"That might just play, Case."

"If David Lang dares to criticize CareFree, who would take him seriously after the state found a legal way for him to move forward? You responded to a snag in the system and corrected it. That takes the wind out of his sails."

"If we act now, he'll never appear on *Insight* next Sunday."

"That would be *imperative*, Governor."

"But what about all the other researchers who'll want to bankrupt the system and undermine our authority?"

"They'll apply. We'll stall things for a while. After the election, you'll see what you can do. Then we won't need to support some of the things we support now, so the priorities will change. When we toss everything in the air after you're re-elected, we'll see how research shakes out."

"Hmmm."

"Think about it, Governor."

As Clark turned to go, Burrow buzzed his secretary. "Mary, who's my next appointment?"

"John Slater," a pleasant voice from the phone's speaker replied. "After that, Tess Olson. And someone arrived without an appointment—"

"I'm not seeing anyone unscheduled."

"Okay, I'll ask Dr. Randall Lang to leave."

"Who?"

"Secretary Lang's son Randall, the hospital administrator."

Burrow and Clark looked at each other, surprised. A curious grin formed on Burrow's face.

"Send him in, Mary. I'll see Dr. Randall Lang after all."

Randy sat in the governor's outer office, staring vacantly at a painting of the Dutch colony of New Amsterdam. Little sleep and a long drive from Manhattan to Albany, following a stressful weekend of memorial services for his father, made staying awake a challenge. Restless with worry, Randy had awakened at 4:00 that morning. As he had sipped coffee in the kitchen, his wife had entered, wearing a black silk robe, her red hair tousled.

"I didn't want to wake you, Beth."

"What's wrong, honey?" she had said, throwing an arm around his shoulders, sitting on the stool next to him at their breakfast bar.

"My job has become an exercise in being a person who's not me."

"I hate seeing you unhappy. I wish you could quit."

"Not until Victoria gets her skating lessons, Stephen his piano training, and Michelle her private grade school, and not until we put all three of them through college."

Beth had nodded. Their three children were gifted, and also expensive.

"Policing David to keep him out of the OR hasn't made my job more pleasant."

"I'm sure."

"David's going to do the second nerve-repair surgery. I don't know how or where, but he'll do it. Unless his experimental procedure is an unqualified success in its first human trial, he'll lose his license, and no other state will accept him. It'll be the end of my brother."

"Now that he's talking to the press, maybe public pressure—"

"The public are whores. They'll respond to David one minute, then they'll demand more of Burrow's programs to take care of them. The only thing that can save David is something he won't do—play Burrow's game."

"What do you mean?"

"I mean we have to be whores, also, to get concessions from the BOM."

"What are you thinking of doing, honey? You're worrying me."

"Never mind."

Randy had not shared with Beth the plan that had brought him to the governor's office. His half-closed eyes suddenly sprang open at the sound of Burrow's secretary approaching. "Dr. Lang, the governor will see you."

Under a historic painting of the Founding Fathers drafting the constitution, Malcolm Burrow sat with his feet up on his antique desk, cutting a hangnail with a nail clipper.

"Good afternoon, Governor. How nice of you to see me when you seem so busy."

"Have a seat, Dr. Lang," said Burrow. Randy sat on a dainty Victorian chair as Burrow lowered his feet and sat up. "So what brings you here?"

"I was in the neighborhood, so I thought I'd drop by."

"How nice. Now what topic can we find to discuss, because you apparently didn't bring one?"

"How about double-crossing?"

"You'll have to talk to your brother about that."

"I heard him say to talk to you."

"You heard wrong."

"That must be it! My hearing's on the blink. I'd better get my CareFree hearing aid."

Burrow smiled pleasantly. "If that's all, Dr. Lang, you will excuse me."

"I came here because I'm concerned about you, Governor."

"And why would that be?"

"If you don't already know it, my brother is crazy."

"So?"

"So his patient's eyes are healing. The nerves are doing what everyone says they can't do; they're growing. My brother's going to restore the patient's sight when he does her second surgery, which will make headlines worldwide. And you, Governor, I'm afraid, will go down in history along with the inquisitors who took pause at the idea of the Earth revolving around the sun and persecuted Galileo."

"I appreciate your concern for my place in history, but you're forgetting one thing, Dr. Lang: Your brother can't do the second surgery."

"I told you he's crazy. He'll do it."

"But no hospital in the state would—"

"He doesn't need a hospital."

Burrow paused, as if genuinely surprised at something he had not considered. "But even if that's true, surgery still requires an operating team, which he doesn't have."

"If he looks hard, he may find a couple of people in medicine who are less than elated with CareFree and willing to help."

"If your brother's success is guaranteed, as you're suggesting, then what's your problem, Dr. Lang? Surely a concern about something besides securing my proper standing in history brought you here."

"I want my brother to do the surgery legally."

"In case he fails?"

"Yes. And you, I suggest, should want him to do the surgery legally in case he *succeeds*. So we have a common goal, Governor."

"We have so much in common, Dr. Lang."

"By the extravagant promises of its charter, CareFree is supposed to support new research and treatments. The best time to establish a research institute would be now. You can name it after my father to pluck at people's heartstrings. The institute will expand the bandwidth so that CareFree can approve experimental procedures it denied in the past. Because my father bent over backward to avoid favoritism, you can say, he was too harsh with his son. In Warren's memory, you can lift David's suspension and allow him to continue his experimental surgery under the auspices of the new institute. Then when David is successful, you can take all the credit. What a perfect media event right before Election Day."

Burrow remained stone-faced, to ensure that his visitor would never suspect that he was already considering such a plan. Only Burrow's eyes showed expression—the intensity of someone stumbling on a mother lode. "I see another matter involved here, Dr. Lang. Because you're so concerned with securing my reelection and my proper place in history, I should think you'd want to squelch those nasty rumors that your father's death was anything other than a terrible accident, rumors spread by your brother."

"I could possibly make a statement about that."

"I should think you'd want to do more than merely make a statement. I should think you'd want to campaign for me to demonstrate publicly your conviction that your father's death was indeed an accident and not triggered by any

double-cross associated with me. I should think you'd want to stand on a platform beside me with your arm around my shoulder."

Randy said nothing. His eyes stared at a spot on the rug.

The governor smiled, leaned back, and locked his hands behind his head in
repose. However, his eyes were not relaxed; they displayed more than their
usual shrewdness. He noticed the pause, the change in Randy's demeanor, the
subtle signs that he was a master of detecting. Those signs told Burrow how to
find the sacred in men, the way a hound sniffs a trail, and how far he could go.

"You have a strong resemblance to Warren. You'll look very good on my platform. Don't you want to campaign for me, Dr. Lang?"

Randy closed his eyes for an imperceptible instant. "I could possibly make a
few appearances," he said, the casual shrug of his shoulders negating an inner
pain.

"I think we may have a deal, Dr. Lang."

Randy nodded, rising from his chair. "When my brother sees me waving your
campaign banner at the same time his suspension is lifted and his research approved, he's going to fling your presents back in your face."

"Why would he be such a fool?" said the governor sincerely.

"For an odd thing called integrity. But because so few of us possess it, it's not
worth worrying about. When David storms into my office to accuse me of col-
luding with you, I'll need to call you on my phone's loudspeaker, so he can hear,
and demand that you not reinstate him for reasons I'll give and he'll understand.
You just have to take his side against me. And you need to act as if we're close
friends, *Mack*."

"It's done, *Randy*." The governor scribbled a number on notepaper and passed
it to Randy as pleasantly as a shopkeeper closing a sale. "Here's my private cell
phone number. You can reach me there any time."

Randy slipped the paper into his jacket. "Okay. And there's also the matter of
getting my brother's staff privileges reinstated by Riverview's board of directors."

Burrow beamed. "I'm sure I can do something for you there." He rose to face
Randy across the desk. "Your brother will be hearing from us soon. And you'll
be hearing from my campaign manager to schedule your public appearances on
my behalf."

Randy nodded somberly and his friend Mack smiled as they ended the meeting with a handshake.

The next day Mack Burrow stood on a podium outside the governor's mansion with his newly appointed secretary of medicine, Dr. Henrietta Richards. He
had summoned the press to make an announcement: "Secretary Lang and I frequently discussed ways of stimulating medical research through the Bureau of

Medicine. Just days before he passed away, we were finalizing plans for an institute to streamline the regulatory process, so scientists could work more productively and devote themselves to cutting-edge research. Today I feel tremendous personal satisfaction at announcing the culmination of our plans." The governor paused, lowered his eyes, and softened his voice in sadness. "I only wish Warren were alive today to see his vision become a reality." He slowly raised his head, as if recovering from his grief. "I hereby announce the establishment of the Warren Lang Institute for Medical Research."

No one knew what the institute was, where it was, or what it did; however, everyone was moved by a grand gesture to a fine man.

The following day the Burrow administration issued a press release:

In view of Warren Lang's distinguished public service, the governor reviewed the recent judgment of CareFree against the secretary's son, David Lang. Governor Burrow believes the verdict to be excessive in levying both the maximum fine and the maximum suspension, as the secretary was obviously trying to avoid partiality. In honor of Warren Lang's memory, the governor has asked Dr. Henrietta Richards, the new secretary of medicine, to consider lessening the suspension so that Dr. David Lang can once again serve his community.

That evening Randy appeared at a political rally in Manhattan with the governor. "The age of unbridled individualism is past," said Randy. "The man best suited to grab the reins on the new stagecoach of humanity is Mack Burrow."

The next day a letter and a visitor appeared in David's office, both from the Bureau of Medicine. The letter notified David that CareFree was lifting his suspension. The visitor was the first to enter David's office in two months, except for Nicole, whose perceptions of light, motion, and color he measured and recorded there. A thin man with a pale, oblong face introduced himself as Dr. Harold Wabash, the director of the Warren Lang Institute for Medical Research, a new department within CareFree. He sat on a dusty chair.

"Dr. Lang," he said, opening his briefcase and producing a document, "I would like to give you an application for admission to our institute. If after careful review we find your proposal acceptable, CareFree will permit you to continue your nerve-repair research by conducting animal experiments and completing the human trial you started."

"Why the change of heart?"

"CareFree is committed to supporting medical research. With the new institute, we can now do that."

"Why choose me?"

"Why not choose you? Your research is in the public interest."

"Why is it in the public interest this week, when last week it wasn't?"

"CareFree is a dynamic program. Its priorities change frequently."

"You mean it contradicts itself left and right."

"You may think what you wish, Dr. Lang, but I'm offering you a golden opportunity."

"Do you mean that if I'm approved, CareFree will let me perform the second surgery on my patient, Nicole Hudson?"

"Precisely."

The disturbing adage about Greeks bearing gifts flashed across David's mind. However, the immense value of doing Nicole's surgery legally—in a hospital, the safest of all places, and without the worry of her running away—drove thoughts of the Greeks away.

"I have to do this surgery right away. I can't wait even five weeks for approval."

"I assure you we can act on your application expeditiously. By CareFree's charter, the federal government will also contribute funds to this initiative through its National Institute of Medical Research. Once we approve you, we'll send your application to the feds for their acceptance. But that's only a formality, just a background check to ensure you are who you say, you did what you claim, and you worked in accredited institutions, that kind of thing."

"What's the catch?"

"There's no catch, Dr. Lang," said Wabash, extending the application to David across the desk.

David did not pick it up. "I'll think about it."

"Very well," said Wabash, rising. "By the way, we also evaluate a doctor's public image—you know, his appearances and statements to the media—to be sure he reflects the vision and ideals of the institute." Despite his casual tone, Dr. Wabash looked at David pointedly.

"So that's it."

"If your public behavior is acceptable," Wabash said pleasantly, "we should be able to approve your research."

"What about a television interview on how CareFree is destroying medicine? How would that look on my application, Dr. Wabash?"

The new director laughed. "You must be joking."

After Dr. Wabash left, David briefly felt the crisp air of late September as he walked next door to the Riverview Hospital office of his brother.

"You've been avoiding me since the funeral and not returning my calls. Last night I saw you on the news *campaigning for Burrow*. Then today I get guardian angels to lift my suspension and approve Nicole's surgery. What's going on, brother?" David stood over Randy's blank face behind his desk.

"I don't know what you're talking about," a toneless voice answered.

"I got a letter from CareFree lifting my suspension, then a visit from the head of a new CareFree research institute that wants to approve my experimental surgery. Why is this happening? Why is it coming right after your appearance with Burrow? And why in hell's name are you standing on his goddamn platform?"

Like an engine with a worn starter, Randy rose sluggishly to face David. "Dad's death was the end of the road for me, pal. My kids were devastated to lose the old man. When Mom died, it was from natural causes, and my kids accepted that. But this was their first experience with tragedy . . . the end of their innocence. And it left me drained, too. I saw how hopeless it was to knock our heads against a brick wall. I'm tired of fighting—with the board, with the regulators, with everybody. What's the use?" He threw his hands up. "Being a CareFree boy scout makes my job much easier. I'm in tight with Burrow now. I know he's using me, but at least I'll get tossed an occasional crumb. You can hate me if you want to, but that's my new life."

David reached across the desk to squeeze his brother's shoulders. "You can't be serious."

"I am."

"This is a trick. You made a deal with Burrow. Why would he send me Christmas presents today? I won't let you do this! You'll get out of his grip now!"

Randy's arms hung limply as David shook him by the shoulders. When David released him, he calmly sat down behind his desk and dialed a number he had memorized.

"Burrow here," the governor's voice sounded over the phone's loudspeaker, with David hearing him clearly.

"Hey, Mack, it's Randy Lang."

"Hi, kid. What's up?"

"That's what I'd like to know. I agreed to campaign for you, Mack, but you didn't say anything about lifting my brother's suspension or approving his new surgery."

"I felt I owed it to your father, Randy."

"I'm sure you also felt safer reeling my brother in, so he doesn't talk to the media."

Burrow said nothing.

"I told you I didn't want David involved with CareFree. If he comes back into the system, he'll break more laws and get into more trouble. The sooner he gives up or gives in, the better off he'll be. I don't want to encourage his new surgery. If it's successful, then CareFree will control it. CareFree will set the terms, pick the patients, fix the fees. David will have to battle the certification officers, the inspectors, the administrators—and when will it end? I don't want my brother dragged through this, Mack. I want you to stop him *now*, before he's beaten— and broken—later by the system."

David gasped incredulously.

"I'm sorry, Randy, but I did what I did. Your father would've approved. Your brother can practice medicine again, and he can apply for permission to perform his new surgery. CareFree doesn't hold grudges."

"Maybe no hospital will give him staff privileges." Randy's eyes avoided David's mortified face. "Riverview won't, if I can help it."

"I think it will. I've already talked to my friend Charlie Hodgeman, your chairman of the board."

"I wish you would've asked my opinion, Mack! I thought I was your new advisor on medicine."

"I've got a stable of advisors, kid. Hey, I'll see you at the rally in Buffalo, won't I?"

"I'll be there."

"Thanks. Take care."

"'Bye, Mack."

Randy stood up to face his brother across the desk.

"I don't believe it! How could you do this?"

"Give up, David. They'll toss you a crumb now, but they'll make you pay later. They'll own you, man."

"A crumb! You're talking about Nicole's life!"

"It's a new procedure. I don't want to see you raise wild hopes—"

"Wild hopes!"

"And I don't want to help them destroy you."

David walked behind the desk. His eyes searched Randy's face for a sign of life but found none. He was trembling when he cupped Randy's face in his hands. "They got Dad. They're getting Marie. I can't let them get you!"

"And I can't let them get *you*. They don't really give us anything. They tease us. They'll pretend to let you do your research, and then they'll tell you to use a black animal with a white spot every other Tuesday. They'll pretend to let you do your surgery, then they'll tell you what patient to take, how to operate, what to charge, what color pill to give on what day. Give in, David. The time for research is past."

"You're depressed over Dad. You'll snap out of it. This isn't you, man!"

"But this is what you wanted, isn't it, David? You told me not to get involved with your affairs. You told me to denounce you. You wanted me to be safe. Now I'm safe. If I support you, I'm not safe. You don't want both of us getting in trouble, do you?"

David's voice shook with a fear he could not control. "That's the same thing Marie says! I couldn't bear to see what's happened to her happen to you. Listen to yourself, brother. This isn't you!"

"I'm tired, David. Very tired."

David loosened his grip around his brother's neck, a grip that was part embrace and part stranglehold. His hands fell slowly, and he stepped back. Randy's face was an impermeable block of stone. David was seeing pathology more serious than anything he encountered in the OR. He quietly turned and left the office.

He did not see Randy fall into his chair, his face sinking to his desk, his hands covering his face.

That evening David discussed CareFree's offer with Nicole.

"Oh, David, I'm so happy you can work again! I'd give anything to have you perform my surgery legally. That's the only way I could agree to it."

The next morning David canceled his television appearance on *Insight* and submitted an application to the Warren Lang Institute for Medical Research.

The autumn chill of the next two weeks deepened the leaves to orange and red. They bristled stiffly in the wind and speckled the tree-lined walkways around Riverview Hospital with the vibrant October colors of sunflowers and wine. Beyond the crimson vines of ivy clinging to the redbrick hospital, color was returning to a surgeon's life. In the manner of a starving man let loose in a supermarket, David gorged himself in the OR. He filled his cart with all manner of tumors, aneurysms, blood clots, tangled vessels, ruptured discs. He explained cases to patients, drew pictures of their insides, showed them their scans, answered their questions, cured their problems, accepted kisses from grateful relatives. He operated at a grueling pace, as if the heady world of the OR were the narcotic he needed to dull the wrenching pain he felt at the death of his father . . . and the living death of his brother.

He received notice from the Warren Lang Institute for Medical Research that his application was provisionally approved. It was sent for final acceptance to the federal authorities jointly funding the project. Dr. Harold Wabash assured David that permission would come in two weeks, after a routine check of his professional background.

A brain scan showed that Nicole's optic nerves were mending, although her visual perceptions were diminishing because of the growing interference of the scar tissue. From his experience with animals, David judged that the best time to perform the second surgery was fast approaching. He would need to operate before she lost all perception of light. Waiting beyond that point would yield failure. However, operating too soon would also be risky because introducing the scar-inhibiting drug would halt the growth of the optic nerve. For the maximum nerve growth, he had to wait until the last possible moment, which was right before Nicole totally lost the perception of light. David concluded that the perfect time to operate would be when the final approval came in two weeks.

One mid-October day, long-legged Nicole, in wool slacks and turtleneck sweater, sat at the end of his examining table. He darkened the room and shone a strong light at her.

"I see light," she said.

He waved his hand in front of the light from ten feet away, a distance from which she had detected motion a few weeks earlier.

"Do you see anything moving?" he asked.

"No."

He moved to five feet from her, waving his hand. "Do you see anything moving now?"

"No."

He moved to three feet. "Now?"

"I see light, that's all."

He stood directly in front of her, waving his hand before two lovely blue eyes that had alertly followed his motion a few weeks ago but now stared vacantly in one spot. "Do you see anything moving now, Nicole?"

"No."

Although she knew what to expect, losing what little perception she had was disturbing. She lowered her head in concern.

He held her hands in comfort.

✻26✻
The Unexpected

Outside the governor's mansion, a few remaining autumn leaves clung precariously to the sugar maples, resisting their inevitable fall. Inside, Malcolm Burrow was trailing in the gubernatorial race, hanging on to the branches of power just as tentatively, on the day when Randall Lang phoned him.

"Need I remind you, Governor, that it's Friday, October twenty-sixth, over a month since we made our gentleman's agreement? My brother needs to operate *now*, but I know he hasn't gotten approval yet."

"I'll get on that right away."

With less than two weeks before the election, the governor wanted nothing to go awry. He called Dr. Henrietta Richards, the head of CareFree. She called Dr. Harold Wabash at the Warren Lang Institute. He called his counterpart at the National Institute of Medical Research, who called his administrator, who called her inspector assigned to review David's application. Dr. Wabash assured Dr. Richards and the impatient Dr. David Lang, who called daily, that approval would come on Monday. Dr. Richards assured the governor, who assured the equally impatient Dr. Randall Lang.

On Saturday night, no moon shone to illuminate the cloudy autumn sky. The thicket of leafless shrubs lining the campus walkways of West Side University concealed a man dressed in black. The whooshing sound of his steps was amplified in the stillness as he trampled through piles of fallen leaves on his way to the William Mead Research Center. He zippered his leather bomber jacket against the biting chill of the season's first cold spell. The parking lots were empty and the windows of the buildings dark. People belonging on the campus had left hours before to meet companions at restaurants, movies, parties, bars. But the man in black met no one save a stray cat that paused to appraise him with a translucent stare, then vanished in a flash, apparently sensing something unsavory.

As he slipped his key into the locked door of the research center, he tried not to think about the scientist who had been arrested and handcuffed in that building on charges of cruelty to animals. An undercover member of an animal rights organization had taken a job in the scientist's lab, compiled evidence of alleged regulatory violations, and blown the whistle. After years of trials and appeals, the researcher had been cleared of all charges, but he was never again given a job by any scientific institution.

The youthful form in baseball cap, polo shirt, leather jacket, jeans, and sneakers—all in black—glided soundlessly through the hallways, looking more like a burglar than a neurosurgeon. But when he locked himself in his windowless lab, about to perform a historic experiment, there was no doubt that the roguish figure belonged there.

An unusual intensity marked the face of David Lang that night as he swiftly and methodically prepared for surgery. He removed one of the five blinded cats from its cage. He held before the creature its favorite toy, a play mouse dangling from a string. Before the cat was blinded, it had followed the mouse with its eyes and poked the toy with its paws. Now the cat lay still, unable to perceive the motion of the mouse before it, a condition that David hoped to remedy. He laid the feline on a cloth-covered patch of counter, placed a mask over its face, and administered an inhalational anesthetic to induce unconsciousness. He set up an IV drip to dispense a general anesthetic to the cat during surgery, inserted a breathing tube into the animal's lungs, shaved its head, and began the operation.

He examined the optic nerves that he had severed twelve weeks earlier. They had grown back! His gasp of delight was muffled by his surgical mask. However, a mass of scar tissue was choking the newly connected nerves. For hours, he painstakingly removed the scar, piece by tiny piece, being meticulous to avoid nicking the glistening new nerves. Then he injected a syringe of scar inhibitor over the area. As lasting protection against the formation of more scar tissue, he implanted a timed-release capsule of the scar-inhibiting chemical on the side of each nerve. Months later, when the timed-release chemical was consumed, the danger of scarring would be past and the capsule would biodegrade. The procedures he performed on the cat matched those that he would perform on Nicole in a few days.

Once David had completed the first cat's surgery, he performed the same operation on the second of the five blinded felines. He worked intently until dawn under a stream of bright light illuminating the cat's palpating brain. Because the optic nerves swelled after the surgery, he would have to wait until later that day to learn the outcome. When the swelling subsided, he would know if he had restored function to transected nerves in the brain, making medical history.

After ensuring that the cats were stable and comfortable following the surgery, David left the research center, his jacket collar raised and his cap lowered to hide his face. Once clear of the campus, he noticed that dawn had given way to a spectacularly sunny Sunday morning. In that moment there was no CareFree, no trial, no funeral for a childhood hero, no rift with the brother he loved. There was only the cloudless sky and crisp wind of a bright autumn day, and the glorious knowledge that his experiments looked promising. He smiled at a newspaper vendor and a passerby, wishing the world well. He walked in the sun, enjoying its nourishing warmth on his face. It seemed Pandora from Nicole's show was sprinkling him with hope.

His serene contentment waned on the drive home to Oak Hills, when he passed his health club. He and Randy had played racquetball there every Sunday morning for years, but they were playing no longer. Randy had switched to a new game, with rules that David could not follow. Stopped for a red light by the club, David closed his eyes painfully, his head dropping to the steering wheel.

The sight of his house evoked dread. To see Marie meant to argue with her. He knew that he had to confront the question of his marriage. Still reeling from the tragic demise of his father and the startling transformation of his brother, he could not yet face another loss. He wanted to understand Marie and the change in her.

The lingering glow of hope, the aftermath of the surgery, vanished from his face on seeing her in the family room.

"Where were you all night?" she asked resentfully.

"At work."

"Ha!"

Fashionably dressed in brown wool slacks and a beige silk blouse, she was standing near the couch, clipping on earrings and about to go out. A television tuned to a news broadcast droned in the background.

"I really was working, if that makes you feel better."

"It doesn't. I'd prefer you had five real girlfriends to that grand mistress you make of medicine. You tell me you're working, and you expect me to feel good about that? Your work killed your father!"

His face tightened at the mention of his father's death, a topic that still choked his voice.

"And your work is killing me, too, David. As you know, after your father died, Paul Eastman and the other owners of my group practice lost interest in making me a partner."

"They were using you for favors they thought my father would do for them. Why would you want to be a partner on those terms?"

"Oh, stop it! You make me sick with your ideals. No, I don't want to be a partner in my group practice. I want to throw my career down the drain, antagonize the entire profession, and lose all my friends. I'll be disgraced and ruined, but I'll have my lofty ideals to comfort me. Is that your perverted formula for a happy life?"

He observed that Marie's attacks had gotten more virulent since his father's death.

"My formula is to succeed, even if I have to struggle along the way. I'm no longer suspended, and I'm getting permission to continue my research. I can act legally now. Isn't that good?"

Marie looked at him bitterly.

"I broke the law and that upset you. Now I can work within the law. Won't you be happy if my experiment is successful and I can restore Nicole's sight?"

"Why should you and that girl get your way?" she blurted out involuntarily.

"What?" he asked in amazement.

"You caused a lot of damage—"

"I think CareFree caused the damage."

"—then you two get your way after all."

"Why does it bother you for us to 'get our way'? Would you rather I be punished more? And Nicole spend her life blind?"

"Don't be ridiculous!"

Just then Randy appeared on the television screen, speaking at a convention, with Mack Burrow beside him. David grabbed the remote and turned off the set. Marie pulled the device from his hand and turned the set back on. She raised the volume so that Randy's voice roared through the family room:

"I support Mack Burrow for governor. He's what today's medical profession deserves."

David reached for the remote, but Marie would not surrender it. He checked his impulse to seize her. With a forced calm, he walked to the set and turned it off.

"Your brother wised up. When will you?"

"Why do you resent me, Marie? I thought it was because I was breaking the law and you were afraid I'd get in trouble. But now I'll be doing my research legally, so why do you still resent me? Are you . . ."—he paused at a thought too inconceivable to utter—". . . afraid I'll . . . succeed?"

"That's ridiculous! Stop accusing me!" She grabbed her handbag from the couch. The fear sweeping her face told David that he had hit a nerve.

"Where are you going?" he asked.

Marie's life was a dizzying maze of meetings, associations, and committees. David wondered which function she was attending and what friends and favors she was seeking.

"I'm having brunch with Mel Brockman. Not that it's any of your business what I do, after you stay out all night! I thought I'd explore a job with the group practice Mel runs, because I'm going nowhere with my own company, thanks to you."

"Why keep reproaching me, when you can see I don't accept blame for the deceitfulness of your employers?"

Marie slammed the kitchen door on her way to the garage. David, too exhausted from the night's surgeries to reach the bedroom, fell onto the couch and slept.

❧　❧　❧

When he awoke in the afternoon, his first thought was of the cats. He quickly showered, dressed, and drove back to the research center. The swelling of the optic nerves would have subsided by then, and he would know!

He cautioned himself to be careful. He had a pass to park in the campus lots, but he opted to keep his car outside and walk to the laboratory. He kept his face hidden under his baseball cap. When he arrived at the research center, there was one lone car in the lot outside. He sat on a distant bench and waited a half hour, until two people left the building and drove away in the vehicle.

He opened the door and took the stairs to the windowless lab on the second floor. Everything was as he had left it in the cramped but orderly room. He scanned the filing cabinets, sink, lab counters, chemicals, lights, monitor, respirator, and other equipment in the small space, assuring himself that the items remained undisturbed. The animal cages, also, were as he had left them, resting on a long, narrow counter. Inside them the cats were clean, well nourished, and comfortable.

The two cats just operated on were groggy from the anesthetic. David placed one of them on a floor mat. He bobbed before it the toy mouse on a string. At first the sleepy animal did not want to play. David nudged it and talked to it until the creature finally opened its glassy eyes. The surgeon swung the mouse before the cat. Then the amazing thing happened. Its eyes followed the toy back and forth, and its paw jabbed at it. "Yes!" David cried out exultantly. *Success!* He repeated the mouse-on-a-string test of visual acuity on the other cat, with the same result. *Success again!* David's glowing face, beholding his little patients, held sheer delight.

A boyish exuberance that he had not felt in recent times seized him. He eagerly recorded notes on the cats' medical charts and prepared chemicals, instruments, and equipment for the surgery that he would perform later that night on the third cat. All the while he played with the newly sighted cats, unable to leave them alone, concocting games to make their eyes follow objects. He moved fingers before them from the right, then made the fingers vanish to the left, watching their heads turn with his motion. He flashed a penlight at them and observed their eyes tracing the tiny beam. The cats became more awake, opening their liquid eyes wider, enjoying their newfound vision and their playmate. When David stopped his games, they meowed for more.

After leaving the lab, David walked to the Hudson River to watch a cloudless sunset shimmering across the waters. His eyes devoured the glistening river, the soaring gulls, and the darkening buildings, as if every perception were sacred in the glorious phenomenon called vision. Wanting to do something special on this, the most important day of his life, he drove to Nicole's apartment.

As always, the dancer's face brightened at his presence. Mrs. Trimbell took the occasion of his visit to make dinner arrangements with a friend.

"There's a plate of marinated chicken breasts ready to cook for dinner," she said, leaving David and Nicole sitting at the breakfast bar.

"I'm hungry. Are you?" asked David.

"Yes."

"Let's go out."

"No!" Fear colored Nicole's voice. "Let's stay here. I'll cook the chicken," she said nervously, rising from the stool.

"Let me help."

"No, I can do it!"

A kindness in his voice responded to a tension in hers. "I'm happy to help."

"I'm tired of being . . . helped. Surely I can place chicken in the oven and throw a salad together. Why don't you listen to music in the living room and let me be, David, please?"

Reluctantly he obliged. Minutes later he heard a crash. He found Nicole sitting on the wooden floor by an open refrigerator, with chicken breasts, a broken dish, and a shattered bottle of wine splattered around her.

"When I reached for the chicken in the refrigerator, the dish caught on a wine bottle that I forgot was there," she cried. "When I tried to catch the bottle, everything fell—including me." She sighed heavily. "I should lay tall bottles down flat. I'll bet I gouged the floor!"

"I know you're feeling frustrated, but you mustn't touch anything. There's glass all over, so get up carefully." He grabbed her arms to help her rise.

She pushed him away and covered her face with her hands. Clad in jeans and a sweater, she was a gaunt figure, all legs, lying like a newborn calf after an aborted attempt to stand. "All I wanted to do was cook dinner!" She cried roundly, releasing what seemed like a thousand pent-up frustrations.

"Did you cook before your injury?"

She stopped crying at what appeared to be a new thought. "Well, no. I never cooked."

"Then why start now?"

She had no answer.

"Do you like cooking?"

"I hate it, actually." A tiny smile threatened to break through her frown.

"Then why are you doing this?"

He locked two sympathetic arms around her and pulled the crestfallen bundle to her feet. She sat on the kitchen stool resignedly as he cleaned up.

When he finished, she had regained her composure. "I'm sorry for the way I acted. Thank you for cleaning up my mess."

"Nicole, you don't have to prove anything to me or to yourself."

She nodded. "I needed your help, even though I wouldn't say so. I always need it."

"Let's go out. I feel like . . ."—*celebrating*, he wanted to say, but didn't—"relaxing."

His suggestion took her aback. They had never gone anywhere together, except to the nearby park. "No! I couldn't," she said apprehensively.

"What's the matter?"

"I'd rather not go anywhere."

"Tell me what's bothering you."

"I feel too . . . clumsy to go out," said the graceful ballerina. "I certainly couldn't go to dinner with a . . . man."

"What'll you do when the Phantom comes to take you out?"

"He's never coming. He just wants to write pretty notes."

"How do you know that? He keeps the floral industry in business on your behalf." David glanced at the Phantom's latest bouquet on the dining-room table. "I think he'll come to take you to dinner one day."

"Why have you appointed yourself as his spokesman?"

"I feel sorry for the poor guy when you pick on him."

"I'm glad he hasn't come around. I wouldn't want to go to dinner with him the way I am now. He'd have to lead me around, explain my food to me, clean up after me when I drop something! I'd feel horrible about that."

"I think the Phantom would see things differently. He'd feel like a kid on New Year's Eve to have you all to himself for an evening. I'll bet he'd like to paint you a picture of the city through his eyes and watch you react. And he'd want you to paint the world for him through your special vision. He needs you to do that, you know. I think he'd gladly help you climb a staircase or walk across a room, not as your nursemaid but as someone who cares about you. The Phantom wouldn't want you to feel pressured to do things you can't yet manage. He would just want you to be yourself."

Giant blue eyes stared in his direction with a child's enchantment at learning something new.

"Maybe you should accept that, Nicole. And to prepare for having dinner with the Phantom, you should practice with me."

She smiled. "David, really—"

"You haven't played it safe your whole life. You've taken chances. I want you to take one now."

Her lips pursed as she pondered the matter. Then she smiled. "I do need to practice having fun."

"We both do."

She disappeared into her bedroom wearing jeans, then reappeared in a backless black evening dress that hugged her body, rising at her breasts, tapering at her waist, and curving around her hips. The dress stopped at midthigh to display long dancer's legs in dark stockings and fashionable heels. In front the dress covered her completely, from chin to wrists, with a necklace of pearls around the high collar at her throat. From behind she was naked to the waist, the soft white skin of her back a stunning contrast to the black dress. She wore dangling pearl earrings with her inch of boyish blond hair. The flawless skin and carved features of her face glowed with a fresh, natural beauty. Embellishing her striking face was a touch of makeup that she managed to apply well. A clutch bag contained the only evidence of her blindness, a retractable cane.

For one speechless moment David surveyed every inch of her exciting landscape.

She smiled at him with a wide-eyed gaze and tantalizing mouth. "Am I put together okay?"

"Is *stunning* good enough for you?"

They stopped at his office, where he kept extra clothing. Leaving Nicole in the inner office, he changed in another room, selecting an outfit of brown and tawny fall tones for a look of casual elegance. When he returned, she was touching his bookshelves. On this occasion, her first nonclinical visit to his office, she wanted to "see" the room in a different way than she had previously.

"What's this book?" she asked.

"The *Journal of Neurosurgery*. There's a whole shelf of them."

Her hands moved along the row of volumes and on to another shelf. "And this?"

"*Vascular Neurosurgery*."

"This?"

"*Neuropathology*."

"This is a very thick one."

"That's the *Atlas of Neurological Surgery*."

"This one smells old," she said, pressing her nose to the binding. "I love musty old books."

"That's from the 1930s, called *Meningiomas*. It's a great read on neurosurgical techniques."

Her hands moved on to touch a picture hanging on the wall. "What's this?"

"It's a portrait of Harvey Cushing, the father of neurosurgery. He's smiling at us."

She did not know why she wanted to linger in the room, to discover its objects, and to know them intimately. Her hands wandered farther along the wall.

"This feels like a glass case. What's in it?"

David opened the door, removed an object, and placed it in her hands. "It's a plastic brain that I used for many years, until it wore out. It comes apart, like this," he demonstrated, "so I can explain things to patients."

Nicole ran her fingers over the pieces of brain. "Why would you put this in a glass cabinet?"

"It was my first model of a brain. My father gave it to me when I was eight."

Her head dropped. "You preserved your first brain the same way I kept my first ballet slippers. But I got my slippers from the trash, whereas you had someone special. . . . You miss him terribly, don't you?" she whispered, her voice heavy with grief.

His hand slipped under her chin and raised her face to him. "I've missed him for years, Nicole."

She nodded sadly, and then continued her leisurely inventory of the office. He watched her silently while putting the plastic brain back in its display case. She felt no need to explain or to hurry. He felt no need to ask for her reasons or to direct her tour. They had always been supremely comfortable with pauses, silence, and their own thoughts in each other's presence.

She passed her fingers over the top of his desk and stopped on a framed picture.

"What's this?" she asked cautiously, expecting the picture to be personal and wondering why it could somehow intrude on the intimacy of this moment with him.

"That's a photo of two normal four-year-old kids," he said proudly.

He told her about Artur and Bernard, the conjoined twins whom he had separated. He described the children and their case as she held their photo. Always fascinated by his work, she listened enthralled, as if a master storyteller were relating a great adventure.

She was struck by the fact that every object in the office seemed to hold a special meaning to its proprietor. The room she touched was like a temple to something sacred in him. He, too, felt a need to linger in the office and to share it with her as a tribute to something too dangerous to divulge to anyone: the glorious event that had just occurred in the lab.

When she finished surveying the office, one question still remained unanswered. "And what do *you* look like, David?"

He raised her hand to his face. She felt a dangerous excitement at her first touch of the object of her curiosity for three months. Her sensitive ballerina's fingers stroked his eyes, nose, and mouth and weaved through the silky strands of his hair. She closed her eyes in concentration, trying to visualize his face.

"Mrs. Trimbell says you're terribly handsome."

"Does she?" he asked matter-of-factly.

She could feel a slight contraction of the muscles on his cheek that produced a telltale rift—a dimple!—telling her he was amused, a fact his voice did not reveal. What untold information could she learn if only she could feel the subtle muscles of his face? How much had she missed about him without this remarkable window into his feelings? She dropped her hand, fearful of the power she had discovered and the thrill it gave her.

Nicole's hand fell onto the soft texture of his sports jacket. "Cashmere," she said, smiling. Then her fingers slipped gently underneath to feel the sheen of the shirt and the warm, taut body beneath it. "Silk," she said, her fingers lingering a moment longer than necessary for her assessment.

The maddening touch of her hand on him made David's eyes dance excitedly over her rising breasts, taut stomach, and slim hips. He was relieved that she could not see a desire that he could not contain.

"Am *I* put together okay?" he asked.

She laughed with the exuberance he knew from the stage. "Yes, David, I think you are."

He took her to a quiet, elegant restaurant in Central Park, where they sat beside each other in a booth.

"We're looking onto a wooden dance floor with a piano on the right. Candlelit tables surround the circular floor. Giant windows wrap around the room, looking out at Central Park. The restaurant has a sparse group of smartly dressed diners who are smiling as they eat and make conversation. The lighting is soft and golden. It makes your face glow."

"Is the restaurant really this enchanting, David, or is it your eyes making it so?"

"It's both, and it's you making it so, also," he said, smiling. "With the room dimly lit, you can see out the windows. The bare branches of the trees are trimmed with tiny white lights. A winding stone path goes behind the shrubs to a place we can't see, maybe a mysterious garden still in bloom." He took her hand and pointed her finger toward the objects he named.

"It sounds as if we're in the woods where the sleeping princess of my favorite ballet lives." Feeling more relaxed, she lifted the menu. "This dish looks good." She pointed to the line naming the chef.

"That's one of my favorites."

She giggled, and the sweetness of her laughter sounded like the first bird of spring to David.

Countless hours of dining lessons with Mrs. Trimbell had paid off, for Nicole ate with grace and dignity. She even had a little wine, a rare indulgence in her efforts to keep her remaining senses sharp. The drink was a testimony to her trust in her companion, to her certainty that she could never be harmed in his presence.

His enduring awareness of her made the evening easier than she had imagined. He walked with her on his arm, describing their surroundings, stopping before steps, directing her to railings, warning her of cracks or other impediments. His assistance was unobtrusive, as if seeing for her were as effortless as seeing for himself.

"David, I'm so glad you made me come here tonight and forced me to have fun," she said, her head thrown back against the booth, enjoying the music and the savory smells of dinner floating in the room.

"The world is still open to you, Nicole. I hope you realize that now. But it's not the reason I brought you here. The real reason is that *I* wanted to have fun, and you helped me do it."

She smiled. "I'm glad that's the reason."

"Are you ready for our next big get-together?"

She knew what he meant. "Yes."

"I want you to come to my office tomorrow, so I can examine your eyes. From there I'll send you to Admissions, and I'll operate on Tuesday."

"You'll operate *legally*, right?"

"I'm supposed to get final permission from CareFree tomorrow." He grabbed her arm, a sudden tension penetrating his hands and voice. "Promise me you won't pull any stunts. The timing of this surgery is *critical*. If we wait any longer than I say we can, we risk losing everything. That means you *must* be in the hospital when I tell you to be there."

"Don't worry. Nothing could keep me away."

"I *must* do your surgery early in the week."

She touched his face—in reassurance, she told herself. It was okay to indulge this fascination she had with touching him if it were merely to reassure him.

"I'll be in the hospital when you say." Her fingers gently brushed his hair, his eyes, his mouth. "Tell me something, David," she said, wanting to change the subject, "in the OR, do you see your patients . . . naked?"

"Momentarily, after they're anesthetized and the nurse is about to cover them with surgical drapes."

"Did you see me naked?"

He paused. She felt a telltale dimple form on his cheek and a smile on his lips. "Yes."

"I suppose you were too busy to notice—"

"I did notice that you were beautiful."

The muscles of his remarkably expressive face revealed an amusement that had not reached his voice. She pulled her hand away, fearing that her game had gone too far. She felt a new, enticing danger in provoking reactions to read off his face.

"Any more questions?" he asked.

"No."

"Then let's dance."

"I couldn't!"

"That's what you said about coming here. Dancing is one thing you can't deny you know how to do."

Hesitantly, she let him lead her to the dance floor. The pianist played a medley of romantic songs. She could feel his eyes on her for a long moment before he took her in his arms and began dancing. Like everything else that evening, dancing was easier than she had imagined. She quickly developed a keen awareness of his body close to hers. She moved when he moved, knowing by the slight shift in his balance and the subtle motion of his limbs where he was leading her. The result, Nicole sensed, was the supremely graceful vision of two bodies moving as one.

They remained holding each other after the music had stopped. Then he led her to a window looking out at the park.

"You can see the skyscrapers in the distance, above the shrubs."

She stood in front of him, feeling the glass before her. He raised her hand, tracing the objects that he described, as if drawing her a picture.

"It's a clear night, with a full moon and a sky dense with stars. The buildings are tall and bold against the bright sky. They look as if they're stretching up to mingle with the stars. The city looks proud tonight."

She leaned back against him as he spoke. He slipped an arm around her waist. She rested her head against his chest and felt his words brush the top of her hair.

"The park is peaceful. It looks as if winter has already passed and it's time for spring. There are wooden benches on a stone walk surrounding a fountain. Maybe the water will spurt at any moment and the birds will come to drink. And I think I see your princess dancing in the woods."

"David, you seem happier tonight."

He thought of two bandaged cats with lively optic nerves firing impulses. "Tonight I break with the Phantom. I'm having no more of his bitterness and discouragement. I look out and see opportunity and hope tonight. The Phantom is too negative a guy for me."

She turned to face him. "I'm thrilled that you're happy, David, but you're wrong about the Phantom. He's had a terrible struggle that's left him disillusioned. I think he's the most desperate man in the city. But I hope it's only temporary. I think he has a great capacity for happiness, so that's why I can't let you call him a negative guy," she reprimanded.

Against her will, her hand brushed his face again. She discovered a reaction his silence had not shared with her. He was grinning.

When they entered the foyer of her apartment, they stood facing each other in one of their long, wordless pauses.

Finally, Nicole spoke. "Thank you, David, for making me feel . . . alive."

She knew he had not intended it. She sensed him turning toward the door to leave when he suddenly grabbed her by the waist and pressed his mouth against hers. Her head fell back, her mouth opened to his, her hands traced the slender lines of his taut body from his hips to his chest to his neck. Her arms flung

around him with the same urgency that she felt in his grip. His hands memorized the soft patterns of her naked back, her hips, her stomach, her breasts, and
his mouth was hot against her face, her hair, her neck.

Then, suddenly, he pushed away. The front door swung open, and like the
Phantom, he vanished.

He drove to the lab, fighting a desire to return to the welcoming arms in the
foyer. The delirious scent of her perfume lingered on his clothes, tormenting him
to return. He had managed to bear his own desire since the first letter that he
had sent to her. But it was beyond his endurance to feel her body answering his,
surrendering to his will, inviting him to do anything he pleased. He reminded
himself that he must perform brain surgery on the source of his torture. He must
remain cool, calm, clinical—just the opposite of the way he felt then. The scientist in him prevailed. The moment passed; he would not return.

He slid through the creaking door of the William Mead Research Center. In
the dead silence, he passed the laboratory where the scientist charged with cruelty to animals had been removed in handcuffs. He thought of the many laws
that he was violating— experimenting illegally, performing multiple surgeries on
the same animal, operating without the presence of a veterinarian and without
an approved OR, keeping the animals outside of the proper holding area. Then
he thought of the dainty, sensitive creature he had held in his arms, and his fears
vanished, replaced by a ruthless determination to accomplish his aim. He would
prepare for Nicole's surgery as thoroughly as he could. He had three cats and six
optic nerves left to practice on. He would perform one surgery that Sunday
night, two on Monday night, and then be ready for Nicole on Tuesday.

As he entered the windowless lab on the second floor, he paused to play with
his newly sighted cats, the most important felines on Earth because they held the
answer to the mystery of the nervous system. Stronger now, they eagerly eyed
their toy mouse and jabbed at it. He thought of Nicole laughing on stage. Her
precious life would soon be restored.

He placed a mask over the third cat's face, and the creature fell limp on the
lab counter. He dripped an anesthetic into its veins, placed a breathing tube
down its throat, hooked it up to a monitor, shaved its head, and began the surgery. He could see Nicole in Pandora's costume. Her white ballet slippers would
be brushing against a Broadway stage once again.

He opened the cat's brain and examined the optic nerves. They had grown
back! So had the strangling scar tissue. With the music from Nicole's show playing in his mind, he painstakingly removed all of the scar. The cat's vital signs
were fine. Its heart beat steadily. The respirator hummed rhythmically. Everything was completely normal. He took a syringe full of the scar inhibitor and injected it onto the nerves.

A screeching alarm pierced the silence. Sudden, erratic readings distorted the monitor. The cat's blood pressure plummeted. Its heart beat irregularly. The animal was in dire trouble. David threw off the cloths covering it and for a few frantic minutes tried every remedy possible to restart the rapidly failing heart, but to no avail. The animal died on the table.

❧27❧
The Raise

Bright-colored heads of hair bobbed like new flowers before Randall Lang. His wife, Beth, and their three children, the blonds and redheads of his life, assembled in his home office for a monthly family ritual. A tall stack of checks placed before him on his desk swayed precariously with every breeze. It was the last Sunday of October: time to pay the bills.

Each month Beth prepared the checks, then passed them to her husband to sign, because she could refuse the children nothing. Each month Randy objected to the small mountain of bills, ranting about the family's spending. But he, too, could subtract nothing from the bulging budget. Although he protested loudly, like a kettle boiling over and losing its steam, he ultimately signed all of the checks.

"I figured we could get this over with early, Dad," explained thirteen-year-old Stephen Lang, "so I gathered the troops when you didn't leave to play racquet-ball with Uncle David this morning."

As he was bringing the stack of checks closer to him, Randy's hand stopped at the mention of his brother.

"Are you guys still playing?" asked Stephen. "I can't remember a Sunday that you ever missed, until this month."

There was a pause.

"No, we're not playing," Randy finally whispered.

He had told no one, not even Beth, about the rift with his brother. The family members glanced curiously at each other. Something was wrong, they sensed.

"Daddy, now try not to get upset when you see my coach's bill." Stephen's twin, Victoria, began the familiar chorus. "The extra ice-skating lessons were absolutely essential to prepare for my next competition."

Randy looked at his daughter listlessly.

"And, Dad, I know you're gonna have a fit when you see the concert tickets on my credit card," said the young pianist, Stephen. "But my teacher wanted me to see those performances in addition to taking lessons. I tried to get matinees, which are cheaper."

Randy nodded numbly.

"And, honey," said Beth, "you'll also see a bill for Michelle's new computer. I can explain . . ."

Beth stopped talking because her husband was not listening. He was signing the checks without protest or commotion. The family members looked at each other incredulously.

Since Randy had begun campaigning for Governor Burrow, Riverview Hospital had entered a propitious period. After a lengthy battle for government permission to reopen its old Stanton Pavilion, its request had suddenly been granted. After another long struggle, it had received permission from the Bureau of Medicine to obtain a new scanner. The agency also had approved the hospital's long-standing request to redesign the Emergency Department. And Care-Free surprisingly had paid eighty thousand dollars in claims previously denied, which the hospital had been contesting.

The board of directors, elated with this turn of fortune, had voted Randy a hefty raise and bonus. "We always knew you had a brilliant business mind, Randall," Charles Hodgeman, the chairman of the board, had said, handing Randy a bonus check. "Now you have the proper attitude and focus to lead us in the right direction." Randy had accepted the check with the enthusiasm of a motorist getting a speeding ticket.

His perplexed family watched him sign the first to last check without a whimper.

"Aren't you gonna yell at us today, Daddy?" asked seven-year-old Michelle.

"No, honey."

"But, Daddy, I don't get it." Victoria stretched her long neck to see the papers on the desk. "Are you sure my bills are in there?"

"They're there, Victoria."

"Hey, Dad, do you have a fever or something?" asked Stephen.

"No, kids, I'm okay. I got a raise and a bonus," he said quietly. Even Beth looked surprised. In the manner of hiding a guilty secret, Randy had told no one, not even his wife. "So now we have the cash flow to cover all this."

The group looked dumbfounded. They waited, but Randy volunteered nothing more.

"That's good, isn't it?" asked Stephen.

"I suppose," said Randy.

Slowly the family filed out of the office, their bowed heads appropriate for leaving a sick man's bedside.

In a windowless lab of the William Mead Research Center, an unshaven David Lang had spent a sleepless night trying to answer the question throwing his life into code blue. Two sighted cats watched him; two blinded cats felt his presence; one dead cat held a secret that tormented him.

Still dressed in surgical scrubs from the operation of the previous night, David sat hunched on a stool on that last Monday morning of October, his elbows propped on the lab counter, his eyes swollen from lack of sleep, his hands holding up his head. He read and reread the medical records of his laboratory cats.

He traced and retraced every step in the fatal surgery on his third experimental feline. He asked himself the same questions repeatedly: What was the cat's physiology? What were the changes in the animal's blood pressure? Was a blood vessel cut? Could there have been bleeding? Was there swelling in the brain? Could the cat have had a stroke? What could account for the shockingly rare occurrence of a living creature dying on the table under his knife? He found no answer.

He considered the new drug used in his second nerve-repair surgery, the scar inhibitor, which he had introduced to the cat's brain immediately before its death. Could something have contaminated the drug? Did anyone break into the lab? Did someone tamper with the substance? In a small chemical lab on another floor of the building, he tested the vial of the scar inhibitor used on the third cat. The results compared exactly to previous analyses, with no trace of a contaminant.

Then he tested the blood of the two cats that had survived the second nerve-repair surgery and compared the results with those for the blood of the cat that had died. He found an unusual chromatographic band in the blood of the dead cat that was absent from the blood of the live ones. He collected that band in a sample jar and carried it across campus to Danzer Hall, home of the university's chemistry department, for analysis by a chemist in a better-equipped lab.

David walked through piles of stiff fallen leaves covering the grassy field between the buildings. He'd neglected to wear a coat, oblivious to the chilly air cutting through his thin surgical scrubs and to the odd stares from passersby in overcoats. He was relieved that he had not scheduled any surgeries or appointments that week, save for Nicole's case. Knowing CareFree, he was prepared to trace his paperwork personally through a maze of departments to obtain final approval for the dancer's treatment. While walking, David telephoned Mrs. Trimbell to postpone Nicole's appointment with him and hospital admission from that Monday until the following day. At Danzer Hall, too impatient to wait for the elevator, he climbed steps three at a time to the office of his friend, chemistry professor John Kendall. David presented the unknown substance in the sample jar and asked Kendall to identify it. Hearing the panic in David's voice, the stocky chemist with the black-rimmed glasses and the kind face agreed to test the substance immediately and to call with the result.

"The sample you gave me contains benzyl alcohol," Kendall told him later on the telephone. "David? Are you okay?"

Benzyl alcohol! David was speechless. Benzyl alcohol was highly toxic to brain tissue. A small amount of it could denature the brain's protein and halt its biological activity. And like an explosion razing a building, the devastation from benzyl alcohol was irreversible.

David drew cerebrospinal fluid from the two sighted cats, whose surgeries were successful, and also from the dead one. He asked Kendall to test the serum-like fluid, which circulates through the brain and spinal cord. The analyses yielded normal results for the live animals, but the dead cat's cerebrospinal fluid contained, in a greater concentration than in its blood, the same deadly poison, benzyl alcohol.

By Monday afternoon, David knew the cause of death: a poison in the brain. But how did it get there? Could something at the surgical site have introduced benzyl alcohol to the cat's brain? He had to find the answer because he would be using the same procedure on Nicole.

David considered the chemicals that he had administered in the fatal operation on the third blinded feline, wondering what reaction could have produced benzyl alcohol. For the second nerve-repair surgery, which he had performed on three cats, David had employed a different general anesthetic on the third cat than on the prior two. The general anesthetic used on the successful two animals was made by Phil Morgan's company, but it was a drug discontinued by CareFree following Morgan's defense of David's experimental surgery. With the supply of Phil Morgan's anesthetic almost depleted after the surgery on the first two cats, David had switched to a replacement anesthetic for his operation on the third feline. Could the new anesthetic have reacted with the scar inhibitor to produce the benzyl alcohol? After all, it was at the moment that he injected the scar inhibitor into the third cat's brain that the animal's heart arrested. Yes!

David phoned John Kendall at Danzer Hall. "I can't tell you what this is about, only that someone's life is at stake. And I can't wait for an analysis from a commercial lab. They're all closing now."

Minutes later he gathered a canister of the anesthetic that he had used to replace Phil Morgan's discontinued drug, along with a vial of his scar inhibitor. He took them across the campus at dusk to Kendall, who had canceled a dinner engagement to run an analysis for him.

Again David wore no coat. Again people stared. Again he felt no sensation of cold through the thin cloth of his scrubs. He felt nothing but the exhilaration of solving a problem that had to be rectified immediately. He would find that the replacement anesthetic used on the third cat reacted with his scar inhibitor to produce benzyl alcohol, which killed the cat. Then he would select a safe anesthetic for Nicole's surgery. And he would have the luxury of sleeping that night, of feeling refreshed for surgery on his precious human patient.

That evening David sat with John Kendall before an instrument. A tiny pen plotted on a chart the chemical result of mixing the scar inhibitor with the only drug used on the third cat that was not used on the first two, the drug that had to be the cause of the third cat's death—the replacement anesthetic.

The chemist's shocking interpretation of the chart reeled David back into a maze with no exit:

"There's no benzyl alcohol produced by mixing those two drugs, David. Your scar inhibitor and replacement anesthetic don't react at all with each other."

On that cheerless Monday night an unfed, unwashed, unshaven David Lang stood before a bright stream of light flooding a laboratory counter. Dozens of shiny metal instruments lay before him. Nicole had already lost her perception of color and motion. She was rapidly losing her ability to detect light. Maybe the third cat's death was a fluke, he concluded, an inexplicable occurrence whose cause eluded him. Two blinded cats remained to have the second surgery. He lifted cat 4 from its cage. He dripped into its veins the replacement anesthetic, because it was one of the shrinking number of anesthetics still available and because John Kendall's analysis proved that it did not react with the scar inhibitor. Following all the usual procedures, David began the surgery. He opened the cat's scalp. He looked into its brain. The optic nerves had grown back! He removed the scar tissue to free the nerves. He injected the scar inhibitor.

The monitor on the cat screeched its alarm, its graphs went awry, its readings plunged into the danger zone. For a few desperate moments, David tried to restart the animal's heart, but to no avail. The fourth cat was dead.

❧28❧
Approval Pending

He was standing on the tracks of a railroad when he heard the clanging of a locomotive. The wheels ground against the track, heading straight toward him. The ground vibrated fiercely. Then he saw the distorted image of his face reflecting off the shiny steel engine. He must get out of the way! But his legs would not move. The train's piercing whistle blasted in his ears—

A startled David Lang awoke to his cell phone's ringing on the lab bench. His neck ached from the awkward position in which he had fallen asleep.

"Hello," he mumbled, still shaken from the nightmare.

"Dr. Lang?" His secretary did not recognize his voice.

"It's me."

"Nicole Hudson is here for her appointment."

"Oh!" The windowless lab hid daylight from him. He glanced at the clock. Ten-fifteen. His new enemy, sleep, had robbed two hours from his life—two precious hours!—when he could spare not a minute. "I'll be right there."

Notebooks, records, and chemicals covered the lab counter. He had rechecked everything, searching for a clue. He had investigated every drug used on Nicole and on the cats: its composition, preparation date, batch number, purity, potency. Earlier that Tuesday morning chemist John Kendall had confirmed that David's latest blood and cerebrospinal samples contained benzyl alcohol. Those samples came from cat 4, showing it died from the same poison in the brain as cat 3. David did not know how the toxin got there.

As he splashed water on his face and walked to his nearby office, his thoughts kept returning to the replacement anesthetic that he had given to cats 3 and 4. But he had witnessed John Kendall's test himself. The replacement anesthetic used on the dead cats did not react with his scar-inhibiting drug. He had to find another cause, and soon—otherwise the train would . . .

"Come in, Nicole," he said to the lovely vision in brown slacks and soft suede jacket.

She rose to approach him, leaving Mrs. Trimbell to wait in the reception area. David had brought a rush of cold air in with him, Nicole thought, when he entered the office. Or was it his voice that was oddly cool and toneless? He seemed preoccupied as he silently escorted her into the examining room. He closed the door, his manner bearing no hint of their intimacy of two days ago. She sat on the end of the examining table while he lowered the blinds.

When the room was darkened, David held a light before her from a distance of ten feet. He turned the knob of the light slowly, increasing the intensity.

"Tell me when you see the light," he instructed.

Nicole said nothing.

He continued to turn the switch, until the light was at full force. "Do you see anything now?"

"No."

She had seen the light from that distance a mere two weeks ago. He moved closer. "Tell me when you see the light," he said from a distance of eight feet, turning the knob and watching the beam grow to its strongest intensity on her face.

"I don't see anything yet."

At five feet he did the same. Nicole had no response.

He moved directly in front of her with the light at its highest intensity.

"I see light," she said finally.

David stared at her, alarmed. He knew that he must operate by tomorrow at the latest. He had never been successful in his nerve-repair experiments when he had waited until all regained function had vanished.

"I want you to check into the hospital now and wait for my further instructions."

"What's wrong, David?" she asked the stoical presence before her.

"I can't talk to you now. I have to go."

She reached up to his face. He tried to move away, but her hand caught the stubble of his beard, revealing that he had not shaved since their last meeting.

"David, what's wrong?"

"Please don't ask. I'm very busy."

She cupped his face with her hands. "Something terrible is wrong. I know it. And it involves my case. All the . . . bad . . . things that happen to you involve my case."

"Nicole, please! I can't take this right now."

He moved away. She felt his body lean against the side of the examining table. She jumped down and reached out to find his hands covering his face.

"David, I must know!" Her voice trembled.

He tried moving away, but she moved with him, tears forming in her eyes, her hands clutching his arms.

"You have to tell me!"

"Don't ask, please."

"Something's terribly wrong and I'm concerned."

"You must let me handle this."

"If you don't tell me, I could get very upset," she cried, knowing she was using the ultimate weapon against him. "I could run away—"

"All right! All right!" She heard anger mixed with caring in the desperate voice. "But if I tell you, then you must promise you won't run away, because I couldn't handle that now. I have other things on my mind."

"I promise I won't run away." The gravity of her tone matched his.

He led her to a chair, and he sat on his doctor's stool next to her. He took her face gently in his hands, the tenderness of their last evening returning to him.

"You must swear you won't tell anyone what I'm about to reveal."

"Of course. I swear."

"After your accident, I duplicated your injury on five laboratory cats. I cut their optic nerves. Then I performed the first nerve-repair surgery on them, just as I had on you." His hands fell to her arms, grasping them tightly. "These experiments are illegal, so no one must know!"

"I see."

"On Saturday night I began doing the second surgeries on the cats."

"And?"

"And the first two cats regained their vision."

"David!" Her face blazed with excitement. "That's fabulous!"

He did not respond.

"What could possibly be wrong?"

"The next two cats died on the table."

Her face flashed with a horror that he wished he could have spared her.

"A poison got into their brains, and I don't know how. I have one animal and twenty-four hours left to find out. That's why I *must* go, so I have to leave you frightened like this! All I can say is don't underestimate me. Don't give up hope."

Nicole's face struggled against an inner turmoil. He watched helplessly, for he had no reassurances to offer.

"David," she whispered finally, "I knew when we began that this was experimental. When I told you that I wanted the surgery, even if my chances of . . . dying . . . were ninety-five percent, I meant it. I know you'll do your best. You don't have to worry about me. I . . . accept the risk."

I don't," he said gently, fighting his own battle. He wanted to wrap his arms around her shoulders and pull her close. "I'll never risk your life. Never! If I don't solve this problem, I won't operate."

"You *must* operate! I want the surgery more than anything. I accept the consequences. After all, two of the cats made it—"

He placed his fingers over her lips. "Don't waste your time, Nicole. There's nothing you could say to persuade me. Some things are more precious than sight."

"Not to me!"

"To me. Your life is precious to me."

The words hung in the air between them.

"I need to count on you to be all right now, Nicole."

"I'm okay." Her voice was almost steady. "I won't make this harder on you."

The dignity in the soft voice seemed to reassure him. He called in Mrs. Trimbell to take Nicole to Admissions.

On their departure, he reached for the wall phone and dialed a number that he had memorized from frequent use. Dr. Harold Wabash, the director of the Warren Lang Institute for Medical Research, answered.

"It took me seven years to develop my new procedure. Is it going to take you that long to approve it?"

Wabash laughed. "Dr. Lang. I was about to call you. The feds have just approved your new procedure."

"Good!" David exclaimed. "My patient is being admitted to the hospital now, and I have to operate as soon as possible."

"There's just one more thing—"

"How can there be another goddamn thing?"

"One more agency has to check one more thing. But you'll have your *final* permission by five o'clock this afternoon, I assure you."

"If you think I'm gonna let your little fiefdom make my patient's life go up in smoke—" He suddenly looked astonished. "*Vapor!*" he whispered to himself. "That's it!"

"What did you say? . . . Dr. Lang? . . . Are you still there?"

The phone he dropped clanged against the wall as David flew out of the examining room. He returned to West Side University, his white doctor's coat billowing in the wind.

David found John Kendall in an organic chemistry lab in Danzer Hall.

"Hey, John."

Kendall saw wild green eyes peering at him from the other side of his lab bench. A face full of tumultuous emotions shone between jars of chemicals on a shelf above the counter.

"What's up, David?"

"When we mixed the replacement anesthetic with the scar inhibitor, the anesthetic was in a pure liquid state, wasn't it?"

"That's right. I took it from the canister where it was packaged as a liquid. Why?"

"In the blood, that anesthetic is in gas–liquid equilibrium."

"Hmmm," said Kendall, his lips curled in concentration. Various anesthetics possessed the property that David mentioned. "That could change things."

"Exactly! In its *liquid* form, the anesthetic doesn't react with the scar inhibitor to form benzyl alcohol. But maybe in a *gaseous* state, the way it exists in the blood, with oxygen and water present, it would react differently."

Kendall nodded thoughtfully. "I still have samples of the anesthetic and the scar inhibitor. Let's try your idea."

The two men were still on opposite sides of the lab bench, talking through the gaps between items on the shelf.

"John, I owe you more beers than I can count."

"Or than I can drink."

Soon after, the two of them sat in a small room before a piece of equipment resting on a table. A pen slowly plotted a graph on a drum of paper. The precision instrument was measuring the chemicals resulting from mixing the scar inhibitor with the gaseous form of the replacement anesthetic used on the dead cats. The device was about to share its secret with two sets of unblinking eyes. The place where the band for benzyl alcohol appeared was approaching on the drum. Would the tiny pen rise to form a nice peak at that point?

It did.

"There it is!" David cried triumphantly.

"That's the band we're looking for," said Kendall. "There's benzyl alcohol in that mixture."

David gave the professor a crushing hug. "My patient's gonna name her first kid after you!"

In the executive offices of Riverview Hospital a handsome blond man in a starched white shirt sat at his desk. Randall Lang took a call informing him that Nicole Hudson had been admitted to the hospital. A check with his compliance people told him that no approval had yet been issued for Nicole's experimental surgery. He called the governor:

"My brother *must* receive approval today. His patient is ready for surgery now, and it can't be delayed. With only a week before the election, Governor, I'm sure you wouldn't want our little deal to go bust."

"I'll call Henrietta and get back to you."

Burrow phoned the head of CareFree, and then returned Randy's call. "Your brother will get approval today. The last hang-up is Animal Welfare. Before any research project involving animals is undertaken, that department has to approve it."

"But Nicole Hudson isn't an animal."

"Still, your brother's research project includes animal studies. The laboratory facility that he uses is overdue for an inspection."

"The William Mead Research Center?"

"Whatever its name is."

"Then will you arrange to have that building inspected *immediately?*"

"Animal Welfare is doing it today. Once that's completed, your brother gets approval. I left strict instructions that nobody goes home today until the final authorization is issued for your brother."

"All right, Governor. I'm counting on you to get that lab facility inspected *at once*."

           ℝ   ℝ   ℝ

Chief Inspector Daryl Denkins of the Department of Animal Welfare wore a colorful bow tie under his colorless face. He opened the valve on the antiquated radiator in his run-down midtown office, waiting for a rush of heat that never came. He threw a woolen sweater over his shirt, swearing at the radiator, at the paint chipping from the ceiling, at the dirty windows, at the shabbiness of his working conditions, at his supervisor, at every supervisor he had ever had, at the city at large, and at all the people who never gave him the consideration he deserved. Daryl Denkins did not like people. He liked them even less that day, because his supervisor had just told him to inspect the William Mead Research Center *immediately*.

He had protested, explaining that he needed to schedule such a job in advance, that he did not have the staff available at that moment, that he would have to drop other pressing work. Why must William Mead be inspected *that day*? Denkins had asked his supervisor.

The superior had shrugged his shoulders. He truly did not know why he had just received an urgent call from a new guy named Harold Wabash at CareFree, followed by a call from the head honcho, Henrietta Richards, herself.

"Who knows why? All I know is that somebody big is involved. If we don't get that job done today, heads are gonna roll. It's *overdue* for an inspection, you know," the supervisor had said pointedly.

"Give me more inspectors, and I'll get the labs checked on time!"

"Don't worry about that. Just get *this one* done *today*."

When his supervisor had left, Denkins had thrown a stapler at the recalcitrant radiator and felt a brief satisfaction from nicking a piece off.

Swearing to himself, he made various phone calls to summon people to assist him. One call was to a medical practice where a young doctor was examining a child's tonsils.

"Marie, it's Daryl Denkins over at Animal Welfare. How are you doing, dear?"

"Hey, Daryl! How nice to hear your voice. I'm fine. How are you?" said Marie Lang.

"I'm in a bind."

"Oh?"

"I've got to inspect William Mead, and I'm short on manpower. I need to call on committee members to assist."

Among her many networking activities, Marie served on the Department of

Animal Welfare's laboratory committee, composed of doctors, veterinarians, community leaders, and government regulators who reviewed standards of animal care, recommended new legislation, and assisted with inspections of research facilities.

"I can help, of course, Daryl. When do you want to do it, next week?"

"I've got to do it *today*. Don't ask me why, because I haven't a clue. Some big kahuna twitches, and the rest of us have to drop everything. You're so close to that facility, Marie, I wondered if you could help me out there this afternoon."

Marie paused. She had a full schedule of patients.

"I called because I know I can always count on you. I was just telling that to Fred Carson the other day. You know, I'm always singing your praises." Fred Carson was the high-level CareFree administrator whom Marie's practice dealt with.

"Well, okay, Daryl. I'll help you out. What time?"

"Two o'clock. I'll meet you in the lobby of William Mead. You're the best, Marie! You're one of us."

From his office, David called the anesthesiologist scheduled for Nicole's surgery. The surgeon described the deadly reaction of his scar inhibitor with a particular anesthetic that must emphatically not be used in Nicole's surgery. David asked his colleague to give Nicole the anesthetic that he had been using from Morgan Pharmaceuticals.

"That one's not available anymore, David. CareFree pulled it from the formulary, and there's none of it left in the hospital."

"I have to work with an anesthetic that I'm certain won't react with my drug. Can you get the agent I want from another hospital?"

"I'll try. Let me ask around."

Later the anesthesiologist called back: "There's none of the anesthetic you want anywhere in the city. Hospitals don't keep much inventory on drugs anymore, with all the changes nowadays. Let me tell you the general anesthetics still available." He rattled off a list of drugs.

"I haven't used any of those with my nerve-repair experiments. What about these?" David named general anesthetics that he had successfully used with his new procedure.

"None of them are left on the formulary."

"What?"

"It's true."

David's face hardened with contempt. He thought of the ancient philosopher who believed that the world was an ever-changing flux, where one could never step in the same river twice. The surgeon felt trapped in that kind of whirling existence, in a current that changed with every political breeze. Could he allow himself and Nicole to be the flotsam and jetsam drifting at sea after the shipwreck of medicine? He could not.

"I'll get the anesthetic I want from Morgan Pharmaceuticals. You'll have it in time for my surgery tomorrow morning. Okay?"

"Sure," said the anesthesiologist.

The next number that the surgeon dialed brought a familiar voice to his ears.

"How the hell are you, David?" said Phil Morgan of Morgan Pharmaceuticals in Ohio.

"Why in hell's name were you such a jerk to defend me? Damn you, Phil!"

David explained that he needed one of Morgan's drugs for his nerve-repair surgery the next day. He felt an instant sense of calm at hearing a competent human being say:

"It's done. It'll arrive at your office by eight o'clock tomorrow morning. I'll have a courier deliver more than you need."

"Would you, Phil?" David sounded like a weary swimmer being offered a life preserver.

"Of course. And save the empty canisters for me. I want to display them in the lobby of our world headquarters, with the inscription 'Morgan Pharmaceuticals provided the anesthetic used in the first successful regeneration of the central nervous system in human history.' I want you to make that happen tomorrow in the OR, you hear?"

When he hung up, the tension had drained from David's body. He glanced at his watch. Two o'clock. He would go to his laboratory to perform the second operation on the final animal. Because he was short on time, he would have to do this cat's surgery in the afternoon, rather than wait until nightfall. He would give the feline the small amount of Morgan's anesthetic that he had remaining. When he injected the scar inhibitor, there would be no adverse reaction with Morgan's drug. Then he would introduce the replacement anesthetic and watch the animal's heart arrest. That would be the in vivo corroboration of the laboratory experiment performed by Kendall. After the cat's surgery, David would get a blissful night's sleep. In the morning, he would awaken refreshed and ready to perform the most important surgery of his career. He phoned Nicole to report his progress as he began a pleasant walk to his windowless lab on the second floor of the William Mead Research Center.

In the lobby of William Mead, Daryl Denkins was giving assignments to his team of inspectors.

"Mark, you take the surgical areas," he said to one of them. "Nancy, you take the animal holding areas," he said to another. "And Marie, here's a master key for you." He dropped the passkey into Marie Lang's outstretched hand. "You take the windowless labs on the second floor."

❧ 29 ❧

Meeting Overdue

David Lang arrived at his lab, his purposeful steps a lively contrast to his sleepless, swollen eyes. He changed into clean scrubs and prepared his instruments for operating on the final cat. He was eager to confirm the cause of the two prior cats' deaths through this final animal surgery, so that he could operate safely on Nicole. Then why was he hesitating? His notebooks were closed; he thought he had left them open. One of the cages looked as if it had been moved. Was he imagining these things? He observed the lab carefully. Everything else looked untouched. Dismissing his suspicions, he finished preparing, placed cat 5 on the cloth-covered operating area, and, with a mask over its face, anesthetized the animal. As he was about to run an IV into the cat, scrub his hands, and begin the surgery, he heard the lock turn in the door.

In utter astonishment, he watched a woman enter. The soft, silky auburn hair and shapely legs seemed overshadowed by the severe lines of her business suit and the coldness of her eyes.

"What the hell—?"

"Don't even think of throwing me out. The Department of Animal Welfare is inspecting this facility. As a member of its lab committee, I was asked to assist. I have a right to be here," said his wife.

"If you have a right to be here, then where does that leave me?"

"Still arrogant?" She said to the man in scrubs standing before an unconscious cat and an array of surgical instruments. "You want to tell me *I'm* wrong, even when I catch you red-handed in the commission of a crime. I know you don't have approval to perform animal experiments."

David wondered why she did not look surprised at her discovery.

"You're still going full throttle, acting as if nothing else existed but you and your work, even after the governor generously found a way for you to do your surgery legally."

"You mean after he backed down when I threatened to expose CareFree on national TV?"

"I think you break the law just to throw your insolence in our faces."

David had noticed a more pronounced bitterness in Marie of late. Gone were the pleas for reconciliation, the lip service to his research, the undertone of apology when he challenged her position, the cries of also being the victim of a system that she liked no more than he. Marie was stepping beyond a point where he could reach her.

"I have every right to shut you down, David."

"Why are you serving on a committee that shuts scientists down?"

"Why must you always have your way? The rest of us have to follow the rules. But you break them anytime you wish. Why should you be above the law?"

"The experiment I'm about to do is essential in making my new surgery work on humans. Don't you want me to succeed?"

"You make me sick!" Marie's mouth fell petulantly. "Why should you get to follow your lucky star while the rest of us can't?"

"You're not afraid I'll fail and disgrace you. You're afraid I'll . . . succeed. Aren't you?" David's eyes widened as if seeing the answer to a long-standing puzzle. Old, confusing impressions flashed before him in the rush of a new clarity. "You once loved singing opera, but you gave it up because it made you an outcast among classmates who couldn't appreciate or equal your talent. You chose to win the approval of mindless kids instead of following your dream. And you once loved cardiology, but you became a general practitioner because it was the more acceptable thing to do. So you gave up that dream, too. You once had standards as a doctor, but you gave them up to practice cookbook medicine and be more popular with the regulators. You could've tagged along with the new order grudgingly, as most doctors do. But instead you twirled the baton in the Care-Free parade. Because you caved in and I didn't, you resent me, don't you? Why did you sell out, Marie?"

"Nonsense! I didn't sell out. I'm doing just what I want to do. And to everyone in medicine—except you—*I'm* the one who's successful. *I* have a future, not you."

"A future of groveling to those in power?"

"You always want me to stand alone, to stick my neck out! I got smashed in court once, so I learned to be careful. There are so many patients, so many decisions, so many ways to fail. The practice guidelines, the administrators, the committees—they help me choose, and they're my defense if I'm ever called on a case."

"Sure, Marie, no one can question your judgment when you don't make any judgments, when your recipe books and administrators call the shots. How can you let others decide for you?"

"How can you decide for yourself?"

In a final burst of clarity, David realized that *this* was the core of the difference between them. He had thought that Marie was a victim, forced to act against her better judgment in the Eileen Miller case and in many others like it. But the truth was that Marie had no better judgment, a voice of certainty inside him cried out.

"I'm not like you, David. You're always trying to make me change, to be like you, but I'm different. Don't you understand?"

"Maybe I finally do," he whispered, more to himself than to her. "If Nicole and I succeed, it will mean that your whole life is . . . somehow . . . wrong—"

"I've heard enough! You're committing a crime, and I'm going to shut you down. You should be begging me not to."

"I don't beg others to let me do my work."

"Of course not! You're above it all! But for once, you're at my mercy." She smiled vindictively. "Tell me why I shouldn't turn you in. And don't spew nonsense about saving our marriage."

"I won't. It's over between us. It was over a long time ago."

"It was over when you took Nicole Hudson's case."

"It was over long before then."

"You're attracted to her."

"Yes."

"You're smitten by her."

"I'm in love with her."

"You bastard! How dare you tell me that? And you expect me to help you now?"

"Nicole doesn't know how I feel. She's innocent. If you want to punish me, then do it *after* her surgery. I must perform an experiment in this lab before I can operate safely on her. And you will not stop it, Marie."

"I won't? You miserable disappointment for a husband, why would I want to help you and your girlfriend?"

"For one reason only. Because it's right. If you forgot about your mindless guidelines and committees and thought for yourself, as a doctor and a human being, you wouldn't interfere with this work."

"Just what do you mean? I have to report you to the authorities."

"Why?"

"Because those are the rules."

"And because you like enforcing them."

"Maybe I do."

"If you take this animal away, I can't find out something I must know to operate on Nicole. You'd be sacrificing a human life to save a cat. Does that make sense to you, as a doctor and a human being?"

"It's the law, David. You have no right to break it!"

"You know perfectly well that a hundred stray cats are put to sleep in pounds for every one used in research. If you take this cat, it'll only be euthanized anyway. Does it make sense to stop a laboratory experiment that could save a human life?"

"It's the law. I respect the law."

"Forget me. Forget Nicole. Don't do it for us. Do it for your own self-respect. I want you to look the other way and not report what you see here—*because it's right*, because you can think for yourself and see that it's right."

"I don't see that it's right to let you off the hook again."

"You wouldn't be rescuing this cat out of any concern for its welfare. Don't delude yourself. You'd seize it out of a bitter resentment for Nicole and me. You'd use an unjust law to cover up your real motive, cruelty. You can't let yourself commit such an unspeakably vicious act, Marie."

She smiled maliciously. "I *can* commit such an act. And I *will*."

"Over my dead body."

He grabbed her roughly, spun her around, and pinned her hands behind her back. He eyed an array of drugs on a cart, mentally selecting one to tranquilize her for a while. Oddly, she offered no resistance, no cries, nothing but a sly grin.

Then he remembered the closed notebooks and the cage askew. "You were in here before I arrived, weren't you?" he said, tightening his grip.

"David, you're hurting me! You'll break my arms!"

"You made your decision already, didn't you? You're just playing with me now, wanting to see me beg. Damn you! I'd like to smash your face and wring your throat!"

The door opened again. David's glance landed on the bow tie of Daryl Denkins, the inspector who had seized his rats on the coldest day of winter. Police officers and other inspectors entered with him. The triumphant voice of Daryl Denkins directed an assistant to take photographs. Denkins was no longer a beleaguered civil servant wrestling with a defective radiator that was a personal affront to him. His face came alive. He strutted around the lab as if it were his personal kingdom. He gave orders to his inspectors. Daryl Denkins of the shabby office had finally achieved the status that he deserved.

David remembered little of the brief, violent scene that was the most desperate moment of his life. Two officers pulled him away from his gloating wife, pinned his arms behind his back, and cuffed the hands that were about to perform brain surgery.

Another officer placed the anesthetized cat, now awakening, back in its cage.

"Don't touch that animal!" David screamed, twisting furiously against arms and cuffs that gripped him.

"Let's bring this cat and its cousins over to the holding area downtown," said one of the officers, removing the cage with cat 5.

"Don't take that animal! I must have that cat! You can't do this! Stop!" David cried desperately. He tried to lunge for the cat, but hands with the grip of a vise dragged him out of the lab and into a police car.

"David Lang, you're under arrest on charges of cruelty to animals. You have the right to remain silent. Anything you say or do can and will be used against you."

✼30✼
No Deal

The music of Nicole's first ballet floated through the earphones of her compact disc player. She lounged on her hospital bed in a white satin robe, her serene beauty more suited to a princess than a patient. She closed her eyes as a triumphant theme swept her back to her first hearing of that fateful tune, at age six. That day, watching her first ballet, her life had been sparked by a desire that had become a life's quest to perform the role of the princess. Years later, on a day that hung like a medal in her memory, she had realized her childhood dream.

Her head rested against the pillow while her body yearned to leap out of bed, to give motion to the sweeping melody, to become the instrument of a joy impossible to express in any other way save dancing. She longed to feel the exhilaration of her own movements. Would she ever be able to dance the princess's role again? she wondered.

Mixed with the grandeur of the music was a voice she had grown fond of. She heard Mrs. Trimbell in the hallway, chatting with a nurse. Another voice lingered in her mind. David had called her earlier with good news. He believed that he had found the cause of death in his laboratory cats. He would perform surgery on the final animal to confirm his findings. She waited eagerly for him to call again, reporting that he had solved the problem and would be operating on her the next morning. The optimism of the music gave Nicole hope. She heard steps approaching her room. Would it be David, with good news already?

The footsteps halted at her door. Her eager rush of excitement froze at the sound of a voice greeting Mrs. Trimbell. David had warned her teacher to screen Nicole's visitors and to permit no one to upset her, but the person at the door was someone whom Mrs. Trimbell trusted and allowed entry. *No!* Nicole wanted to scream. *Don't let this person near me!*

"Hello, Nicole, dear. How are you feeling?"

"Go away."

"Why?"

"I don't want to talk to you."

"You know I always tell you the truth, dear."

"Why?"

"Excuse me?"

"Why have you made it your job to tell me . . . upsetting things?"

"Someone has to be honest. Your doctor seems to lack the courage to tell you the plain truth, but you're entitled to know it."

The words pounded Nicole's heart. She knew that she must listen, just as she had listened when the same visitor had informed her of David's suspension and of his father's death, events that had made her . . .

"Your doctor is . . . unavailable, so he won't be telling you much of anything." Nicole waited.

"What happened was inevitable, you know, dear."

An ashen face belied Nicole's forced calm.

"You can't break the rules and do as you please. Life isn't like that," continued the visitor. "That policy was bound to catch up with him . . . and you."

The voice seemed to want to be prodded, but Nicole waited quietly.

"Why should you two be better than the rest of us?"

Nicole noticed that the voice she dreaded was different this time. It lacked any pretense of wanting to help her and was more obvious in its malice.

"Why should you always get your way, while the rest of us have to put down our dreams and take what we're given?"

"Why do you want to put down *his* dreams?" asked Nicole.

"Your doctor's arrogant disregard for the law is what put him down in the end. Do you know the old Greek myth about the boy who stole the chariot of the sun god? Remember what happened to him, dear?"

Nicole stared into the dark void of her existence. The light she had been able to perceive was fading into duller shades of gray.

"He came crashing down from the heavens in the end," said the visitor.

Nicole detected a note of triumph. She could listen no more. "Why is David . . . unavailable?" she whispered, trembling.

"He was performing illegal animal experiments this afternoon. His lab was inspected and he got caught. I understand that he was waiting for approval to do your surgery. I'm afraid that approval will never come now. You see, dear, David was arrested," said Marie Lang.

In a gunmetal police station, David Lang was booked, fingerprinted, given a number, and set before a camera for mug shots. The bitter eyes captured in his photos matched those of any hardened criminal. In a jail behind the station, a cell door slid shut behind him. Like a restless animal, David paced the width of his cage incessantly.

He had to operate on Nicole before another day passed. But how? After his arrest, CareFree would never grant approval for Nicole's surgery. Could he perform it illegally? Where? Riverview Hospital surely had heard about his arrest and was off-limits to him. Could he operate outside of a hospital? Before performing Nicole's surgery, he needed the last cat to confirm the cause of the problem that he had encountered. But the animal had been seized. How could he retrieve it? Nicole was rapidly losing her perception of light, and he needed to act fast. But he was behind bars!

This storm of disturbing thoughts funneled in his mind while his lawyer arranged for a bond hearing to release him. His trim form moved fitfully from side to side in the small cell. He knew that if he were stopped from performing Nicole's surgery, he would loathe everything and everyone from that day forward in a blind, searing hatred gripping his soul for the rest of his life.

Still reeling from his father's tragic demise and Marie's betrayal, David yearned for yet another . . . enemy, a man who would surely smash any remaining hope of performing Nicole's surgery. Nevertheless, David kept a thousand childhood pictures of this man framed in golden memories. *Randy*, he cried to himself in desperation. *Where's Randy?*

An officer arrived to announce that he had a visitor and to take him to another gloomy place. The gray walls and wire-mesh window of the new room resembled a cloudy sky. A dividing wall with a glass partition sliced the room, separating David from the outside world. When the door on the other side of the barrier opened, David gasped. "Randy!"

The brothers had apparently forgotten their differences, because they both pressed their arms against the partition, each like a mirror image of the other. The men lowered their arms slowly, reluctantly, and sat down facing each other across the glass.

"I'm the reason you're in jail." Randy's voice drifted to David through slats in the divider.

"What?"

"After I made a deal to campaign for the governor in exchange for your getting permission to do Nicole's surgery—"

"You what? You mean you didn't . . . really . . . join Burrow?"

"Hell, no."

"I thought you—" a stab of pain cut David's voice.

"I never sold out, David, not consciously. Although what I did amounts to that. I made a deal with Burrow. I had to make you think I turned against you; otherwise, you'd never accept CareFree's offer. But did I win any *right* for you to work without CareFree's blessing? No. Did I win any *right* for the hospital to be free of Burrow and his inspectors? No. My deal did nothing but get you a *favor*, which can be taken away just as capriciously as it's given. That's what everybody in medicine does today. We bargain for a crumb, but we never contest our feeder's power to decide who eats and who starves. I did the same thing as Dad did, really. I tried to combine you with CareFree.

"And my deal backfired royally. In order to approve your experiments, the bureaucrats had to inspect your research lab. That's how you got caught. I was screaming for Burrow to have that lab inspected. Now look at the bind you're in!"

"You tried to *help* me? You were on *my* side?"

"Of course, pal. I'm sorry I had to pretend—"

"Forget it," said David, smiling broadly in his eagerness to erase his agony over Randy's betrayal. "I did the same thing you did, brother. Instead of blowing the whistle on Burrow to the media, I went along with the farce. I put Nicole's life in his hands by leaving the decision about her surgery to him and his gang. Now I've got to take control. I must operate within twenty-four hours, or she'll never see again. I need a cat I was experimenting on, which was seized during my arrest. I ran into a problem, and that cat holds the answer. I can't operate on Nicole without getting it back."

"The police probably brought the cat to the animal facility downtown, the one that was broken into last winter."

"They said they were bringing it there."

"Hell, I can get the cat back." Randy whispered, so the guard in the room would not overhear. "I'll break in the same way the vandal did last winter. The papers described the whole affair. I never mentioned this, but I've always had my suspicions about who that vandal was. Weren't they holding some of your rats at the time?"

David grinned.

"I don't think I'll need to do quite the same job as the vandal did of smashing all the windows and trashing the place."

David's grin widened.

"But I'll get the cat. Your lawyer is here. He'll get you out on bail or on your own recognizance, depending on how dangerous a character the judge thinks you are."

"He should only know."

"Then I'll meet you at Riverview and get you an operating suite."

"But you'll lose your job. I can't have that. I've got to find another way."

"Your arrest was announced in the middle of our board of directors' meeting this afternoon. The board, of course, revoked your staff privileges. But I didn't go along with it. I did something that made me happier than I've been in years. It's amazing how all the tension I was living with suddenly disappeared."

"What the hell did you do?"

"I told them that if you go, I go. So I quit."

"No!"

"Oh, yes," Randy said, laughing gaily. "I'll be officially replaced tomorrow, so you *must* operate on Nicole *tonight*, before my resignation is announced. Tonight I'm in charge. In my final act as president, I'll get you an operating room, brother."

"I can't let you do that! You'd be open to who knows what charges—"

"You *must* let me help you, David. Not for your sake but for mine. When I quit, I felt tremendously relieved and . . . free. I told the board to go to hell. I told them that you'd be the first one they'd look for if they needed brain surgery. I told them they were cowards and hypocrites, but I wasn't going to be like them anymore. You know, no one argued with me. They *knew* I was right. But they wouldn't budge.

"Even the bonus and raise I got for being Burrow's fair-haired boy gave me nothing but grief. To get that money, I had to promote a cause and a man I despised. Now I've got a chance to do something really important. You can't take that away from me, David. What's the old saying, that a life lived in fear is a life not lived at all?"

David closed his eyes in relief and deliverance. "I love you, brother."

"I love you, pal."

They pressed their hands together against the glass.

"Nothing can stop you now, David. Everything's going to be okay."

David's eyes held hope. Everything was going to be okay. Could he believe it?

❧31❧
Everything's Going to Be Okay

The third-floor surgical suites of Riverview Hospital were quiet at 6:00 that Tuesday evening. An attendant washed the floor of a vacant corridor, an orderly wheeled a bin of laundry through a darkened hallway, a nurse carried a tray of equipment into an empty room. The day's scheduled cases had been completed and the night's emergencies not yet begun. No one noticed two masked men in scrubs inside the only lighted operating suite. David and Randy were looking at a small creature on a table, cat 5, which Randy had mysteriously retrieved.

With equipment suitable for the animal, David anesthetized the cat, hooked it up to a respirator and monitor, and then opened its skull. A tiny patch of exposed brain was the only part of the feline visible on a blue canvas of surgical drapes. The surgeon explained the procedure while his brother observed.

"See those optic nerves?" said David excitedly. "They grew back! Look at them, man!"

"Incredible!" Randy smiled under the mask.

"I'm giving the cat an IV of Phil Morgan's general anesthetic, which is the safe one. Now, I'll inject the scar inhibitor over the nerves." David drew a solution in a needle, then sprayed the liquid over the cat's optic nerves. He waited. "There's no adverse reaction. The cat's vital signs are okay. But CareFree removed Phil's anesthetic from the formulary, so there's none left, except this small amount, which isn't enough for Nicole's surgery. Phil is shipping me more, but it won't arrive until tomorrow morning."

"Can't you use another anesthetic?" asked Randy.

"I used a few different general anesthetics safely on animals in combination with my new drugs, but they've all been pulled by CareFree."

"We can't wait for Morgan's anesthetic to arrive. In the morning my resignation will be announced, and I won't be able to issue an order to remove the garbage."

David nodded. "In my early attempts to use this treatment, I experimented on the optic nerve of rats. I employed a *local* anesthetic, which numbed the scalp while the patient remained conscious. Because there's no sensation of pain in the brain itself, as you know, local anesthetics are sometimes used for brain surgery, such as in cases where the patient's conscious response is needed. I thought that after I had freed the rats' optic nerves from the scar tissue, I could immediately check their vision during the surgery. But the optic nerves swelled and the animals didn't regain sight instantly. When I realized I couldn't find out the results during the operation, there was no reason to keep the animals conscious, so I switched to general anesthesia."

He took a vial from the anesthetic cart near him and pierced its rubber seal with a needle. "This is the local anesthetic I used on the rats, and which I can use tonight on Nicole." He injected the drug into the cat's scalp, then waited. "Nothing abnormal," he said, watching the monitor and listening to the cat's steady heartbeat. "The local anesthetic is working fine with my scar inhibitor, as it did with the rats."

Then David took another bottle from the cart. "This is the general anesthetic that I used as a replacement when CareFree pulled Phil Morgan's drug off the formulary. This drug, I believe, reacted with my scar inhibitor to kill two of my cats. I want to prove that by injecting this cat with it." He injected the suspect anesthetic into the cat's IV tube. "The scar inhibitor is already in the cat's system, so let's see if there's a reaction."

In moments the electronic monitor sounded its alarm. The graphs showing the animal's heart activity and other vital signs lost their regular pattern and rapidly became flat. "The cat's dead," said David, relieved. "Now I can do Nicole's surgery."

Smile lines beamed above two masks.

From a wall phone David dialed Nicole's hospital room.

"Hello, Mrs. Trimbell," he said to the familiar voice that answered. "There's been a change of plans. Instead of operating tomorrow morning, I'm going to have Nicole brought to surgery right now."

"Oh, I see," said Mrs. Trimbell.

"Can I speak to her?"

"She went for a walk."

The smile lines suddenly disappeared from around David's eyes. "I thought you weren't going to let her out of your sight."

"Oh, this is different," Mrs. Trimbell said cheerfully. "You needn't worry. She's with someone trustworthy."

"Someone apparently trustworthy got to her twice before and drove her to—" David's mind suddenly made a chilling connection. "Is Nicole with . . . my . . . wife?"

"Why, yes, she is. How did you guess?"

"You've got to find her right now, Mrs. Trimbell, and get her away from Marie!" Mrs. Trimbell did not recognize the desperate shriek that was David's voice.

After the surgeon raced to Nicole's room, and after he, Mrs. Trimbell, Randy, and the nurses searched everywhere—in the corridors, the bathrooms, the visitor's lounge, the other patients' rooms—but could find no trace of Marie or Nicole, everything was emphatically *not* okay.

❧32❧
The Phantom's Plea

David, Randy, and Mrs. Trimbell stared at Nicole's belongings in her hospital room. Apparently to avoid being caught, the dancer had vanished in her robe without taking the time to dress or to gather her purse, phone, or other possessions. Riverview's security guards had combed the medical complex for the missing patient, but to no avail. Mrs. Trimbell had checked Nicole's apartment but returned to report no sign of anyone having been there.

According to Mrs. Trimbell, Marie was wearing a long coat. The others surmised that she had placed the garment over Nicole's robe so that the two of them could leave the hospital unobtrusively. David dialed a variety of phone numbers in an attempt to reach Marie. He dialed her pocket phone, their home, her office, her car; but his wife did not answer. Using unrepeatable words, he left messages, but she replied to none of them.

He called Reliable Car Service, the company used previously by Nicole, and learned that she had not requested a car that evening. Had Marie dropped her off somewhere? David tried to discover where the car service had taken Nicole when she had disappeared previously. The dispatcher, however, did not have the information; the owner was not there; the dispatcher would call the owner; yes, he would stress that it was an emergency; the owner was not answering his cell phone; the dispatcher would call David as soon as he made contact.

The surgeon sat on Nicole's hospital bed, nervously glancing at his watch. Seven o'clock. Exasperated to have come this far only to be stopped again, he called the private detective who had searched for Nicole after her previous disappearance. The investigator responded immediately, arriving to find the troubled faces of David, Mrs. Trimbell, and Randy. The stoical man with astute eyes listened as the others gave an account of Nicole's disappearance.

"Does she have any close friends or relatives?" asked the detective.

"She has a few girlfriends," said Mrs. Trimbell, "but I already called them, and they haven't seen or heard from her today."

The investigator handed the others a copy of the background report on Nicole, which he had generated during her earlier disappearance. "Is there anything in this report that strikes you? Any person or place that Nicole might have mentioned? Anyone she might still be in contact with?"

David looked at the chronology of a child named Cathleen Hughes being shuffled from one foster home to another. "Nicole never mentioned any of these foster families or case workers to me."

"Nor to me," said Mrs. Trimbell, thumbing through the pages.

"All right," said the detective, "I'll visit the car service and contact the people she worked with at the theater."

"Wait a minute. There *is* someone Nicole mentioned," David said, recollecting. "A Sister Luke. Nicole knew her as a child and liked her. There's no mention of her in the report, but there is a reference to a St. Jude's Parish, where the case workers retrieved her after she . . . ran . . . away—" He sprang from the bed. "I have a hunch. I'm going to try St. Jude's." He turned to the detective. "Could you get me the address?"

In a streak of blue scrubs and white coat, he left the room before receiving an answer.

David hurried to his car. He drove past the tree-lined streets with the restored brownstones in Nicole's elegant neighborhood. The detective called with the address of the parish, and David turned south to find it. The scenery soon changed to a forgotten neighborhood on the West Side, a tattered patch of New York with potholed streets and deserted tenements. This was where Nicole was born. He saw stolen cars, stripped and abandoned along the curb. Many of the buildings had no windows or doors, only wooden boards and the charred remains of past fires. Dingy lights flashed inside other structures, revealing bare walls and chipped ceilings. He saw a rat sniffing garbage from an overturned trashcan. A homeless man chased the rat away so that he could have first pickings. A child in torn clothing sat on the curb of an unswept street, playing with empty beer cans. The thought of another child, named Cathleen Hughes, a little orchid struggling to grow in this wasteland, appalled him.

He parked by a tall building resembling a bundle of spears frozen in stone and pointing to the heavens. *St. Jude's Parish*, read an old inscription carved above the massive front doors of the Gothic church. He entered a hollow chamber lined by stained-glass windows and smelling of incense. An old man lit candles at the base of a statue. A woman knelt at a brass railing before a marble altar. David walked down the aisles, his eyes surveying every pew, side chapel, and nook. He irreverently opened the confessionals, but they were empty. Nicole was not there.

He walked around the outside of the church, finding no one among the leafless shrubs of late October. In the cool autumn air, he heard organ music and the sweet voices of women singing hymns. The sounds were coming from a building behind the church. Could that be the convent? he wondered. Would he find Sister Luke there? His eyes followed the line of the five-story structure up to a towering, lighted cross on the roof. Next to the giant crucifix, he saw a smaller figure moving, a human form. It was a dainty young woman in a white satin robe!

The sight galvanized him. He reached the door and found it unlocked. He entered the old building and walked past a candlelit chapel where a cluster of veiled heads bowed in prayed and enchanting voices rose in song. Engrossed in their service, with their backs to the door, the nuns did not notice the sleek stranger who ascended the staircase three steps at a time. As he climbed, David dialed Randy on his pocket phone.

"Call off the search party. I found her."

Earlier that evening, Nicole had gone to Sister Luke of St. Jude's Parish, as she had when she had run away the first time after her surgery. The nun immediately took the visitor in, bringing her to the small room where she had slept as a child, her cot and nightstand still intact. For a while Nicole lay on her old bed, smelling the pleasant scent of fresh laundry from the sheets. When the sisters retired to the chapel for their evening service, the dancer found her way to the stairway and climbed to a favorite place of her childhood. It was a solitary spot where she had gone to forget the bleak world around her and dream of a better one. Her special place was the roof. From it, the child could see the lights of Broadway and come tantalizingly close to her future. Nicole remembered gazing longingly at the distant explosion of lights that was the theater district.

The grown woman searched in darkness for the bright spot of her childhood. With her arm on the waist-high cement wall encircling the roof, the blinded dancer moved along the perimeter, feeling her way, until she reached the point where a large cross was fixed. This was the spot where she had seen the sparkle of the great New York stage. She felt heat from a spotlight illuminating the twelve-foot high cross; however, she could perceive no more than a faint trace of its light. Soon that final flicker would be extinguished. She wanted to be at the spot where she had first viewed the brilliance of Broadway when the last light that she would ever perceive faded.

Nicole heard the gentle voices of the nuns singing to something sacred.

> Let my footsteps slip not
> In the path to glory.

She had once traveled a path to glory, and her footsteps had not slipped, she thought, her face to the wind, her satin robe shimmering in the darkness.

> Let my spirit arise
> And my heart rejoice.

Her spirit had indeed arisen, and her heart had rejoiced. *No one can ever take that away from me*, she thought.

> Let me fly on thy wings,
> Oh, glory in the highest.

I once flew on wings. I once knew a . . . glory . . . in the . . . highest.

In thy presence is
Fullness and joy . . .

Let me never forget the fullness and joy I once knew, she thought, facing the dazzling Broadway lights that she could not see.

. . . Darkness turned to light,
And pleasures evermore.
Deliver my soul,
Oh glory in the highest.

Let that sustain me, my memory of a darkness turned to light . . . of a glory in the . . . highest.

Nicole lifted her head, remembering how the immense power of the Broadway lights illuminated a vast circle of sky and kindled a fire in her soul. Hearing the nuns' hymn, her mind did what it always did at the sound of pleasing music. She thought of how she would dance to it, of the steps and tempo that would express the exultation in the music, as if dancing were synonymous with feeling, as if the two had irrevocably meshed within her long ago. *I must never feel sorry for myself,* she thought, imagining herself dancing to the hymn, *because I once knew . . . glory.*

Suddenly the door of the roof sprang open and urgent footsteps moved toward her.

"Nicole!"

Startled at the sound of a voice she had not expected, she jumped onto the top of the narrow cement wall that encircled the roof. She held onto the vertical bar of the crucifix, its crossbar over her head. The spotlight now hit her own body, revealing her willowy shape under the translucent, windblown robe. She heard a gasp from her visitor and the abrupt cessation of footsteps.

"Don't jump! Don't move!"

"How did you find me?"

"Your feet are an inch from the edge, Nicole. Don't move a muscle." She heard fear in the measured whisper of David's voice, despite his attempt to control it.

"I'm not having the surgery, David."

"That's fine. I won't force you to do anything. Just stand very still while I get you down."

"No! Stay away."

"I swear, Nicole. You have my word. You can do as you please." She heard him cautiously approach. "No one's going to make you do anything you don't want to," he said soothingly.

Then her body jerked at the sudden pull of two strong hands around her hips. In one startling, violent motion, she was yanked from her perch. She tumbled down, falling against David. She felt his trembling arms embrace her, stroking her back, her arms, her head. She heard a cry of relief from the lips buried against her neck.

He guided her away from the edge of the roof. Then, as if in proof of his vow not to force her will, he released her. She stood facing him, her robe shining like the brightest star in the night. Her body trembled in the cool fall air. He removed his white coat and placed it around her shoulders.

"Tell me why you're about to cast your dreams and mine to the wind." His voice was harder now.

"You were arrested for experimenting on the animals, weren't you?"

"Yes."

"And you'll break the law again if you perform my surgery, won't you?"

"Yes."

"I said all along that I wouldn't have the second surgery if it were illegal."

"I said all along that I would do it no matter what."

"You'll be thrown out of medicine for good."

"There's no place for me in today's medicine. I'm glad to be thrown out."

"I know you love medicine desperately. I can't take that away from you, David. You'll end up as I am now. You'll hear music and ache to dance, but you'll be unable to move."

"Do you think CareFree is the tune I want to dance to? Is that what you're saving me for? *Your surgery* is the music I hear."

"But if my surgery fails, then you'll be ruined. You'll go to jail, won't you? I couldn't stand that."

"I may go to jail, but I won't be ruined. Some things are worth going to jail for. My work means to me what the Phantom's dream means to him. You said he was the most desperate man in the city because he was about to lose something precious to him. You said that the Phantom shouldn't confine his dreams to the world he sees on the stage but fight for them in real life. Do you want me to confine my dreams to make-believe? And are you going to confine your dreams to a few fading memories?"

"That's different. I didn't mean that we should destroy other people for our dreams. I can't destroy your future, David, for the sake of my own."

"I want to do your surgery not to destroy my future but to raise it to new heights—in my eyes, and to hell with what the world thinks. I want you to accept that. I know you want this surgery more than anything."

"I'll survive without it."

"You'll be crushed."

"I'll get used to a new life."

"You'll hate your life if you give up without a fight."

"I'll manage."

"You'll be miserable."

"I'll get by."

"You'll be devastated. Say it!"

"I'll adjust."

"You want this surgery more than you ever wanted anything. Be honest and say it."

"Okay, I want it."

"You more than want it. You want it desperately."

"Yes! Yes! Damn you, David, I want it so much I could kill for it!"

"Then why don't you live for it?"

"I must let it go to give you your life. You'll have other chances, other patients, if you let my case go."

"I want to operate on *you*, because that's immensely important to me."

"Can my surgery mean that much to you?"

"It does . . . and you do," he said softly.

The nuns' delicate voices fluttered like those of songbirds in the background.

> Lift up your hands
> Toward the sanctuary.
> Lift up your eyes
> Toward the heavens.
> Reach out and embrace
> The best within you.

"Your surgery, Nicole, is the best within me."

His words lifted her body. She breathed deeply, as if inhaling his every syllable.

"You can't keep running away when something upsetting happens. Give yourself the same advice you gave the Phantom. You can't confine your dreams—and mine—to make-believe. If you do, there will be nothing left of us, and the things you fear for the Phantom—that he'll end up bitter and desperate—will be our fate." He momentarily thought of Marie. "What's left of people after they give up the best within them?"

He paused for her protest, but she made none.

"Will you quit running away, Nicole, for your sake and mine?"

She raised her head in a bearing that was pride itself. The muscles of her mouth shifted subtly into a Mona Lisa smile. She extended her willowy ballerina's arm to him. He kissed her hand and curled her arm around his waist. He raised his arm around her shoulder and pulled her close. She felt the exciting warmth of his body through the thin surgical scrubs. Then they walked to the stairway, arm in arm, two people who dared to follow their dreams.

❧ 33 ❧

Necessary Treatment

An orderly wheeled an unoccupied stretcher through the double swinging doors of the Department of Surgery. A janitor cleaned a vacant lavatory. The operating suites were dark that evening, save for OR 3. In the hallway outside the lighted room, two people in surgical scrubs stood over the sole patient in the area, a young woman lying on a gurney.

"I was an OR nurse once, so I'll be assisting with your surgery," Mrs. Trimbell said to the patient. "I told Dr. Lang from the beginning that he could count on me. I'm here because I want to be, child, because it's right."

Nicole nodded, her silence underscoring the depth of her appreciation.

"I'm here because I want to do what a hospital president is supposed to do—support the best medicine," Randy Lang said to the patient. "Without CareFree, your surgery would be damn good for our business *because* it's good for you. Only CareFree could make what's good for you bad for the hospital. I don't want to look into that carnival mirror anymore." He fondly squeezed her shoulder. "I'm here to watch and to help if I can. But mainly, I'm here to handle anyone who might question your surgery."

Nicole smiled at the two, understanding for the first time what it meant to have a family. "Thank you both, more than I can say."

The two moved away when David approached. The surgeon was smiling, his eyes as fresh as morning, the strain and exhaustion of the past few days vanishing from his appearance. He turned to Nicole, taking her hands in his.

"We'll be wheeling you in as soon as we finish setting up."

"I'm ready," she said, smiling radiantly.

"I have to explain something. I don't have access to any of the general anesthetics that I used successfully in my lab experiments, but I do have a local anesthetic that worked with this surgery on animals."

"Did you say a *local* anesthetic? Will I be awake?"

"Yes. It seems odd, but there's no sensation of pain inside the brain, even though it's the root of all sensations. Only the scalp and the outside of the brain can feel pain. So once I numb those areas with a local anesthetic, I can perform the brain surgery while you're conscious, and you won't feel anything. I've done many craniotomies with local agents for one reason or another. It's the best way for us because it allows me to use drugs I have complete confidence in. And it'll be easier for Mrs. Trimbell and me to monitor you with a local, because we won't have an anesthesiologist. With the surgery being unauthorized, I couldn't involve any of them."

"Okay, David."

"I'll of course be with you, talking to you."

"I'm not afraid to be awake. I'm so thrilled to have this surgery that nothing can scare me."

He squeezed her hands, which she knew meant *Listen—this is important.*

"Nicole, you will have to stay perfectly still. No coughing, no sneezing, no moving. This is *very* important."

"I understand."

"I can't have *any* sudden movements."

She squeezed his hands reassuringly. "I have experience with that kind of role. I'll be as still as I was when I played the princess who slept for a hundred years."

"Good!"

Soon Nicole was wheeled in and slid onto a table. An overhead light warmed her body, then cool linens covered it. The muffled voices of Mrs. Trimbell and David spoke to her through masked faces. David placed patches over her eyes to prevent the optic nerves from firing impulses during the surgery, he explained. An IV line pricked her hand. A liquid dripped into her veins to calm her. An electric razor shaved her scalp. A pungent solution painted her bare head. She felt the intense but brief pain of needles injecting the local anesthetic into her scalp. Holding pins gripped her head in a vise. She heard the sonorous beep of her heart on a monitor. At one point, David left to scrub. When he returned, she heard the whoosh of a gown placed around him and the crisp stretch of rubber gloves sliding over his hands. Soon she heard the piercing whine of a drill and smelled the stench of scorched tissue as a superbly calm, matter-of-fact voice announced the cutting of her skull. *You just lie still like the sleeping princess,* Nicole ordered herself, while the roar of the drill and its furious vibrations resonated through her head. *We can't confine our dreams to the world we see on the stage.*

Her head shook as David pried a block of bone from her skull like a brick from a wall. Nicole knew that the top of her head had become an open window. More clatter of instruments followed until the voice of science announced that her brain looked beautiful, palpating with her every heartbeat. As the clock on the wall pointed to nine, the narrator of the drama declared with ruthless self-confidence: "I'm going in now. Remember, Nicole, you're to stay perfectly still."

Outside the building, a man walked into the hospital parking lot. He was someone who arrived for work with the surgeons, used the surgeons' lounge, parked his car with the surgeons' vehicles, and received the same deferential treatment as the surgeons. He even commented frequently to friends about having a hard day in the OR. But he was not a surgeon. He was CareFree's Inspector Norwood.

After working earlier in Riverview Hospital's Department of Surgery, Inspector Norwood had left his car in the doctors' parking lot while he met friends for dinner nearby. One of his companions, a fellow inspector, told him the late-breaking news at the agency: David Lang had been caught performing illegal animal experiments and arrested. Inspector Norwood was elated at the misfortune of the brazen surgeon who had pulled a knife on him in the OR. His joy was marred only by his feet, which throbbed in a new pair of shoes. As he returned to the hospital to retrieve his car after an evening with his friends, he was limping.

He recognized an ER doctor having a smoke in the parking lot. "How's it going?" the inspector asked casually, as one colleague to another.

"Oh, hello, Inspector," replied the doctor, surprised to see the official at that hour. "It's slow tonight."

"Oh?"

"All we've seen are a few guys needing to sleep off a drunk," the doctor added, as if justifying his cigarette break to a supervisor. "But it's not yet midnight, so anything can happen."

The inspector smiled courteously, and then continued limping to his car. He wondered how many blocks he would have to walk when he reached his home in Brooklyn. He did not have a garage, and finding a parking space on the street at that hour would be difficult. He suddenly had an idea. He could change into his work shoes, which were inside his locker in the surgeons' lounge. This would make his trip home more comfortable.

He entered the hospital and took the elevator to the third floor, avoiding the looks of people who might ask him for information. His aloofness, combined with his business suit and speckled gray hair, gave him the air of a doctor with weighty concerns. He exited on the third floor and passed the swinging doors leading to the surgeons' lounge and the operating suites. He noticed a light from OR 3 beaming across the otherwise dim hallway. He knew that no operations were scheduled that evening, and the ER doctor apparently had sent up no patients. *Curious.*

OR 3 resembled an overexposed picture with glaring white walls and pale blue linens. The only dark streaks in the whitewashed room were the trays of instruments by the operating table. David and Mrs. Trimbell attended the patient, and Randy stood farther away.

Nicole listened to the whispered monologue that David was having for her benefit. After hearing his voice remain steady for the entire time, she thought she detected the first subtle rise in his tone to punctuate something of particular importance.

"An aneurysm has formed on an artery near the trauma site, Nicole. This can happen sometimes in an injury like yours, where a fragment of broken bone can come loose and nick an artery. This weakens the wall of the artery, so it balloons out from the pressure of the blood. The danger is that the aneurysm could burst and cause a bleed. I have to put a clip around the neck of the aneurysm, so that it will be cut off from your bloodstream and never cause trouble. I suspected that this might occur, so I prepared instruments to clip the thing. It's nothing to worry about."

Nicole answered his soliloquy with the only response he wanted: a completely silent, motionless, accepting body.

The aneurysm was nothing to worry about—provided he could clip it before it burst, a condition he did not verbalize to Nicole. David paused to consider the best way to reach the aneurysm and the most suitable clip to use. From an instrument tray with an array of clips, David selected one. With a suction device in one hand and the clip at the end of a holder in the other, he approached the aneurysm.

Mrs. Trimbell and Randy quietly listened to David's whispers. Then the surgeon, too, fell silent. Everyone sensed that this was the tensest moment in the surgery. There was no movement in the room, except for the subtle maneuvering of David's hands, finding the best way to perform a critical task in Nicole's brain. There was no sound except for the beep of Nicole's heart monitor.

Inspector Norwood walked down the corridor to find the reason for the lit surgical suite on a night when there should be no activity. He quietly peered through the window on the door of OR 3. To his astonishment he saw a figure resembling the man whom he most despised . . . performing surgery! This was the man who had humiliated him at knifepoint, the man who had just been arrested and had no right—

Inside OR 3, David was about to clip the aneurysm. He approached it cautiously. It was difficult to reach, but he had it. . . . He thought he had it. But no, he did not have it at all! Before he could clip it, the aneurysm burst.

David quickly covered the tear in the artery with a suction device. Everything was under control. Provided that the sucker held the opening, there would be no hemorrhage, no flood of blood to wipe out his field of vision and leave him with no control at all. He had the sucker on the aneurysm and the clip in his other hand. He needed to get the clip around the aneurysm.

"Nicole," he whispered almost inaudibly. She loved the way his baritone voice pronounced her name. Even then, she felt pleasure in hearing it. Even then, he pronounced it with softness. "This is the most important time . . . to . . . stay . . . still."

Suddenly the swinging doors to the room flung open with a thump and a shrill cry pierced the calm. "Just what do you think you're doing, Dr. Lang?"

❧34❧
The Wake-Up Call

Mrs. Trimbell gasped. Randy jumped, startled, then leaped in front of the intruder.

"I'm Inspector Norwood of CareFree, and I'm calling my supervisor. He'll be interested in learning how a surgeon who was just busted got back in the OR!" yelled the inspector, his cell phone out and ready.

"I'm the administrator of this hospital, and I say you'd better not make that call." Randy stood before the inspector, blocking him from advancing further.

"It appears that you're the accomplice to a crime, and I'm going to report it," said the inspector proudly, like a man earning a medal.

"Turn around and leave. We'll discuss this outside," Randy ordered.

Ignoring the remark, the inspector began dialing a number on his phone.

In a violent twist of his body, Randy grabbed a knife from David's instrument tray and lunged at the intruder, warning, "Don't move a muscle."

It was déjà vu for the mortified inspector.

Mrs. Trimbell seized the phone from his hand.

"You can't do this to me! I'll have all of you thrown out of medicine!" The inspector's voice was still threatening but less steady than before, the knife's presence rattling him.

"Shut up!" ordered Randy, forcing the intruder into a corner of the room, away from the patient.

"But Dr. Lang was arrested today. He can't operate. He has no right—"

"Say one more word and you'll have no throat!" The knife danced like a serpent's tongue around the man's vocal cords.

Mrs. Trimbell surveyed the anesthesia cart, and Randy, glancing her way, guessed her thoughts. She filled a hypodermic needle with a potion.

"Lie down on your belly, nice and easy," Randy directed the inspector.

"But . . . but—"

"Shut up and do what I say!" Randy's menacing knife silenced the inspector, who kneeled, then lay facedown on the floor.

Mrs. Trimbell pulled off a sleeve of his jacket, rolled up his shirt, and injected the liquid into his arm. "Have a nice nap. You'll wake up later," she told him, but his eyes had closed before she finished speaking.

She and Randy dragged the limp body into a small connecting room. Then the two took a step back into the OR—and back in time, it seemed, for David and Nicole were in the same positions as before.

"David," Randy asked tentatively, as if afraid to hear the answer, "what happened to . . . the . . . aneurysm?"

"It's clipped."

Randy and Mrs. Trimbell marveled at David.

"Nicole, dear, are you okay?" asked Mrs. Trimbell.

"I'm fine," said a cheerful little voice beneath a tunnel of linen.

"You're a good sleeping princess, Nicole. You're doing very well in your role!" said David. Then he looked at his team proudly: "We all did very well."

Triumphant laughter puffed out all three surgical masks, and smile lines appeared above them. Randy, Mrs. Trimbell, and David looked at one another, a mutual salute apparent in their vibrant eyes.

"The rest of this is going to be a walk in the park," the surgeon said, relieved.

In disposing of the intruder, Randy and Mrs. Trimbell had broken the sterile field, so the operation had to be halted. After changing their clothing, removing contaminated instruments, and replacing them with sterile ones, the two rejoined David and Nicole to resume their tasks. The rest of the surgery proceeded just as David had hoped—uneventfully. The inspector awakened, but only after Nicole had been wheeled into the recovery room.

At 4:00 in the morning, a bleary-eyed, barely awake, but supremely happy surgeon sat at the edge of his patient's bed in the recovery room. He performed various tests to ensure that Nicole was in good condition, with no neurological deficits following the surgery. Despite her head being wrapped in a gauze turban and her eyes being patched, the sublime beauty of her face still resembled a princess in repose.

"With the manipulation of the surgery, the optic nerves swelled. I want you to keep the eye patches on for now. I'll remove them later in the morning when the swelling subsides. Then we'll know the outcome."

As he spoke, long, graceful fingers stroked his face with the lingering joy of one touching a favorite sculpture. The fingers found their favorite spots: the smooth arc of the eyebrow, the warm lips, the elusive dimple on the cheek that vanished and reappeared as he spoke. In a departure from classical ballet, it was the reposing princess who raised her head to kiss the leading man. His head slowly followed hers back to the pillow, the bond of their lips unbroken. Exhaustion softened the urgency of her kiss and claimed her. A moment later, she was asleep.

Pajamas, disheveled hair, and yawns greeted Randy in the dining room of his home that morning. A grandfather clock in the corner chimed to announce

4:30. The weary father sat at the head of the oblong dinner table. His suit jacket was flung haphazardly over the back of his chair, his shirtsleeves rolled, his tie loosened. The way a soldier ignores a bullet wound to finish a battle, Randy had tried not to think about this moment during the tumultuous events of the past fourteen hours. Now he faced the confused, sleepy eyes of his wife and three children, whom he had awakened for an emergency meeting. They waited while he struggled to choose his words.

"Honey, you're so pale," his wife said finally. "When you called to say you would be detained at the hospital, I never imagined you'd be out all night. What's wrong, dear? What've you been doing?"

"I've been changing our lives, Beth. Now I owe you and the kids an explanation."

Thirteen-year-old Stephen shot a questioning glance at his twin sister, Victoria, as if to say, *What's up?* She raised her shoulders in bewilderment. Seven-year-old Michelle, the diminutive figure sitting on an adult's chair, stretched sleepily.

"Today I quit my job and broke the law."

Four sets of sleepy eyes suddenly sprang open.

"After what I did, no other hospital will hire me, and I could be arrested at any time."

The family listened, stunned, as Randy related the astonishing story of his deal with the governor, his brother's arrest, his resignation, the illegal surgery, and the incident with the inspector.

"I know you kids are at critical stages in your lives," Randy continued. "You're accustomed to having important things to groom you for your futures. Victoria, I know you want to be a champion figure skater, because you told us so when you were five years old. You work very hard at it, and you need costumes, competitions, travel, and coaches to develop your talent.

"Stephen, your gift is the piano, and you need the best teachers and the finest opportunities to develop that. When I see the thrill on your face while you're giving a recital, I imagine you looking that same inspired way in the concert halls of the world.

"And Michelle, my baby, there's something special sprouting inside you, too. You love your microscope, and you devour children's science books the way other kids read nursery rhymes. You need a special school to nourish your talents.

"And Beth, honey, I know that you're a serious painter, but you work in commercial art for the money to help fuel our kids' futures. You'd rather be doing the fine art that you're talented at and enjoy more."

Each family member listened intently when addressed but did not interrupt. Even Michelle, the most talkative one of the group, seemed to sense that this was a time to listen.

"One talented child would be rare enough for a family, but having three of you very special and very expensive kids is more than your mother and I ever imagined. My job, especially my recent raise and bonus, provided a good share of what you kids need and of what we want you to have.

"But that money is tainted. To get it, I have to betray everything I believe in. I have to support people and causes I disapprove of. My job requires that I feed not only your uncle to the wolves but also every doctor and patient who want something different for themselves than the system forces on them.

"And there's no making deals about it, either. I thought so, but I was wrong. The deal I made meant only that if I followed their course, they'd throw me a few crumbs. The deal didn't mean that I could oppose their course and choose my own. My deal is what put your uncle in jail."

Widened eyes and dropped jaws faced Randy.

"You see, kids, while you're getting your special training, I'm doing something that makes me feel ashamed. But yesterday I felt different. I told the board members what I really thought of them. I felt as if I had crawled out of a cave and could breathe fresh air. And the air smelled even sweeter when I let David do his surgery. I felt like Victoria when she does a triple jump or Stephen when he plays Chopin or Michelle when David takes her to the lab. Kids, I felt excited about doing something I really wanted to do! My own dream flashed before my eyes, the dream of running an unusual kind of business in which great medical innovations would be made and brought to market. It's one thing to manufacture a new carpet or car or television. But to produce new discoveries that restore health and life to very ill people, well, that's the concerto that's been playing in my mind for years. Last night I saw my music *performed*, instead of only hearing it in my head. For the first time in years, I can't wait to go to the hospital. I can't wait for David to remove Nicole's eye patches and find out the result. I can't wait to go to work and not get paid for a job I no longer have.

"I lost everything, but I feel great about what I did. I only regret what it's going to do to you. We now need to live on just a fraction of the money we had before. I don't know how long I'll be unemployed or what disasters this will cause for you. I only know that I had to do what I did . . . because it was right."

At first, no one spoke. Everyone seemed to be chewing the large bite they had just been fed. No one looked at anyone else; everyone seemed to be judging the matter privately.

Stephen was the first to break the silence. "Give 'em hell, Dad."

Victoria followed. "I'm glad you quit that awful job, Daddy. It was making you mopey."

Then Michelle chimed in. "I want Uncle David to do a new operation."

"I don't need a new number for my next competition," added Victoria. "I'll skate to my old number, with my old costume and choreography. And I'll be fantastic!"

"And I can take a job working in a band on the weekends," said Stephen. "It'll be good practice for me, and the money will pay for my lessons."

"Daddy, I can go to public school with Betty and Sarah. Then my tuition won't a-salt you. Is that the word you use, Daddy?" said Michelle.

"Honey," said Beth, with all eyes turning to her, "if we're as gifted as you say we are, then we should be able to use our talents to find a way to manage. We want you to do what's right. Don't we, kids?"

"Yeah, Dad!"

"We're with you, Daddy."

"Hey, guys, let's hear it for Dad and Uncle David," said Stephen.

Then Randy's family did what it had always done when one of them reached a new milestone. They cheered and they embraced.

The final day of October began with a deliciously nippy fall morning. Hanging in a cloudless blue sky was its only daytime ornament, a fireball burning in the eastern horizon. Like Venus on the first morning of her life, the island of Manhattan seemed to be rising on a seashell amid sun-streaked silver waters. Skyscrapers stretched horizontally in long angular shadows across the avenues of the city. The east windows of Riverview Hospital, like mirrors, shot the sun into the windows of the building across the street so that the west, too, could share the abundant light of a new day. A patient with patched eyes lay inside the hospital, warming her face in the early morning sun and wondering if she would ever see its light again.

By midmorning, the shocking news of David's arrest and illegal surgery, along with Randy's resignation, rocked the hospital and the city. In the hallways, locker rooms, and nursing stations and even over unconscious patients in the OR, staff members talked of nothing else. The board of directors waited for CareFree to make a statement before preparing its own. CareFree waited for the governor to speak first. Reporters hovered outside, wondering whether David Lang would be thrown in jail or declared a national hero. As he ate breakfast six days before the election, Malcolm Burrow waited, also. He waited for two small patches to be removed from someone's eyes by a man he cursed between bites.

Without having had general anesthesia, Nicole was wide awake. Publicity about her case had necessitated her move to a secluded room, leaving her alone with her thoughts . . . and hopes. Members of the hospital staff visited to wish her well. Whenever footsteps sounded outside her room, she lifted her head from her pillow, hoping it was her doctor. Her dainty body, a robe wrapped twice around it, barely made an impression in the bed. As a tube dripped liquid into her arm, she waited for the man who could infuse life back into her soul.

Finally, two familiar warm hands reached for hers.

"David, you're here! You weren't . . . arrested again?"

"They wouldn't dare. Not yet, anyway. But we weren't going to worry about that, were we?" His voice was lighter, happier, as if being an outlaw agreed with him. He squeezed her hands. "How are you feeling?"

Ignoring the raw, throbbing wound that was her head, she smiled softly. "I feel fine."

"You're doing fine, very fine. The surgery went well."

"And now, is it . . . time?"

"Yes."

The muscles of her face tightened.

"It's almost time. First, someone gave me this for you." He reached for something that he had set on her bed stand. He held it before her as she sat up in bed.

"It's a vase," she said, her hands circling a glass hexagon, her fingers stopping at the sharp, pointed corners that told her it was crystal. "This feels beautiful. Did you say someone *gave* this to you?"

"Yes."

"You mean the Phantom?"

"Yes."

"He's *here*?"

"Oh, yes."

"In the hospital?"

"Yes."

"Is he *really*?"

"Yes, really."

"Why doesn't he come to see me?"

"He's coming."

Her dainty lips pursed in puzzlement, but David said no more.

"What kind of flowers did he send?" Her fingers touched the arrangement in the vase. "There are lots of flowers! One blossom on top of another. They're in tall clusters on stalks that feel stiff and tapered, like swords." She stretched an arm high to reach the top of the arrangement. "There are twenty stalks and each one has about ten blooms on it. That's two hundred flowers, isn't it?"

"I suppose."

"Could they be gladiolas?"

"They could indeed."

"After we've already had the first frost?"

"The Phantom apparently thinks it's summer."

She laughed with a child's delight.

"The flowers are a mixture of whites, pinks, yellows, and lavenders, Nicole. All pastels."

"The Phantom is out of sync with the season."

"He's in a season of his own."

"I adore gladiolas. They're tall and bold. They assert themselves."

Her hands lovingly brushed through the hardy arrangement. Then her fingers paused on an envelope. She gave it to David.

He pulled a flower from the vase and placed it in her hand, then set the others on her bed stand. She could hear the crisp sound of paper tearing as he opened the envelope. He could see the eager smile, the attentive tilt of her head toward him, the hands that caressed the flower. Sitting on the edge of her bed, he read to her:

Dearest Nicole,

Today I plant my own garden for the rest of my life. From now on I will gather only bouquets watered by my own hands. Before, when my garden was overrun with the forced blooms of others, I smelled no fragrance. I had scrawny hothouse attempts at bloom too dull to catch my eye. Those flower impostors lacked the color and perfume of my own hearty patch. It was you, Nicole, who gave me the courage to plant new seeds in the fresh air. And the world has never looked more breathtaking than from the special plot you helped me nourish.

Now, everywhere I go I see summer. It follows me around like my new companion. I heard the curling wind of an autumn storm and mistook it for a robin. I saw the first white patch of frost by the river and thought it was a swan. I felt the little lights that decorate the trees for the winter and thought they were new buds.

When you open your eyes, Nicole, the man who hid from you and the world will be there. Whatever the outcome of your ordeal, we'll face it in an embrace. You'll be mine, all mine, for today I come to claim you.

Nicole listened intently as if hearing a stirring love song. She held the flower to her breast, stroking it tenderly.

"The Phantom's changed, David. He doesn't sound like the most desperate man in the city."

"He doesn't sound desperate at all."

"Not anymore," she said, her voice solemn, her head raised in a salute.

"Are you ready, Nicole?" She detected a slight tremble in his voice.

"David, the Phantom is the second person I want most to be with me when I open my eyes. The first is *you*. Would you tell the Phantom that this is our moment together, yours and mine?"

"We'll have to see how this works out. He's pretty insistent."

David lowered the blinds to block the glare of the direct sun. He took the flower from Nicole's hand and returned it to the vase.

The softness on her face disappeared. No trace of a smile remained. Her mouth tightened as if to brace for anything. She propped herself up with pillows. Her swanlike neck seemed to stretch even longer, like a pedestal to display her bandaged head. Her shoulders tensed to form a square base for the pedestal.

David lifted a hand that had begun to sweat and squeezed it. Nicole did not respond, as if the intensity of her thoughts was all consuming. She felt the quick sting of bandages pulled swiftly from her face. Then the patches were lifted off her eyes. The cool air of the room hit her lids.

"Your eyelids may feel as if they're stuck. It may take a little work, but they'll open."

He walked to the door. She heard it close.

"David, are you still here? Did you leave? . . . David?"

He did not reply. He looked at her as a doctor and as a man, staring intensely in both capacities.

She tried to pry her eyelids open, but they stuck like stubborn clams. Her brow wrinkled as she gave the task a second try. The lids loosened. But lashes from the top and bottom still intertwined. Nicole kept trying. Then her eyes slowly opened. A liquid smear glistened before her. She blinked several times.

Suddenly she was thrust back in time. She was standing at the corner of a street, across from a flower shop. A man stood outside the store looking at her with an unusual intensity. The upward tilt of his head told her that she was a goddess he would worship. The downward sweep of his eyes over her body told her that she was a woman he would possess.

"I . . . I . . ." The small cry that was her voice struggled to gain volume. "I can see you! I can see you! I . . . can . . . see!" Just as she found her voice, it was muffled again, this time buried in the arms and chest that urgently fell against her. "I see this room! I see you! I see everything!" she screamed, her cries a sublime mix of laughter and tears.

His hands stroked her face, her neck, her bandaged head. He seemed to want to laugh wildly but was suppressing the urge to make a sound.

The radiant Nicole of the stage exclaimed, "You came for me after all! And I can *see* you! Oh my, I can *see*! But I must see my doctor now. Where is he?"

The man before her grinned boyishly.

"Where's Dr. Lang? I must see him!"

He laughed quietly.

"Why don't you speak?"

His eyes, those green lasers that seemed to burn her skin, never left hers as his mouth widened in yet more laughter. The Phantom was enjoying the moment.

"Talk to me, won't you?"

Her eyes held curiosity; his, amusement.

She reached out to touch his engaging face, to cup it in her hands. "Why won't you talk—?"

She paused as a thought took shape. She studied him curiously. Her hands began trembling.

"Wait a minute," she whispered.

Then she closed her eyes. She touched his brow, his eyes, his mouth, his cheek. Her fingers paused on the telltale dimple. She opened her eyes, incredulous.

She mouthed a word, shaped it on her lips, for she could find no voice to utter it. Then she gasped, "D-David?"

"Yes, Nicole." She heard a familiar baritone voice heavy with affection for her.

Two arms wrapped tightly around his neck. A tear-stained cheek rubbed against his face. "David, I'm thrilled!"

"You said the Phantom was the most desperate man in the city. Who better fit that description than me? The *old* me?"

"David, I'm so glad it's you! I'm so happy the Phantom is you! I wouldn't have wanted him to be anyone else!"

His lips landed on hers, choking her voice. He slipped his arms around her body, his eager fingers racing over her back and shoulders. Then they heard the ringing of a phone, and he reluctantly released her.

"Hello," David said into his cell phone.

"What's happening in there?" asked Randy.

"Does anybody have an eye chart?"

The door of Nicole's room burst open. Two optic nerves that had been dormant for months were now firing rapidly to capture the lively scene that followed. Dozens of people barged in. They wore scrubs of various colors, white coats, or business suits, many with stethoscopes swung around their necks, all with hospital name badges clipped to their clothing. They cheered. They opened champagne, poured the bubbly liquid into plastic cups, and clicked them together as if they were fine crystal. They shook David's hand and embraced him. They squeezed Nicole's hands and expressed their happiness for her. David's triumph was in some way a victory for them all, a deliverance, a rekindling of the dream of practicing a noble profession that had inspired them in the early days of their medical schooling. Their wild cheering for David and Nicole was also a glorious tribute to medicine as it might be and ought to be and to themselves as healers.

An austere-looking woman with joyful tears streaming down her face embraced Nicole.

"Mrs. Trimbell!" the patient exclaimed.

A man who closely resembled David smothered him in a robust embrace, then grabbed her face, and kissed her cheek.

"You must be Randy," said the radiant Nicole.

Though Nicole observed the dizzying spectacle, it kept moving to the periphery of her vision, the way scenery whizzes by a carousel rider. Her eyes, as though drawn by a magnet, kept fixing on the new joy of their existence, on the tall, handsome figure who looked at her with a boy's amusement and a man's passion.

Word of the surgery had spread through the university, and chemist John Kendall came to congratulate both patient and doctor. "Now I know what those analyses were about!" he said jubilantly.

Resident Tom Bentley gazed at David with a look normally reserved for icons such as Louis Pasteur. "Dr. Lang," he said, "how did you keep from giving up on your research? After all the obstacles you encountered, what kept you going through it all?"

The commotion in the room ebbed as the others turned to David to hear his response.

"A wise woman once told me that we can't confine our dreams to the world we see on the stage. We can't just idly dream about the things most precious to us. We have to act to gain them in real life."

David winked at Nicole. She smiled at him in return.

❧ EPILOGUE ❧
Should a Man Receive Flowers from a Woman?

Wearing the feather boa given to her by Hope, Pandora seized Zeus's torch and burned the ropes binding Prometheus. The valiant couple, armed with fire and hope, fought the woes that Zeus had unleashed on mankind through Pandora's box. To the orchestra's climactic notes of victory, Pandora and Prometheus chased all of Zeus's plagues back into the evil box and saved the human race.

The sun shone on the Earth. The mortals rejoiced. A corps of ballerinas joined the first men of Earth in a jubilant dance of life. With a trembling hand, Pandora touched Prometheus's arm, his hair, his face. She moved about him with the fragility of a ballerina and the sensuality of a woman. He lifted her high in the air to begin their final pas de deux.

The playbill for the hit Broadway show *Triumph* concluded: "Man discovers woman and enters an age of innocence, goodness, and joy."

The audience clapped, whistled, and roared. A radiant Nicole Hudson bowed appreciatively, threw her fans kisses, and gathered the bundles of flowers lovingly tossed to her on the stage. As she smiled at the people she had stirred with her dancing, she, in turn, was moved by their cheering. She felt a burning rush of liquid fill her eyes and wondered why happiness could hurt. Basking in the warmth of the spotlight, she knew that finally she, like Pandora, had entered a period of innocence, goodness, and joy, and that nothing greater was possible to her.

Backstage she leaped into the waiting arms of David Lang. He raised her off her feet and whirled her around. In him she had found a new passion, one that was never sated but grew more intense the more she indulged it, like a sweet addiction nourished on itself.

A taxi took David and Nicole to the restaurant in the park where they had spent their first date. It was a place that held a special fascination for the couple. This time it was Nicole who described to David the enchanting scene outside the glass walls. She could now understand the exciting mystery of the woods that David had so vividly imagined on their first visit. However, the park no longer contained the bare shrubs and barren grounds that David had seen the previous autumn. The wooded patch now held lush trees with delicate spring leaves of yellow-green, along with fragrant bushes and tulips in full bloom. Many changes had occurred between autumn and spring.

The charges against David of cruelty to animals were quietly dropped. And no one ever arrived to punish him for performing Nicole's illegal surgery.

The day that Nicole regained her sight was not a good one for Governor Burrow. His agencies had banned a revolutionary new treatment and arrested a surgeon who had to break the law to make medical history. "OOPS!" read a glaring headline over Burrow's picture in New York City's leading newspaper. In the aftermath of David's wild success, the governor's popularity, always precarious, plummeted. Six days later at the polls, a dispirited Mack Burrow lost his bid for reelection.

The voters also defeated a referendum calling for new taxes to bail out the financially troubled CareFree. A failure to meet its payroll, combined with further curtailments in service, threw the agency into chaos and enraged the citizens. Following David's example, other doctors began ignoring the rules and providing their own independent services. A cottage industry of private medicine was developing, and the politicians, intimidated by the popularity of the new movement, were forced to ignore the lawbreakers. The steady deterioration of Burrow's pet program and the rumors of its imminent collapse sent shockwaves through the CareFree-created physician groups, such as Reliant Care, which released half of its doctors. One of its employees, the recently divorced Dr. Marie Donnelly Lang, was a casualty of the layoffs.

With the financial backing of drug company president Phil Morgan, David and Randy leased a small, closed hospital and reopened it as the Lang-Morgan Institute for Neurological Research and Surgery. There was no public announcement of its opening because it technically did not exist. More accurately, it existed in violation of countless regulations. It had no permits or licenses. It passed no inspections, save the rigorous ones of its vigilant owners. "We'll just work until somebody comes to arrest us," David said to his partners. No one did.

Somehow the people of the city heard about the establishment despite the lack of signs, advertising, and announcements of any kind. Ambulances carried victims of spinal cord injury, stroke, and other nerve trauma to the institute. As if they were abandoning children at the doorstep of a church, the ambulances dropped the patients off secretly, then quickly sped away. Word spread beyond the city of the revolutionary work being performed. Desperate patients flew to New York, their plane seats replaced by stretchers, to reach the place that did not exist.

Like a death-row prisoner never knowing which meal might be his last, David ravenously performed his nerve-repair surgeries. He feasted on this new banquet of his life. As the first spring crocuses broke through the soil, he completed the second operation on his first wave of patients. Hopelessly injured people were amazingly restored to normal lives. One was a young quadriplegic who had been living on a respirator after a football injury. After David's treatment, he breathed and walked normally. He took his first tearful steps toward David, whom he almost crushed in an embrace. Other victims of paralysis stood up, folded their wheelchairs, and walked away. A teenage victim of a stab wound that severed his optic nerve regained sight through David's new treatment.

Neurosurgeons began going to the institute to learn the new technique. With Phil Morgan's backing, Randy's business management, and David's clinical skills, the institution that did not exist was rapidly becoming famous.

Contrary to CareFree's policies, the patients at the institute paid for their treatment. For those on a budget, Randy offered financing plans to make medical care as affordable as automobiles, furniture, and other widely purchased goods. He had viable ideas for low-cost insurance, which he said was not the kind mandated by a myriad of regulations, making the premiums soar, but the kind offering a myriad of innovations, real choices, and solid financial protection against a serious health problem. Contrary to the CareFree way, the rich received special treatment at the new institute, with luxurious private rooms, gourmet food, and other amenities—and they paid extra for it. Their money increased the profitability of the institute, which benefited all patients, as well as employees and owners. The institute also practiced private charity. The greater its success, the more it could afford to be generous. The only people it would not consider as candidates for charity were those who claimed they had a right to it. Treatment at a reduced fee was available from surgeons learning the new procedures, with their work performed under supervised conditions that were safe for the patients. These policies were molding a top-notch clinical institution that was also a profitable company.

Each time David successfully completed a case, Nicole sent flowers to him at work. As his accomplishments multiplied, his office became a solid blanket of blooms. "This place smells like a brothel," Phil Morgan commented on one visit.

After their dinner in the park that spring evening, with the scent of lilacs heavy in the garden outside Nicole's brownstone, the couple climbed the stairs to her apartment. When the door closed behind them, David faced her in the foyer, her short hair glowing like newly minted gold, his eyes burning like liquid metal. Through every bite of their food, every dance, every sound of her laughter that evening, he ached to crush her body against his. He grabbed her by the waist, confessing a desire that had become the urgent need of his life. His mouth covered hers. She felt her head falling back, her mouth opening to his, as she traced the firm lines of his body, from his hips to his chest to his neck. She flung her arms around him with an urgency that answered his. She felt the exciting thrill of his hands dancing over her back, her hips, her stomach, her breasts. She felt his mouth hot against her face, her hair, her neck.

He no longer had to vanish as he had done on their first date. He lifted her in his arms and carried her into the apartment. The lights burning on the theater marquees and in skyscrapers beyond their window were the majestic fire of their gods and a backdrop to their own glorious celebration of a new spring.

About the Author

Genevieve (Gen) LaGreca is a former pharmaceutical chemist and now a writer in the health care field. She lives in Chicago. *Noble Vision* is her first novel.

Give the Gift of
NOBLE VISION
to Your Friends and Colleagues

Check your leading bookstore or order here

Yes, I want _____ copies of *Noble Vision* at $27.95 each, plus $5.00 shipping for the first book and $2.50 for each additional book.

Illinois residents, please add $2.45 in sales tax per book. Canadian orders must be accompanied by a postal money order in U.S. funds. Allow 15 days for delivery.

My check or money order for $ _____ is enclosed.

Please charge my   ___Visa   ___MasterCard

Name _____

Organization _____

Street Address _____

City, State, Zip _____

Phone _____ E-mail _____

Credit Card # _____

Exp. Date _____ Signature _____

Please make your check or money order payable and return to:

Winged Victory Press
P.O. Box 11307
Chicago, IL 60611

www.wingedvictorypress.com

OR CALL IN YOUR CREDIT CARD ORDER, TOLL-FREE: (800) 844-2114